WiTCH GiRL

WiTCH GiRL

Tanvi Bush

Published in 2015 by Modjaji Books
PO Box 121, Rondebosch, 7701, Cape Town, South Africa
www.modjajibooks.co.za

© 2015

Tanvi Bush has asserted her right to be identified as the
author of this work.

Edited by Karen Jennings
Cover artwork by Tammy Griffin and Toni Olivier
Book layout by Andy Thesen
Printed and bound by Megadigital, Cape Town
ISBN 978-1-920590-61-1
Ebook ISBN 978-1-928215-00-4

To the other Goon, my Dad and indomitable lodestar,
Mike Bush.

And my friend, Teelo 'Who's The King Of The Jungle' Ross,
the best drinking buddy I ever had.

The Silver Box

1.

It is a monstrous bruise of a sky. Thunder pounds the horizon, sending vibrations through the slumbering city. Luse twitches in her sleep but doesn't wake fully. She is semi-standing, lodged uncomfortably against the huge concrete curve of a storm drain, her feet planted firmly on the sandy earth, head lolling uncomfortably. The concrete has been storing the blazing heat from the sun all day and is now gently releasing it into her lower back and buttocks and so, in spite of everything, including the fact that she is supposed to be on watch, Luse has fallen asleep. Another low rumble of thunder is followed by a burst of wind which ruffles the electricity pylons overhead and causes a sudden eddy of dust that knocks down the large pile of assorted rubbish Luse has been collecting for the fire. It slides apart, plastic bottles rolling in all directions, but she doesn't wake. In her sleep she is dreaming of food, of soft steaming cakes of nsima, of gravy, chicken meat glistening in groundnut relish. *Ahhhh...* her mouth drops open. She pants slightly and a tendril of drool creeps down her chin.

Plop!

The raindrop hits Luse right between the eyes, spilling in perfect symmetry down each side of her eye socket. She is instantly out of her sweet slumber and into her aching, eleven-year-old body.

She turns and yells the alarm into the darkness of the storm drain, 'Rain! Rain! Rain!'

Her voice echoes off the curved walls and she is already running, kicking out at the soft shapes that are packed together like warm sacks, one on top of the other, in the utter blackness.

'Your fucking mother is a baboon,' hisses a sleepy voice in Bemba as she trips, plunging head first into a mass of writhing bodies.

'Get up you idiots!' Luse screams again. 'Rain! Rain!'

As alarm begins to spread among the ragged piles, movement erupts all around her. Children shout and call to each other in Bemba, Tonga, Nyanja, Lingala, English. Luse pushes and pummels her way back through the melee. Over the racket, she can already hear the low roar of storm water from all over the city rushing like some filthy, furious beast down a thousand pipes towards this main drain. Her feet are now sloshing through foul sewage water gushing from the ground pipes. It is rising fast. She steps on something sharp with her bare foot and she yelps, nearly falling over, but there is no time to check the damage. She wades further in.

'Joshua!' she shouts. 'Josh! Josh! Where are you?'

Luse doesn't know exactly how many kids have been sleeping in this particular drain. She would guess a couple of lorry loads. She has passed the big knife-toting boys who keep to the front fifteen feet of pipe. This ensures their escape should there be a police raid, a fire... or a storm. The girls – at least the ones not being utilised by the big boys – the new kids, the sick kids and the smaller ones are stuck behind the bigger lads back here in the deep dark with the rats, cockroaches and snakes... and the occasional dead thing.

'Joshie!' Luse gasps, holding her sides. She can't wade any further and is left looking into pitch black with the water rising to her shins. She screams into the darkness as the last of the small children splashes past. Something is rising inside her, a rage more terrible than anything the storm can imagine. If she has lost Joshua she will not be able to contain it.

Then a small sticky hand slips into hers.

'Luse?' says a small voice. 'Luse, I'm here. I'm frightened.'

Luse bends down and sweeps Josh up into her arms, dragging his special smell of honey and firewood into her lungs. She turns, slipping and sliding in the water that now pours from the side gutters. He buries his head into her shoulder and Luse staggers back up the culvert towards the light of the night sky, the storm and the writhing, crackling five-thousand-foot-high filaments of lighting.

2.

The city of Lusaka is twinned with no less than Los Angeles, the money-sodden City of Angels. The doctor often wonders if anyone in LA has even heard of Zambia, let alone its capital. She lies in her bed thinking about America, about England, about leaving. The thunder rolls and the intermittently blasting wind sends raindrops exploding against the window.

In another life she would have got up and watched the storm from the glass patio doors overlooking the garden, and in such a fearsome tirade as this one she might even have put on her wellies and dashed out to dance in it. She usually loves these torrential African storms, the noise, the danger, the drama, but not tonight. Tonight she lies sullen, about as animated as her duvet, watching the eerie sheet lightning cast shadow puppetry onto her bedroom wall.

Dr Georgia Shapiro has been working in Zambia for eleven years. She arrived fresh from completing her residency in London, keen to get her teeth into the HIV pandemic engulfing sub-Saharan Africa. Originally she thought she would only stay a year or two, but she loves her job, a mash-up of general practice, tropical medicine and minor surgery. She also loves Zambia, this odd gentle country spread like a butterfly on the navel of Africa, speared from above by Congo and bolstered from beneath by its sibling Zimbabwe. Or at least she used to love it...

The storm rattles the mosquito grills in her windows and there is a sharp crack as a branch breaks off and falls from the towering bracystigia tree outside. Still Georgia lies, gazing up at the spider webs around the ceiling vent, feeling the blood moving through her body. A mosquito whines nearby, desperate for that same blood. *Take it*, thinks Georgia.

The whine stops and she twitches, feeling the scratch near her collarbone. Outside the rain thunders and pauses. She understands that she is depressed – has even considered medication – but in the end couldn't face asking her colleague for a prescription. She keeps hoping she will start to feel better.

Harry. It is all to do with Harry. Just a few months ago she was called to the University Teaching Hospital to identify a body and found that it was her best friend. He had been in a car crash on the Kafue Road. It would have shaken anyone, but Georgia just couldn't get past numb. None of it made sense. Harry, her friend, should have been far, far away on the night of the accident. He should have been in South Africa cheering the

4

Zambian football team as they battled Bafana Bafana at Thulamahashe Stadium. She knows this because she was the one who dropped him off at Lusaka airport with three of his clients from the advertising agency, all of them hyped up on local lager and adrenalin, chanting 'Chipolopolo! Chipolopolo!' and happy, excited.

Four days later there was Harry, in the morgue. He had been driving a battered pick-up truck that had gone out of control and plunged off the escarpment just 100km south of Lusaka. *But how*, thinks Georgia over and over, *could he have ended up there, like that, with his dreadlocks running blood?* He didn't even own a pick-up truck...

Georgia blinks, but no tears spring into her eyes. None of it seems real. Her cell phone vibrates on the bedside table. Slowly she sits up, swinging her legs over the edge of the bed and picks it up.

'Hello, Dr Shapiro here.' She has to raise her voice over the noise of the storm.

The voice is faint and tinny, a strange accent. 'Doc, sorry to call you so late. This is Danny. Can we meet?'

3.

It's mid-morning and the sun is already hot and happily sucking up the storm water, the evaporation causing everything to steam gently. Little Joshua leans sleepily in the crook of the tree, his thumb in his mouth and one round cheek smeared with flour from the bun Luse had 'found' him for breakfast. The large jacaranda tree grows alongside the ditch which circles the Northmead shopping centre. Luse watches her brother from the far side of the ditch, her head cocked to one side.

'Will he be okay?' asks Bligh anxiously. From where he stands he can see the lone tree with its thick roots and the little boy sheltering in the shade. There is not another soul around. 'Shouldn't you leave him with someone?'

'He is kind of with someone, Bligh. I've told you already. Ba'Neene – Gran – watches over him.' Luse clicks her tongue when she sees Bligh's expression. Luse's grandmother has been dead for over a year. 'Ach, man. I tell you he'll be okay. We aren't going to be long and he knows what to do if anyone comes near.'

Bligh isn't entirely convinced by the dead grandmother, but he trusts Luse. As they head towards the line of shops he doesn't glance back at the lone little boy snoozing under the tree.

Bligh himself is a mess. His head is too big and his prominent front teeth force his mouth open in a continuous 'oh' of confusion. He's rake thin and taller than the rest of the twelve-year-old boys, his arms dangle and his knees knock together. Constant starvation, combined with an addiction to sniffing petrol, makes his eyes bulge and water.

Yet Bligh's ugliness has bizarrely kept him alive for the four years he has been on the streets. He is not approached for sex, he is not hassled to help with thefts or muggings due to his wretchedly wasted body and tangle of clumsy limbs, and he is a most proficient beggar. He only has to stand, looking gruesome and mournful, near a group of tourists or next to a family trying to eat at an outdoor restaurant or perhaps hang around outside a shop, and you can guarantee within minutes someone will be paying him to get the hell away. But begging isn't enough. Bligh is always desperately hungry. He hates to sleep because his dreams of hot nsima, of fresh kapenta, of beans and bread, make him cry and his stomach bleed. His body desperately wants to grow, to move on through puberty but is stumped by lack of sustenance. He has discovered that petrol stops the worst hunger pangs. Like other street kids, he drips it onto the cuff of his sleeve and sniffs at it all day. When he can afford it that is. There are other drugs too, but these are harder to find when one is desperate and penniless.

His stomach makes a mewling sound and he raises his stinky sleeve to his nose.

'Stop it!' hisses Luse, batting his arm down. 'I need you to be full force, okay?' She glares up at him and wheels away.

Bligh sighs, stomping after her. *Bossy bitch*, he thinks, but with a resigned fondness. Luse is his heroine.

He is the only other kid on the street, apart from little Josh of course, who knows Luse is actually a girl. She wears faded T-shirts and torn shorts – same as all the other boys – and keeps her hair shaved close to her skull. She is strong too and can look after herself in a scrap. Bligh looks down at his own concave chest and shrugs. If she wants to stay in disguise for the time being that is fine with him, as long as they can stay friends. Because with Luse he knows he might actually get something good to eat once in a while. He may be a decent beggar, but Luse is an outstanding thief.

They appear to be walking towards the Lebanese supermarket and at first Bligh has high hopes, but when he sees where they are actually heading his heart sinks. On the far block from the supermarket is a row of smaller shops and businesses. They are on course for the entrance with the red cross and the sign 'Chipitala/Clinic' outside the door.

'Awww no, Luse,' wails Bligh. 'We already checked there three times. They are going to get mad.'

'They said they would make enquiries,' says Luse over her shoulder. 'They said someone might know a Doctor George Shapi at the University Teaching Hospital. They said they would get back to us.'

'That's what people say when they want you to go away and never come back. "We'll check"? Yaaa vaaa! It's shit.' Bligh stands still, his bony arms akimbo.

There is silence but for the stumping thump of Luse's feet walking away. She doesn't look back.

'George Shapi, George Shapi! What the hell is wrong with you?' Bligh mutters. 'What is so damn important about this doctor anyway?'

'I told you,' he hears Luse shout. 'The Rasta told me to find him. Now shut up or I won't steal us anything for supper!'

Bligh slumps, but steps up his pace to catch up, his poor famished stomach overruling his sense of unease.

4.

The alley ends in crumbling concrete steps that lead down to a large blue metal door. Over the door hangs a hooded light-bulb that serves only to cast odd shadows against the whitewashed breeze block wall. This is the entrance to the World Famous Danny's Bar (and Grill) and Georgia sticks out her hand and pushes open the creaking door. The stench of urine from the men's toilets hangs thick as a velvet curtain and she shoulders her way through it, holding her breath.

Danny's Bar is always dark. Outside, clean African sunlight could be idly burning holes through car windows and casually dehydrating the already scuffed brown grass on the football field, but down here sunlight penetrates feebly through vent shafts in the corners of the purple ceiling and Danny's Bar is cool as a cave.

Georgia steps in with a mixture of relief and apprehension. Once past the stench, her eyes reopen and slowly adjust, familiar objects gradually seeping into her vision like a developing Polaroid; the long cracked bar top on its thick brick base, glittering bottles and winking glasses behind it, and the rickety tables with the odd chairs and mismatched broken-topped barstools leaning like drunks.

She expects to see the figure of Danny himself, a small bespectacled Chinese man who usually sits unsmiling on a high chair behind the bar, tutting and clicking his tongue at the barmen and running his fingers through the sweaty kwacha bills they hand him.

Of the barmen she likes Chibeza best. Chibeza is tall, from Northern Province, his skin so blue-black that in the constant gloom, Georgia has only ever known him as a beautiful set of white teeth floating high above the bar. Watson, the second barman, is an ex-tsotsi from Cape Town, the whites of his eyes mottled by brown spots and his skin a gravelled mess of acne scars.

Today only Chibeza's pearly whites are visible, floating Cheshire Cat-like as he wipes glasses behind the bar. He is singing a reggae tune, just the two lines over and over,

'Me hungry but me belly full.

Me hunger makes me an angry man.'

Georgia loves the song. She would love the thumping sweet bass to flood out of the two cracked speakers over the bar. She wills with all her heart for her dear friend Harry to be right here, shaking his dreadlocked head and swinging his skinny hips, his hands up in the air, ash floating from his endless cigarettes. Shutting her eyes for a moment, she can almost feel the pounding beat, the crush of people all around calling 'Harry! Harry! Harry!' and Harry up on the bar, singing into his beer bottle. She hears his roar of laughter and she is breathless from dancing and woozy from Malawi gin, breathing in the sharp grassy smell of ganja hanging like a blessing over the heaving crowd.

Then she shivers and is alone with Chibeza in the cold, dirty bar with its stink of urine and vomit exposed by the lack of smoke and mirrors. Colder than the bar is the grief that almost opens her inside out.

'Well hello there, Doctor!' Chibeza beams at her, but then his smile flickers. 'Are you alright, madam? Do you need to sit down?'

Georgia waits for the dry lump in her throat to stop threatening to choke her. She coughs, and sighs, 'Hey Chibeza. No, no. I'm fine. Too long in the sun perhaps. Could you fix me a Coke? And one for yourself?'

Chibeza's smile flares back on and he bends down to un-padlock the fridge, emerging with two glass bottles glistening with condensation. He looks over her head into the dark far corner, 'You want another cold one, Bwana?'

Georgia is not the only one in the bar after all. A heavy-set white man in a shirt and tie is sitting with his head in his hands, right under the official picture of the current President. Georgia recognises him from a function she attended three days previously. He is aide to some ambassador, Georgia can't remember which. A very young woman, face cream-lightened, sits opposite him, shivering a little in her tiny tank top. Georgia has seen her before; one of the bar's working girls, a waitress with benefits. The girl is filing her nails and sighing with boredom. The man, immersed in a slightly drunken daydream, raises his bloodhound face from his hands and looks, unseeing, across the room, 'Yah. Another one, Mr Chibeza. Tak.' He lowers his head again and the little prostitute sags.

Chibeza plucks an ice cold lager from the fridge, pops the lid and carries it over on a tray to the Dane.

Georgia turns her back on them, gulping the Coke until she belches gently. An ambassador is not unusual in Danny's Bar. Nothing is. She once came here to treat a burn victim at 6am. The woman turned out to be the CEO of a major pharmaceutical company, and had been out all night with a bunch of UN officials – and Harry of course – before setting her hair on fire when doing Sambuca shots at dawn. Another time Danny banned firearms in the karaoke room after one of the local government minister's sons had shot a hole through Danny's prized Elvis mirror.

Georgia drifts. She is very tired and terribly sad. Since Harry's death nothing has seemed the right colour or intensity. Everything is muted and blurred.

She jumps when a hand grabs her shoulder. Danny's specs glitter in the dim light. He is a small, slight man but his grip is bruising.

'Doctor Shapiro, what you do here? Is there a medical emergency?' He laughs without smiling. Georgia wonders if the man has eyelids. Lizard-like, he never seems to blink.

'Hey Danny. You called me, remember? What's up?'

Danny glances around, and for a moment his glasses are mirrors. Georgia sees her face, hair a dark knotted mess, eyes red and heavy with shadows. Danny pinches her shoulder again. His head cocks to one side in the direction of the depressed Danish aide, 'Not here. You follow me.'

She follows the little man back behind the bar, through the large open space used for the disco and into the foul little kitchen reeking of burnt cooking oil.

'Come, come.' Danny is disappearing into what Georgia has always thought is a pantry.

Cautiously, she follows. The pantry is much bigger inside than it looks. Danny has cleared the bags of rice and vegetables to one side and piled the tins and bottles against the other. The rest of the room has been converted into an office. He has somehow stuffed in a huge metal filing cabinet, a squat black safe that could have been a set piece in a 1920s bank heist movie, and a dark wooden desk. A large hole in the ceiling exposes several rafters and the tin roofing slats above. Enough sunlight filters through the cracks and the holes in the roof to ensure the spiralling dust is visible. Food hygiene is obviously not a particularly high priority.

Danny settles himself into a large office chair behind the desk and reaches underneath. 'You sit,' he says, nodding at a wooden stool.

Georgia pulls it over and sits gingerly. The stool has one leg shorter than the others. Danny pulls out a bottle of Black Label whiskey and two glasses. He doesn't offer, just pours two drinks and thrusts one across the desk at her. Georgia has known Danny for five years. She has never ever known him to hand out a free drink. She hesitates. It is mid-afternoon.

'Drink,' Danny flicks his hands at her. 'You look like shit. You still missing that crazy bastard. You drink.'

Georgia blows breath slowly between her lips, picks up the tumbler and takes a swig. The amber liquid burns a pleasant hole all the way down to her heart.

Danny nods. 'Now, Doctor. We need a serious talk.'

He turns and crouches in front of his safe, fiddling with the lock and swearing softly in Cantonese. His bald spot gleams from the hair oil he uses. Georgia, now whiskey-warm, is mesmerised.

'Hai!' Danny finally gets the creaky safe open and pulls out a large packet, which he places carefully on the desk.

'What...?' Georgia opens her mouth, but Danny holds up a slender ink-stained finger. He picks up the envelope and, running a long nail under the gummed flap, slides the contents out onto the table, delicately and with great distaste, as if releasing a scorpion. There are three things that slip out of the padded sleeve onto the desk. The first is a European driver's licence. The picture of a severe-looking young white man stares out of the top right corner. The licence itself is stained and torn, and water has got under the laminate making the paper bulge. The man's name is indecipherable. Coiled next to the licence is a long, thick silver chain with a heavy wooden black cross attached by a silver ring. Beside that is what looks like a dried mopane worm, the black caterpillars that are a local delicacy. Georgia looks quizzically at Danny and reaches to pick it up.

'No, no! Stop! You no touch!' Danny's voice comes out in a screech and Georgia freezes. It isn't a caterpillar. It is a mummified finger.

'For fuck's sake, Danny!' Georgia stands up appalled, and the precariously balanced stool falls over.

Danny shakes his head apologetically, sighs deeply, throws back his whiskey and pours himself another.

'I told him not get involved,' he mutters, his mouth twitches with disgust as he looks at the contents of the envelope.

Georgia waits perfectly still. Dust glitters gold to grey, spiralling down.

'Two months ago I am here and your friend come charging in. "I must speak with you, Danny," he said.'

'Harry?'

'Yes, that one. He was... not himself.'

'I don't understand...'

'He wasn't happy Rasta. He was crazy and he was...' Danny scrunches up his face trying to think of the right words. 'He was mess up. Nervous. Blood on face and shirt. He was scared. He speak to me in here alone, hand me the envelope and ask me to hold it in the safe for him.'

Georgia shakes her head. 'No way. He would have told me if something was scaring him.'

Danny looks up at her, unblinking, but there is something like pity in the downturn of his thin grey mouth. The whiskey is turning to acid in her gut.

'Look,' he continues. 'All I know is when he come, your friend he ask me to put this thing in my safe until he collects it. Said it was evidence for something. Of something. He say nothing more. I ask if it was evidence why he not go to the police but he looked at me like I was the crazy. He offered me money. He even offered to pay his bar tab.'

Harry's bar tab was famous throughout Zambia. It must have come to millions of kwacha. It had been a point of honour for Harry that somehow he always got away with signing for his drinks.

'Why didn't he...' begins Georgia, but her voice falters.

'Come to you? I don't know. Maybe I just take money and don't ask questions,' says Danny pragmatically. 'I don't ask what was in the envelope. I just put in the safe. I wait for him to come and take it back. Then I hear about the accident. I do nothing for a while and then I think maybe it is something like money in that envelope. Only then I look in the inside and I know I don't want this... juju... in my place. No – it must go immediately!'

Danny pauses and twists his neck sharply, cracking it, releasing the tension. He doesn't make eye contact now but looks down at the desk. 'He was like your family I think so I offer it to you to take... or I will burn it.'

'Why did it take you so long to call me? Harry died months ago, Danny. If you were so keen to get rid of this...?'

Danny shrugs, looking uncomfortable. 'I tried speak to you at funeral but...'

Georgia reaches across the desk for the whiskey bottle to pour another shot. She holds the liquid in her mouth briefly, feeling it burn, then she swallows.

'What else do you know?' she asks, her voice quiet but insistent.

'Look at licence,' sighs Danny.

Placing her hands carefully on either side of the items on the desk, Georgia leans in to look at the photograph. She holds her breath but even so she gets a momentary glimmering scent of dried blood. Standing, she looks wide-eyed at Danny. 'It's the Danish filmmaker – the one who disappeared in November?'

Danny nods and his glasses mist up. He takes them off to wipe, revealing huge dark circles under his eyes, his skin sallow and almost translucent with fatigue. Georgia's inner doctor wonders about his health; the Chinese are prone to liver disease, hepatitis... something else...?

Then she remembers the aide in the other room.

'Shit Danny, there is someone from the Danish embassy in the bar... aren't they related? Should we...?'

Danny stands up, pushing his glasses firmly onto his nose. His mild manner is gone. He is enraged, bristling like a cat. 'This is my bar! Mr Bisgaard is customer. You don't do in *my* bar.'

'But...'

'No, Doctor. I give you one choice. You take this filth out of my bar or I take outside and throw in incinerator. I won't speak again. You go to the Zambian police, to the Danish embassy... you go to the fucking CIA if you want, to the Queen, but I don't want my name associated. No one investigates here. No one!'

Georgia is too confused to do more than stand and stare. She wants Danny to take the envelope and the foul things and burn them. She wants to go home and go to sleep, but in her heart she has always known Harry's death was wrong and now there is proof that he was involved in something much deeper and darker than she could have possibly imagined. Should she turn away, let the dead sleep?

Danny takes a rolled up newspaper from the side of the desk and scoops the licence and the chain back into the envelope. He has to chase the dried finger around the slippery surface before trapping it and sweeping it in. They both shiver with relief when the envelope is shut.

Danny formally hands it to her and after a tiny moment she takes it. It feels heavy.

'Do jeh... thank you.'

Danny wipes his hands on his shirt even though he hasn't actually touched any of the envelope's contents, throws the newspaper into the dustbin and breathes out, immediately more relaxed. 'Right. Good.'

He moves around the desk and flaps his arms, shooing Georgia backwards towards the door. She stumbles over the fallen stool and bends to pick it up.

'You no worry about that... just go now, go now.'

Georgia, disorientated, puts her hand on the door handle.

'No wait.' Danny whirls back to his desk and, turning back, slaps the large bottle into her free hand. 'Keep the whiskey,' he says, and shoves her out of the door.

5.

Northmead shopping centre is a hodgepodge of odd architecture. A central square of shops – small businesses in front and Lebanese supermarket behind – is circled by a road, so pot-holed and rutted that cars will sometimes sink almost out of sight. Both lanes of traffic have to use the same areas of relatively drivable tarmac, so there are constant jams, hooting and howling as car blocks bus blocks jeep blocks wheelbarrow and on and on. Car fumes in the heat make the air ripple.

To the left of the supermarket are two Indian restaurants, a chicken and chip shop, and a strange dark place that sells seafood, which considering Zambia is one of the most landlocked countries in the world, and several thousand miles from sea in every direction, would explain the eye-watering expense – and smell – of the fish.

To the back is an outdoor local market selling Zambian and Congolese tat: masks and fetishes, cloths and ornaments. There are stalls of vegetables – mostly tomatoes and beans – dried river fish that hum with flies, cobblers, tailors, several tinsmiths bashing strips of metal into charcoal braziers and saucepans, and of course the traditional healers with stalls laden with various roots, dried powders in wonderful colours, and glass bottles full of un-nameable things in oil.

To either side of the market are more shops: chi-chi dress shops, pharmacies, sweet shops, cake shops, all thinning out to grotty housing blocks with broken glass in the lower windows and overflowing cesspits out the back.

Luse and Bligh negotiate the chaotic traffic, trying to look all ways at once. It is luck more than anything else that gets them to the far pavement. They are heading to the little clinic on the corner. The walls are freshly white and the door is open.

Outside Luse pauses and looks critically at Bligh. 'I think you better stay outside... on watch,' she says.

'Watching for what?' asks Bligh, secretly relieved.

'I dunno. Trouble. Stuff. You know.' Actually Luse worries that Bligh with his ghastly face will cause havoc in the clinic. Someone will probably try and give him first aid. She just wants to get the information and get out.

Bligh shrugs and leans against the wall. A passing woman widens her eyes in shock at his appearance and takes large steps around him, shaking her head with pity. Bligh sticks his tongue out at her retreating back.

Inside the clinic a dilapidated ceiling fan makes chunk-chunk sounds and the sharp smell of antiseptic hides something nastier. The floor is freshly mopped and the linoleum gleams – as does the middle-aged receptionist who sits all shiny with her vaselined skin and a nylon wig on her head. She wears a wide pink kaftan and bright orange lipstick. Luse's heart sinks. The woman is a stranger to her and looks quite unlike the warm young nurse she has spoken to before. She bites her lip, thinking, and then takes a step forward.

The reception area is almost empty. A grizzled old Indian man and his wife sit on the left of the reception desk. The wife is in a blue and purple sari, her flaccid flesh overflowing and her face grey, lips the colour of cooked liver. The man has heavy, thick glasses balanced precariously on his bulbous nose. Grey hair explodes from his ears and nostrils. Luse tears her eyes away from the old man's nose hair and, wiping her hands nervously down her T-shirt, walks up to the desk. She limps a little without realising she is doing so; the infection in her heel is worsening. It feels as though she has a couple of tiny glass splinters in the skin. She shuffles closer. The orange-lipped receptionist does not look up.

'Mulibwanji, madam.'

The orange lipstick glistens like wet paint as the woman's lips tighten. She takes her time, shuffling her papers, stapling something, then she looks over the desk at Luse. 'Bwanji mfana. What can I do for you?'

She runs her eyes over Luse's rags and down to her bare feet. The top lip curls, the lipstick making a slight sucking sound.

'I am sorry for taking your time, madam,' Luse speaks politely, perfectly and without shame. She holds eye contact for just long enough before letting her eyes slide to the side as is traditional. She may be dressed as a street kid but her manner is that of a chief's child. 'Nurse Banda asked me to come in. Is she here?'

'Nurse Banda?' The woman blinks. Surprised out of her condescension by the child's precociousness, she checks the desk diary. 'Nurse Banda is in Livingstone at a conference this week. You should come back another time, boy.'

'Oh dear, that will be a bit difficult, madam,' Luse says. 'Nurse Banda was the sister of my aunt's cousin who died last Tuesday. She promised to help us with funeral costs.'

The receptionist looks both baffled and upset. In Lusaka there are hundreds of funerals each week, mostly AIDS-related. It isn't unusual these days for even very distant family members to seek out those lucky ones with jobs and ask for assistance with funeral expenses.

'She told me I could pick up an envelope from a Dr George Shapi but she forgot to tell me which clinic,' Luse improvises desperately.

'Dr George Shapi? I have never heard of a Dr Shapi and I know many doctors.' The woman begins shuffling papers again.

Luse's forehead creases. 'A white doctor. Muzungu. Please, madam. Maybe you will remember a Shapi from the UK?'

The woman purses her lips. The slick lipstick makes more swamp noise. 'I told you child, I don't know such a one.'

'A white doctor from UK?' A voice comes from the bench on the left. The old Indian man is blinking at them with eyes magnified to ten times their size by his glasses. He looks like an eagle owl.

'Oh dear, Mr Bannerjee, please don't let a street boy bother you,' says orange-lips hastily, her wig slipping slightly as she shakes her head.

'It's no bother,' says the old man. 'My wife must have seen every doctor in the whole of Lusaka. Come here, child.' The man blinks again. His wife seems asleep.

Luse steps closer, aware of the receptionist's eyes boring into her back. She gives the old man a slight bow and he nods, and then elbows his fat wife in the ribs, hard.

'Wake up, you hippo,' he demands. 'Tell this child the name of that white doctor at MedCare clinic.'

His wife comes out of her reverie and peers at Luse. 'You can't give names of important people out to just anyone,' she simpers.

'You are a stupid warthog,' says her husband calmly. Luse has to agree, the similarity is there.

The wife bristles and then sags back into her skin. 'MedCare... there are two British doctors. One is a woman and one is a man.'

Luse waits while the woman thinks. Thinking, it seems, is quite hard going. Luse's hands become fists at her sides. The old man looks as if he is going to poke his wife in the ribs again.

'The man... Dr... Peterson. The woman is Dr... um... Shapiro.'

Shapiro. Shapi. Luse must have heard the Rasta wrong. He had said Shapiro. George Shapiro was a woman.

'MedCare is easy to find,' interjects Mr Bannerjee. 'Half way down Cairo Road. Next to the United Arabica Bank.

'Yes. That doctor,' his wife continues, 'she was the one who treated my gout last year. An okay lady but so expensive. These ones are for sure unmarried...'

The woman warbles on but Luse is no longer listening.

6.

Georgia emerges shakily from the depths of Danny's Bar and finds herself blinded by white sunlight. Holding up the padded envelope to shade her eyes, she feels the things inside slide down towards her fingers as she walks to the car. The sensation is unpleasant and she holds the envelope away from her body as she approaches her dusty green Toyota. Unlocking the high cab, she pulls herself up onto the driver's seat and sits still. A few minutes pass and then she jumps back out, leans over and throws up the whiskey she has drunk onto the red-grey dust. She is still bent over retching when she hears someone approach.

'You need a doctor, Doctor?'

It is Watson, the South African bartender. He has been filling beer crates on the porch and must have seen her come out into the car park.

'Drinking on the job surely is a bad idea for a medic. Boozing could ruin your looks.' Watson's pockmarked face looms over her shoulder, his mouth still stretched wide with his own joke. In trying to help her to her feet, he manages to pinch her breast. 'Oh sorry there, Doc.'

Georgia straightens up, already feeling better now that the whiskey is out of her system. She wipes her mouth and then grabs his shoulder to haul herself up, deliberately leaving an unpleasant smear on his white T-shirt. The smile disappears from his face and his blood-flecked eyes narrow.

'Oh sorry there, Watson,' she says, clambering back into the car. She has thrown the envelope and bottle of whiskey on the passenger seat. As she reaches out to shut the door, she sees Watson's face change. His scowl deepens and the marks on his face darken, suffused with blood. He is looking over her shoulder at the envelope.

'Watson? Do you know anything...?' But the stocky man turns away sharply and strides back towards the bar. His hands are balled into fists and Georgia doesn't call after him. Instead she starts the Toyota and reverses quickly out of the car park, sending a cloud of red brown dust into the air.

In minutes she is heading out towards the Great East Road, her mind untwisting as she gears up. She is a good driver; it soothes her to feel almost part of the machine, her foot balanced on the clutch, her eyes slipping from road to mirror to road again. Her heart slows and she allows the memory of Danny's conversation to bubble up and burst on the surface of her conscious mind. Harry was in trouble, scared. He lied to her and the others at the airport that day, but why? And what was he doing with the Danish lad's driver's licence? And that mummified finger? There are too many questions but they all lead back to one. Was Harry kidnapped and then murdered?

She squeezes the clutch and smoothly drops from fifth to second gear, idling at the traffic lights at the pedestrian bridge, ignoring the stream of hawkers touting brightly coloured plastic toys, imported fruit and Obama T-shirts. Her air conditioner roars, dampening the noise of people milling on the roadsides, weakening the powerful smells of roasted maize, diesel and sewage from outside. A man knocks lightly on her window, waving a cutlery set and an Arabic Monopoly board. She gazes through him, thinking hard, and then she remembers.

'Father Bernard,' she says aloud. The hawker outside cups his ear and Georgia smiles and shakes her head. 'Not you, buddy. It's Father Bernard we need. Now there's a priest who knows his witchcraft!'

7.

'Well that's it then,' says Bligh when Luse tells him about Dr Georgia Shapiro and where the clinic is located. 'You'll just have to let it drop now. It's far too dangerous. The Twins will kill you, chop you into pieces and throw you to their dogs – or worse, right back to the Priestess – if they see you. Even if they smell you or your little brother.'

'I can't let the Rasta down, Bligh. There must be a way to get past them,' Luse responds sulkily, knowing Bligh is probably right. She scratches her heel and winces. Her whole leg aches. They are squatting behind the low wall of the car park outside the Lebanese supermarket, scouring the crowds, Luse now with a freshly-washed face, a vaguely clean T-shirt and unbroken flip-flops carried along especially for the occasion. She can hear Bligh's stomach growl and knows he is beginning to lose focus.

'Maybe we should try Shoprite...' he starts to say, stretching, but Luse grabs his arm and pulls him back down behind the low wall of the parking lot.

'Them!' she says triumphantly and points at the mark before leaping up and running forward to the entrance of the supermarket.

The family Luse has selected is headed by a solid but weary-looking woman in large designer sunglasses. Her pretty, gold, high-heeled sandals are a couple of sizes too small so that her cracked dry heels stick out over the backs of the shoes, but her hair is perfectly and expensively shaped. A large and ugly handbag has the letters D and G making up the buckle. Behind her a young nanny, scarcely older then Luse, is making heroic and mostly futile efforts to herd together five very young children. Luse runs smiling through the entrance on the heels of the distraught little nanny and under the radar of the shop security that stand at the entrance, slapping their thick wooden sticks in their palms.

It is a very simple scam but difficult to pull off, and Luse has worked hard on her technique. She follows discreetly behind the family, still giving the impression to other shoppers and security that she is part of the group. The fat, weary woman doesn't bother to take off her sunglasses as she moves mechanically down the aisles grabbing things from the shelves and lobbing them into the large trolley with one hand, her other hand occupied with a cell phone she holds plastered to her ear. Occasionally she lowers the phone to yell instructions or abuse at the poor nanny, but pays no attention at all to the children who are running riot, grabbing packets of crisps and cereals and sweets and shrieking, exactly what Luse is relying on.

'Ya va! These little ones!' Luse exclaims in her posh voice, helping the nanny drag one of the little boys away from the mountain of cauliflower he is about to dislodge. 'My mum is a friend of your madam. She told me to see if you needed help.'

She points vaguely in the direction of a crowd of women gossiping near the dog food. Luse hasn't a clue who the women are, but it doesn't matter. The nanny's eyes are rolling in her head in her efforts to keep track of the children, and she just nods gratefully at what she takes to be a nice young boy and the son of a family friend. Luse is in.

Under the pretext of helping the nanny, she subtly stows several extra bits and pieces in the trolley, another loaf of bread, a third pack of sausages, some tea and so on. As the manic group led by the world-weary mama approaches the checkout, Luse whizzes around the fat woman to the front to help pack the shopping, seamlessly blending into the faceless young people who stand at the end of the checkout aisles packing customers' groceries. She is able to carefully slip one loaded plastic bag out of the trolley and onto the floor by the checkout, kicking it just out of sight underneath the till.

The fat woman, still on the phone, pays and without even glancing at Luse, signals to the nanny. The family move off, Luse skipping childishly along with them to the security. Now it is all in the timing. She waits until the family is past security before peeling off and rushing back into the shop, calling out, for the benefit of the security guards, 'Don't worry, I'll get it!'

She grabs the full plastic bag she has stashed moments before and runs back outside, veering off in the opposite direction from the family to join Bligh. He begins a crazed, silent, victory dance, one arm raised above his head punching the air, the other rubbing his concave belly in anticipation.

8.

That night a motley collection of children joins Luse, Joshua and Bligh for bread and sausages in the safety and relative shelter of a half-built and now abandoned church that leans precariously against the outer wall of the national football stadium. They have bartered a few sausages for some charcoal and the loan of the mbaula – a little charcoal cooking brazier – from the ancient, half-blind night guard, and have begged half a bag of mealie meal for nsima from one of the local bartenders. It is a good haul and the children feast silently at first, intensely focused on getting the food into their starving bodies, eyes and greasy lips shining in the firelight. The night is dark and cloudy and thunder rumbles far away, briefly silencing the tree frogs in the nearby thicket and the crickets in the grass.

The kids have built a large fire from collected rubbish and sit close to each other in a semicircle passing food, burping and smiling. Flames crackle and spurt sparks and smoke. Occasionally the stench of burning plastic makes them all cough, but mostly they revel in their full stomachs, the warmth of the fire and the camaraderie. Replete for once, they chat, trading local gossip. The Banda sisters say that one of the Lebanese madams is offering good money for virgins. She will take virgins of either sex and any age. Hope says she has been a virgin three times already. A seed explodes in the newspaper roll of ganja being passed around and nearly takes Bligh's eyebrow off.

'Tchaaa! You roll the newspaper too loosely, you Congolese idiot!' Bligh snaps at Franco, before spitting on his finger and dabbing at the singe mark. Franco ignores him. He is trying to remember if it is his birthday, and counts on his fingers but gets stuck after ten.

'How many is it if I was ten five fingers ago?' he whispers to Joshua but Joshua isn't sure and is being distracted by little Kenneth who has been given a scratch card for the local lottery by a compassionate stranger. He has scratched it to pieces and is furious to find it still doesn't turn into money.

Only Luse remains separate, sitting a little further from the group, rubbing her leg. The calf muscle feels hard and she can see in the flickering light that tiny spidery black lines have appeared on the inside of her foot – tendrils of infection from her heel. She can't eat, and passes her sausages over. They disappear in less than a second.

Her ears prick up when Bligh starts quizzing the group about the Twins.

'What's the word on the Cairo Road Gang, bro?' he is asking Franco.

'The Twins?' Franco spits. 'Shit and more shit, those crazy psychos. I heard they killed a tourist outside the Lusaka Hotel last week.'

'What?'

The other children lean in to listen. All of them at one point or another have been forced to brave the territory of the Twins, and not all of them have come off unscathed. The Twins own the three main streets that form the backbone of the concrete city, and encompass an area running from the railway station to the bus station and all through the centre of town. Any lone child arriving in the city has two choices; either they pay to pass through to the relative safety, but less financially appealing, city suburbs, or they join the Twins' gang.

'Yeah, some guy from Nigeria,' continues Franco. 'They didn't even bother to rob him. Just bashed his head in. Apparently he was a newspaper guy or something.'

'I don't understand how they get away with it.' Susan, the eldest Banda sister, shakes her head, holding her other two sisters close. Their eyes are dark with fear. Each sister still bears the mental scars from their initiation into the city.

'Their older brother is the second-in-command at Police Station Central. He takes a cut of everything.'

'Eh heee!' The children blow out their cheeks, nodding with comprehension. It makes sense. That is how the Twins get away with all that they do.

'Didn't you have a run-in with them once, Luse?' Hope asks, her eyes glowing as her face turns in the firelight.

Luse jerks away from the sudden attention of the children. She doesn't like being looked at too closely. She is still Luse the street boy to all these youngsters, apart from Bligh. Any flaw in her camouflage could be fatal to both her and Joshua. But she can't think straight; the pain in her leg is beginning to make her feel nauseous and dizzy. The thunder in the distance is closing in. It sounds as if it is pounding the distant hills to pulp. She has a flash memory of cowering in a crowded room whilst one of the Twins holds Joshua upside down by one ankle and tells her quite calmly that he is going to tear Joshua's leg off and eat it like a chicken drumstick.

The other children watch as Luse wets her lips and tries to sit up straighter, but at that moment Joshua runs up and puts his small palms over her eyes, crying out, 'No, no, no, no! Don't tell!'

She pulls him into her arms and cuddles him, whispering, 'It's okay Joshie, I'm not going to tell. Shhh.'

Over his shoulder she shakes her head at the others and they turn away.

9.

That night Luse dreams that she is still lying on the ground of the ruined church, but now she is alone. All the other children are gone; the fire is years dead and the old football stadium has crumbled into dust. She lies with her back against an ancient anthill and stretching in front of her is endless empty, harsh scrubland without a living thing in sight. Along the black line of the horizon the roaring wind whirls a million dry, dead things into a tornado. Above her a low half-moon hangs sideways in the blue-black night and the sky is berserk with stars.

In the dream she is cold, almost unbearably so. Realising she is naked, she clutches herself tightly, trying to pull her knees into her chest – but her right leg sticks stiffly out in front of her, nerveless and solid, a stump of blackened wood. Far away a woman's voice, huge and deep, is intoning the Lord's Prayer.

'Our Father who art in Heaven
Hallowed be thy name...
Hallowed... hallowed...
Kingdom come...'

Luse hides her face from the approaching storm, but at her back there is a sound of splitting earth and the termite mound cracks open. She tumbles backwards into the darkness and falls down for a long time, twisting and turning in the endless space. Then far below she spots a tiny flame and as she plummets towards it she sees it is a fire at the very bottom of the cavern. Standing next to the fire is a woman with her arms held wide to catch the falling girl.

It is her grandmother. Her Ba'Neene.

And in this dream Luse does not crash to the rocky ground but lands softly in her dead grandmother's arms, feeling the wonderful warmth of the fire flooding her body. She clings tightly to the old woman and does not want to let go. Her grandmother settles her on the ground, wrapping her in a sheepskin, and leans her wrinkled face close, kissing Luse's tears away and soothing her.

The fire burns huge, bright and hot, the only light source in the pitch blackness. Over the fire are slung several cooking pots of all sizes, and the old woman moves between these, lifting lids and stirring. As she cooks, moving around the pots or using her long stick to prod the fire, she leaves a ghostly trail behind her. Within the trail Luse can make out the faint echoes of other people; another arm lifts at the same time as her grandmother's, another leg steps forward, another face turns towards her.

High up above something is tearing like a hyena at the remains of the termite mound. Luse looks up and sees dust and dislodged pebbles raining down towards the fire. That terrible voice howls into the dark chamber from far overhead.

'Hallowed be thy name,
Give us this day our daily bread,
Give us our bread!'

Her grandmother pauses, shaking her head with disgust, picking up two small pots and pouring them into a third, which steams, sending the smell of acrid herbs into Luse's nostrils.

Placing this pot on the ground, she takes a knife from her skirt and slices the gnarled pad of her thumb, letting several large dark drops of blood splash into the mixture. Before Luse can react, the old lady has filled a gourd from the pot and is pressing it against Luse's lips. Luse drinks and gags as larger chunks of rock begin to fall down into the cave.

The hole above is widening and the tearing wind streams down towards the fire. Flames surge up and flap angrily. The old woman snatches the pot from Luse's hands and with her two long middle fingers scoops out the dregs and flicks them at the girl's blackened stump of a leg. The drops sizzle and smell of sausage fat.

Another roar from above and a boulder smashes down, narrowly missing them both. The web of ghosts behind her grandmother seethes in indignation. Luse feels a pull on her hand and looks down as the old lady scrawls quickly in the red dust of the cave floor. She can just make out the shape. It looks like a bus... a box with wheels... and then the wind hits the bottom of the cave and the fire explodes out in every direction.

Luse wakes up feeling disorientated but refreshed. Her fever has broken and her leg feels better, although the pain is still intense when she puts any weight on her heel. She has slept a little later than the other children who are already packing up their camp and preparing for a day of begging and parking cars for small change. It has rained in the night and puddles glint in the early morning light. Luse dips fingers into fresh clear water that has pooled in the brickwork of the abandoned church and wipes her face.

Joshua skips over to her, grinning widely, lips greasy. He holds out a cold sausage squashed sideways into a bun.

'I made you breakfast!' he tells her proudly. 'And there is even tea!'

Luse hunkers down munching, and as she swallows the dregs of her sweet tea, swirling it in the bottom of the recycled plastic bottle, Bligh comes over to ask her about the day's plan of attack.

'I'm going to go into Cairo Road and find Doctor Shapiro,' says Luse. The words take her by surprise as much as they do Bligh. He stands shuffling uncomfortably.

'I thought we agreed you'd give it up.' His tone is sullen, but Luse can see in his face both fear and guilt. She knows immediately that Bligh isn't going to come.

'I could stay here and look after Joshua if you like,' he says tentatively.

Luse looks at him without rancour. If anything happened to her, Bligh would do his level best to look after Joshua, but he would never manage to keep focused. He would get stoned eventually and forget to feed Joshua or keep him clean and safe. And Bligh's stomach would always come first.

'It's okay, Bligh. It's okay,' she says. 'He has to come with me this time. We'll be fine, I promise.'

'Why are you being so stubborn? How can you possibly get across without someone reporting you to them?'

Luse chews her lip. 'I just know something is going to come up...' She tails off, feeling daft.

'Oooeee, you just "know", eh?' Bligh shakes his fingers at her and makes a face. 'You going to ask your grandmother?'

Luse shrugs, knowing Bligh is being mean because he is upset and worried he is going to lose them. It's time to get moving, although she really doesn't know where to. They don't say goodbye to Bligh. They pretend they are to meet up later around supper time. It is easier that way.

'Here,' says Luse, handing him the plastic bag with the last of the tinned food in. 'You better keep this for us.' Bligh nods and draws the back of his hand across his nose, sniffing loudly.

'Promise you won't trade them for ganja?' she calls after him but he has already walked out of earshot.

10.

Luse takes Joshua by the hand and they begin the long trudge to the main junction where the minibuses swarm. They get to the bus terminus at lunch time. It's hot and crowded with irritated passengers craning their necks to see which buses are going in what direction. There does not seem to be much in the way of a timetable... in fact not much of any kind of order or plan at all. Each bus has a driver, usually sporting a thick gold chain and a baseball cap worn backwards, and at least one conductor responsible for touting for custom and collecting the money. Buses don't leave until full and conductors are often flexible with the truth about their routes in order to ensure every square inch is occupied.

Some of the minibuses are gang-owned and the conductors are often rough, rude, stoned or drunk. Luse has enough money for her and Joshua to share a seat into town but she isn't sure which buses will get them closest to the MedCare clinic and it is too dangerous to be wandering through the city.

They are standing in what might be a queue, baffled and buffeted by the din of the shouting men and revving vehicles. A drunken conductor leans down from the open sliding-door of a packed bus as it veers past and makes a grab at a woman's breast as she waits in front of the children. She shrieks in anger and steps backwards into a puddle. Mud splatters her skirt and oozes into her sandals.

As the bus speeds off, the drunken conductor lurches around laughing and catches sight of Luse and Joshua. His face changes, his gaze sharpens and he shouts something but Luse doesn't hear it.

'He knows us,' she thinks, panicking, turning around and almost falling into the mud herself. 'How can he know us?'

'I don't want to get on a bus,' says Joshua, pulling at Luse's hand. 'Those men on them are too rough.'

Up ahead the bus with the drunken conductor looks as if it is slowing down. It lurches forward then stops.

'You are right, Joshua! Quickly now!' The children peel away from the crowd, running and dodging across the road to find themselves gasping for breath and back at Northmead, right opposite the Lebanese supermarket. Luse's foot aches and her mouth is dry. She knows there is a public tap behind the market. If it is connected to the mains they can get a drink at least.

At that moment she hears a siren.

An ambulance screams up, lights flashing and horn burping. Traffic parts and the ambulance drives through the cars in front of the shocked children. Luse watches as it speeds through the junction and around into the pot-holed car park. On its side she reads 'MedCare Clinic Emergency Service.'

'Come on, Joshie!' she yells, and they run after it, Luse hopping on her good leg.

The ambulance pulls up outside the Singing Dolphin Seafood Restaurant and two paramedics with kit leap out from the front and dash into the building. A third man in his smart blue uniform walks to the back of the ambulance and opens the doors to allow for the gurney. A crowd begins to gather immediately, drawn to the drama, the possibility of blood.

'Stand back please,' orders the third man importantly, holding his hands out at the gathering. 'Let our boys do their work.'

The crowd shuffles backwards a little, but Luse pulls Joshua forward. She can see the third man is enjoying himself. He is short, his legs slightly bowed, but his chest is puffed up like a pigeon. He makes clicking noises with his tongue as he leans into the back of the ambulance and then there is a big show of pulling on plastic gloves. The crowd 'Ooee', impressed. Luse and Joshua edge forward.

The door of the seafood restaurant opens again and one of the paramedics comes out and speaks to the Pigeon quietly. Something about 'That judge again...' The Pigeon looks somewhat deflated. He leans into the ambulance without his previous verve, dragging out a folded wheelchair. Then he disappears back into the restaurant with the other medic, forgetting to secure the back.

Luse sees her moment. The crowd is watching the door of the restaurant and no one has yet noticed that the back of the ambulance is hanging slightly ajar. Luse pulls Joshua to the door, hoists him up and crawls in after him, leaving the door slightly open behind them. They slither as far into the back as they can go, burying themselves under a pile of silver blankets and glove boxes that have been stuffed under the wheeled bed. Luse holds her breath but Joshua is giggling.

She hears the crowd murmuring and guesses that the paramedics are emerging from the restaurant again. The children keep very still, watching through the open gap of the back door. They see the wheelchair pushed forward, buckling under the weight of a plump elderly man who clutches his gut, glistening with sweat. He is wearing a suit that is a little tight for him and his flesh bulges out at the collar, the wrists and the waistline. A hard-faced young woman in massive platform heels and a tiny halter top teeters in the restaurant doorway looking more bored than anxious. The paramedics appear a little confused.

'Please, Your Honour,' Luse hears the Pigeon hissing, away from the crowd and into the old man's ear. 'There is really nothing wrong with you. There is nothing more we can do, Bwana.'

The man groans dramatically, his face in a rictus of pain, but Luse can see a glistening beneath the lids as he keeps an eye on the crowd. Making a pretence of clutching at the paramedic's arm, he whispers, spittle glinting in the sunlight, 'Can't you just pretend to defibrillate me? If my wife gets to hear about this.'

'Oh, isn't that your...?' The paramedic stops himself mid-sentence.

The girl in the heels bats her mascara-heavy eyelashes at him, 'Will... Daddy... be okay, sir?'

The Pigeon sighs and the fat man pulls at the medic's arm again giving another groan.

'Please!'

Anxious that the medics are going to allow the man into the ambulance, Luse pushes Joshua deeper under the pile of boxes and lies flat herself. She thinks she hears the Pigeon saying something about the time and that perhaps they should just bring the Justice in, but at that moment the old man farts with such force that the ambulance rocks and the crowd cheers. The man isn't having a heart attack after all.

Voices continue outside for a moment, some raised, then the door is opened, the folded wheelchair flung up into the back, and the door firmly slammed shut. The ambulance heaves gently to one side as all three of the paramedics climb back into the front cab. To their credit they don't collapse into snorting, braying laughter until they have turned out of the car park.

11.

The ambulance has been parked for some time, the hot engine pinging and creaking as it cools. Hunched in the back, Luse is beginning to feel odd again, as if she is floating.

'Can we get out now?' Joshua is uncomfortable and sweaty. He needs to pee and Luse is beginning to snore. He shakes her by the arm.

'Please Luse...'

She wakes, groggy, mouth dry, leg aching. Although the closed ambulance has heated up like a furnace and sweat dribbles off her top lip, she has begun to shiver.

'Yeah okay, but quietly. Let's have a look.'

Crawling carefully out of the pile of glove boxes, she peeks out of the window. They are in a car park – a clinic car park. The sign on the main wall of the building reads 'MedCare – taking care of YOU!' in large red and blue letters with a life-size mural of a grinning nurse with a terrifyingly large hypodermic syringe held aloft.

Luse peers around. There are several cars parked nearby, mostly empty. In a battered Daewoo a man sits reading a newspaper, door open and local radio gently hissing rumba from the dashboard. In another, a silver Pajero, a weary but well made-up woman gesticulates with one hand, holding her cell phone to her ear with the other. Her mouth opens and shuts, but with all doors closed she makes as much noise as a goldfish.

Some of the clinic staff stands in a group in the shade of the only tree, sharing cigarettes and gossip. The Pigeon medic has just finished telling a story and the group breaks into raucous laughter; a man claps him on the shoulder and another laughs so hard he has to grip his knees to keep standing. Everyone looks happy, self-assured, engrossed.

Luse shivers again, confused for a moment. Her calf muscle is rigid again and whatever her grandmother gave her in the dream is quickly wearing off. Joshua is jiggling and squirming.

'Luse, I need to weewee...'

Cautiously, Luse cracks the back open. Two of the paramedics have come sauntering back from the emergency ward and join the others under the tree. The acrid smell of cigarette smoke and the sound of male laughter float up into the afternoon sky.

Luse helps Joshua slide down to the ground and then grabs his hand, ready to make a dash for the main door.

'Hey? Iwe! Wafana!' A woman's voice comes from behind them. It is the gate guard, a very pretty young woman in army fatigues. She waves a black baton at the children but Luse doesn't stop, just turns slightly and raises her hand in a thumbs-up gesture. Her confidence causes the guard to hesitate and that is all they need. Luse and Joshua are through the door and blinking in the brightly-lit, chilly air-conditioned reception.

'Please, madam. We really need to see Doctor Shapiro.'

For the second time in 48 hours a clinic receptionist looks down at Luse with that particular expression of pity, disgust and boredom.

'We run the clinic for street kids on Thursdays between twelve and two,' she says, her eyes flitting over the children and then back to her computer screen. Her face is absolutely smooth, milky-brown and without a line. With her dark hair pulled back, her pale eyes and almost non-existent eyebrows, she could be made of plastic.

'Luse!' Joshua tugs at her arm urgently.

Luse looks up at the impenetrable face of the woman and opens her mouth to plead, but at that moment the reception telephone rings and the woman answers. She no longer sees the children. They might as well have become invisible.

The sign for the toilet is pointing to the far end of a low-lit waiting room and Luse pulls Joshua swiftly away from the front desk. In the bathroom she helps him with his trousers and then leaves him to pee. She runs water in the sink, splashes her face. She needs to come up with some way to get past reception, but instead she is seeing lights flickering at the edges of her vision. She thinks she can hear her own brain sloshing around in her head. It hurts.

Quietly returning to the waiting room, out of sight of the reception desk, Luse finds a seat on the cushioned bench that runs along three walls. A low table covered with ancient magazines and newspapers takes up the middle of the room. There is also a large jug of water and several plastic cups next to a vase of roses. Without needing to be asked, Joshua slips off his seat and pours water for Luse, slopping a little on the floor as he brings it back to her.

'Thanks, Joshie.'

The water is glorious but she can only sip a little. Bang! Bang! goes her poor head and she rests her forehead against the cool grey wall.

'Why are you breathing funny?'

Joshua is standing against her knees, holding her hand. She hasn't realised that she has been panting.

'Luse?'

She hears his voice tremble but she doesn't know what to do. She has not thought ahead, has no plan past getting to MedCare and finding the doctor. She just wants to rest for a long, long time.

'Did I hear you need to see Dr Shapiro?'

A very dark-skinned old man with wire-rimmed glasses is sitting quietly next to them. He is wearing black, and in the gloom Luse has not noticed him. Now she sees a gleam of white at his collar.

'Yes, Father,' she croaks.

Joshua has narrowed his eyes and is standing with little arms akimbo. 'We must see the doctor Shapi, Bwana Father. But that lady won't let us.' His eyes blaze in the direction of the receptionist.

'I see...' The priest seems to be thinking.

A nurse comes into the waiting room, glances around and sees the elderly man. 'Father Bernard? She's free – she asked to see you now.'

The priest stands. He is frail and bent over. He holds out a hand to Luse, 'Come on then, son. Let's go and see Dr Shapiro.'

12.

Georgia is hunched over her desk scribbling a prescription when the door opens.

'Father Bernard,' announces the nurse.

'Wonderful!' says Georgia. 'Come on in, Father...'

She stands up, dropping her pen on the desk and extending her hand to the old man but his are occupied. On one hip he holds a little boy with soft cheeks, wide dark eyes and a snotty nose. His other hand holds that of a ragged skinny kid of about ten or eleven whose eyes glisten with fever.

'Georgia!' he says with warmth. 'Lovely to see you!'

'Father?'

'These are friends in need. This here is Joshua and this is... Luse, I think. He doesn't look too good.'

The boy sways and his eyes glaze briefly then sharpen.

'Doctor Shapi? I mean Doctor Shapiro... I have to speak with you.'

His English is perfect, unaccented.

Georgia moves forward quickly and takes Luse's hand. The palm is almost crackling, dry heat coming from the child's body as if from sun-baked concrete.

'Now come here, Luse.' Georgia puts an arm around the child, leading him gently towards the examination bed.

'No... I'm okay...' Luse says weakly. 'I have to tell you...'

'Can you climb up on here?'

Clumsily Luse tries to climb onto the examination table, but there is something badly wrong with her coordination and she can't work out how to move her legs. She remembers the blackened stump from her dream.

'Don't chop my leg off...' she begins, her words coming out in a muddle of English and Tonga.

Georgia registers the word 'leg'. Swiftly she puts her arms under Luse's armpits and lifts the child up onto the disposable sheet. She takes a temperature, quickly checks ear, nose, throat and chest glands and begins to palpate the child's legs, asking questions gently all the while.

'Where does it hurt, Luse? Does this hurt? Did you have a fall or cut yourself?'

Luse is still trying to speak but the words coagulate in her throat and she chokes and then convulses, eyes rolling back into her head.

Georgia has the primary source of infection in seconds. The heel wound is septic. The black tendrils of infection are creeping swiftly up the child's leg; a deadly tattoo.

Georgia calls for the nurse then moves straight back to Luse, holding the fitting child firmly to ensure a clear airway. The fit passes and Luse looks groggily up at Georgia as two nurses run into the room.

'We are going to need Cephalexin, Valium and a fluid replacement drip, and clear me a bed in the emergency ward.'

Georgia has already picked up Luse without waiting for a wheelchair and races to the door.

'Will you excuse me, Father? This child needs immediate care!'

Father Bernard steps back, hugging Joshua closely as Georgia rushes past into the corridor and along into the triage ward.

'Luse!' wails Joshua, burrowing his head into Father Bernard's shoulder.

'It's going to be alright, little one. Your brother is getting the best treatment in Lusaka!'

13.

It is some time before Georgia returns to her consultation room. Bernard and Joshua have found the stash of children's toys that she keeps to calm nervous youngsters, and both are sitting on the floor behind her desk doing a jigsaw puzzle. The nurse has organised tea and juice and a large plate of biscuits, which Joshua has in a neat pile next to him on the floor. Riveted by the puzzle, he sticks out a hand and feels for the pile, patting the top biscuit, and then returning his hand to the jigsaw.

Bernard stands up when Georgia enters and, seeing Joshua is happy and calm, joins her at her desk.

'Jesus!' says Georgia and then blushes. 'Oh sorry, Father.'

'How's the boy?'

'Girl, actually,' says Georgia. 'Turns out she is a little girl.'

'But how?'

'I think she was in disguise, Father. If she has been on the street then disguise must have been very sensible. Anyway, we have caught the infection. She'll be on a drip for a couple of days but she'll be fine. I couldn't see anything else wrong apart from some minor abrasions and bruises. There is evidence of a couple of old injuries – nasty ones – on her back and shoulder, but they have healed well and the scarring is minimal.'

Georgia sits back, stretches, then looks quizzically at the priest. 'How did they come to be with you, Father? Are they from your street child project in Chelstone?'

'Actually I just met them here in the waiting room. The boy – the girl – asked to see you urgently. She was very polite but adamant it was you and no other doctor that would do. Your receptionist turned her away. Told her to come back on Thursday for the street kid clinic. The child was beside herself and I could see she was ill so I thought you wouldn't mind them using a little of my time...'

'Bloody Brenda! A little compassion for God's sake. If the kid had gone away she would have gone into a coma in a few hours. She'd have died.' Georgia makes a mental note to have words with the receptionist. 'I wonder why she wanted to see me.'

'I wonder why *you* wanted to see *me*.'

'Oh goodness, yes Father!' Georgia is contrite. 'I need your expertise on some artefacts that have come into my possession. They are somehow linked to Harry's death.'

'Harry... Ah, your poor friend who died in the accident?'

'Yes. But perhaps we should talk about it another time?'

Joshua has become aware of them and realising it is Georgia back in the room, has clambered to his feet and come shyly over to the desk. Father Bernard picks him up and sits him on his lap.

'Your sister is going to be fine, Joshua. She is just going to have to rest for a couple of days and then she'll be all good as new again, okay?'

Joshua slips his thumb in his mouth. He is looking at Georgia with huge eyes. 'You are Doctor Shapi?' he asks around his thumb.

'I am Georgia Shapiro,' says Georgia, leaning forward and beginning an instinctive check up on the boy. She's glad to see minimal malnutrition. His sister must have been looking after him very carefully.

'Luse says I must give you this,' Joshua pulls on a string that is hidden under his T-shirt. Father Bernard helps him unwind it from under his armpit and they pull it out. At the end of the string is a pouch fashioned out of a scrap of T-shirt. In the pouch is a silver cigarette box with a lion motif on the lid. The box is well used, chipped and marked. Father Bernard turns it over curiously.

'It's engraved,' he says.

'I know,' Georgia's voice is flat and odd. Bernard looks up surprised and is shocked by her face. It is white, drained of blood.

'It says, "Who is the King of The Jungle? With all my love, Georgia". I gave it to Harry for his birthday five years ago.'

The Blood of Christ

1.

Luse floats in cool cotton sheets, feeling the morning sunlight warm on her closed eyelids. Drowsily, she wonders if she needs to get up and collect the eggs for Mum. The hens will probably need water too. She sighs and turns over, thinking she can just have a few more minutes in delicious comfort, but then a strange feeling of unease filters through her sleepy fog. Isn't Dad sick? No... not just Dad. Mum collapsed at work. Luse needs to go to her... where is she? Mum?

She tries to call out but her mouth is full of termites and dust and then...

And then Luse remembers it all as she does every time she wakes, and she sighs as the huge weight settles on her chest again. She opens her sleep-sticky eyes properly and looks around the sunny bedroom. She has a vague memory of being carried in here by the beautiful doctor, Georgia Shapiro. This must be Georgia's home. Luse feels calm and safe, although she has no real idea how long she has been asleep. The sun is strong against the glass windows and she guesses it must be nearly midday.

On a camp bed next to her lies Joshua sound asleep, his arm flung out of the yellow blankets over his head, his thumb poking from his fist ready to pop back into his mouth. She wonders if she should start telling him to stop the thumb sucking. Mum once mentioned that it could damage his teeth if left too long. Luse yawns and drifts off again briefly, her thoughts all jumbled up into a mess of memory and dream.

The room is large and the curtains are orange with blue flowers. They billow a little as sweet fresh air blows in through the open windows. The room is pretty, with two chests of drawers and a large wardrobe with a full-length mirror. On each wall are bright paintings; landscapes and townscapes from all around the city. Luse recognises the National Stadium and the huge central Shoprite supermarket. She feels a slight weight in her bladder – the need to pee – but as she turns she finds her hand and wrist wrapped with tape and something sticking into the back of her hand. Something sharp that is attached to a thin plastic tube line that snakes across to the bag hanging from a metal frame over her head. In her half-sleep state she is unperturbed.

A tentative knock comes at the door, making Joshua stir and stretch. 'Luse,' he says instinctively, still mostly asleep.

'Right here,' she replies.

The doctor comes in. *She is so pretty,* thinks Luse, looking at her long, dark hair tied in a bundle at the back of her head, calm, grey eyes and a funny snub nose. She is older looking than Luse's mother but there is a similar vibration about her, a kindness. Luse can feel it. She blinks as the doctor approaches, bringing her more sharply into focus.

'Oh good, I see you are awake!' Georgia whispers. 'I just wanted to check up on you and see if you are hungry. Is that okay?'

Luse nods shyly and Georgia gently pulls Joshua's bed to one side and sits next to Luse. 'Pop this under your tongue, Luse,' she says, shaking a thermometer and slipping it into Luse's mouth.

Georgia takes Luse's pulse and looks at her eyes, feels her neck, eventually taking the thermometer and nodding, pleased, before finally placing a chilly stethoscope against Luse's chest and back. Luse knows it is a stethoscope because she once played the doctor in a play at school and Mum borrowed one from work for her and even showed her how to use it. She heard her mother's heart thump-bump, and demanded to hear her father's and Joshua's, who had squirmed and cried with annoyance.

'Can I hear my brain working?' she asked her mum, holding the stethoscope to her own forehead.

Her mother laughed. 'Everyone can hear your brain working, Luse!' she said.

Georgia is leaning over her now and Luse can smell apples and coconut from her hair.

'This might sting a little, but I think you are well enough to come off it now,' Georgia is saying as she gently un-tapes the sticky stuff from Luse's wrist and removes the needle from her hand. She helps Luse sit up. Joshua, now fully awake, also clambers onto the bed and wraps his arms around Luse's neck.

'Gently, Joshua!' laughs Georgia. 'Your sister needs special care for the next few days. Only the softest hugs!'

Luse sleeps again and then, in the late afternoon, when she has bathed and dressed, she slowly makes her way out of the bedroom and along the corridor to the narrow wooden staircase that spirals down into the living room.

The priest from the clinic is downstairs, sitting on a chocolate-coloured sofa. When he sees Luse he leaps up and comes to help as she reaches the last step, clucking around her like an old hen. His name is Father Bernard, he tells her. He's very happy to see her so well recovered. Joshua has grabbed the priest's hand and is refusing to let go, which means Bernard can only gesture and guide with one hand. He grins apologetically but doesn't complain, and Luse thinks it good of him not to be irritated. Joshua is almost dragging him over and the old man already has a stoop.

In the kitchen Yvonne, Georgia's maid, serves Luse a little tomato soup, and when she has had enough, Georgia helps her back to the living room and makes her comfortable under a blanket on the couch across from Father Bernard and the now dozing Joshua.

For a while they sit quietly while Georgia and Yvonne discuss shopping and cooking for the additional guests, and then Yvonne heads off to catch her bus and Georgia comes through, wiping her hands on a dish towel.

'Can I get you anything, Father? Your usual?'

'Thank you, Georgia. It is indeed that time in the afternoon.'

Luse watches as Georgia pours gold liquid into glittering little glasses. As she hands one across to Bernard, Luse catches a whiff of it – acrid, strong. Into Luse's foggy mind comes a sudden thought as pungent and sharp as the smell of the liquid. 'Joshua gave you the silver box, didn't he?' she asks, anxiety causing her voice to squeak a little. She coughs.

The adults turn to her immediately as if they have been waiting for her to speak.

'Yes,' says Georgia with obvious relief that the questions have begun. 'Luse, the box belonged to a very dear friend of mine. I can't believe you found it!'

Luse feels strangely empty with relief. It is over. They have handed over the Rasta's box to the right person. There is no more that can be done.

'He gave it to us,' says Luse. 'The Rasta. He was hurt...'

Georgia blinks rapidly, leaning forward, 'Wh... when did you see him?'

'Wait, Georgia,' interrupts Bernard calmly. 'One thing at a time.'

Georgia bites her lips, swallows, and sits back nodding.

'Luse, where are your parents? Can we contact them?' asks the priest gently.

Again the memories are confused; time squashes and stretches and Luse begins to feel sick, as if she is in a boat on choppy water. There were empty beds, the constant dull murmuring of chanted prayer, shouted prayer, anger and fear.

She tries not to gag, swallows spit. 'My father is dead. My mother... I think also. I don't know. We – Joshua and I – we were taken away by the church.'

'By the church?'

'The Blood of Christ Church. My father... he joined them and they told him to stop his medicine, his HIV medicine. They said he would be protected by God, but he wasn't protected and then he just died.' She pauses, trying to get the shards of memory into some kind of order. 'So they – the Church and the Priestess – took away the house where we lived.

My grandmother's house in Siavonga. Then they took away my mother. Then they took us...' Her voice trails off, remembering blood under her fingernails and the smell of burning.

'I don't understand,' Georgia presses her. 'Who are The Blood of Christ Church?'

Again the deafening sound of chanting wells up in Luse's ears, causing her to squeeze her eyes shut.

'There was the church leader lady, the Priestess. She said we were possessed by the devil. That Joshua and I killed our parents. Then they... they just took us... away from the house. In sacks. Joshua nearly choked.'

'Do you remember when, where?'

'I know it was the dry season still.' Luse, thinking back, can see the birds flying in the early evening sky, little soft bodies silhouetted against the sunset.

'After my birthday... so I think the end of September. I don't know where we were taken – but far... out in the bush. Near Monze. A school.'

Luse's teeth chatter in a tiny spasm and she bites her tongue, tastes blood, sees the tall man broken in the ditch. 'That man... your friend, the Rasta. We found him and he helped us to Lusaka... but then... he didn't come back...' Luse looks down at her hands twisting in her lap and wonders why they are shaking.

Georgia gently reaches over and feels Luse's forehead. She makes a small tutting noise. 'Oh dear... it's time we got you back into bed.'

To Luse, Georgia's voice is strange, deep and slow like when her old story tapes got stuck in the tape player when she was little. She wants to be more helpful. Georgia and the Father need to know more of course, but Luse can't keep the memories in her head. They hurt her – like staring into the sun.

'I'm getting muddled. I want to remember but it isn't... good yet.'

'It's alright, Luse. You are running a temperature again. You need to take a little more medicine and get some really good rest. I promise you will feel better tomorrow, okay?'

'Don't you worry, little sister. You need to rest.' Father Bernard speaks softly, but when Georgia turns to look at him she is surprised by his expression. His face is twisted in suppressed rage. He looks like he might explode.

Georgia takes Luse's hand and squeezes it tight. 'Come on, kiddo. Enough for tonight, eh? Let's get you to bed. '

She signals to Father Bernard and he gently picks up the sleeping Joshua and leads them in a procession upstairs to the bedroom.

2.

Once Georgia has settled the children, dosing Luse with more antibiotics and paracetemol and tucking Joshua firmly into his own bed, she joins Bernard in the corridor outside the bedroom. She hears as he lets out his breath in a long, whistling hiss, 'Dear Lord!' He leans his forehead on the wall, his bony shoulders shaking, 'In the name of Jesus...'

Georgia doesn't know what to say. She has never seen her friend so agitated and she wants to put an arm out to steady him, but isn't sure of the etiquette with elderly Jesuits.

She can't quite understand the ferocity of his reaction. Although she too is deeply saddened by the idea that The Blood of Christ Church has potentially pulled apart Luse's family, she isn't entirely surprised either. As a doctor she has seen many of the consequences of fear, stigma and superstition that cast a murky fog around the treatment of HIV and AIDS. She has treated other children and adults cast out by their families through fear and shame, has seen first-hand the wounds and scars inflicted by fake traditional healers on sufferers too. Far too many unscrupulous men and women set up as doctors and healers here, faking cures for money and making fortunes out of blood and death. Ironically, it is often the unsterilised razors and sharpened bones the fake witch-doctors use that spread the HIV infection – along with tetanus, septicaemia and false hope.

As Georgia waits for Father Bernard to regain his composure, she remembers that at the clinic, just a few months back, she saw a young man who had been told by some quack doctor, unregistered of course, that the only way to cure his HIV was a full blood transfusion. The man's sister had brought him to the clinic, furious and upset, begging Georgia to talk him out of going through with it. The young man just sat patiently on the examination table, legs dangling, eyes on the floor while his sister raved and wept.

'This trickster treated our cousin, doctor. It cost her very much but she did not live and now this crazy boy wants the same blood exchange!'

Georgia, shocked, had told the lad that a blood transfusion was not an appropriate treatment; that antiretrovirals and a good diet would potentially ensure he stayed healthy, but he sat, sullen, saying nothing.

Did he know where the blood would come from? Did he know anything at all about the doctor who would be treating him? She felt utterly helpless in the face of this man's refusal to see the danger.

'You will die,' Georgia said bluntly. 'You stay with me, we treat you here at the clinic and you live, or you go to this unregistered crook and you die.'

The young man got up, put on his jacket and, passing his sister without a word, walked out of the room. Georgia felt like screaming in frustration.

Neither he nor his sister have come back. Georgia has thought about the episode a great deal, has wondered about trying to find the quack and telling the police. But when Harry died she just lost impetus. Her depression has cauterized her keen sense of outrage, numbed her.

Now it is a church group feeding on people's fear and superstitions, telling them that God is the only cure for HIV. She is not an idiot. She knows that many religious groups veer away from Western medical treatment; Jehovah's Witnesses, Christian Scientists, many of the more radical fundamentalist groups. But hearing about people being bullied off their life-saving drugs always enrages her. However, there is something more than this in Bernard's knotted back.

'Bernard? Do you know this group?'

Now downstairs, her friend is standing in front of her looking bewildered, and worse, frightened.

'Have you heard of Blood of Christ, Bernard?' she asks again. She feels the pulse beat in her throat and regrets the sharpness of her tone. The old man takes off his glasses and rubs his face hard.

'May I sit?'

'Bernard! Of course.'

'I fear I may not only know this particular group. I may well have been, unwittingly, a key ally in their campaign in Zambia.'

Georgia sits quietly, waiting while Bernard fidgets and coughs. Finally he meets her eyes and speaks, 'A few years ago several videos were released in Nigeria. They were made by a production company originally called Evil Eye Productions Ltd. Evil Eye has been producing low budget horror and action films for many years, but they marketed this particular series of videos under another name. They called it the Faith Matters Series and targeted the films at church-based organisations across Africa. The films were cheap and nasty slashers in keeping with the horror genre, but themed around biblical interpretations of demon possession, witchcraft and worse. I believe the Bible is quoted throughout.'

'Really? Sounds unpleasant.' Georgia raises an eyebrow. 'Why would a horror film company find religion?'

'Mammon, Georgia. Simply an excellent money spinner. As you are aware, God's business is booming across Africa. Any righteous man, or woman for that matter, can set themselves up as a pastor and preach the word of God. It doesn't require an exam, just a loud voice and usually an edge on the competition, you know. Something that makes your new church group better than the other guy's down the street. The bigger the congregation the more...'

'The more donations to the cause.'

'Exactly. And competition is fierce.'

Georgia feels more than a little circumspect when it comes to things religious. Her parents were non-practising Jewish academics and she has grown up to consider herself above religion, and is inherently suspicious of it all. She can see the irony, of course – trading one form of superiority for another – but she prefers basing her life-changing decisions on the known, the scientific.

Bernard continues, 'These films are an inspired business move by the CEO of Faith Matters. New church groups snap them up and encourage their congregations to watch them over and over. She sold the distribution rights for one film in particular, *Witch Children*, for a vast amount of money to an evangelical organisation, The Blood of Christ Church.'

'What?'

Bernard nods, '*Witch Children*, when first shown in Lagos, triggered a massive hysterical response and led to many thousands of children being victimised, tortured and killed. But the congregations expanded exponentially. People joined these churches fearing that they too would be accused of witchcraft if they did not.'

'That's appalling.'

'It took the courage of a small children's charity, a very brave Nigerian journalist and a small Danish film crew to expose it and to raise the issue of child demonisation in Nigeria and the Niger Delta as a whole.'

Georgia scratches her head. 'Danish filmmakers... the same ones that were here with Harry do you think?'

'I would think it most likely. The video was banned in Nigeria and the production company has gone back to mainstream horror, but the film has continued to sell in other places, distributed by...'

'Our Blood of Christ? Here in Zambia?'

'It seems they have been circulating the videos amongst their congregations for over a year now. Luse and Joshua are not the first children to report incidents of victimisation... although the school and the kidnapping is a new one to me.'

'If you know about it, Bernard, why don't you stop it? Aren't you on the advisory board of the Council of Churches?'

'I...' Bernard puts a hand to his throat as if finding it hard to swallow. 'I made a mistake. There was a meeting with the Council of Churches and the Zambian Ecumenical Council and a motion was made to have the films banned and The Blood of Christ Church branded as a cult. I had just come back from three weeks travelling and hadn't had time to view the film.'

His eyes flicker behind his glasses as he remembers. 'A woman came to see me, saying she was a pastor with The Blood of Christ Church... came to speak to me a few minutes before the meeting and assured me that the films were an important audio-visual tool in her ministry and had been used to raise debate about superstition, not to encourage it. I am afraid I was impressed, there was something compelling about her, and she seemed to have a thorough, balanced knowledge of biblical text. She quoted Mahatma Gandhi at me as well as Leviticus, and I was tired and easily swayed. I went into the meeting and, in ignorance, voted that the film should not be singled out. I even suggested that doing so could be compared to a book burning. Ach... if only I had just waited until I had time to think it through.'

Bernard picks up his whiskey glass but puts it down again carefully on the coaster. 'My vote meant the motion to have the film withdrawn from distribution failed. Afterwards... Georgia when I saw a copy...' Bernard shakes his head. 'The film is cheaply made, sure. But there is something different about it. The children, covered in white make up and coated in fake blood, eat their parents alive. It's abominable.' He pauses and wipes his mouth with his handkerchief. 'The woman pastor who approached me that day was the same CEO of Faith Matters and Evil Eye Productions, one Selena Clarke. She is also known as the Priestess.'

'You mean Luse's Priestess?'

'Sounds one and the same.'

Bernard's face is grey. They sit in silence for a while, then Georgia claps her forehead and stands up.

'Those Danish filmmakers?' she says. 'Harry was working with two young filmmakers when he died. I have one of their driver's licences...'

She whirls around, wondering what to do, and immediately sits down again feeling dizzy. Father Bernard, sitting on the wicker and red-cushioned chair, looks equally spent.

'Food, Father Bernard. We both need to eat. How is pasta for you?'

Bernard blinks, slightly taken aback by the change in direction of the conversation. 'Err... I love pasta. But Father Michael always overcooks it.'

'Not me.' Georgia stands slowly but with renewed purpose. 'Al dente with fresh tomato and basil sauce. And we still have three-quarters of a rather good bottle of whiskey.'

3.

After Father Bernard has gone, Georgia goes in to check on the children. Joshua has climbed into Luse's bed and now lies across it sideways, pushing Luse almost over the edge. Both the children are deeply asleep and Georgia gently moves Joshua back onto his own camp bed.

She and Bernard talked only a little more over their supper, beginning to put together the jigsaw. The Blood of Christ Church obviously migrated south to Zambia. The Danish filmmakers must have been here primarily to expose their continued distribution of the film *Witch Children* and the subsequent exploitation of children. They employed Harry as a fixer – a guide and translator. He was the best after all. But why the secrecy, and what happened to the Danes?

Georgia told Bernard about the envelope and the three things inside – the blood-stained driver's licence, the ugly black cross and the mummified finger. She asked if he wanted to see them but he insisted that she not touch the envelope again until he came back the next evening. 'These things are used to infect people with fear. They could be coated in something poisonous or hallucinogenic. Just don't touch them till I get back, okay?'

Georgia nodded.

Now she stands quietly in the children's room, listening to their slow, relaxed breathing. The sky has clouded over outside and small storms rumble away in the distance. Luse moans in her sleep and curls over into a foetal position and Georgia pauses, watchful, until the girl relaxes again.

She doesn't want to go into her study where Harry's cigarette box lies on her desk next to her computer, and where, locked in the desk drawer, lurks the envelope from Danny's Bar.

'What next?' she thinks, gazing out of the window into the blackness of the garden. A rusty scream tears a small hole in the night as a screech owl hunts in the garden and unseen things rustle high in the trees. Far away, as ever in this rainy season, the thunder seems to be closing in. Georgia looks at nothing, thinking about her friend, missing him, wondering what she should do. At last she picks up her phone and dials a number in Ndola.

4.

Luse is allowed up for breakfast. She is wearing a T-shirt and jogging pants from Georgia's gym collection; bright blue and orange and too big. She loves them and is hopeful that Georgia might let her have them when it is time to leave. Now she has found Dr Shapiro, there is nowhere really to go apart from back on the street. Maybe Georgia would help her get to Canada and to Aunt Miriam? Luse still feels weak, and things drift in and out of her head. She knows Georgia and Bernard want to hear more about the Rasta, but it is still all tied up inside her.

Meanwhile Joshua is being followed around by Yvonne's five-year-old daughter, Marta. The two little ones are in the garden in their pants making mud pies. Georgia has gone in for an early shift, leaving Yvonne in charge, so once Luse has had a mug of sweet, milky tea and a couple of pieces of bread and jam, she feels safe to wander around the house in her bright new clothes.

Georgia's house is pretty and simple, one of six semi-detached houses in the complex. The front door opens into the large living room, and a wooden step leads down to the dining room and kitchen. Glass doors at the back open out into a garden that runs nearly twenty feet down to a solid white wall embedded with bits of broken glass along the top. Most people have razor wire these days, so there is something a little old-fashioned about the glass that warms Luse. Her parents' old house had a back wall stuck with glass too.

Dark, warped, wooden steps in the corner of the living room spiral upstairs to three bedrooms, one of which Georgia has converted into a study. Light streams into them from the east and trickles along the walls of the upstairs corridor.

Yvonne is in Luse's bedroom, sweeping the wooden floor. She looks up and smiles. She is a bright, warm woman only a little taller than Luse, with breasts and hips so wide she rocks from side to side when she walks. She has a large hanky, that she dabs her round face with, and light brown eyes that twinkle.

'Do you want to sleep, child?' Yvonne asks kindly in Chinyanja, indicating the bed. 'I can come back and finish later.'

'Thank you, madam, but I am okay. May I keep looking around?'

'Of course, dear,' Yvonne dabs her cheeks and puffs on with her work. The doors are open downstairs and Luse can hear the little ones shrieking with delight as Wilson the gardener turns on the hose.

In Georgia's messy bedroom sunlight streams through the large windows and tiny rainbows spin and bounce off the walls from the crystal prisms hanging from the curtain rails. Luse is captivated, entranced. Then her eye falls on a silver frame that holds a large photograph. In the photo the Rasta stands in a boat with a laughing Doctor Shapiro, holding up a huge and fearsome tiger fish. He looks so happy and relaxed, a wide grin shining through his raggedy beard, huge solemn eyes glowing. She knows now that he is dead and her heart twists.

'Luse?'

Luse moves to the top of the stairs and peers down over the bannister towards the front door.

It is Georgia back from the clinic and there is someone with her. A tall Zambian man with hair cropped close to his skull, wearing a dishevelled brown suit. He looks at Luse from where he stands in the front doorway and something about his eyes makes Luse stop and slowly sit down on the wooden steps. Joshua, dripping wet, slides across the wooden parquet floor, making Yvonne shriek with annoyance. As Joshua comes level with the tall man, he stops still and regards him seriously.

'Are you the Rasta's...' Joshua narrows his eyes trying to find the right relation.

'Brother?' The man's voice is low, melodic. He smiles. 'Yes, I am. My name is Augustine but you can call me Gus.'

'H'okay,' says Joshua, ducking out of the towel that Yvonne is trying to smother him with, before skidding back out into the garden again, leaving a puddle of muddy water on the floor.

Georgia, walking through to the kitchen, glances up and sees Luse sitting mesmerised on the stairs. She understands. It is hard not to stare at Gus. He doesn't look much like Harry physically. He is older, thicker set and hasn't the arrogant, slender grace of his brother, nor the dreadlocks, the tangled little beard or the laughter lines... but those eyes are the same.

'Come on in Gus!' she calls over her shoulder. 'That was Joshua and on the stairs the heroine of the hour, Luse.'

Gus clicks his heels and salutes, and Luse gets the giggles.

It is Gus that Georgia rang the night before. Although she knows very little about him, has only in fact met him a couple of times – once at a party and again not so long ago at Harry's funeral – she felt it imperative to let him know about Luse and the silver box. She knows that Harry said Gus disapproved of him, thinking him irresponsible and impetuous, but at the funeral she saw Gus bent double with grief. He wept openly throughout the eulogy. There had been much love there.

She knows too that Gus is the elder brother and that he spent much of his life abroad with the military, that he now lives in Ndola and works as a consultant to the UN in some kind of security or intelligence. If anyone can help them unravel the strange circumstances of Harry's death it has to be him. He has connections, surely?

She watches him out of the corner of her eye as he walks over to the living room. He takes his time, chooses a hard-backed chair to sit in, and doesn't relax into it but sits stiff and straight, waiting.

'Can I get you a drink? I'm going to throw together some sandwiches for lunch, but in the meantime I can fix you some tea or coffee, or a cold drink?' Her voice comes out too high, squeaky. She loved Harry as a friend, never really considered him handsome, but Gus... He catches her staring and Georgia feels pink dapple her cheeks.

'A cup of tea would be lovely,' says Gus and smiles, and Harry smiles through him.

Turning quickly to hide her emotion, Georgia beckons to Luse, 'Come on down kiddo and give me a hand with the sandwiches?'

Luse nods and clambers down the stairs in her bright, floppy, clothes.

While Yvonne gets Joshua and Marta upstairs for a quick rinse, Georgia and Luse fill buns and pile the table high with all kinds of snacks and at least three different types of fruit juice. When the two little ones come down, scrubbed squeaky clean, Yvonne and Georgia cannot help laughing at the expression on Joshua's face – his immense delight at the ham and cheese buns, boiled eggs, crisps, bananas and fruit juice. Luse looks at the food without appetite. The lovely colours and smells and textures are wonderful to her. It is as if she has never seen food before. For months all she has done is think about food – how to find it, how to make it last, how to find more. Now here is a magical feast in front of her and she has no appetite at all. Not so her little brother, who takes handfuls and mouthfuls of everything all at the same time, making Yvonne roll her eyes in mock horror at the mess.

A knock on the mosquito screening at the front door announces Father Bernard and a round-cheeked, young man in army fatigues who stiffens and salutes when he catches sight of Gus.

'At ease soldier,' says Gus.

The man relaxes and raises his hand to the group around the table.

'Sergeant Edward Mwansa,' begins Gus.

'Just Eddie,' says the man. 'Yo!'

'Eddie is my current aide.' Gus gestures him over to the table. 'I hope you don't mind but he has brought over the lab's forensic emergency bag for us.'

'And he was kind enough to give me a lift over too,' says Father Bernard, slapping Eddie on the shoulder.

Joshua jumps from his seat and runs to Bernard, arms outstretched, mouth full of crisps and hands sticky with pickle. The priest catches him up in a bear hug. 'I see you have begun lunch without me, little brother?'

'Mulibwanji, Father,' says Yvonne clucking sternly at Joshua and steering him back to his seat at the table whilst at the same time handing the priest a wet wipe.

Bernard dabs at the handprints on his shirt but without rancour. He winks at Joshua. 'How's your day been going, little brother? Busy?'

'Eeehey!' Joshua sighs. 'There is a lot to do in this garden. I am training Marta in dam-building.' Joshua gestures casually towards Marta with a carrot stick. The little girl gazes at him with undying love.

'Ah and you,' says Bernard, extending his hand to Gus, 'must be Harry's brother, Augustine?'

The conversation is easy. The drone of small talk lulls Luse and she almost drifts into sleep, thinking for a fleeting moment that she sees her grandmother come in from the kitchen before her shape fades, becoming indistinguishable from the dusty sunlight. She is half-woken by Yvonne reaching over her head to collect the plates.

'The children look like they could do with a rest,' she says firmly. Joshua tries to sulk but his heart isn't in it and soon all three children are up in the sunny orange bedroom drifting away.

'Perhaps now would be a good time to have a look at the contents of that envelope?' Bernard looks at Georgia.

'Oh hell.' She pinches her nose briefly to concentrate and then gets up. 'I'll go and fetch it.'

Yvonne is on the stairs. She looks down at Georgia and sucks her teeth. 'I'll stay upstairs with the children,' she says. 'And Georgia, please... no juju around my daughter. Let the men take those things from the house when they are done.'

Sighing, Georgia goes to her office and plucks the envelope from the desk, carrying it with distaste down to the three men standing around the now cleared dining room table.

Gus and Eddie lay down a newspaper, cover it with a sheet of plastic, then with white paper. They have both donned rubber gloves and surgical masks, and Eddie has opened what looks like a fishing tackle box to bring out several clear small plastic bags and lidded pots.

'Shouldn't I just take this to the police?' asks Georgia. She is becoming perturbed by the drama of it all.

'Madam,' says Eddie. 'My brother-in-law has a satellite television and CSI is my favourite show. I study it every day. I am telling you I am better than the police. One day I will be even better than those ka-dudes in Vegas.'

'What on earth are you talking about?' grumbles Father Bernard, holding a mask to his face and peering over Eddie's shoulder.

'Do *not* listen to Eddie,' says Gus, smacking the lad on the back of the head. 'He is actually studying hard at the University Teaching Hospital with a forensic scientist the military were able to pull over from Japan for six months.'

He looks over at Georgia, his light brown eyes disconcertingly clear over his mask. 'Georgia, I work with the police here and trust me, if you took this to them now they would do one of three things; laugh at you, throw it away in fear or...' he pauses, cocking his head towards Father Bernard who is stooped low over the table.

'Or call Father Bernard?' Georgia is surprised but it makes sense. 'Really Bernard? Do the police call you?'

'If they had speed dial at Central Police, my dear, I would be on it.'

Georgia isn't sure if she is being teased again. She bites her lip and tucks a strand of hair behind her ear, sees Gus watching her do it. Her face tingles as if he has touched her.

Eddie, meanwhile, unseals the envelope with a scalpel and gently shakes out the contents onto the white paper; the heavy black ebony cross, the stained driver's licence and the mummified finger. He blows out through his nose and Bernard crosses himself, nodding sombrely.

'This is serious juju used to silence an enemy.' Bernard points at the mummified finger. 'Usually a child's index finger or thumb, it can be cut up and used in a potion or inserted into the mouth of the intended victim. Either way it is supposed to cause the tongue to wither or the throat to close up in a matter of minutes.'

Gus raises an eyebrow.

'Cool,' says Eddie and prods the finger with the blunt end of a scalpel. 'It has mummified to black but I think it is a Caucasian finger... not a child's either.'

Georgia shudders.

'I think it is coated in some residue,' Bernard says peering at the blade of the scalpel, sniffing. 'Possibly *Datura*. Moonflower to you and me. Hallucinogen. Very powerful.'

I have moonflowers in my garden, thinks Georgia. She wonders what other plants growing out there are potentially poisonous, maybe even fatal.

Eddie sprays chemicals on an ear-bud and wipes a corner of the driver's licence.

'Positive for blood,' he says. 'Won't be able to tell if it's human until we get it back to the hospital lab.'

'Blood on the licence? Jumping to conclusions, but could that possibly be the licence owner's own blood. The Dane's?' Georgia squints over

Eddie's shoulder. 'He was one of two Danish filmmakers and they both went missing last October. This one – the one on the licence, Emil – was never found.'

'The other?'

'The other, Jens, they picked up in a terrible state somewhere near Pemba. He couldn't speak. Still doesn't. I believe he is in a hospital or a kind of asylum in Copenhagen.'

Silence. They all think it but no one says it aloud.

'The Danish... filmmakers you say?' Gus directs the question at both Georgia and Bernard.

'We are still not sure. They were tracking the same religious group that Luse has mentioned, called The Blood of Christ Church. I think they were filming a follow-up on a documentary they shot in Nigeria. I know that Harry was approached by them as a fixer at the beginning of last year but he told me he wasn't going to take the job. He said the Danes took too many chances, would get the whole crew in trouble.'

'What's a fixer?' asks Eddie.

'The fixer on a film crew is the local guy or girl you call for local advice, translation, access, and so on. They organise customs, permits, speak to the cops, help set up interviews, that kind of stuff. Pretty invaluable.'

'Yes,' Georgia concurs. 'And Harry loved it. Had quite a good track record and was on the books for the BBC, CNN and several other news crews. That would have been how the Danes found him.'

'But you say he declined the work?' Bernard raises a greying brow.

'That's what he told me. We saw the two Danish lads getting sloshed one night at Danny's Bar. Harry went over, bought them a drink and said "no hard feelings". But perhaps he changed his mind.'

Perhaps that was for my benefit, she thinks to herself. *Did he know I wouldn't have approved of him taking the job?*

They all lapse into silence as Eddie sprays another chemical on the cross. Georgia glances at her watch. It is getting on and she has to nip back to the clinic for the late shift and to pick up some more antibiotics for Luse.

Gus catches her arm. 'Could you take me over to the hotel?' he asks. 'I'll leave Eddie to collect and bag up and he can drop off the Father when they are through.'

5.

They drive silently for a while, Gus gazing out at the city.

Georgia glances over at his profile, wondering how old he is, if he is married, has children. It doesn't feel appropriate to ask, given what they have just been looking at.

They drive alongside Kalinga Linga, one of the oldest and most frenetic townships. The sides of the roads are crammed with welders, furniture makers, charcoal sellers and market stalls. The Fizzy Bizzy Nursery School has the letters of the alphabet painted into bright murals along its walls. A is for Avocado, B for Bread. Further along, G is for Gun and R for Rat. The wall turns a corner and Georgia does not get to see what Z stands for. Zambia, she guesses.

They cut through past the stylish frontage of the Alliance Francaise and the battered, ugly UN buildings with their speed bumps and unfriendly 'No Visitors' signs, and emerge at Longacres with the glass-walled bank and the chicken eatery renowned for its salmonella. The hotel is close, its marble facades, tinkling water features and soothing air conditioning in view.

Gus shakes his head as if to rouse himself. 'Look, I am sorry. There is something I need to tell you.'

Georgia nods without looking at him.

'I did know that Harry was... fixing, or whatever it is called, for the Danes. In fact I was the one who insisted he take the job back after he had decided that the Danes were getting in over their heads.'

Georgia is shocked but says nothing, concentrating on slowing down as they go over a speed bump. She pulls into the car park of the hotel and finds a space far from the entrance then turns off the engine and waits.

Gus rubs his top lip and shuts his eyes for a moment. 'I told him he needed for once in his wasted life to commit to something. I told him I wanted a brother I could be proud of.'

'Even so, his death wasn't your fault, Gus.' Georgia is embarrassed, doesn't want him to feel he has to explain, but he shakes his head.

'The thing is... I needed him to get involved with The Blood of Christ Church. There have been rumours of child trafficking at the UN – an eye witness testimonial from an ex-member of the church. At around the same time, the government was contacted by Interpol about some body parts that had landed up in Paris – human body parts. Children's body parts.'

Body parts? Georgia can't believe it. 'That's crazy. How did they know they were from Zambia?'

'They didn't. Just that the parts were from children indigenous to this region. The Interpol alert went to all Sub-Saharan countries.'

With the engine and air conditioner off, the car heats up quickly and Georgia opens her door to let the cool air flood in.

'A police commander, a friend, came to me last year to say he had picked up a young man in one of the compounds outside Kitwe. The man had been arrested after a minor drug bust but it was the cold box he was carrying that caused the upset.'

Georgia doesn't want to hear about the cold box. Gus tells her anyway.

'The man said the meat in the cold box was from a monkey but it was quickly discovered to be human. Heart and liver, human, small. Under interrogation the man confessed to being a witch. Said he had bought the parts for his practice; bought them on the black market from a man he called the Red Chinaman. We called the Ministry of State Security in China and they were going to assist us with the investigation. However, by the time my friend arrived at the police station with a forensic crew from Lusaka there was no cold box, no evidence. The other police out in that part of the bush were superstitious. Said the witch had made it disappear. In the end they had to release the man. He was later found dead. Shot – not bewitched.'

'I don't understand...'

'The young man was a former member of a new church group.'

'Blood of Christ?'

'Yes.'

A brown and orange butterfly rests briefly on the bush next to Georgia's window. It seems to be catching its breath, its delicate wings pulsing.

'There are so many stories about this kind of thing,' Gus murmurs, looking up at the wide blue sky. 'Cannibal witches and wicked Chinese. At least once a week someone accuses someone else of something ridiculous. I wouldn't have thought much of it if The Blood of Christ hadn't already been flagged as potentially linked to child trafficking. When Harry said he was working with the Danes on their documentary, I encouraged him. When he tried to back away I pushed him, wanting an insider, but I didn't tell him about the Interpol warning. I didn't want him to tell the Danes and blow our investigation. I think...' Gus shuts his eyes again. 'I think it is my fault he is dead.'

Georgia breathes out at last, and sees the butterfly flapping unsteadily onwards. She takes off her seatbelt and turns fully to Gus, seeing in him the weight of guilt.

'You are saying that you knew Harry was potentially in more danger then he knew.' Her voice rises, 'But if you were already investigating why didn't you insist he had back up, some kind of protection...'

Gus makes a terrible noise in his throat. Words tear out of him, 'The investigation was a shambles. I went from one police contact to another and each time there was a problem with information. Witnesses withdrew statements, disappeared along with evidence. The Blood of Christ's accounts were spotless; their charity work was remarkable only in its extent and efficiency. The Police Commander-in-Chief came to see me in Ndola and said they thought it was all a red herring. He said money was short and they were closing the investigation for the time being. It never occurred to me that there might have been something amiss with the police doing the investigation themselves.'

'So what happened?'

'So... I got busy with other things, distracted. When Harry went off that night with the Danes instead of going to see the football in South Africa, he didn't warn me. I was in Rome when I got the news of his "accident".'

'But now? What now, Gus?' Georgia is trembling with anger. 'Surely you knew he had been killed – that it wasn't a damn accident? Have you, has *anyone* investigated his death? What have you been doing all this time while your brother rots in the ground?'

Gus bangs his hand on the dashboard and the car rocks a little. Georgia is silent, chews her lip. Her skin feels too tight and she wants to push Gus out of the car and drive away. *Fucking coward, stupid fucking idiot coward*, she thinks.

'I am not a detective, Georgia. I am a liaison officer. I teach, I write papers on multi-initiative government police strategies and UN funding policies.' Gus can't look at her.

'You gave up? *You gave up?*'

Georgia is almost shouting now and Gus's fists are clenched. A gardener weeding the nearby lawn has stopped work and is standing looking at the car. Georgia covers her face, feels the hot tears and sweat leaking through her fingers. She doesn't feel anger now, just grief and shame. After all, what has she done since Harry died? Nothing. Thought of running home to England. *Who is the coward now, Georgia?*

'I miss him, Gus. He was my best friend.'

Gus puts an arm around her shoulder. She allows him to, feeling the weight of his arm along her back, warm and solid, and rests her forehead briefly in the crook of his neck.

'Georgia, he always spoke about you as the one person he could trust. It was you, not me, that was his real family.'

'Well, then,' Georgia sits up sniffing, wiping at her face with her hand, 'you can make up for it. Now. You can help us find who did it. And we need to find Luse and Joshua's relatives.'

She takes a tissue from her pocket and pulls down the visor to dab at her ruined make-up.

'You say Luse and Joshua saw Harry days before he died.'

'Yes.'

'Okay,' Gus turns his amber eyes on Georgia. 'I wonder if I could speak to Luse about it. I don't want to upset her, but the key to all this could lie in what they have seen and heard. And...' Gus's face is pale now and Georgia wants to reach out and rub the darkness from around his eyes. She knows what he is going to ask. 'I'd also like to visit Harry's grave. Will you take me?'

Georgia is running late, so she accelerates out of the traffic and swerves into a road on the right, cutting through the north end of town to try to avoid the bumper-to-bumper peak hour traffic that clogs up Church Road. At the clinic she is irritated to find the entrance gate is barricaded shut. She cranes her neck but the guard is nowhere in sight. She hoots, never comfortable with getting out of her car in this part of town when there are fewer people about, and irritation creeps in. It is accepted that many of the gate guards supplement their meagre income by selling phone scratch cards and occasionally disappear to do business. Georgia is about to step out of the car and try to haul up the barrier herself, when she sees the pretty young woman in the brown uniform running towards her from the other side of the busy Cairo Road.

'Sorry, sorry, Madam Doctor!' she says, panting, contrite. 'I went to sell talk-time.'

She gestures vaguely at the street where two massive, fat men stand on the dry grass island, staring impassively back at them. The men wear matching dark green track suits, each with a trouser leg rolled up the calf, street style, with the glister of bling at their necks. Even from this distance Georgia guesses they are identical twins, except the one on the left has a spidery scar across his face that closes his eye in an eternal puckered wink. *Tweedledum and Tweedledee... with teeth*, she thinks, pulling into the car park. And then she forgets about them in the rush of work that the late afternoon shift has brought.

6.

Luse dozes on the bed, listening to the muted voices echoing from downstairs. Georgia has told her to rest and will call for her when supper is ready. It feels odd being upstairs in a muzungu's house, like a holiday from her real life. What would Bligh say if he could see her here? Bligh... his haggard, buck-toothed face swims through her mind. He would be appalled that no one seems to eat nsima in these muzungu places. Not that Luse minds. The smell of chicken stew and rice is making her mouth water, but she has work to do before she can face opening her eyes, let alone brave going downstairs. She needs to bring the sweepings of her memories together, to slot them into some kind of order so that she can speak clearly about what has happened to her family, to the Rasta. Her head feels swollen with memories. They bulge behind her closed eyes, but they scare her and she resists them. Finding the right ones and the safe ones is like trying to pluck a single ant from a nest. Others always end up crawling up your arm no matter how careful you are...

Downstairs someone takes the lid off a beer. She hears the crack and fizz, hears Daddy sip the foam off the top of the bottle and raise it to Mum saying, 'Eish, thank goodness for Friday!' and Mum smiling. No... she can't hear Daddy... not now... that was ages and ages ago. *Come on Luse*, she tells herself firmly. *Think. We are here in Georgia's house. The beer is probably for...* She rummages through faces... *Yes, that one. The Rasta's brother. Gus.*

Voices merge again. She can't make out what they are chatting about in the kitchen but it sounds fun, easy. Several people calmly chatting as if everything is normal in the world. Occasionally, one of their voices punctures the general hum with a laugh or a raised question.

Then Luse hears 'Demon'. Fingers point, red nail polish glistens. Luse twists in the bed, brings her knees up to her chest, heart juddering. *Stop it,* she thinks desperately. *That was before, not now!* Another bark of laughter from below and she flinches again.

The people chatting downstairs will stop talking when Luse brings her story to them. They will scowl and Georgia's face will change, darken to blue-black. 'Get out of my house!' she'll scream, and maybe the men will chase Luse and Joshua with mealie sacks and electric wires...

For a fleeting second she wonders if she can cut out her own tongue. It would be better to never talk about it. Or think about it ever again. Georgia only cares about the Rasta anyway. The dead man in the ditch... only he wasn't dead then.

There is Bligh's face again. Or is it Eli's? Luse moans. They are taking Joshua away and she is too tired to stop them.

'We can sell him to the Twins,' they are saying. 'We are so hungry... maybe we can even eat him ourselves...' But it can't be Eli. Eli lies dead on the side of the road with his tongue stretching out all white. Or is that her father, all bones and covered in flies?

'My mother is dead, my father is dead, all dead dead dead...' Luse croons to herself.

She steadies her ragged breathing and imagines a fish eagle flying in the sky above her. It circles slowly. And then Luse is the eagle. She is floating on a hot updraft above the house, separate, alone. From up here she can just about bear to look down on the house in Lusaka in 2002 where she lived with her parents, Bertram, and Gran.

The Shrine

1.

'I am six and I am six,' sings Luse from up in the jacaranda tree. 'I am six and I am six and before I was six I was a baby and then I was one and then I was two and then I was three...'

From her position in the crook of the massive tree, she can look down and see the black and white patio front of her house and the three neighbouring houses that all share the same scrubby garden. The houses are separated by a low myrtle hedge that Luse thinks needs a haircut. A discoloured, white wall circles the plot, blocking the view of the quiet, tree-lined road.

Noises are coming from her house. Voices from the living room, raised in anger. It is very hot, and there is no breeze at all, even up here in the tree. All around her are the munching, clicking, whirring noises of little insects at work and up above her the long branches reach high into the bright, blue sky.

She is up high enough to see through the windows of all the houses. Old Mrs Malambo is watching television in her living room. All her family go out during the day and leave her alone, but she doesn't even notice. She sits in the same chair all day and all evening watching TV. Luse knows, because she went in to visit with Mummy once, that Mrs Malambo smells of wee. The house opposite the Malambo's is empty again and looks sad and dark with no curtains or flower pots outside to make it pretty. They had lots of funerals at that house. The last people there went away in an ambulance in the night.

Luse peers around the branch and sees Bertram, Daddy's cousin, digging a trench next to the fence where it keeps flooding. Bertram is funny because he is scared of everything and hardly speaks. Mummy says he is special but Luse can't see what is so special about him. He sleeps in the kitchen and doesn't even have his own clothes, but has to borrow Daddy's. He glances over at her and she sees the whites of his wide, worried eyes. He is supposed to be keeping an eye on her in case she falls out of the tree, which Luse feels cross about. She has never fallen from this tree. Not ever.

'Bertram is a silly poo-poo...' she sings, but quietly. She doesn't mean it. Bertram is okay. He makes her little figures out of grass that smell nice and that she can play with in her doll house. And he doesn't kill the big night moths that bumble into Luse and Gran's room. Instead he carries them outside gently, cupped in his big hands. He tells Luse that if you knock the moon dust off a moth's wings they cannot fly and that makes him sad.

Across the unkempt green lawn and the pffing cluck-cluck of the single sprinkler, she can see in through the glass doors of the house and watch her mother who is standing very still with a hand over her mouth to hold her words in and her other hand on her swollen belly. Luse hears Daddy shouting, 'Why did you tell her? How could you?'

There is a small crashing sound as the glass doors are flung open, and one of the plant pots topples over onto the patio and cracks. Luse looks up to see her father come out from the living room and stagger into the middle of the garden. His smart, grey trousers are getting wet from the sprinkler, but he doesn't notice. He just stands looking up at the blue sky with his hands on his hips and his tie all twisted to one side of his white shirt. He is all puffy-looking and his face is blotchy, and then Luse sees he is crying. She wants to wail but she is too scared.

Instead she moves a little and her father glances over at the tree. At first he doesn't see her, but then he spies her through the leaves. For a moment he just stares blankly, then he wipes his face and comes all the way across the lawn and up the mound and plonks himself down at the bottom of Luse's jacaranda tree, with his back against the trunk so that she can use his shoulders as steps when she needs to clamber down. He taught her how to climb the tree this way, although now she can manage to haul herself up and drop to the ground on her own. He sits silently and waits. She can see his head beneath her with the shiny, hairless spot on the top that he says he doesn't have because he can't see it. She lowers herself down from the tree and steps on his shoulders with her dirty feet and then uses his warm back as a slide to get to the ground.

When she is down, he hugs her and he is heavy and his face is sticky from sweat, but Luse doesn't pull away. He still smells nice, of tobacco and spice. Over his shoulder she sees Mummy and Granny in the doorway watching. They don't come out but it seems as if everything is calming down, slowing down.

'Taata, can I ask you a question?' she whispers in his ear.

He nods, puffing out his cheeks in readiness.

'Why were you yelling at Baama? You shouldn't yell at her. It's naughty.'

She waits and tries to wipe her dirty toe-prints from his white-shirted shoulder. Her father sighs.

'Your poor old Mummy puts up with such a lot from me,' he says. 'It's true. I shouldn't have shouted. There was no need. She just told Granny something that I had wanted to keep a secret, something I hadn't wanted your granny to know about yet.' He sighs and scratches at his head, looking at Luse like he is a naughty boy. 'Actually your Mummy is very sensible. We will need Granny to help us when the baby comes. I thought we could do this on our own but your Granny is going to be a great help. I tell you what, I will go and say sorry to Mummy. How's that?'

'And Ba'Neene?' Luse waves her finger at him.

'And Granny,' he says.

He glances over at the house, at the now empty doorway, and shivers like he is cold. Luse strokes his arm. She knows about the baby coming. Now that Mummy's tummy is so big, it is not easy to forget. Everyone talks about it all the time. Mummy is always tired now and sits down in a funny way with her hands on her back and her face all pouty.

'Why don't you want Ba'Neene to know your secret, Daddy?' Luse asks, fascinated. 'Will she be cross?'

She loves her grandmother but she is a fearsome old thing too. She has a gap where her front six teeth should be and her nostrils are really, really big because she says she used to wear a big stick through them. Except she called the stick a chisita. With her bony elbows and wrinkled face, Granny could easily have been a witch from one of Luse's books. And now that Luse thinks about it, Granny is always boiling things up and chopping things and shredding things. She makes smelly potions that she puts in bottles that no one can touch. *Maybe she is a witch.*

'Daddy, Daddy is Ba'Neene a witch?' Luse asks, and is so excited that she has to get up and do some skipping. Her father watches her, smiling, but shakes his head and gestures for her to sit back down next to him again.

'She is a great herb-a-list, Luse.' He stretches out the word and she repeats it, 'Herb-a-list.'

'That means she can brew potions from herbs and roots, even bones. But she only uses them for good medicine. She would never hurt a soul. Remember when you had tummy ache? She gave you that yellow root to chew and you stopped feeling sick.'

Luse can't remember that, but she understands more about her Gran now. No matter what her Daddy says, it sounds as though her grandmother is a witch all right. A good one maybe, but still...

2.

Just after Joshua was born, when Mummy was still weak and spending most of the day in bed, it was Luse who heard the strange, half-choked cry and the terrible crashing in the bathroom. It was Luse who ran in to find Daddy stretched out on the floor making funny twitching movements with his arms and legs and with his mouth full of yellow sick. He had cut his head and there was bright red blood all around his shoulders like a cape, oozing across the white floor tiles, and Luse screamed and screamed.

She cried for ages afterwards, burying herself in Gran's lap.

'Daddy's knocked his head off. Daddy's knocked his head off,' Luse kept telling Granny, not wanting to let go of her hands.

Gran had said, 'Shuuussshhh, Luse. He cut his head but it was only a small cut. Just lots of blood came out that's all. The doctors at the clinic will fix him quickly.' She gave Luse special tea to sip and sat next to her on the sofa until she became sleepy.

Luse slept, and when she woke up she felt relaxed and hungry, and by the time she had some lunch Daddy had come back from the clinic, still woozy, but he waggled his eyebrows at her and smiled in a funny way with his sticky-out ears all shiny as if he had had his head polished.

Later, Mummy called Luse into the bedroom. Mummy said that Daddy had fallen over because he couldn't get used to the new medicine he was on.

'What medicine?'

Her mother made a gesture with her hand, a kind of pushing away, *not now*. They would change it, give him different tablets and he would be all better again.

Daddy came quietly into the bedroom, smiled at Luse and went to put his new medicine in the small fridge in the corner. Luse had been told never to touch that fridge. She would get a smack. Now she understood that the medicine inside could be dangerous. She watched him as he hunkered down, unlocked the small padlock, and unpacked several long cardboard boxes from the paper bags he was carrying. He sighed, and turning, looked at his wife in such a loving, gentle way that Luse quietly got up and left them together in the grey room.

She went straight to Gran who had, as usual, been boiling something unspeakable in the kitchen. She didn't say anything – there was no need. Gran took one look at her face and opened her arms for a hug.

'Little Luse,' she sighed, kissing the top of her head. 'Things are going to be hard for a while but you are going to be fine. Come and help me with this.'

Gran always had distracting tasks for Luse to do these days and usually it involved shucking and crushing seeds or cooking up various leaves and pods. When Luse was little she would get bored quickly and hop off her kitchen stool to play with her Barbie doll or go leapfrogging through the sprinkler, but now that she was six-and-a-half she found she not only enjoyed working with Granny, but that she was learning too. She could already identify most of the plants in the garden and several of the trees and was beginning to get an idea of what was safe to eat raw and what had to be cooked, what plants helped if rubbed onto the skin and which ones could be drunk for stopping things like diarrhoea and vomiting. Daddy had protested on occasion, scared that Luse would poison herself by mistake, but Granny had reassured him that Luse learnt fast and knew never to taste anything without asking first.

Anyway, Daddy was away a lot that year, travelling to local bank branches around the country, running workshops. Luse had asked him once what he did all day and he said, 'Count money and teach other people how to count money.'

'You could count it here, Taata. I could help you!' she had suggested in all seriousness, and hadn't really understood why he had laughed so much and called her a clever girl. When he was home he always went to the fridge for a beer and then to the desk in the living room with his files. He was boring these days, Luse decided, and Granny was anything but.

After Joshua's birth, it was Gran who was there to help Luse get ready for school in the morning and who fed her and helped her with homework in the evening. Gran was surprisingly good with maths and spelling. When she was a little girl all the children in her village had been sent to a very strict missionary school run by several European Jesuit priests known as the White Fathers. It was there that she had first met the man she would eventually marry.

'The White Fathers would kaa-crack our fingers with rulers if we got our sums wrong,' she told Luse. 'There was one priest who used to walk around the classroom with a sjambok whip made of hippo skin. Aiee, that hurt! He would go quietly, quietly along the desks...' and here Gran crouched low and crept around the dining room table where Luse was trying to do her homework. 'And then he would bring it down on your head chaaa if you were naughty.' And Gran suddenly banged the table, making Luse jump and giggle with terror and pleasure. 'Eh, that priest was a bad man! Once, when your grandfather was only a boy, the priest hit him with that sjambok right in the face and his nose bled for two days.'

Luse's eyes opened wide. Her mouth too. She swallowed.

'So your grandfather collected lots of buffalo bean from the bush. You know buffalo bean is that hanging creeper that has the tiny red hairs in its leaves that stick like fishhooks in the skin? He wrapped it carefully between rushes, hid it in his shirt and took it to school. During the lunch break he broke into the White Fathers' living quarters and found the mean old priest's room. He quickly rubbed buffalo bean into all the man's shirt collars and all his underwear.' Gran mimed rubbing the buffalo bean into Luse's T-shirt, tickling her until she was gasping between giggles. 'He ran back to the classroom and rubbed the last of it into the handle of the priest's sjambok and then he went quickly to his desk and sat there looking as innocent as a duiker calf.'

Joshua, next to Luse, gurgled in his high chair and waved his hands.

'Eh hee, Joshua. The man did dance! You know that the more you scratch at buffalo bean the further it goes into the skin. Hunters who have foolishly walked into patches of buffalo bean have been known to jump into muddy waterholes full of crocodiles just to try to cool their skin.'

Gran waved her hands in the air like Joshua. 'Oh, that priest danced and screamed and howled and cried and grabbed for his sjambok which only made it worse! Ach, we laughed and laughed at that mean old muzungu! They had to take him all the way to the mission clinic in Choma and he didn't come back for weeks.'

Luse couldn't get enough of that story. She imagined the man in his priestly vestments whirling around covered in red blotches and howling.

'Did Kaapa get in trouble?' she asked.

'He was never found out. Not one of us would tell on the other. We were all threatened and each of us got a ka-crack with the ruler but we were happy.'

'Kaapa was clever, wasn't he, Ba'Neene?'

'Yes he was, Luse. He was the smartest boy in the school and the most handsome.'

There were photos of Granny and Granddad but not from when they were young so Luse had to imagine them. She found it very hard to think of Gran as a young girl, as her own age. She was almost too shy to ask about the teeth. Gran was missing her front six. When were they knocked out? Did boys like Granddad, smart and handsome, like girls with no front teeth? Luse felt her own with her tongue. She still had little teeth, not big ones like Mummy, but they were wedged in very tight. It would take lots of strong pulling to get even one out. And it would hurt!

'Ba'Neene?' she wasn't sure if she could ask this. 'Why do you have no teeth in the front?'

'Do I need them?' Granny wrinkled her wrinkles. 'Joshua doesn't have any teeth in the front.'

Luse knew she was being teased. She pointed at Granny's mouth. 'Come oooonnnn, tell me,' she whined.

'Yah vah... okay. Luse, tell me what you see.' Gran leaned her elbows on the table and pushed her face forward, half-closing her eyes. Her hands were up behind her head in two finger fans that resembled ears. She slowly lowered and raised her head and made a low moaning sound. Her tongue came and slurped at her bare gums and then she chewed, and chewed and chewed.

Luse shrieked with laughter. 'You are a moo cow!'

Granny straightened up and the cow impression slipped from her until she stood sharp and straight again.

'For many years my family raised cattle on the plateau. They were more precious to us than anything. My family was very good at raising cattle and made a lot of money back in those days. My grandfather, your great grandfather, even traded with David Livingstone, the white man who told everyone in England about Mosi O Tunya. We women would knock out the front teeth to mimic – that means to be like – the cattle, to show our love and respect. It doesn't happen anymore of course. Times are all different now, but in the old days there were lots of women like me.'

Luse reached over and pushed up the thin lip. Her Granny's gum was a bright, healthy pink, but thickened and callused where the teeth should have been. Luse pushed her finger against the pink until it went white and her Granny didn't even blink. It felt almost as tough as a bicycle tyre.

'Did it hurt?'

'Oh yes! It had to hurt! There was a special ceremony and the teeth were knocked out with an axe! But we were the bravest, strongest women in Zambia. We told everyone that to us the pain was like a mosquito bite! They were amazed at our strength and they respected that. It didn't hurt for long though. They would rub special porridge in to stop the bleeding.'

The idea of blood and porridge, pain and axes is beginning to make Luse feel sick.

'When you are older I'll tell you more.'

'No now, Gran, noooww.'

'No – later.'

3.

Luse found that there were a lot of things that Gran would 'tell her later'. Not too long after Daddy's accident, Mum began to get stronger and when Joshua moved on from bottles to mashed food, Gran said it was time for her to head back to the farm.

From then on they would make the drive out of the city, over the escarpment and down into the heat of the Zambezi valley, to visit Gran. Luse loved every kilometre of that drive. Each time they drove the road, Luse would see more and more houses being built along the route. Breeze block walls, flapping plastic sheeting on the roofs, and improvised sewage ditches everywhere. Eventually the houses would peter out, giving way to bush and farmland and the long road opening up to Kafue.

On the road Mum always talked about car accidents. When she was young there were so many killed on this road that people said it was crowded with ghosts and nobody liked having to walk it at night time. Mum said there used to be car skeletons from crashes and breakdowns all the way along the road and through the bush to Siavonga, until the Chinese came and collected all the scrap metal.

Luse always scanned the roadside market as they whizzed through Kafue township, waving forlornly at the sad queue of long-horned cattle awaiting their doom at the roadside abattoir, and being dazzled by the bright, second-hand clothes flapping in the breeze. Kafue Bridge would take them over the wide river and Luse would feel the air around getting hotter, drier.

And then came the escarpment, the slender road climbing precariously up and down the craggy hillsides. Often the really big lorries carrying freight between Durban and Dar es Salaam would break down or jack-knife on the climb. Many times on that familiar drive, they would peer over the edges of the precipices to see recent wrecks crushed to a pulp on the thorny rocks below. But the landscape was glorious and in the wet season the undulating green was dotted with shiny-skinned baobab trees, massive figs and mahogany trees sticking their heads out through the outrageous ferns and carpets of creepers. In the parched browns and greys of the dry season the white-gold melele trees glittered and the odd stink of the potato bush would flood in through the open window.

They would pass through villages with thatched huts, grain stores on stilts and goat kraals. Sometimes people would be sitting by the roadside waiting patiently for lifts into town. They might wait all day, longer. Occasional stalls of seasonal fruit and vegetables lined the road – pumpkins, tomatoes, mangos – people waved from the backs of bicycles. Sometimes there would be just endless, baking hot, empty road. They would sink lower and lower into the Zambezi valley as the heat grew around them. Sometimes geese or egrets would fly past in arrow-shaped formation. Above kites and crows kept watch in the warm updrafts for road kill.

4.

Then came the September when Luse turned eight.

A few weeks before the holiday, the thing happened at school, the thing that turned her inside out, her and her whole family. Turned them all upside down and shook them all like pepper from a pot. And ever since then Luse had been very angry. In Lusaka she no longer played with her friends or climbed the jacaranda. She was meant to watch Joshua, but refused to either look after him or to help with any chores. Instead she spent a lot of time in her bedroom with her Barbie dolls and her Hannah Montana DVDs.

When the time came for them to drive down to see Granny, she didn't pack for the trip properly and Mum lost her temper and shouted, breaking the early morning chill with hot words. She immediately regretted it as Luse sulked, dragging her feet to the car, refusing to say goodbye to Daddy. She lay in the back and slept all the way down to Siavonga rather than ride up front.

But that drive, like all the others, ended when they passed through another set of hills, and emerged to see Lake Kariba, turquoise-blue to the horizon, and Luse felt a familiar rush of happiness in spite of herself. Granny's house was along a turn-off before the actual town of Siavonga itself, with its little market and holiday homes for the Lusaka elite. The road ended abruptly and Mum drove carefully over the sharp edge of the tar and down onto the rocky, dirt track that led through Lusaka jesse bush, up higher into the hill above the town and back down again towards the lakeside. The driveway was steep and lined with old trees, and the house itself, although a little dilapidated and ragged, was large and airy, built by Granddad in 1979 from the money he had made in the transport business. That had been before his 'Kapenta Fish Empire'. Granddad had been something of a phenomenon in the valley, a local celebrity, the Tonga man who beat the wazungu in business. Luse knew these things because people were always mentioning it.

'Ah, you are Luse Ha'angomba? Not Chipo the Kapenta Man's family? Heh, that man beat the wazungu at their own game! He made more money out of kapenta fish than even those ka-fat Zimbabweans! That man could fish for real!'

Luse had never met her grandfather, but always imagined him as that crafty little boy with the buffalo bean in his pocket, sitting on the juddering kapenta rig in the middle of the lake at night, like a pirate.

Gran's house was set in the hillside with a sweeping veranda made up of large, irregular pale stones encircled by a white, wooden balcony. From the patio the view was lovely, the ground sloping away in large, terraced-garden blocks all the way down to the thick, concrete walls and uneven stone steps that led onto the rocky lake shore fifty feet below. Granddad and Granny's handprints, names and the date 1987 were imprinted into the concrete of the top step. The first thing that Luse usually did when they arrived was to run over and put her hands into Granddad's prints, feeling the cool concrete under her palms. Then she would scamper down to find Puss, Gran's three-legged cat, and the yellow dogs, Mosi and Shake Shake. Shake Shake, the bitch, always had hanging teats and golden-eared pups flopping about in the dust. There was also the terrifying bantam cock called Bwana, whose long feathers were as gorgeous as any peacock's, and a dizzy brood of hens that followed him around as if he were a pop star.

However, this September Luse refused to get out of the car. A baffled Gran helped Mum, taking a sticky, smiling Joshua onto her hip and hefting a bag over her other shoulder. She looked quizzically at the car, at the pouting Luse.

'Leave her, Amai,' Esther said, irritation criss-crossing her lovely face. 'She has been like this all month.'

Granny paused, watching as Luse, with a furious expression, leaned over the front seats and locked all the car doors. Gran sighed and followed Esther down to the house.

The car was parked in the shade, but it was still stifling hot and Luse stayed as long as she could before miserably dragging open the door and flopping like a beached fish on the rocky driveway. Sweat and rage poured from her. Slowly, sliding on her bottom, she bumped down one step at a time to the cool house, leaving the car door wide open for the mosquitoes, her bag still on the seat.

After two days of this behaviour, Gran told Esther to have a break, sending her with Joshua for a leisurely lunch at one of the grander hotels in town. The hotel was Luse's favourite, with a wonderful round pool and the best chicken and chips for miles. She was so angry at not being allowed to go that she threw her shoes at Esther and nearly hit Joshua. That earned her a couple of sharp smacks on her legs and banishment to her bedroom, where she sat twisting the head off her blonde Barbie and chewing at the plastic stump.

'Right. Are you going to tell me what is going on in your head, little Luse?' her grandmother asked. She stood in front of Luse, hands on hips. 'This behaviour is unacceptable in my house.'

Terribly ashamed, Luse finally told Granny what happened at school. A kid in her class, a skinny boy called Ahmed Ali, had come up to her one break time. Luse was on the swings and about to kick off with her legs when Ali blocked her. He put his arms out and held the metal chains, stopping the swing dead, and then leant towards her and spat in her face.

'Your Daddy's got AIDS,' he shouted as she sat with the disgusting spittle dribbling down her cheek. He pushed her and she fell to the dirt, winding herself. Ali's shouting and the sudden violence aroused the interest of several of the other children in the playground. 'Your Daddy's going to infect everyone he touches! You are an AIDS baby! AIDS baby!'

The chant was taken up until Luse was encircled by a group of children screaming 'AIDS baby!' at her and spitting.

'It's these bloody Indians, spreading lies about AIDS, not educating their children,' Esther said afterwards, furious. She had taken Luse from the school and driven, without thinking of the consequences, to Ahmed's cooking-oil-stinking house and sat on the sofa opposite Ahmed's mother, still quivering with barely concealed fury. Ahmed's mother was an exquisite, long-limbed, raven-haired woman in a turquoise and gold shalwar kameez with delicate gold hoop earrings and pale pink nail polish on her fingers and toes. Luse had thought her mother, usually the most gorgeous woman in the room, looked dishevelled, sweaty and ugly compared to the movie star sheen of Mrs Ali, and she began to get stomach cramps of embarrassment.

It didn't go well. Esther accused Mrs Ali's son of being an ignorant bully. She said she was horrified by his attitude and expected him to be punished severely. Mrs Ali was cool and polite, nodded and apologised, but then ruined it all by saying that it was hardly Ali's fault – that there were people all around the country infected with AIDS and they should be separated from the rest of society and taken somewhere where they wouldn't infect other people. Luse's mother had gritted her teeth and tried to explain a few basics. She tried to explain the difference between HIV and AIDS and the reasons why it was essential people neither feared it nor stigmatised those who had it. Mrs Ali hid a yawn behind her pretty fingers.

'Luse's father's HIV status is private, just as yours is, Mrs Ali,' Esther had said in a strained voice. At that Mrs Ali's lovely dark eyes had widened.

'Wha... what?'

'I mean,' continued Esther, 'if you or your husband is infected, and there is no way anyone could tell unless they tested your blood, but *if* you were, I would respect your privacy and insist that my children behaved with respect and consideration. HIV is *not* contagious. It can only be caught through exchanges of blood or bodily fluids.'

A slight pink flush appeared on Mrs Ali's fine cheekbones at that point and soon Luse and her Mum were back in the car going home. Esther swore all the way back, mostly at herself for acting without thinking.

Nothing changed at school. Ahmed just whispered his taunts instead of shouting them. They never had a formal apology from either the Ali family or the school, and Daddy came back from work earlier and earlier looking strained and pale, his mouth tight. The occasional beer became several shots of liquor before supper. This made Luse mad. But what made her maddest of all, more than anything in the world, was what Ali had called her. Because what no one, *no one*, had told her, was whether she really was an AIDS baby after all. A pig-sick, disgusting, infectious AIDS baby.

All this Luse told Gran, slowly and with lots of pauses because it was the first time she told anyone about it. Gran's face was solemn and she waited until Luse was finished. 'Luse, listen very carefully. Your Mum and your Daddy have HIV but neither you nor Joshua has the HIV virus. Do you hear me? You are a totally healthy, normal girl. And you need never have the HIV virus if you are as careful and clever as I know you to be. Do you understand?'

Slowly Luse let the words filter into her mind and deep into her body. She let out a breath, the longest breath ever. She was healthy. Joshua was healthy. They were not going to die any time soon. She should have asked Mum right at the beginning. She should have just asked.

Granny said nothing more for a while. Instead she got out some of the fruit jelly she made from the marula trees outside and cut some bread, and they sat together quietly munching.

5.

Back in the bedroom in Georgia's home, Luse is awake, her head a little clearer. There is the sound of cutlery clinking. 'Supper!' calls Georgia from the kitchen. Joshua comes thumping up the stairs in his bare feet and thunders into Luse's room, excited, hungry and hopeful.

'Luse,' he says, hopping from one foot to the other in agitation. 'Are you all better now? Are you hungry? Are you coming? Can I help you?'

She is slow, swinging herself off the bed, pausing on the edge like Daddy used to do when he first got sick. Joshua looks at her blankly and Luse wonders how deeply he has, like her, blocked out all of the last year. She tries to stroke his face but he is too quick, dashes to the door and back like an over-excited puppy.

'It's chicken stew, ' he says reverently. 'Can I hug you after?' He tells her that Father Bernard is teaching him dominos and that Georgia says he can watch a DVD after supper. He chatters on as Luse pulls on a top and the soft moccasin slippers she has been lent and follows him slowly.

Georgia is on the stairs waiting, wearing a purple dress. Her exposed arms and legs are tanned a honey colour and her thick dark hair hangs loose around her shoulders. Georgia would never squat over an open sewer with nothing to clean herself with after. She would never steal from fat women in supermarkets. Luse gets the familiar twinge in her guts of shyness, anger and self-revulsion. Compared to Georgia she is a bloated tick, a street rat. When Georgia smiles she has a dimple in her cheek in exactly the same place as Baama. *My mother was beautiful too*, thinks Luse.

Georgia notices Luse's hesitation at the top of the stairs. She tucks a stray curl behind an ear and smiles reassuringly up at her, briefly reaching out to put a hand on Luse's forehead. 'You feeling like company?'

Luse nods, lying, and Georgia pauses, seeing the lie.

'I'm fine... Georgia.' She has been told that she can use Georgia's first name but it still feels odd, too intimate. 'Really. It's just...' Luse twists her mouth in an apologetic grin and shrugs and in that shrug is a whole universe. Georgia can only nod. She takes Luse's hand, squeezes it.

After the stew, when Joshua has been settled upstairs in the bedroom with the DVD player, it is Luse who turns to Father Bernard, Georgia and Gus.

'I wasn't sure what you would want to know,' she says as Georgia ushers them all into the living room and they settle comfortably on the chairs and sofa. Georgia sits next to Luse, but not too close as she doesn't want to seem over-protective. Gus sits on the hard-backed chair next to her and puts an ankle on his knee exposing a bit of blue sock. Bernard sits opposite, leaning in to pat Luse's shoulder.

'Can you tell us how your family got involved with The Blood of Christ Church, Luse? Can you start there?'

For a moment Luse panics, the carefully collected memories almost scattering again.

'It was a few years ago...'

Bernard smiles encouragingly, 'That's fine. I think just start there and go on as far as you can. As long as you feel safe and comfortable. And remember there is plenty of time too. If you need a break just say so.'

Gus clears his throat as if a bit embarrassed. 'Details are... err... very useful. I might stop you sometimes and ask for details.'

'That's okay.' Luse is clenching and unclenching her fists without realising and it occurs to Georgia that Luse seems to be talking as if slightly sedated, as if looking down on herself. Georgia wishes she has more paediatric psychiatry under her belt. She runs an eye over her library for any books that she might pluck out to read. Something on post-traumatic stress might be useful. She can phone her colleague working in paediatrics at Chinama hospital. She catches Father Bernard's thoughtful expression. He too is aware of the weight of this child's memory. *We should have discussed it in advance*, she thinks, cross with herself. It's too late now though.

Luse takes a little breath. She is aware that telling all she remembers – and is remembering, even now, on the couch – will only confuse them, maybe even make them think she is crazy. Instead she tells little bits, skipping across the flood of memory like the flat stones she and Daddy used to flick at the surface of the lake.

She begins with the banner.

6.

It's 2006 and nine-year-old Luse is nearly finished. The banner is spread out on the ground with a rock at each corner, and the slogan in red paint reads 'ABC! Abstinence. Be Faithful. Use Condoms!' Her friend Rachel reads the words out slowly, standing slightly bored, twisting her new braids and sucking her thumb which she thinks makes her look cute. Luse thinks thumb-sucking at nearly ten years old makes her look really dumb.

'What do you think?'

'Yeah... whatever...' Rachel is distracted. 'Ab-stin-ence... Why do you think you have to *tell* people not to have sex? I mean it's stupid, isn't it? I mean why would anyone have sex if they were going to get HIV?'

'Duhhh... people don't *know* they are going to get it, stupid. You can't tell if someone has it unless they get a big rash on their face or get really, really skinny or something...'

'Why would you have sex with a man with a rash on his face? Gross.'

'That's not what I mean.' Luse is getting confused. 'People just have sex a lot without knowing... that's all.'

'Well I'm not going to have sex until I am married.'

'How will you know if you want to... you know... do *it* with your husband if you don't try it first?'

'I'll just know. If the kissing is good, you know... like in *Pretty Woman*, then I will know. Anyway, my wedding Aunties will tell me everything before... that's how it should be done. I can't believe your Mum is always talking to you about stuff. It used to be taboo you know...'

Luse rolls her eyes. 'Well even then you should wear...' and Luse points to C, condoms.

Rachel gets the giggles. 'Condoms go over a dodo.'

'Only babies say dodo.'

'Nu uhh.'

'Uh huh.'

'Well what do you say?'

Luse hasn't thought this through. 'It's pen-is.' She says it quickly, embarrassed.

'Well a *condom* goes over a *pen-is* then! If you know so much, how does it fit on then?'

This is a constant worry of Rachel's. She and Luse often see used condoms in the sewers, sometimes just on the side of the roads, especially when they go through the compounds. They look like shed snake skins, all white and floppy and greasy.

'I would vomit if I saw a man with one of them on his *pen–is*.'

Rachel looks at her nails. Yesterday they painted them pink but they are already a bit flaky. 'Can we redo our fingernails?'

'Nope. No time. The HIV/AIDS peer group meeting is here this afternoon. Everyone will be arriving in a minute.'

Luse is thinking that Mrs Chanda might bring her son with her again. Christopher. Just thinking about him makes Luse's mouth go dry. 'You have to go home.' She says this casually, but Rachel knows better.

'Christopher Chanda is coming, isn't he?'

Luse feels blood rushing into her cheeks.

'Chris and Luse up a tree, K. I. S. S. I. N. G!' Rachel sings gleefully and Luse grits her teeth.

Esther comes out, calling, 'Your mother is here, Rachel. Have you got your school bag?'

'It's inside...' Rachel dashes around Luse's mum and heads for the house. 'Byeee Luse. Have a nice sexy evening with Christopher!' she shouts over her shoulder.

Luse looks at her mother and her mother looks at her. There is an embarrassed silence.

Esther tucks a sprig of unruly hair back under her wig. She is dressed for the AIDS Day march in a red T-shirt and jeans. Her wig is expensive, sent from Canada by her younger sister Miriam.

'Is Dad coming?' Luse asks quickly and then realises it is the wrong question. A light goes out of Esther's eyes.

'I don't know, Luse,' she says. 'He went out. I'm not sure if he will be back in time.'

There is time... just enough, thinks Luse and tells her Mum she is going to see if Samba wants to come along. But she doesn't go towards Samba's house. Instead she crosses the street and heads east over the football field. It takes her across the main road that bisects George Compound. She has to scramble over the ditches and cross the concrete culverts, being careful because they are full of rainwater and sewage, flowing fast.

Blue minibuses sweep past, honking, and the pavements on both sides of the road are crowded with people in Saturday mood, walking easily and slowly, slapping handshakes and laughing.

The far side of the road is lined with small businesses, barbers, carpenters, welders, vegetable sellers, and everywhere bright signs promote Maximum condoms and talk-time for cell phones.

At the third telephone pole she cuts away from the road and plunges in amongst the houses. The paths are irregular and narrow with tree stumps, roots and ditches full of rubbish to work around. The houses vary in size, shape and stability and everyone's front step is someone else's back door. Many of the stronger buildings have several single-windowed extensions built on in concrete and mud brick with provisional plastic or sacking roofing. These are rented out and everyone with an inch of space is a landlord. Luse has seen families of twelve sharing a single-windowed concrete space half the size of her bedroom.

Electricity and running water are not usual here and communities share standpipes and latrines. Washing areas are shielded partially from prying eyes by swaths of plastic sheeting tied around a couple of poles, but privacy is a luxury. And children are everywhere – four-year-olds look after babies, while kids her age cook, clean and keep an eye on the four-year-olds. Women sweep constantly, dig sewage ditches and clean at this time of year. The red mud gets everywhere and there is always the fear of cholera.

A woman sitting on her front step shucking peas stares at Luse as she runs past and Luse is conscious of her pristine red T-shirt and jeans. Girls should wear skirts or at least wrap themselves in a chitengi, the traditional wraparound cloth, in this neighbourhood. No one wants unnecessary attention here.

A stream of sewage and plastic detritus comes out at another tar road junction. Across this she can see a high thick concrete wall covered in once-bright murals of people dancing. 'Flight Deck Cocktail Bar' is emblazoned on the wall, although the word 'cocktail' has been squeezed in and looks more like 'coktil'. At this time of afternoon the red metal gates are still open and the sound of rumba music floods tinny and thin out into the road. A couple, dressed for church, passes Luse as she pauses outside.

'That is not a good place for children,' says the woman sternly.

'I am collecting someone,' says Luse, still reluctant to go in.

The woman's face softens. She has seen it all before. 'Would you like my husband to go in with you?'

Her husband smiles, but it is without the woman's warmth and Luse shakes her head and thanks them, waiting for them to disappear around the corner before taking a breath and going through the gates.

Because the entire bar, including the outdoor seating area, is enclosed by the high concrete wall, it is hotter and smellier than outside. Luse feels prickles of sweat on her face and under her arms as she scans the outdoor tables for her Dad. The layout is basic. The bar itself is inside a large ugly building with a door in on the right and a door out on the left. Most of the clients prefer to sit outside on the odd mix of metal and plastic chairs that line the large courtyard. It has a partial roof that provides shade around the edge and there is a step down to a central well where people dance in the evening when it is cooler.

Luse sees her father almost immediately. He is outside at a long wooden table with a woman and a man, neither of whom Luse recognises. She is relieved that she doesn't have to go into the dark interior of the bar itself to find him. A few weeks ago when she was rushing to find Dad, she went in without thinking. She was grabbed right by the door and pushed into a corner by a sour-smelling man who fumbled in the dark with his trousers saying, 'Oh yeah baby girl, you so fresh and fine... now come close... I want you to suck it. How much just for a suck?'

Her Dad is not one of those drunks, not yet anyway. He is what he calls 'a social drinker' and this bar is in his old stomping ground. He used to rent a room nearby when he was a student and once helped the owner, Masauso, out with a loan.

'Your father made this all possible,' Masauso says all the time, rubbing Dad on the head or hugging him and handing him fresh beer. Masauso isn't around now as Luse approaches the table where her father is deep in conversation. Again she is relieved. When Masauso smiles, he looks at her like she is game meat.

'... yes I would call myself a Christian man...' her father is saying as she approaches the table. The woman looks up and Luse is surprised by her clear, unclouded gaze. Not a drunk then? Her skin is very dark, high cheekbones wing out below hooded eyes and large, gold cross earrings dangle from under her stylish cap. Her tailored black T-shirt has a silver sparkling dove with an olive branch flying off her shoulder.

'Ah, this must be your eldest, Paul,' her voice is deep and there is a distinct foreign accent. 'You must be Luse. Your father has told us so much about you.'

Luse feels oddly shy, and squeezes around the back of the table. The woman tracks her with her bright, dark eyes.

'Well, Luse. What do you say?' her father is irritated but not with her. *It must be the conversation,* thinks Luse.

'Mulibwanji madam,' says Luse, dipping into a shallow curtsy and clapping her hands in respect. She curtsies to the man, keeping her eyes lowered. He grunts in acknowledgement. His nostrils are slightly flared as if his nose can't quite believe the stink of the place.

'Daddy, are you coming home for the march?'

'Luse, I am busy...' he begins, but the foreign-sounding woman cuts in.

'Now Paul, please don't let us keep you. I have to get back to my flock anyway. We have a service in an hour and of course I will need to change into my vestments. It's been such a pleasure meeting you and your delightful daughter.'

Luse colours. The woman says the word 'delightful' as if she is making a joke and the man opposite even smiles.

'Do you often come to the bar to get your father?' asks the man, raising his eyebrows at her.

Luse doesn't respond and her father, woozy with booze, doesn't notice. 'Luse is a good girl, aren't you, love? She is the only one who really understands me.'

Luse hates it when he starts to whine like that. The next thing will be him talking about how Mum is so demanding and mean. It gives her a lumpy, disappointed feeling in her stomach.

'Come on, Taata. Mum is waiting for you.'

The woman's poise is unsettling; a graceful intent stare, hands under her chin. With her deep-set eyes and flat high cheeks, her face is like an African mask and her perfume is very sweet and doesn't mix well with the bar stench of stale cigarettes, latrines and spilled beer.

'Which way are you heading?' The man has turned to Dad. He is young, also well-groomed, sweating away in a nicely cut shirt and waistcoat, but he is fat and his skin bulges out from his shirt cuffs and collar. 'Perhaps I could walk with you and we could discuss the Good Book some more...'

Now at last Luse sees the Bible in the man's lap and understands. It is not unusual for missionaries to come to bars, even cesspits like this one. Luse's Mum says there are more evangelists in Zambia than in all the southern states of America. 'Ever since President Chiluba declared this place a "Christian nation" you can't take a walk without running up against some Bible-bashing-speaking-in-tongues nutcase,' she says.

Luse has had her fair share of them at school. So many of her good teachers died of AIDS last year that they ran out of trained replacements and have now resorted to hiring Sunday School teachers whose only inspiration and method is teaching Bible verse, usually parrot fashion with no explanation or discussion.

The woman stands and so do the men. Luse is impressed by her height. She is almost level with Daddy and he is over six foot.

'Madam Priestess,' her Dad says, taking the woman's hand and doing an odd little bow that nearly tips him over. 'Madam, a pleasure.'

'Yes,' the woman leaves her hand in his momentarily. Her fingernails are bright, hot red against Dad's brown skin. 'Remember, Paul, you say you are a Christian man but do you really know God? I mean really know him, as I know him, as Thomas here knows him? Our Bible says in 1 Corinthians 13,

"When I was a child, I spake as a child, I understood as a child, I thought as a child: but when I became a man, I put away childish things." I believe it is your time to put away childish things, Paul. You know where we meet. It would be more than good to see you there.'

She squeezes his hand and then disengages herself, turning on elegant two-inch-heeled boots and sashaying towards the red gates. She is wearing a tightly-fitted calf-length leather skirt which should be demure, but with the heeled boots, emphasises her lean backside. Luse does not like the way her father and Mr Thomas stare at her bottom as she leaves.

'Come *on*, Daddy!' she hisses and pulls at his shirt sleeve. She can still smell the woman's cloying perfume. It's stuck on everything.

'Yah...' but her father has the look of a man climbing down an unsteady ladder from a great height. He grips the table and seems as if he might weep.

'Put away childish things?' he whispers, 'Oh Lord, forgive my sins.'

Luse glances across the table and sees a smile on Thomas's face. He looks like he has just won the lottery.

7.

It is about a week after the encounter in the bar with the Priestess and Thomas. Dad has been very subdued and Mum says she thinks he is 'contrite' about missing the World Aids Day march, but Luse isn't so sure. In the morning he tunes the radio away from Station Eagle and their favourite chat shows and pop music, to Christian Mission Voice with its wailing hymns and chirpy, American-style religious music.

Luse knows Dad has better taste than this and sees him squirm slightly at the white woman's voice belting out the hymn. Yet the whole week it is church music. And the next too. And the next. Then Dad says to Mum that he is joining the church choir.

'That strange man, Thomas's, church?' asks Mum looking surprised.

'Thomas is not strange,' her father snaps. 'He is saved!'

'Saved?' Mum shakes her head. 'From what? What on earth are you talking about?'

But Daddy has stalked off, and Mum, catching sight of Luse, bites her lip and smiles saying, 'Oh don't worry about your Dad. It's just a phase. A lot of people find they need to turn to more formal... errr... forms of religion when they are going through hard times.'

Luse hasn't got a clue what her mother is talking about. 'But Daddy is Christian already,' she says.

'Yes, love. But there are different ways of showing you are a Christian.'

Dad's way of showing he is a Christian seems to now include insisting on the family reading the Bible together after supper. It doesn't work. Luse always has homework and Mum usually disappears to bath Joshua.

8.

After several attempts, Dad invites Thomas over. That night is cold and dry. Thomas arrives in another smartly tailored suit with a waistcoat. Joshua wants to know what is in all the little pockets, but it is apparent that Thomas is not a man particularly fond of children.

'The pockets are empty, little boy,' he says without looking down, as if Joshua is a kid in the street. 'Best to just leave them alone, eh?'

As usual, Luse is plugged into her cell phone, listening to music.

'Do turn that music off,' says Mum wearily. Luse pretends she hasn't heard and then catches a look from Thomas to Daddy. It is a look that says, *Have you no control?*

Daddy rises to his feet, reaches over the table and roughly swipes the phone from Luse's hand. Shocked, she looks up to see his face contorted in anger.

In the uneasy silence that follows, Daddy apologises to Thomas, Joshua giggles and Mum begins handing around the food. Luse sits stunned, tears burning in her eyes, blood boiling in her cheeks.

'Please begin,' Mum says.

'Oh, I am sure you will want to lead grace first, Paul,' Thomas interjects, and there is something in his tone again, a challenge.

'Oh yes...' Daddy clears his throat. He will not look at Mum. 'Come on now everyone. Join hands.'

'Luse won't hold hands,' Joshua whines.

'Never mind, Joshua,' says Mum sharply and Luse can hear that she too has had enough of the evening.

'God bless this food and this house...'

After supper, untouched by Luse who remains furious throughout, Dad suggests they go into the living room for Bible study.

'Can't we just get it ov... I mean, do it here at the table?' whispers Mum.

'We have a special guest this evening.' Luse's father is adamant and they troop through to the living room, leaving Bertram to clear away and wash up.

'How come Bertram doesn't have to come in?' hisses Luse.

'If you would like to go and help him wash up, love, I am sure we could fill you in later,' says Esther, a dimple appearing in her cheek. Luse huffs but follows her mother through.

Thomas leads the study in a self-conscious, overbearing kind of way that irritates Luse more than ever. As he reads from Chronicles, Joshua wriggles and fidgets on the sofa next to Mum. The evening drags on and on, and when Thomas finally leaves, she sighs with relief and says, 'Never again!'

Long after she has turned out her light, Luse can hear her parents' voices raised in anger.

9.

There is no let up from then on. Dad insists on having his way with the evening study and even extends it to breakfast readings. All are to attend and be inspired by the lesson of the day that he reads out before they eat. He begins to pray morning and evening for hours at a time. He never makes a single decision without consulting the Great Book, as he calls it.

He brings more church people home too, all smart-suited, serious, rather cold people who gather in the living room holding soft drinks and reading Bible passages to each other. Luckily Mum has made it very clear that the children are not to be involved in these late night studies and so Joshua and Luse sit in the kitchen with Mum and Bertram, Luse doing homework and Joshua colouring-in with his bright, new felt tips. The upside is that the TV and DVD player get moved into Luse and Joshua's bedroom. The downside is this means that Luse can't watch anything after Joshua has gone to bed at 7pm. She spends a lot more time at her friends' houses and it feels as if she hardly sees her Dad at all. If he isn't at work, he is at church or in a church meeting or in the living room discussing church business.

'You know they do a lot of great community work, Esther,' she overhears Daddy saying one day. 'They have all these impressive street kid programmes. They could really do with a nurse as skilled as you.'

Mum is ironing. The iron huffs and steams. 'For goodness sake, Paul. I already volunteer at two different places. I just don't have the time to do anything more. You know this.'

'Yeees... but maybe you could stop at the Red Cross and do something with The Blood of Christ instead?'

'Why on earth would I do that?'

'Well, then we could spend more time together.'

'What?' Her mother's voice has hit a new tone. 'You, Paul, are the one who leaves our family to be with those miserable church people. Every night, Paul. Every night I am alone with *our* children. And now you expect me to find another few hours in my day to help other people's kids when our own are stuck at home with hardly a parent between them? Are you insane? God, I preferred you when you were drinking.'

'How dare you talk to me in that way! I am your husband. I demand some respect...'

84

'Husband? When were you last a husband to me? You are more of a husband to that skinny bitch priestess.'

'How can I be a husband to you? We are unclean. Us both. At least I am trying to wash my sins.'

'HIV is *not* a curse or a sin, Paul. How could you say such a thing after all we have been through together? How dare you!'

Louder and higher the voices ring around the house, echoing bitterly from the walls and unavoidable in Luse's bedroom even with her headphones on full volume.

10.

Luse still loves her Dad though, and when he turns to her and pleads, 'Please, my daughter. I really need a friend on this one,' she sees in his eyes that he means it. 'This church feels right to me, Luse. I just wish you could see what I see.'

'But Taata... you have become so... stern.' Luse actually wants to say 'cruel' but that isn't quite what she means either. And she feels guilty. She has been angry with him for so long and now, seeing his sticky-out ears and solemn boy eyes, she thinks perhaps she could have been a little more flexible. It is just a church after all.

Feeling a little like she is betraying her mother, Luse puts on a bright yellow T-shirt and a plain blue skirt and goes with her Dad to The Blood of Christ Celebration Day. It is being held in a big marquee tent in the field behind Shoprite on Manda Hill, and the Priestess is going to be there to talk about the Church's expansion in Zambia.

The field is half full of parked cars and music is blaring from the inside of the marquee. The vibrations from the four massive speakers make the tent poles quiver and give the slight impression that even the marquee is dancing. The music is Christian pop mixed up with local religious songs and hymns, but it is hard to make the lyrics out over the buzzing reverberation from the bass. Luse feels her teeth fizzing with it too.

There are hundreds of chairs in rows facing a raised front stage made of scaffolding and wooden planks. Flowers and bright white cloth have been draped all around and there is a sweet smell of flowery incense mingled with the smell of tarpaulin and mown grass. Crowds of people mill about talking and taking it all in. Some sit immediately and go into fast-rocking prayer, but generally the atmosphere is relaxed and upbeat.

There are several stalls selling crafts and one selling videos, DVDs and CDs. Luse and her Dad drift past and Luse picks up a video with the title *Witch Children* written in fake blood over a photo of a zombie child with black eyes and white ash on its face.

'It's a horror film, Taata,' she says, bemused at finding such a thing at this event.

'That is not for children,' hisses the woman behind the stall and Luse hastily replaces it in the pile. Her Dad has already moved away towards some people he knows, a couple of whom Luse recognises from the meetings at her house. They blink at her like owls but don't greet her.

Children really aren't wanted here, thinks Luse, and it is odd, the obvious lack of children. Luse sees only a couple of woman with babies on their backs, two or three other teenagers and no toddlers at all. She is about to point it out to her Dad when there is a terrible screech of feedback and a voice comes over the tannoy.

'Good Day! Good Day! I would like to greet you all warmly, and invite you all to join our first prayer circle.'

And at first it is uneventful; the usual muffled praying followed by a couple of songs and some more prayers led by various church members. Luse is deadly bored and begins to wonder if Dad would mind if she slipped away to Manda Hill Mall for a while. She has enough kwacha for an ice cream.

'And now,' gurgles the compere. 'May I bring to the stage our inspirational leader, Madam Selena Clark, or, as we fondly know her, the Priestess.'

There is thumping applause as people stand, clap and stamp their feet. For a while Luse's view of the stage is blocked, but gradually the clapping dies down and everyone resumes their seats. The Priestess is wearing some kind of flowing, purple kaftan and a white sleeveless coat over it like a priest might wear. Her headdress, also purple, rises in a plume from her intricately knotted hair. It is an impressive combination, but the speech itself is boring, mostly statistics, figures and account details. Every now and then there is a cheer as she talks about a new location, additional funding and so on, but Luse drifts off, looking around at the people who have gathered.

She catches the eye of a young man, a boy really, but tall, who seems equally uninterested, and for a second their eyes lock and he smiles. Luse feels blood rush to her face but manages to grin back quickly before ducking her head. *Jeez! He is really handsome*, she thinks. *Wait till I tell Rachel*. She sneaks another peak and yes, he is still looking. Luse feels flustered. She wonders how much longer the Priestess will go on for.

The Priestess has begun another prayer but this one is different. It goes on and on and her voice becomes louder and louder until she is shouting down the microphone and the whole marquee is quivering and trembling. Luse holds her hands up over her ears and sees people beginning to stand up and sway all around her. They have their eyes closed and their faces are naked with pleasure.

'Taata...' she begins to say, and looks up at him to see that he too is in some kind of semi-trance. He is talking out loud, but it sounds like a mishmash of words, not anything real. She swings around looking for someone, anyone who is still normal and is beside herself with relief to see the tall young man is looking at his mother with confusion as she too sways and mutters, holding her hands up above her head.

Then there is a brief wail of feedback and the Priestess's voice booms out, 'There is a demon in this place!'

The Priestess's words cut through the sweet-smelling tent like ice water on a fire. 'I said, my people, there is a demon in this place.'

One by one people seem to come to, opening their eyes, focusing on the stage.

'Among us right now walks a hound from hell!' The purple Priestess has come forward to the front of the stage and several men are helping her onto the grass. She begins to walk along the central aisle, her right arm held out, the fingers pointing along the sea of faces to her left and right.

'Who here has suffered torment, who here has suffered death?'

A few voices cry out 'Madam!' 'I have, madam!' but she ignores them and walks on.

'I see a very particular death. A true follower who was set upon by the beast in his own home!'

Gasps from the crowd. Luse grabs at her father's hand but he seems shocked, his hand lies cold and heavy against his side.

'I tell you I have seen it, in my dream. In dreams and prophecy! A demon in his own house!'

And then her finger points and is still, the purple nail polish bright. She is pointing at the mother of the young man.

'Emily Ngoma. Your husband was taken from you this very week was he not?'

The woman is terrified, gripping her son's arm, nodding until her headdress slips forward. Her son is angry. Luse can see it in his face. He stands in front of his mother, protective; reaches to straighten her scarf.

'Mrs Ngoma, your husband, our good follower of Christ Jesus, was killed by a demon from within your own house!'

More gasps, exclamations. People around her back away, exposing her and her son to the Priestess's glare.

'And that demon resides... in YOUR SON!'

Now the crowd really does step back. There is a five-foot ring of clear air around the boy and his mother.

'Didn't you wonder, Emily, why whenever your son was in the house your husband got worse? Why, when your son fed him, cleaned him, he would get weaker and not stronger?'

'This is not true!' the boy shouts in horror at the Priestess, but also at his mother who is looking as if she has been shaken by a giant hand. 'I loved my father! Mother, you know how I loved him!'

'Of course you did,' the Priestess is as soothing as a snake. 'You had no idea that the demon had entered you. Or maybe you did? Did you begin to dream of wickedness in the night? Of girls and of unspeakable acts?'

The boy's face darkens; he is shaking his head. 'What are you doing?' he cries staring at the Priestess. 'You came to the house. You saw how it was.'

'I am exposing and casting out the demon!' screams the Priestess, throwing up her hands, and the feedback screams too, and Luse screams, and the crowd screams, and when she opens her eyes Luse sees the young man has tears flooding down his face.

'Why are you doing this?' he asks again, and Luse doesn't understand what is going on or why the people around the boy and his mother are not helping them. Surely her father...? But when she turns to her Dad she sees he is as caught up in the drama as the rest of the crowd.

'Come here and be cleansed!' demands the Priestess, and the people sway forward as if wanting to push the boy forward, and he turns to his mother and in her eyes sees the doubt that Luse can feel tearing his insides apart.

'Mother?' He is gasping for air. It is all happening so quickly, there is no time for him to breathe, to think. But his mother steps away from him.

'We can take the demon from you,' says the Priestess more quietly, but still loudly enough for all around her to hear. 'Surely you want to be cleansed before you suck the life force from another innocent?'

The boy stands tall, shakes his head. Tears fly and the drops sparkle in the light. 'I loved my father.'

'You will be an outcast until you are cleansed. Fear him all you faithful. Fear him.'

The boy turns and, keeping his back stiff and his head up, he walks away from his mother and away from the tent. No one stops him or goes after him. When he is out of view his mother sinks down onto the ground and that seems to release the crowd who run forward to lift her up and fan her face.

The Priestess is satisfied. Luse can see the twisted contentment in the woman's face as she flaps the wings of her purple kaftan.

Luse's father reaches down and pats her head, as if pleased with her. As if she has passed a test... and then Luse knows that her father brought her here deliberately. That he was offering her up to the Priestess, that he believed – may still believe – that she too could be infected with a demon, that she too could be full of evil.

The very next day, Luse's father takes his packets of antiretrovirals out of the paper bag and starts emptying them down the kitchen sink.

Mum leaps up and screams, 'What are you doing? Paul! What?'

But he just laughs and winks at Luse and Joshua as he rips at the little boxes and pops the pills one by one from their foil. "'If you diligently heed the voice of the Lord your God and do what is right in His sight, give ear to His commandments and keep all His statutes, I will put none of the diseases on you which I have brought on the Egyptians. For I am the Lord who heals you.'"

'Paul...?' Esther's voice has dried in her throat. Her hands are on her head, her eyes huge and horrified.

'I put my whole trust in the Lord my God, Esther. I have been for weeks now and I feel stronger and happier every day. I cannot believe I was so blind.'

11.

'It's too hot.' Aunt Miriam is fanning herself with *The Post* newspaper, which flops, its stiffness defeated by the sweat she is producing. 'Why haven't these people got a goddamn generator? It's goddamn 2006 for crying out loud, not the Stone Age.'

Luse makes a soothing noise, not really listening. Auntie Miriam has flown all the way from Canada, thousands of miles, to be with Esther, Luse, Joshua and Ba'Neene. Later there will be food and dancing but right now the village is deathly quiet and the heat so oppressive it is hard to catch a breath. Luse loves the heat, loves almost everything about the village, apart from the lack of cold running water, and finds she is a little irritated with her aunt's lack of enthusiasm. Luse first came to stay in the village with Gran when she was a toddler and now is very quick to settle into the rhythms of village life. She knows that Auntie Miriam stayed here too as a child and she and Mum always talk about the village with such fondness, but now here, Miriam seems to have forgotten all the funny stories. The heat has warped her sense of humour and without it she can be a bit of a mean old cow.

However, to be fair, it is so hot that the tar on the road has become soft and sticky, clumping to people's flip-flops and shoes. No one goes anywhere anyway at this time of day. Looking around, Luse can see a dozen children, several adults, and assorted dogs dozing in the shade of their verandas or under the nearby trees.

'It's too hot to doze,' snaps Miriam when Luse suggests this.

There are only a couple of families who live in the village all year round now. It used to be a big, crowded place but most people have left to live in the cities like Granddad did in the seventies. Gran says that back before the dam was built the village was famous for its cattle and its rainmaker, the sikatongo, Gran's mother-in-law. The village had a prime location up on the ridge, with the flat plain at its back, and was used as a trading post by many other villagers from all over the area.

Now there are only three small compounds, each with their own grain store on stilts and a couple of kraals and no cattle, only goats and sheep. The huts are still lovely, large and cool with intricate carvings in the wooden frames and fresh thatch. The headman's first wife lives with him in the central hut and his two other wives each have their own family quarters.

Luse wanders around a little, drifting around the ruins of the hut that Granddad built for Gran when they were newly-weds, the one he gave to his youngest brother when he and Gran left the village. The walls are crumbling now and there is a huge hole in the thatch where Luse can see wisps of white cloud and the fingernail of white moon. Several large black wasps with yellow stripes drop silently from the high thatch and zoom out of the doorway into the sun. Luse used to be scared of the wasps, but Gran told her that they were usually too busy to be bothered with people. They only get angry if sprayed with insect repellent or if someone is playing the wind-up radio too loudly. It is the same for the saucer-sized rain spiders that appear from holes in the earth floor after a storm. Ignore them. They do their best to do the same.

She can hear a brood of chickens dusting themselves outside and a child calling. Auntie Miriam is with Mum, Gran and Joshua in the current headman's hut. They will be talking about the ceremony as usual. Tonight the drummers arrive and once they get going the news will spread all across the valley that there is going to be a funeral and then a feast at the village.

It is cooling off very slightly as the sun tips down, but there is still a simmering heat coming from the ground. Luse wants to go and collect water with the other girls from the village and she hurries towards the main hut, but hears someone call her name.

'Luse!'

It's her mother. She waves her over to the doorway of Gran's hut. Esther looks relaxed in a grey and blue T-shirt and wrap. Her skin is freshly oiled and gleams, speckled with sweat. She flaps her hand at the flies.

'Hot enough for you?' she grins.

As Luse's eyes adjust to the gloom inside she sees Miriam, prostrate on a reed mat in her knickers and large beige under-wired bra. She is having a sneaky cigarette and the smoke smells sharp and sweet at the same time. Joshua sits next to her playing with some ancient Tonka toys; a yellow earth mover and truck that used to belong to Granddad.

'Luse,' says Gran. 'I want to go over the ridge. Will you come?'

Soon it will be evening and the ridge is a long hike down the craggy hillside. She looks with surprise at her mother, but Esther is not listening. She is sewing beads onto Gran's belt and in her face Luse reads both deep love and terrible sadness. Tonight is Gran's last.

'Yes, I'll come,' she says. She glances down and sees her dusty feet in her pink flip-flops. 'I'll get my proper sandals.'

Gran walks swiftly and silently along the dirt track, weaving through the trees and around the thickets. Luse follows a few feet behind. It is the best way to walk in the bush and the safest. There are still a few wild animals about; the headman's second wife saw an elephant nearby a couple of months ago, and of course there are sudden drops, poisonous plants, and it's very easy to get lost. The shadows are lengthening and Luse listens to the soft thump of Gran's steady feet in the sandy soil. Far off a ke wee bird calls, its alarm sounding like 'go away, go away!' fading among the trees.

They emerge into a small clearing where several men are shaping a long piece of musangu tree into a canoe. They have lit a fire for their scraping tools and one man is bent over with his chapunga knife raised when Luse and Gran appear. He straightens up and gives Gran a sort of salute and a lovely smile. His teeth are very large and white in his bearded face, and, like the other men, he is shirtless. Luse notes the muscles roping around his arms, the sweat dripping from his back. His stomach is concave, each rib prominent, but his smile is full.

'Greetings, madam. How is your last day? How is your family?'

'Greetings to you, Benne. All is well, thank you. My family are fine.'

'That is good, madam.' He smiles again, this time at Luse. 'Your grandmother taught me all about the bush, little sister. She is better than the whole National Archive up in Lusaka!'

Luse ducks her head shyly, grinning. She imagines Gran with the man when he was little, like her, talking to him about the trees and the animals. She is both proud and a tiny bit jealous. Gran is hers after all.

Gran and Luse walk on, and now the trees become sparser and the ground more rocky. They are climbing down from the ridge and for a while the air gets close again. Sweat drips into Luse's eyes, blinding her briefly, and she trips and falls on a sharp rock. Gran pauses but Luse waves her on, holding her breath until the pain passes. She is going to be brave today, tonight. For Gran. She gives up trying to be as swift and gracefully balanced as Gran and slides on her bottom over the most treacherous, slippery rocks, keeping an eye out for scorpions and snakes. They have been hiking now for over an hour and far below she can see the glint of the greasy Zambezi. She can hear it too, the river is sluggish now but still noisy and the sound of rushing water bounces up the valley, bringing with it an occasional fetid, fishy smell. They are still higher than the swallows that dip and flit beneath them chasing insects, but the hillside plants are becoming denser, lusher, as they edge slowly down.

Gran pauses, hands on her hips, looking over to her left as Luse comes up alongside. Three white and gold melele trees stand guard at the mouth of a large cave. This is the shrine and this is the first time Luse has seen it so close. Normally she would have to wait at the ridge whilst the adults clambered to the cave mouth. Luse takes Gran's hand, Gran squeezes her fingers and they walk the last few yards to the cave opening.

The mouth of the cave is wide but not very high. Anyone taller than Gran would have to stoop to enter. Before they go in, Gran takes some herbs, a bottle and a torch from the bags slung around her waist. She pops the cork of the bottle and takes a swig, handing it to Luse. *It definitely isn't water*, thinks Luse, sniffing it suspiciously. *It's got that alcohol smell.* She takes a small gulp and just manages to swallow. The liquid burns all the way down. She gasps, feeling it hit her empty stomach.

Gran nods and places a small, dry twig in her mouth and hands one to Luse, gesturing for her to do the same. Luse holds it between her teeth and tastes spicy resin. Gran has told her that the stick stops any spirits from entering the body through the mouth. She watches as Gran then turns to each of the three melele trees, greeting them formally, curtseying, asking permission to enter the cave. She dribbles some of the noxious liquid from the glass bottle at their roots and then, replacing the stick in her mouth, nods to Luse and together they duck into the cave.

Luse isn't sure what to expect. She has never been in a cave before. It is pitch black and stinks of animal dung. She would prefer to breathe through her mouth but has to hold the stick, so she is forced to take in the pungent stink through her nostrils. It is also cold, especially after the baking heat outside. Goosebumps rise up in rashes all over Luse's body.

She shivers, waiting for her eyes to adjust to the darkness. Gran, however, clicks on the torch, swinging the beam in a wide arc to show Luse that the cave is a long sausage-shaped corridor that narrows towards the end. The walls are jagged and sparkle with mica in the torch beam. When the torch hits the ceiling, Luse sees it move and realises that it is a furry mass of tiny bats. Gran then shines the beam down and jerks it. The floor is thick with bat droppings and large, raised flagstones have been carefully placed in a line like stepping stones. Gran doesn't hesitate and so neither does Luse, although she can't imagine where they are going. It looks as if the cave ends in about twenty feet. She concentrates on the beam from the flashlight, trying not to think about the creatures hanging with their tiny teeth, claws and soft little bodies in their thousands over her head.

There are thirty stones and by the midpoint Luse notices a strange glow coming from the end of the tunnel. As they get closer to what she expects to be the back of the cave, Gran pauses and shines the torch for Luse to see that the end of the cave is actually a raised shelf that becomes a crawl-through space. The glow is coming from whatever is beyond this. Luse's heart is beginning to slam in her chest. She thinks she can hear someone breathing in the darkness behind her and has to fight the urge to turn around and run back out from the cave. *Keep right behind Ba'Neene,* she thinks. *You can do it for her... This is for her...*

Gran heaves herself up onto the shelf and crawls forward, waving the torch behind her to encourage Luse to follow. It is a bit of a struggle but Luse manages to pull herself over the lip of the shelf and follows Gran's feet and they slide along the floor. Then Gran begins to turn a corner and the torch light ebbs. For a second Luse feels a strong hand close around her ankle and she turns, twists and kicks out violently, heart pounding, but there is nothing there. She has nearly dropped the stick from her mouth. She growls over her shoulder and, quicker now, shuffles along the smooth rock floor after Gran... emerging into sunlight and bird song!

Gran clambers down from the rock shelf and takes the stick from her mouth.

'Look, Luse,' she says. 'Isn't it beautiful?'

The small tunnel has opened out into a spectacular space right in the middle of the hill. The roof of the cave must have fallen in hundreds of years ago and sunlight floods down from the huge, gaping hole above their heads. This sunlit cave is the width of at least two football fields. A slender waterfall twists and gushes from the roof of the cave to a deep, blue-black pool at the bottom, edged with wide grassy banks. The walls of the entire place are lined with a multitude of plants, trees, creepers, orchids, and more. The noise is incredible and Luse is amazed that she didn't hear it before. Amazed that it doesn't pour out of the mouth of the cave and rock the hillside. A cacophony of bird song. Every wall is lined with nests and nest holes. Bee eaters, weaver birds, kingfishers, swallows, waxbills and fire finches, hundreds of thousands of birds flitting, flying, calling, singing, joyfully feeding. It is the most wonderfully magical thing that Luse has ever, ever seen in her entire life.

Gran is grinning from ear to ear.

'You can take your stick out of your mouth now,' she says, and although there is a tumult of bird song and water, Luse can hear her as clearly as she could outside. 'But keep it safe. You will need it for going back.'

Gran has clambered down to the pool and is standing at the bottom of the waterfall. The glass bottle is in her hand again and she sings to the cave and to the birds, 'Spirits of my ancestors, welcome and protect us. Spirits we salute you!'

She pours liberally from the bottle into the pool and then takes another swig herself, before stripping off her chitenje and white vest top. The rock face behind the waterfall is pitted and at waist height there is a large, hollowed-out rock that she uses like a sink. She splashes water over her face, drinking deeply, and Luse does the same. The water is very cold and refreshing with a slight earthy taste. Luse follows Gran's lead, washing her face and then her feet.

'What now?' she asks, wondering if she can just lie down on the sunny bank and watch the birds, but Gran hands her a broom made of long, fine sticks bound together with twine.

'We haven't long,' she says and leads Luse to the side of the cave where the walls meet the earth banks. Feathers, twigs and fallen flowers cover a wide area of newly turned soil. Gran and Luse begin sweeping. In a few minutes they have cleared a good-sized area and uncovered a large reed mat that has been placed over a recently dug trench about six feet deep. Luse notices that all around the edge of the cave are large stones, hundreds of them, stretching all around the pool, each one about the size of a large loaf of bread and obviously carefully placed by hand. In front of each stone is a small, cleared patch from which broken bits of pottery, bowls, plates and spoons stick out. *I am standing in a burial ground,* she thinks, and at the same time understands at last what the trench is for. Gran.

She stands for a moment letting this realisation sink in all the way to her toes, but she is not sad. She cannot think of a more wonderful place to be buried. It is almost with joy that she begins vigorously sweeping again. They clear the whole area from the pool to the cave walls. Afterwards they rinse the headstones with water.

From high overhead, above the open roof of the cave, comes the keening call of a fish eagle echoed by its mate. *Heeeeee ee ee eeee.* Gran straightens up and looks at the sky.

'It's time to head back,' she says, and looking around, nods her head with satisfaction. 'Well done, Luse.'

'Ba'Neene, this is the best place in the world!'

Gran smiles, exposing her bare gums. 'Yes. I think it is. And so did your grandfather.'

She leads Luse over to the line of headstones and kneels down next to one with a fishing net half-buried in the ground. 'Chipo,' she says, 'meet your granddaughter.'

13.

Back at the village, Luse sits in the doorway of the hut watching sparks from the fire rising in clouds of thick, black smoke and listening to the strange thrumming noise of the namalwa and the intricate rhythms of the budima drums.

The men have pulled all the drums into a central ring around the fire to heat the skins and tune them and now are throwing rhythms to each other and calling out to the people. At least one or two of the drums must have been playing all afternoon because people are arriving on foot, appearing from out of the twilight like ghosts. Most are elderly. Luse can see that several of the old women are missing their front teeth and have the reed chisitas through their noses. They separate from the men and move to one side of the fire, sitting in a group, smoking from large pipes that they pass around.

Luse is waiting for Gran to come with her to the fireside, but Gran is taking ages. Luse hears her make a funny sound inside and turns around.

'Are you ready, BaNeene?'

'Ach, Luse... I feeling very tired suddenly.' She looks like she is winking, but she isn't smiling and the left side of her mouth dips down as if half her face has already fallen asleep. Her voice is slightly slurred.

'Luse, I think I am going to lie down for a while. Could you go and find Baama. Let her know I'll be along later.'

'But–'

'No, little one. You must take Joshua and go and have a good time tonight.'

'Okay, Ba'Neene.'

Luse is still thrilling from the excitement of the day and desperate to get to the dancing. She dashes through the throng to find Mum, sweeps up Joshua and runs from the hut, plunging into the pulsing beating of the drums, whirling him around and around until he is dizzy and laughing. She keeps him dancing until he is toppling over with exhaustion and then they lie with the old women on mats by the fire. Luse sleeps deeply and without dreaming and when she wakes she knows Gran is dead.

14.

Life back in Lusaka city, without Gran and with Miriam back in Toronto, is duller, but Luse is quickly immersed in school. She starts a new term and is bumped up a grade which means that she is in the same class as Rachel. Rachel's older sister is getting married and Luse and Rachel are allowed to go to the kitchen tea party and are to be in the parade of dancers during the Machibito – the presentation of food to the bridegroom's family – and, even more exciting, to be in the group of dancers at the reception leading in the newlyweds. So for two evenings a week Luse gets to stay over at Rachel's and go to the dance rehearsals. They talk about dresses a lot. Her family is really strict so they will have to wear long skirts which Rachel is trying to negotiate a side slit into so that they can at least dance a bit more easily.

'Come on, Daddy,' she says. 'We will fall over in these curtains.'

Her father is a large, heavy man who rarely smiles except at his daughters. He smiles now but it is a smile that even Luse can see means a slit in any skirt isn't ever going to happen.

That week she gets dropped off at home on Saturday morning. Mum and Dad are waiting for her. Mum is beaming, her skin is dewy and soft and to Luse she looks stunningly beautiful. Dad obviously thinks so too. He keeps glancing down at her as if he is the luckiest man in the world. *Which he is,* thinks Luse grouchily. Ever since Gran's death Luse has tried, really tried, not to let his Bible stuff depress her. He has been better, there is no doubt about that. He still goes to church a lot – three times in the week – and he still does his Bible readings in the morning at breakfast, but it makes him happy and Mum doesn't seem to mind. He rarely brings his church friends around now, which is a huge relief. The church stuff is more like a hobby now, like Luse and her dancing; only there is still something Luse can't put her finger on. A week ago she got dropped home early after swimming class and Dad was in the kitchen talking on his cell phone. He had been speaking loudly, obviously a bad line, and Luse had heard him before he saw her.

'... Yes Madam, I agree it would be a great honour... yes Madam... but I have told you how it is now... no... no! I am taking precautions... I am watching them... I...'

As Luse walked into the kitchen, he stopped, phone held to his cheek, and stared at her first with annoyance and then with what began to look like fear.

'Rachel's Dad just dropped me...' she began to explain and then momentarily she hated him entirely. His pathetic expression enraged her. 'Whatever!' she said when he didn't respond. She dropped her wet swimming costume and towel on the kitchen floor and went to her room. Behind her closed door she sat on the bed, furious and confused by her feelings.

But now Luse's troubled thoughts are interrupted by her mother.

'We have something to discuss, Luse. We thought we could have a treat, go for lunch at Nando's restaurant and chat there.'

Luse really wants to go to the mall with Rachel and Samba, but she thinks she might be able to get dropped off after the lunch and at least that way there will be chicken and chips.

'Yeah, okay,' she says without much curiosity or enthusiasm, and follows Joshua over to the car.

They go to the Nando's restaurant in Kabalonga, which is already crowded, and Luse sits in a plastic chair texting Rachel.

'Can you put the phone away just for lunch, honey?' Mum asks, and Luse sighs hugely.

Have 2 put fone off. Laters L.

As usual Joshua takes handfuls of food from everyone's plate.

'Gross, Joshua!' says Luse as he licks ketchup off a chip, then lays it gently back on her plate.

The bombshell comes over ice cream.

'Your father has been invited to become the manager of the Betabank branch in Siavonga! It's a great opportunity for him and it looks as if I may be able to get work at the private clinic there.'

They will be leaving Lusaka for three years, moving into Gran's house by the lake.

'Isn't that wonderful?' Mum has tears in her eyes, but Luse just happens to glance across and see Dad's expression. It makes her think of something... a pirate... a pirate look... furtive.

'But what about school? I am halfway through a project!'

'Luse, love, we know it will be hardest for you but they have a pretty good school in Siavonga town itself.'

'It's not just about that, Mum. What about my friends? What about Rachel and Samba? I will die without Rachel.'

'Don't be so dramatic, Luse,' her Dad butts in. 'No one is going to die without Rachel.'

Luse doesn't like the way he says that. It is almost like he is mocking her. Even Mum in her bubble of bliss seems to wince a little.

'Well I am not going and that is that!' roars Luse. 'I am going to pack my stuff and go and stay with Rachel.'

But in the end of course she does go because she is only ten years old and there is no way that her Mum would let her stay in Lusaka with Rachel or Samba or anyone for that matter. And no amount of sulking, swearing or yelling is going to change the fact that they are leaving the city and moving to the lake house. So in the end Luse bows to the inevitable and even helps with the packing, wrapping glasses and plates in newspaper, helping Dad collect brown boxes from his friend at Shoprite, deciding what clothes to bring and which to give away.

Bertram says he is going back to Northern Province to get married. Luse is so amazed that her Mum has to prod her with an elbow to get her to close her mouth.

'When did you meet her?'

'Oh, you know,' Bertram is shy. 'She is a cousin's daughter.'

He won't be drawn, but Mum and Dad are delighted and Dad offers to pay something towards the lobola, the bride price. Mum kisses him on both his cheeks and Bertram smiles with pleasure.

So Bertram won't be with them in Siavonga. Luse calculates that this will mean she will get her own bedroom after all, the one closest to the bathroom. She is beginning to have to fake the fury she takes to school with her to share with Rachel. She is beginning to enjoy the idea of being in Gran's house again.

15.

They move the Sunday after Rachel's sister's wedding, at the beginning of the Christmas holidays. It is raining when they arrive and the house seems gloomy, echoing with emptiness, longing for company. The familiar smell of reed matting and wood smoke makes Luse's stomach tighten with guilt as she realises that she hasn't thought of Gran for weeks.

They camp the first night, waiting for the truck with their things to arrive, and Mum goes around the house checking that all the lights are working and the water is running from the borehole. Rain is leaking through the roof in a couple of places and Dad finds buckets to catch the drips. Gran's stove went to Old Dominic, her only staff, so until theirs arrives they rig up a barbecue on the veranda and Dad does the chicken while Mum stands next to him trying not to burn the two pots of nsima and relish. They have brought the wind-up radio and listen to golden oldies, getting all lovey-dovey. They stand close over the fire, giggling together like teenagers, knocking elbows and bums and basically annoying Luse to the point where she goes to her room and lies on the bed, listening to the rain gently plinking against the window.

Joshua comes in.

'This is my room Joshua. No boys are allowed.'

'But Luse, where is Ba'Neene going to sleep?'

Luse sits up and is about to be rude when she sees he is actually quite upset. 'What's wrong?'

'If Baama and Taata are in Ba'Neene's bedroom, where will she sleep?'

'Joshua, Ba'Neene is dead. She is sleeping forever in the hill at the village. Remember?'

'But I heard her singing outside.'

Luse gets a chilly feeling and swings her feet off the bed and onto the cold floor. She cocks her head and for a second she too hears a soft cooing coming from out in the rain. A lovely, watery low note, then another, then a trail of them, descending into silence, dro dro dodododododo...

'Joshie,' she says, relief rushing through her, warming her face. 'That isn't Gran, I promise. It's a chiburuburu, a wood dove that sings just like Gran used to when it rains.'

Luse loves that the knowledge is still there, just below the surface of her memory. 'Gran taught me the song. It goes "My mother dead, my father dead, everybody dead dead dead..." Listen... there it goes again.'

They listen to the lovely woody notes as they slip down the scale into silence.

Witch Girl

1.

Luse stops now and yawns until her jaw cracks and Georgia is amazed to realise it is nearly eleven. Luse has been talking for almost two full hours but the little group has been entranced, horrified and moved in turn. Luse is a remarkable story teller. She speaks slowly, only occasionally hesitating to bring her thoughts into focus, her hand movements are small and her child's voice mesmerising.

A moth buzzes and bumps against the fluorescent strip in the kitchen and she hears the rusty-throated screech owl outside again. Gentle rain has begun falling and brings a waft of moist night air in through the mesh door. Luse yawns again.

'Luse, you have done so well this evening. I – we – are so grateful to you for sharing all this.'

But Luse is already half asleep and Bernard smiles and puts a hand on Georgia's shoulder and a finger over her lips. 'Let's get her upstairs.'

Gus, stretching, goes out to the gate guard to organise a taxi and Bernard and Georgia half-steer, half-carry Luse to bed.

'I'm not finished...' Luse mumbles.

'You can carry on tomorrow if you feel like it.' Georgia helps her into the bed and waits a moment to see her breathing deepen. Luse sighs and turns over on her side. Joshua is snoring sweetly, thumb at the ready.

'Taxi's en route,' says Gus as Georgia and Bernard return to the living room. He picks up Bernard's notebook. 'What do you think?'

He asks this to both Georgia and Bernard. They shrug simultaneously.

'I think I want to find out more about this Aunt Miriam in Toronto,' Gus says, tapping the pen on the pad. 'I should be able to track her down. Get her and the kids in contact again. I wonder if she is aware of what's been happening?'

'We still don't know what happened to the parents though.' Bernard scratches his head, suddenly looking elderly and frail. He steadies himself on the thin bannister. 'I will need to do more research on this Blood of Christ Church; try and find out where exactly they are getting their funding and how much influence they have in the various dioceses. I am afraid I'll need more information from Luse for that, poor child.'

Both Gus and Bernard look at Georgia. She tries to think of an alternative but can't. They will have to ask Luse for more of the story.

'Tomorrow?'

They nod, agreeing to meet the next day.

At 5am Luse wakes screaming. Groggily Georgia runs to her room, flicks on the light and finds Joshua crouching by Luse's bed. He blinks in the glare from the bulbs and holds his hands out to Georgia. She sees that he is calm in spite of his sister's tortured shrieks.

'She is having a nightmare,' he says over Luse's wailing. 'But don't try and wake her up. It makes it last longer.'

Georgia crouches down next to Joshua and sees that Luse is indeed still deeply asleep, propped up on elbows but eyes half shut with the whites showing at the bottom.

'It isn't a long one,' Joshua says over the shrieks, his palms on his knees and his face too taut and lined for a six-year-old child. And in a few more seconds Luse stops and slumps down on the bed. Georgia checks her pulse and temperature, but Luse seems perfectly alright and is breathing normally, unlike Georgia, whose heart is racing like a train.

'Are you alright, Joshua?' she asks the boy.

He nods wearily, like an old person. 'She does it sometimes,' he says again. 'It's worse when you wake her.'

'I'll remember that. Do you want to sleep in my room?'

'Oh no. I am okay. I am used...' He yawns. 'Can I have chicken sandwiches for breakfast...?'

'Err...' begins Georgia, but Joshua is already asleep.

Birds are beginning to sleepily chirrup outside by the time Georgia climbs the stairs again. She isn't going to get any more sleep and has brought a cup of steaming tea with her into the study where she cracks open the laptop and boots up. She cannot let go of the image of Joshua calmly crouching by the bed as Luse screams, waiting, keeping guard with that old man's face.

2.

The next afternoon Georgia's cell phone rings. It's Brenda, the clinic receptionist.

'There is a policeman here,' she says. 'He wants to talk to you about some missing street kids.'

Georgia blinks rapidly and feels strangely cautious. 'Thanks, Brenda. Get his name and a contact number and I will call him after the weekend.'

'Alright.'

'And Brenda...'

'Yes, Doctor?'

'Do not give him any of my personal information. Is that understood?'

'Of course, Doctor.'

Unsettled, Georgia turns to Yvonne, but is interrupted by the arrival of Gus and Bernard. Joshua bounces downstairs and leaps across to Bernard. Gus bends down to kiss Georgia's cheek. His lips are soft and he smells of hotel soap and toothpaste.

Luse is waiting, eager to begin, and Georgia is pleased to see that she looks rested in spite of her troubled night. They settle outside on the patio, Joshua and Marta disappear off into the garden and Luse, taking a deep breath and smiling bravely at Gus, focuses and takes up her story again.

3.

Luse isn't impressed with the school in Siavonga. The other kids are idiots.

'Isn't there anyone there you could make friends with?' Mum asks as Luse is once again lying on the couch with her headphones on. 'What about going for a swim at the old clubhouse?'

'Mum,' snarls Luse, 'that place is for prostitutes and druggies.'

'Oh really?' Mum looks worried. 'Gosh. I will have to stop swimming there then...' She grins but Luse scowls. 'Oh come on, Luse. It's not forever.'

The mesh door creaks as Dad arrives in the kitchen and Mum turns eagerly from Luse to go and meet him. *As if you even care that I have no friends,* thinks Luse sulkily. She is about to text Rachel when she hears a glass smash and a sharp shout from the kitchen. It's Mum. She tears off her earphones and runs towards the noise, bumping into a sleepy Joshua in the corridor.

Dad is standing at the kitchen table, still wearing his jacket. Now that Luse looks at him she sees that the shoulders are too wide, the jacket is too big. Odd. It's the same jacket he always wears. Mum is on her hands and knees sweeping up a shattered glass from the stone floor with a dustpan and brush. There is something in the stiffness of her back, the jerkiness of her movements that radiates terrible upset.

'You lied, Paul. You lied to me. To all of us,' she is muttering under her breath as she sweeps. Joshua begins to go to her but Luse catches him.

'There is glass, Joshie,' she whispers. 'You have bare feet.' She picks him up and steps a little backwards into the frame of the door.

'I never lied to you, Esther,' Dad says. 'I didn't tell you because I knew you would react in this ridiculous, childish way. Becoming a pastor is a real honour for me and should be for you.'

'What?' Mum sits back on her knees. 'An honour to become a pastor in a church that demonises children? That doesn't believe in western medicine but instead makes victims out of those suffering?'

'Enough!'

'Paul, you cannot give up your job to become a goddamn pastor in an illegitimate church! I won't let you! It's insane. Obscene. You must have lost your mi...'

She doesn't finish her sentence. The crack of his palm across her face echoes off the empty, unfurnished walls like a gunshot. In the silence that follows Luse watches from the corridor where she and Joshua are now crouching as her mother raises a hand slowly to her face. Her father too puts out his hand, his eyes wide and horrified, his mouth working as if trying to apologise, but Esther backs away from him, still on her knees.

Then Luse sees something happen to her father. He straightens and his eyes go dead as a goat's and in a strange, monotone voice he says as if in a play, 'Wives, submit yourselves unto your own husbands, as unto the Lord. For the husband is the head of the wife, even as Christ is the head of the church: and he is the saviour of the body. Therefore as the church is subject unto Christ, so let the wives be to their own husbands in everything.'

He stares down at Mum and then across to Luse and Joshua. 'I *will* stop working for Mammon. I will be a pastor here for The Blood of Christ Church. I will become a servant of the Lord and...' here he holds out his finger and wags it at Mum, 'I will be respected in my own household. Now pull yourself together.'

He walks around Mum where she sits still holding a shaking hand to her cheek and slams the door of the bedroom.

4.

From this point on the fracture in the family becomes a full shattering of bone. Life is relatively normal during the day, but in the evenings Dad's church friends descend on the lake house to read, pray and sing, sometimes for hours. Mum resists with silence and with as much grace as she can muster, putting out refreshments in advance to ensure that the kitchen at least is free for herself and the two children. Mum and Dad no longer seem to ever be in the same room and at night Mum sleeps with Joshua.

The church people offer money and bring groceries over, but Mum always refuses them, and on a single salary finances get tight quickly. Luse's phone now has to be shared and there are no more trips into Siavonga town for Cokes and Fantas at the clubhouse pool.

And Dad gets thin. Horribly thin, almost overnight. Coughing and wheezing all the time, huge rings around his eyes.

'Daddy's sick,' Joshua says over breakfast as they all watch him double over with the pain of his racking coughing. Luse looks desperately over at Mum but Mum just stares at her plate. Luse wonders if she cares at all anymore but then, in the car, Mum asks for Luse's phone. She calls her own doctor in Lusaka, Dr Kaunda. He already knows some of the situation.

'Could I crush the pills and put them into his food?' Mum asks, but the answer is that it is too complicated and risky with the doses. Also unethical. If he doesn't want to take his antiretrovirals...

'But he could die,' Mum protests, and Luse hears the tinny voice saying just two words, 'I'm sorry.'

5.

It is a year since Gran died and it's oppressively hot. All around are the electric pulses of cicadas and the creak of crickets. Joshua is whining about the flies that keep landing on his face. He bats at them and cries and the moisture of his tears attracts more flies. Luse is hot and thirsty too and she ignores him, raising the binoculars again instead. Through the tunnel of the binocular lens she scans the steep side of the valley. The scrub is thorny and brown with occasional bursts of green from the tamarind trees and mukuyu. Far below, at the bottom of the valley, runs the Zambezi River, brimming with tiger fish and humongous crocodiles lazily swirling in the slow muddy water. The river is very low and subdued at this time of year and from up here it looks and moves like a python, all glittering, scaly muscle.

She plays with the binocular focus and swings it too far at first and then back. There! Three white-gold bare trees in a circle stand out brightly against the dark greens and browns of the bushes. Underneath them is a black hole in the rock; the entrance to the shrine.

There is a flash of colour at the entrance of the cave and Luse concentrates through the binoculars. Her mother emerges slowly with Auntie Miriam. They are laughing, standing up and waving at Luse and Joshua. Auntie Miriam gulps from a metal water bottle and hands it to Mum and they stand, hands on hips, getting breath back. A few small, dark shapes slip from the darkness of the cave behind them. Bats. Mum ducks, and even though Luse can't hear her from this distance, she knows she will be giving her high-pitched shriek. They wave again and signal that they are going to trek back towards the children and the car.

Auntie Miriam has flown from Canada again to be with them for Gran's year memorial. This time it is just a small family ceremony and they have stayed only one night at the village, bringing gifts of beer and a goat for slaughter. Luse could have gone with Mum and Miriam but it is still too dangerous for Joshua to clamber down the thorn-strewn hillside in the sickening heat of September to place offerings, prayers and libations. Instead, Luse waits with him on the ridge within sight of the dirt track and the now filthy car. She doesn't mind. She went the day before with Benne to the shrine to sweep and wash the headstones and her head is still full of the flocks of gorgeous birds, the waterfall and the flowers.

Luse picks up Joshua, heaving him onto her hip and jiggling him.

'Shhh shhh,' she says. 'Mummy and Auntie Miriam are coming back now. No need for crying anymore, right?'

Luse has the keys for the car, but even with all the doors and the boot open it's still too hot to get inside. Instead, she pulls the cool box out from the back and over into the shade of the nearby acacia thicket, popping the tab of a bright orange Fanta for Joshua and a Coke for herself. The fizzy drinks are cold and sweet, frothing on their tongues as they wait panting in the dappled shadows.

Joshua now stands up and solemnly dribbles a little Fanta onto the ground where immediately several ants and a couple of hard-shelled beetles bundle towards the evaporating puddle. Luse raises an eyebrow at him.

'It's for Gran,' he says. 'In case she is thirsty too.'

'Is Gran in the cave?' Joshua asked earlier.

'Sort of,' Mum replied. 'Her body is there, Joshua, but her spirit is all around us, in the air, in the ground, in the Zambezi too.'

Luse sighs and then she too drips some of her drink onto the dust. The sugary smell of sun-baked cola rises up into the air. Flies whine excitedly.

'Luse!' Mum's voice rings out from just below them and Luse and Joshua jump up and run into her arms. Auntie Miriam with her lovely, soft brown eyes and cocoa-buttery skin is gasping for breath, her enormous bosom heaving between the straps of the rucksack. Sweat is dripping from both the women's faces.

Miriam's white T-shirt is filthy with red dirt from the scramble and she looks down at herself and laughs, 'Esther, promise me we don't have to do that every year?'

Miriam has been visiting for two weeks, staying with them in the lake house. Since she has been here the house has been full of light and laughter. Luse's mum has been happy again and funny, and the deep lines in her forehead and under her nose have smoothed out. Luse is dreading her aunt leaving next week. She sighs, drawing Miriam's attention.

'Hey girl. What you worrying about now, hon?' Luse is pulled into a sweaty breast and kissed on the top of the head. 'Your gran told me that she thought you were the smartest kid she had ever come across. Did you know that?'

Luse is surprised and instantly suspicious. 'When did she tell you that?'

Miriam laughs. 'She didn't come to me in a vision, kid, if that's what is worrying you! We did speak on the telephone, you know!' Her warm laughter is familiar, that cackle just like Ba'Neene, and when Mum joins in so too does Luse, and then Joshua, until they are breathless and wheezy.

'Ahhh Miriam,' Mum gasps. 'I have missed you so much.'

They crack open a couple of beers and Mum hands round little packets of homemade biltong. Luse chews the dried meat in with her Coke so that the salt and the sugar rocket across her taste buds.

The sun is beginning to gently lower itself down to the horizon and the shadows have elongated, the air cooling slightly. Luse is happy and doesn't want to go home, but it isn't long before they are packing up the cool box and buckling themselves back into the old land cruiser.

The lights are on at the house. As they pull up, they all see the other vehicle parked alongside Dad's car – a single cab pick-up with 'Blood of Christ Church' printed in black letters along the side. Mum gives an audible sigh and Miriam leans over and squeezes Mum's shoulder. Joshua is sleepy and Mum has to carry him in. Miriam and Luse get the cool box and the rubbish from the boot, so they both have their arms full when the front door opens and her father stands with his arm raised in the doorway. Before Luse or Miriam can make a sound or jump forward, he brings his arm down hard as if striking Esther and Joshua who are in silhouette in front of him.

'Cast out the demons!' a shout comes from behind him – not one voice but several. Luse drops the rubbish and rushes to her mother's side to stand, trembling with fury, looking up at her father. He hasn't actually touched Esther, but instead has brushed her fiercely with a large, black cross in his right hand and now splashes something over her from a bottle in his left. Some of the liquid lands on Luse's face. Water.

For a long moment the family stands like this in the doorway, Dad blocking the way, his face contorted with concentration and something else – not drunkenness, as he no longer drinks, but similar.

'You fucking asshole,' says Miriam. Cool box still in her arms, she pushes Luse's dad out of the way. He is so slender now that she doesn't need to touch him. Just the force of her pushes him aside. He coughs and coughs.

'Paul, you are a damn idiot. Your wife has just come back from her mother's memorial and you perform a fucking exorcism? You sick bastard.'

Dad staggers slightly, blinking in the harsh porch light, and leaves enough space for Esther, Joshua and Luse to get past him.

There is something magnificent in Miriam's casual deflation of the drama and her dismissal of her sister's husband. If Luse were not so embarrassed and angry with him she might even feel a prickle of sympathy, but she chooses not to. She doesn't even look at him as she steps over his feet and stalks away with the women to the kitchen.

She can hear Dad's church cronies in the background. They were too pathetic to even come with him to the door. Luse turns her head just a little and sees her father slink back to join them in the living room. He begins to close the door, but Frank – one of her father's mates – shouts, 'No Paul, leave it open! When they hear the word of our Lord they will be healed.'

Esther and Miriam are huddled in the kitchen when Luse comes in. They open their arms and Luse rushes over and the hug is fierce and sad. They know from experience that the church group will be here for hours, singing, chanting prayers, perhaps even talking in tongues. No one will get much sleep tonight.

'Well, what did you expect, Esther?' Miriam asks. 'Mother was a healer. To them that's another name for witch. In a way they are trying to protect you.'

Esther shakes her head. 'If only that were true,' she says and then she stands for a moment, shoulders slumped, and Luse holds her breath wishing with all her might that she could comfort her. But the lovely Esther doesn't cry. She straightens up and then does a funny little twirling dance and begins to rumba to the deafening 'Onward Christian Soldiers' coming from the other room. She rumbas over to the door and shuts it firmly with her bottom.

'Supper!' she announces to her surprised family, grinning. 'We witches have to eat!'

6.

The birds explode from the nearby lantana bushes; thousands of tiny bodies scattering like coffee grounds flung up into the sky. For a brief second they are in chaos and then with a brrrrumph of wind and feathers they twist around, turning in on themselves, closing ranks like a fist and flying away northwards to the hills in tight formation. The quelea. Flocks can get so large that they strip fields of newly-planted seed in seconds.

Joshua loves them. He stretches his arms out towards them and then follows their bafflingly intricate flight paths with his hands, looking as if he is directing a choir. It is good to see him calmer after the terrible morning. His face is still marked with small white patches of dried tears and Luse herself is not far off crying.

They should be having a good morning. They should be. Today is her eleventh birthday after all. Although Dad is too sick these days to have many visitors, she and Mum planned pancakes for breakfast and were going to soak them in the last of Miriam's maple syrup. They can't afford to go to the nice hotel for supper, but Mum said that they would put together a picnic at the weekend and perhaps even go for a sundown lake cruise with Granddad's old partner Randolf, who still keeps a small fleet of banana boats.

Dad's church people come less frequently now that Dad is unable to get out of bed, needing almost constant nursing. Mum refused to let them sing and pray too loudly around his bed and this infuriated Frank so much that he rounded up the others and stormed off, to Luse's immense relief.

Lack of money means that Mum has to do a lot of Dad's nursing herself, with occasional help from two of Old Dominic's daughters who look after him whilst she is at work. Mum has been coping, just about, although she has become a little forgetful. She can never find her handbag. She has twice forgotten to pick up Joshua from kindergarten, and yesterday Luse found her car keys in the fridge.

And then last night Luse woke up feeling thirsty and came into the kitchen to find Mum sitting at the kitchen table staring at her hands. She sat alone; in front of her was a kidney-shaped metal bowl with the cotton cloths she used for giving Dad his bed baths. She looked like she had been sitting there for hours, very still, palms facing up in her lap. In the quiet of the night Luse could hear Dad's breath rasping through the house. Over the last few days she had become used to the sound and could even sleep through it without a problem, but now, with Mum so still and hunched in the dark, it sounded very loud, as if someone was sawing wood in his bedroom.

'Baama?' Luse came through in her bare feet, wading through the pools of moonlight on the stone floor. 'Baama?' she said again louder, and she saw her mother's shoulders tense as if she had only just heard. Her head came up a little and swayed on her neck as if it was very heavy. The swaying motion made her mother look weird, like a blind creature, a new-born kitten. With the moonlight and the noise of her Dad's tortured breathing echoing in the quiet house, Luse was deeply afraid.

'Baama?' This time her voice trembled and she felt she wanted to run into her bed and pull the blankets over her head.

'Luse? Oh... baby... I am... tired. I am so tired...'

'Come to bed, Baama.' Luse walked around the table and reached out for her mother's shoulder. It was cold and hard, bones poking through. *Mum is not eating enough,* Luse thought, realising that she had not seen her mother actually sit down to eat for several days. *I will give her so many pancakes tomorrow that she will feel stronger again.*

'Come to bed,' she said again and this time Esther stood up and, leaning heavily on Luse, allowed herself to be led away to Luse's old room opposite the main bedroom where Luse's dad lay crumpled and wheezing in the big bed. She hadn't even tried to undress herself, just lay down, closed her eyes and was asleep before Luse had even pulled her sandals from her feet and arranged the mosquito net around her.

Luse left the door open and went back to her warm bed in Joshua's room.

Now she has woken to bright sunlight and Joshua sobbing.

'Wha... what's wrong, Joshie?' she asks confused. She must have really overslept. Why didn't Mum wake her up for pancakes?

'Mummy went to work without her shoes...' sobs Joshua, and Luse sees that he is still in his pyjamas, unwashed and as confused as she is. She swings herself from the bed and runs through to the kitchen, but Joshua is right. Mum has already gone to work and there, in the middle of the doorway, are her white work pumps.

She runs over to the wall clock. Nearly 9am and now there is no way of getting herself or Joshua to school. And there is something else. Dad.

She hasn't been into his room for several days, not since he went into his deep sleep and Mummy said there was not much more anyone could do. Mum has been nursing him around the clock, usually sleeping on a mattress on the floor next to the bed, getting up during the night when he needs her, washing him, turning him, changing his dressings. Luse has been aware of the seriousness of her father's illness but hasn't felt connected to the drama. Mum has been dealing with it. Mum has been coping.

When she opens the door, the smell makes her gag and she has to turn back for a moment. Joshua is standing behind her, his Winnie-the-Pooh pyjama top is on backwards and his eyes are wide and sparkling with tears.

'It smells pooey,' he says.

'Joshie, will you do me a favour? I am going to make us pancakes for breakfast and I will need eggs and milk. Can you get them from the fridge and wait for me?'

Slowly Joshua nods. Luse sees the idea of pancakes becoming real for him, his mouth relaxing from its anxious pout. He goes back into the kitchen and Luse takes a deep breath and goes in to her dad. Opening the curtain and the windows, pulling back and tying up the big mosquito net, the stench quickly lessens. Luse looks down at the man in the bed, seeing and not seeing her father. It could be a different man, half her Taata's height and weight. The man in the bed is hairless, his skull showing through the skin of his head, eyes sunken. Under the thin sheet he is shirtless, every rib, lump of cartilage, tendon, muscle is obvious. Luse has a book on human biology that has pictures of people without skin to show the structure of bone and muscle. The man in the bed, her Dad, could be an anatomy lesson.

Every breath he takes sounds as if it is tearing him inside. Luse cannot bear it, wonders how her mother can bear it and realises for the first time that maybe her mother can't bear it and that is why she isn't here on Luse's eleventh birthday to make those pancakes.

I don't know what to do, Daddy...

His eyelids flutter, the lashes look so long on those enormous dark lids, but his eyes don't open and Luse is relieved. She pulls back the sheet a little and the smell pours out, making her grasp her nostrils shut and blink. There is actually not much mess and it is very watery and almost clear. It just smells gruesome. Like something rotting. But she can manage, she thinks, and she goes to the bathroom to get a new bowl and some cloth.

She isn't prepared for the bedsores and one glance at the suppurating holes in what remains of her father's bottom sends her reeling backwards, vomit rising in her throat. The gassy, rotten stench is coming from the holes in his body not from the watery poo after all.

'Sorrydaddysorrydaddysorrydaddy...' she chants, hot tears and sweat dribbling, pulling the sheet up and backing out of the bedroom.

She washes her hands over and over again, panic rising in her like bubbles in a shaken cola bottle. In the kitchen Joshua is waiting. He has put the eggs, milk and flour on the table and is sitting very straight, being good.

'Good boy, Josh!' Luse tries to keep the tremble from her voice. 'I am just going to make some calls and then I'll cook, okay?'

'Why didn't Baama take her shoes?'

Luse ignores the question and flails around looking for the cell phone. Her mum has one and the other is the joint one they usually leave in the small entrance way next to the crackling old dial-up. She rings her mum's phone and it goes straight to voicemail. Hearing her mother's calm voice panics Luse more. *What now, what now?*

Just then there is the sound of a car outside and hope wells up in her. Mum is back! And it is Mum's car but Mum is not driving. She is sitting in the back seat between two people and there is a policeman driving the car. Luse can see his hat through the windshield. Driving close behind them is a battered pick-up with the words 'The Blood of Christ Church' on the side door.

Luse runs up the steps to meet the cars, nearly tripping over the top step.

'Mum, Mum! What's happening?'

The policeman parks Mum's car and gets out. He is young, very skinny and his uniform looks several sizes too big as he comes solemnly forward to Luse. 'Now you must be the daughter?'

Luse nods, not trusting herself to speak. Her mother is being gently pulled from the back of the car by two policewomen.

'Come on now, madam,' says one. 'What you need is some rest and you'll feel much better.'

But her mother is staring at the sky unblinking and her arms hang heavy at her side. She doesn't move and the policewoman on her left slips an arm around her shoulders and pushes her gently forward.

'We found her like this on the main road,' says the young policeman. 'She drove off into the ditch and was just sitting there with the engine running. Luckily these people were on their way to your house and recognised her.' He gestures at the three people clambering out from The Blood of Christ Land Rover. Frank, his fat wife Mulenga, and her friend Nelly. They look concerned and more than a little excited.

'Don't worry, Bwana sir,' says Frank, almost bowing. 'We'll take it from here. This poor girl's father is very sick in bed and now this affliction has befallen his wife. We know the family well and will take care of them.'

'No, no...' Luse tries to speak but there is no stopping Frank.

'Come on, girl. Now quickly prepare a bed for your mother.' He blocks her from coming any further up the steps. She is about to yell at the policeman to please call an ambulance when Joshua, who has come outside to see what is going on, catches sight of Esther and starts screaming.

Luse has no choice but to gather up her terrified brother and carry him back into the house with Frank, the policeman close on her heels; the women, almost carrying Esther, follow slowly behind.

Luse makes up her own bed with fresh sheets and Mum is brought through by the women. As they help her towards the bed, Esther starts to thrash around, shouting incoherently and swearing obscenely. Luse is horrified and stands back, shocked, not knowing what to do. Then Mulenga and Nelly shove Luse out of the way and take over. Mulenga holds Esther down whilst Nelly roughly undresses her and then they cover her with the sheet, tucking it in tightly to stop her moving around. Now Esther lies still, her hair matted, her skin dripping with sweat, her eyes following invisible people around the room. Luse tries to go to her but Fat Mulenga shakes her head, shutting the bedroom door.

'What she needs is rest, dear,' she says, not unkindly. 'You need to look after your brother while she does so.'

As there is no getting around Mulenga's wide hips, Luse is edged back into the kitchen. Meanwhile Frank has barged into Dad's room and calls Nelly and Mulenga in to clean him up too.

The police stand at the kitchen table drinking sweet tea and looking around at the house.

'Soooo...' says the young man. 'This is Chipo the Kapenta Man's house?' He has taken off his hat respectfully. The two women officers also plonk their caps on the table and listen out for noises from the bedrooms.

Luse just nods. She worries that if she opens her mouth she will be sick. Her heart thumps in her chest and the hairs stand up all over her body.

Finally Frank, Mulenga and Nelly come out from Dad's room with sleeves rolled up and several dirty towels. They reek of antiseptic. Nelly's face is twisted in revulsion, making her already saggy jowls even uglier than usual. She spends a long time at the sink making a big play of washing her hands and sighing hugely.

'It's a terrible thing to see,' she huffs and puffs. 'Two young people cut down like this in their prime.'

One of the policewomen comes over and pats her broad back. 'You are a good neighbour, madam.'

'We can take it from here.' Frank is all gruff self-importance, chest out and bandy legs wide. 'I'll drive you back to the roadblock.' He begins to herd the police towards the door, but Luse springs after them, grabbing at the young man's hand.

'I think my Mum needs to go to hospital...'

'Now that's enough of that,' says Frank, rolling his eyes at the cop. 'Your mother is just overworked trying to look after you and your brother as well as your poor sick father. Rest is what that woman needs! She works at Siavonga hospital, right? Well I will head there after dropping these fine people off and let them know she is... indisposed.'

Still Luse holds the cop's hand. He looks down at her and, seeing something desperate in her face, cocks his head and pauses.

'Well... perhaps...'

'No!' Mulenga's voice rings out from behind them. 'That girl makes trouble all the time, officer. Trust me. We will call our fellow church members and there will be so many volunteers to help here, you will see...'

Frank yanks Luse's hand from the policeman's and, clapping him on the shoulder, steers him out of the door. Helplessly, Luse wheels around and is face to face with the two blocks of flesh and bone that are Nelly and Mulenga. All pretence of kindness is gone. They stare at her with both unconcealed dislike and irritation.

As they listen to the sound of the Land Rover revving up and driving away, Mulenga reaches out and picks up the cell phone that lies on the table. She holds it up to her nose and nods, 'I think I better keep this safe, don't you Nelly?'

'Look at all this food on the table.' Nelly indicates the milk, eggs and flour that Joshua pulled out earlier.

'It's for pancakes,' whispers Joshua in the corner of the kitchen where he has been sitting. 'It's Luse's birthday today. We are going to have pancakes.'

The two fat women ignore him and Luse sees his eyes glisten with tears again. She goes to him and opens her arms and he climbs up. *He is heavy,* she thinks. *He has grown while I wasn't looking.*

She swallows back her fear, hardens herself, closes down her face as her Gran taught her to do. No emotion must show through. She turns to the women. 'Thank you very much for all your help,' she says.

Nelly blinks rapidly and Mulenga stares.

'I would like to thank you by making up these pancakes. You must be hungry?'

The women look at each other. Nelly's jowls flap slightly.

'There is still maple syrup from Canada.'

The clincher. The women nod. Nelly sucks her teeth. 'Can you even cook?' she asks ungraciously. 'I don't want charcoal.'

'Ach, sister. Let her do some work.' Fat Mulenga eyes the eggs and milk. 'You better make them quickly before Frank comes back with the others. There is not enough there for many people. Bring them to us in the living room. Come, Nelly, I want to rest my poor legs.'

Luse cooks quickly and hands the first pile of steaming pancakes lathered with maple syrup to her brother. He kicks his feet and hums as he eats.

The mixture for the second batch she spits in, twice. She gets Joshua to spit in it too. Then, when they are cooked, she carries the pile of pancakes through to the two women who have taken off their shoes and are sprawled on the sofa.

Nelly sniffs the pancakes suspiciously. 'There is not much maple syrup here,' she says.

'Sorry, madam,' says Luse, 'I will bring sugar instead.'

The third batch is smaller and perfect. She looks at Joshua. 'You must be very quiet and you must be very brave. No more crying, okay?'

Joshua, sticky and full, solemnly nods and together they run around the back of the house and in through the main bedroom door.

'Don't wake Taata,' says Luse. 'Just run and open the door for me.'

Joshua does so, sprinting past their father, managing not to flinch at the tearing, gasping breaths coming from the bed. Clutching the plate of pancakes, Luse dashes after him and through the door and across the corridor. Together they crack open the door to Luse's room where Mummy is lying in the bed. Luse can hear the two women in the living room have switched on the television. The reception is not good here and they have turned the volume up. This is good, meaning she can speak rather than whisper. She takes Joshua's hand and they approach the bed.

'Mummy, we have brought you some pancakes.'

Esther is lying on her back, with one arm still pinned under the sheet. Her eyes dart from side to side and she moans softly, but she doesn't appear to be scared anymore. Her skin is cool to the touch. Luse helps Joshua up onto the bed, reminding him, 'Don't be scared or you might scare Baama. You must be brave, okay?'

She pulls a chair over as quietly as possible and sits near her mother's head and cuts off a piece of pancake smeared with maple syrup. 'Come on, Mum,' she says. 'It's yummy.'

Joshua joins in. 'Yummy pancake for Mummy,' he encourages. And, after a couple of attempts, Luse manages to get some into Esther's mouth. She instinctively chews and swallows.

'Good Baama,' cheers Joshua. 'More, more!'

Slowly they manage to feed Esther two of the pancakes before she turns her face away and closes her eyes.

'Mummy has had enough,' says Joshua sadly. Luse takes a corner of the sheet and wipes the maple syrup from Esther's mouth and chin. Her breathing is slow and strong. Luse helps her brother down from the bed and gives him a long hard hug.

'She is sleeping now, Joshua. You did really well. You are really good at nursing.'

Joshua is calmer now, happy to have seen his mother, to have helped. Luse stuffs the leftover pancakes in her own mouth and they sneak back out the way they came. As they come round the front of the house, Luse hears the sound of the Land Rover approaching again.

7.

Luse stops her story for supper and a breathing space. Gus and Bernard take plates out onto the verandah and so when Georgia comes out of the kitchen, the living room is almost empty, with just Luse on the couch. Georgia can hear Gus outside on his cell phone and Bernard chatting to Joshua upstairs. Luse's pose is calm, relaxed, but when she looks up at Georgia there is something contorted in her face, the skin pinched around her mouth.

Georgia sits next to her. She can smell onions and garlic on her own skin and thinks of her mother in London. It's Friday, not too late to call. She clears her mind to focus on Luse.

'Georgia...' Luse speaks very quickly and quietly. 'I have to tell you a secret thing. I can't tell everyone.'

'Yes? Tell me anything.'

'When Miriam went back to Toronto she told me just to ignore Dad. That I was to live my life as happily as I could. That I should just think about Mum and Joshua.'

'Yes... I can understand that.'

'Well you know Dad was sick.'

'He had stopped taking his medication, Luse. He would have been very sick. Yes.'

'I think... I think I killed him... that it was my fault he died...'

Georgia is silent. Luse doesn't look up from her knees.

'I... I came home a week... something like a week... before my birthday and he was alone in the living room. He looked like a skeleton by then. He was so ugly. He had a sore on the side of his mouth that had pushed up here.' Luse pushes her top lip up high above the gum, eyes twitching. 'It was gross, full of pus. But he wanted to speak to me.'

'When had you last spoken?'

'I can't remember if we had spoken at all since that day when he tried to exorcise Mummy. I kept away from him. Joshua did too.'

Georgia waits.

'He made a kind of croaking sound... that's how I knew he wanted me to come over. And... and I did go over to him but I made out that I was in a hurry. I was really rude. I said "Come on," when he didn't speak fast enough. He was saying something I couldn't hear but I didn't want to bend close to his horrible face to listen. I didn't want to...'

She pushes her hands against her mouth. Georgia puts an arm around her and Luse continues, her voice a whisper, 'I think he was asking for his medicine. I think he said, "I'm sorry, Luse. I'm sorry. May I please have my medicine?" I just went out. I went down to the lake and I swam on my own which isn't allowed... and... I know it Georgia. He asked me for his medicine...'

Georgia gets down on her knees in front of Luse and puts her warm hand on the girl's thighs. 'Okay, Luse, I am going to tell you something and you have to promise to really listen.'

'Okay.'

'Luse, your father was in the late stages of AIDS. You would not have been able to prevent his death. He died because he chose to, or was convinced that his medicine was not going to save him and he stopped taking it. You couldn't have helped him, do you understand?'

Luse doesn't respond.

'Luse love, I have seen hundreds of people die because they refused to accept they had HIV in the first place. Your father knew he had the virus. He understood the risks.' Here she takes Luse's chin and turns her face so that she has no choice but to make eye contact. 'Even if your father realised he was dying and asked for your help, it would have been too late. What I really do think is that he was trying to say sorry. And that is the most important thing for you to remember. Your father loved you and even if he made mistakes and got confused along the way he knew he had wronged you and he wanted to say sorry.'

Luse thinks her heart is dead. She feels nothing now. She wants to believe Georgia but the words are as comforting as a wooden blanket.

8.

After dinner, Luse continues.

The church people are mostly strangers, but they all act as if they have lived in the house for years. Luse and Joshua are gradually squeezed out of the living room, out of the kitchen and out to the far end of the veggie patch in the garden. From there they watch people moving back and forth in front of the windows. It is coming on evening and the smell of cooking begins to filter into the pinkening light of sunset. Luse wonders if it would be possible to go back inside, if they could sneak into the bedroom with Mummy.

And that is when the birds fly up as if they know something is about to happen and the Priestess arrives in her long black Mercedes. Luse and Joshua hear the rumble of the engine over the beating of the birds' wings. The car turns into the drive and the church people inside the house begin shouting to Jesus.

The Priestess is already inside the house when Joshua and Luse are called in for supper. The ladies from the church have made nsima and groundnut relish with chicken. The delicious smells saturate the house and dozens of tin plates are being filled from the large pots on the kitchen table. Luse counts ten people from the church. Most of the women are in the kitchen. The men sit stiffly in the living room with their Bibles and bottles of Coke and Fanta, sternly waiting to be served. Standing in the middle of the living room, the Priestess is talking into her cell phone. She turns around when Luse and Joshua are ushered in.

Luse shudders. She is unforgettable; a tall woman with skin so dark it is hard to make out her features in the gloomy room. Today she wears a traditional long dress, only it is cut tighter and shaped around her long lean figure in a way that would alarm the older local women. Her headdress of bright red and yellow African cloth is twisted differently too, into a flattering shape that fans out like a huge orchid over her head. She looks to Luse a little as if she is playing dress-up.

'Ah, Paul's children,' she says, lowering the phone and scrutinising them. She is handsome, mannish, and she stands like a man, hands now on her hips, dominating the space.

Luse feels dark, greasy fear at the Priestess's presence. She wants to go and find her mother but the Priestess steps in front of her, obscuring Luse's view of the back corridor.

'Paul's children,' the woman says again, and crouches in front of them, kneeling so as to be eye-to-eye with Luse. Those black eyes seem in that instant calculating, weighing the children up, but she smiles brightly and her gestures are graceful and soft.

'I was just so sorry to hear about your poor father... and now your mother. May the Lord have mercy.'

'Mercy,' echo the men in the room. They all stare up at the Priestess as if she is coated in gemstones.

'You know you just mustn't worry about a thing. Your parents have the Lord in their lives and Jesus in their hearts. Together we will get through these dark times. I will take care of them, I promise. And of you. Suffer the little children. Praise Jesus.'

'Praise Jesus!' intone the men.

'Where's Baama?' says Joshua and begins to cry.

The tall woman immediately pulls back the long, red-tipped finger she has been caressing his cheek with so that her skin won't make contact with his tears. She sighs and gets to her feet. 'Mary!' she calls through to one of the kitchen ladies. 'Take the children through to see their mother.'

9.

Luse's father dies that night, surrounded by the people from the church, who kneel around the bedside praying loudly and weeping. Luse and Joshua are allowed in briefly, but they have no privacy and the church people grip their hands and heads so hard during their keening that both children have bruises. In the midst of all the hysteria, her father lies under a white sheet with every bone showing through his dry skin. They have shut his eyes, but Luse can hardly recognise him anyway. The room stinks of air freshener which doesn't mask the sewage smell of death. It only seems to make breathing more difficult and the hairless skeleton in the bed more frightening.

There is another thing that has begun to worry Luse. It is the way the church people look at her and Joshua, from the sides of their eyes, snatched glances. Earlier she overheard one of the gruff old men talking to the Priestess.

'How long do we wait?' he was asking. 'Isn't it dangerous? We could all be affected.'

Worse than that, she has seen several of the church folk removing the family's possessions from the house. The gruff old man, whom Luse overheard in the kitchen, openly wheeled out the bed that her father had died on and loaded it onto the back of his truck with two sets of drawers and the bedside table. *Like vultures,* thought Luse. Were they waiting for her mother to die too? Surely not? Her mother wasn't anywhere near death – still strong, just lost and confused.

10.

The Priestess comes to see her flock later that week and to pray for Luse's mother whose ravings have subsided into unconsciousness. In the early morning she strides into the house, bristling with energy, wearing a starched white shirt and a long black skirt, her hair woven into hundreds of tiny long braids and dragged back into a tight ponytail that makes the bones in her face sharper than before. Over her shoulders she has hung a thick scarlet silk scarf embroidered with two crosses and a dove with a bleeding heart. A chain with a heavy black cross swings from her neck.

There are four men from the church choir who have moved in and are sleeping in the living room. Several women have moved mattresses into the now empty main bedroom. Luse and Joshua, who are, so far, still being treated with polite formality, have taken to sleeping on the floor next to their mother. Luse trusts no one else to feed or wash her. Sometimes Esther has night terrors and wets herself and Luse needs to be there to rock her and soothe her.

It's so early that the chickens are still roosting. Inside everyone is still in semi-slumber, and the Priestess is forced to stride over the bodies of her drowsy church members. At first quietly, then louder and louder, the Priestess begins to quote from the battered black Bible she carries in her right hand, 'And crying out with a loud voice, he said, "What have you to do with me, Jesus, Son of the Most High God? I adjure you by God, do not torment me." For he was saying to him, "Come out of the man, you unclean spirit!" And Jesus asked him, "What is your name?" He replied, "My name is Legion, for we are many... we are MANY!"'

The Priestess's voice booms out and everyone leaps up, rubbing their eyes and pulling on shawls and trousers and shirts, stumbling forward to join in with the responses.

'We hear you, Lord.'

'We praise you, Lord.'

Joshua is frightened and Luse has had enough. As the elongated shape of the woman flings open the door of their room, Luse stands defiantly in front of her mother and Joshua.

She takes a deep breath and speaks loudly and clearly, 'Madame Priestess, my mother needs a medical doctor. I think she will also need some peace and quiet to recover. And she will need her medicine. Her antiretrovirals...'

The Priestess pauses in the doorway, her eyes flicker and for a moment she seems unsure. Luse thinks, *She has finally seen me... she will stop all this now.* But then the Priestess takes up the heavy black book and hits herself in the face with it. Hard. Luse jumps backwards, shocked as the woman lowers the Bible, whispering, 'Lord, give me the strength to do Thy will. Give me the strength. They appear frail but they are infected with evil.' The skin on her cheek and forehead is even darker now from the blow and her eyes are glazed as she moves forward. Luse backs into the room ahead of her.

'Enough. Your mother is in a state of sin. She needs the Lord's mercy. Only our Father can release her from her torment. Torment you have brought upon her this day.'

'She is NOT in torment!' yells Luse confused. 'She is sick! She needs a doctor.'

Behind her Joshua begins to cry quietly. She hears him crawl onto their mother's bed and beg her to wake up.

The Priestess's eyes roll and she points a long, red-tipped finger at the bed. 'Look! Look! Bear witness. The witch children are feeding!'

Several of the church members crowd in behind the Priestess and see Joshua with his arms wrapped around his mother's neck and his face buried into her shoulder.

'He sucks her blood!' one of them screams. Several of the church people begin rocking and clapping their hands in prayer, their eyes rolling in their heads.

'No, no, no!' Luse holds out her hands beseechingly towards the people milling in the doorway. They back away from her, looking terrified. Only the Priestess still smiles.

'We knew there were demons in this house. First Paul was slain and now you feed on your own mother's life essence. The exorcism is justified, oh Lord!'

Everything happens too fast. Two men rush into the room with a sack and, pushing past Luse to Joshua, begin to prise the terrified child off his mother. Luse is almost incoherent with rage and leaps onto the bed, flinging her arms around both Joshua and her mother, screaming with fury, 'No, no, no! Get away from us!'

But the Priestess quotes from her Bible again and this seems to encourage the men, who surge forward, grabbing first for Luse and then for Joshua. Luse twists and writhes and manages to get free but then Frank has Joshua and is dragging the child by his ears away from their mother. Luse clambers without thinking onto Frank's back, kicking and biting, inhaling the stink of cigarettes and old sweat from his T-shirt.

'Get off my brother, you crazy stupid...' she howls, and then bites down. Her teeth make contact with the man's cheek and he pulls his face away, leaving skin between Luse's teeth. Blood spurts into the air. Now the Priestess grabs Luse's hair and pulls, but Luse clings onto the man with her knees and fists, screaming, 'Baama! Baama! Wake up, wake up!'

Frank spins in a circle, clutching at his bloody face, then loses balance and falls over, his head smacking down on top of Luse.

And then there is just darkness.

Luse comes to with a terrible headache and gingerly reaches up to find a lump on the back of her skull. She is still in the room, on the mattress and next to the bed where her mother was lying. But now her mother is gone and only Joshua's small body lies on the stained coverlet. The curtains have been drawn against the morning and hang heavily, the windows behind also firmly shut. The room is boiling hot and Joshua has a sheen of sweat on his naked skin.

Luse sits up slowly, the pain in her skull ricocheting from one temple to the other, and then gradually calming into a steady nauseating thump in the back of her head. She is thirsty. She and Joshua are alone in the room but voices can be heard indistinctly from other parts of the house. Chanting. She wonders what time it is and how long she has been out. Minutes? Hours? Tears still glisten wetly on Joshua's plump cheeks.

'Joshie?'

His eyes open but he doesn't move.

'They took Baama,' he says in a small voice. 'She was crying, Luse. She didn't want to go with them and they pulled her and she was hurting.' Then he closes his eyes again. Luse doesn't press him. Instead she climbs over him and draws the curtain to look out into the driveway and little vegetable plot.

A couple of the church men sit outside smoking. They look more like sentries than parishioners. One of them is Frank, the ugly flat-faced man that Luse bit. She notes with a little satisfaction that he keeps wincing and touching his torn cheek. She tries the window, but it won't budge and even if she could get it open, she knows she won't be able to squeeze out between the burglar bars. She clambers down and pads over to the door, knowing before she even pulls on the handle that it is locked.

'They said Taata gave them the house. That he wrote it down. That it's their house now.' Joshua's eyes open again and spit gathers at the corner of his mouth as he speaks. Luse sits beside him and gently wipes it away.

'They said we are witches. We killed Taata. They say we are bad people.' Joshua can't cry anymore. Tenderly Luse strokes his sticky face and shoulder. If she had a gun or a machete she would kill every last one of them, starting with Frank and the Priestess. Her hands tremble and she clenches them.

'We are not bad people, Joshua. Baama and Taata love us... loved us... very much. They, those horrid church people, that Priestess, *they* are the bad people.' *Where have they taken Mum,* she wonders, willing herself not to cry for Joshua's sake.

11.

They are left in the room for two days and two nights. Luse has no choice but to break one of the windows so that a breeze can lift some of the weight of the grinding heat. She thinks the sound of smashing glass will bring someone in, yelling and cursing, but there is no reaction. Her head is very clear and she feels no fear, only a kind of low burning rage in her guts that continues to make her tremble slightly. All she will allow herself to think about is how to get Joshua through this. She improvises, using the flowery wastepaper basket as a toilet. The stink of their own piss is at first horrible, but after a while they stop noticing. They are not given any food and no one attempts to talk to them. Luckily a glass of water was forgotten on the bedside table and they take tiny sips every hour or two. By the second evening, with only a stale dribble in the bottom of the glass, their thirst is becoming painful.

On the third morning Luse can't wake up properly. She knows something is terribly wrong and that she and Joshua are in danger, but her body will not respond. She lies on the rug next to the bed with her arm around Joshua, hearing the sound of people's feet outside the door. The chanting has finally stopped but instead of relief, Luse is terribly afraid. She can't open her mouth to cry out and her eyes will only half open. 'Wake up!' she screams at herself. 'Wake up – they are coming!'

And then, just like that, Ba'Neene is in the room. The wonderful wood, reed and tea smell of her fills Luse's nostrils and seems to break her free from her paralysis. Luse can hear birds singing, the flutter of feathers.

'Ba'Neene,' she says, her voice just a puff of breath between parched lips as she sits up. Her grandmother is both there and not there, a dusty fragmented shape, leaning down over the children and encircling them with her arms. She has no face and no mouth but Luse hears her speaking inside her head.

'Luse,' says Gran. 'These people are very dangerous but they are frightened of you so you can find a way to use that.'

Joshua's face contracts and he doubles up, suddenly awake, coughing.

'Luse?' he asks groggily, but before she can respond the bedroom door is flung abruptly open and several men rush towards her. In the split second she has, Luse realises that they are holding white meal sacks in their hands.

'Do not hurt them! We have defeated their demons,' yells the Priestess from behind the door. There is no time and Luse has no strength to resist. Instead she holds Joshua's hand as long as possible, speaking to him calmly and as loudly as she can, telling him that he will be alright, that they are going to be alright, and she carries on talking even as she is dragged away and the sack closes over her head.

She knows they are being carried to a car. The bastard Frank is shouting orders and throwing his weight around. Other church members have begun chanting again. Luse feels the man's shoulder cutting up into her stomach and wants to vomit.

They are outside, the sunlight hot on her bare legs. She hears the Priestess's voice speaking, 'Now Frank, I am trusting you to make the delivery on time. Make sure they get there undamaged! And I want a goddamn receipt for the additional supplies this time! Right, call me when you get back. I have to go and speak to my lawyer about the estate. God be with you.'

She begins talking distractedly into her cell phone. A car door slams shut and her voice is gone. An engine purrs into life. The Priestess's Mercedes, Luse realises. This means they will be going in the other vehicle parked out at the front of the house – an old Land Rover with The Blood of Christ logo on the side. She feels rough hands on her again and then she is thrown into the back exactly like a sack of maize, amongst the rough rolls of tarpaulin and the spare cans of diesel. She feels the thud as Joshua is thrown in behind her, and immediately she starts talking to him again, 'I am right here, Joshie. This is all going to be over soon. Keep taking nice slow breaths...'

The Land Rover lurches as several people clamber into the front and the engine churns, whines, dies, churns again and roars to life. The driver drags at the gears and they jerk forward. Luse tries to manoeuvre herself closer to Joshua. When she can feel him through the sacking, she curves her body around his to protect him from the jolting and bouncing.

Then, she doesn't know how many hours later, the Land Rover pulls over. Luse becomes aware of the stillness of the vehicle, the ghost of the rumbling engine ringing in her ears. She hears the voices of Frank, Mulenga and an old man, and the crunching noises of their feet in the dirt. They gather at the back of the Land Rover and on some unseen signal begin chanting together before pulling back the tarpaulin. Luse hears the stiff kcccrrr as the velcro is pulled back and cool fresh air blows onto her bare legs. She keeps very still, trying to guess what her captors are going to do. Then with a wrench she is dragged upwards and out, her legs bashing the metal edge of the Land Rover. She hears the woman grunting as she does the same to Joshua, who has begun sobbing softly again inside his sack.

Then there is a glorious sweet rush of air and light as the sack is pulled over her head. She staggers, her legs buckle and she kneels, sucking in air, blinking.

Frank pulls her up by one arm and turns her to her brother, signalling. He doesn't speak, just continues the low monotonous chanting through his clenched teeth. His cheek is inflamed and Luse's teeth marks are clearly visible. It looks painful, and Frank's eye is red and watery. This lifts Luse's spirits a little.

They are frightened of us, she remembers.

While Fat Mulenga and the old man stand back a little, Luse gently removes the sack from her brother's head.

'Right then,' says the old man, brushing dirt from his trousers. 'Don't let them out of your sight. I'm going for a piss, praise Jesus.'

'Iwe,' Mulenga says to the old man. 'Get the stove.'

It seems they have stopped for the adults to eat lunch.

'Where are we?' Luse asks. 'Where is our mother?' The man and the woman pause and then carry on, ignoring her.

'Please may we have some water? Madam Mulenga, please? Just a bottle of Manzi for my brother?'

Mulenga twitches but says nothing.

Luse tries another tack. 'Why have you kidnapped us? Where is our mother?'

She tries to make her voice sharp and strong. She wills herself to sound angry and not scared. 'I asked you a question, Mulenga. What is going on? You were a friend of my father and now you are abusing his children?'

She sees Joshua's eyes rolling too late and turns as Frank strides up, sand rising around him in clouds. 'The Lord is my light and my salvation; whom shall I fear?' he mutters, and punches Luse in the face.

Luse is lucky that Frank has little purchase in the sand and the blow only glances across her jaw, but she is still stunned and falls over on her side.

For a while there is nothing but muffled noise. Gradually she becomes aware of the smell of cooking and feels Joshua shaking her shoulder, whispering her name in terrified squeaks.

'It's okay, Josh... I'm okay I promise.'

Luse wonders if she has gone mad. She feels no pain at all anymore, not a bruise, not a bump, and even though she can see by Joshua's horrified expression that her face must be bloody, she feels only rage running through her body like electricity.

She leans against Joshua, swings her legs under her body and pushes herself to her knees. Fat Mulenga, Frank and the old man are cooking on a portable stove under a tree across the road from the children. They have relaxed, it seems. The old man has his back to Luse. Frank has sprawled out on the sand while Mulenga bends her vast body over the mess of stinking fish and oil in her saucepan.

Luse tips her head back and screams. The sound is shocking even to her, and ricochets through the bush like an explosion. The three adults are frozen, their heads turned towards her, their eyes huge. Luse lets the scream ebb away.

'I curse you, Frank!' she says, quite calmly and clearly.

The three around the stove don't move for a while, and then Mulenga bursts into loud tears. 'Why did you touch her, Frank?' she wails.

'Shut up,' says Frank, but he doesn't take his portion of food and instead goes a little way away to smoke.

Mulenga and the old man mutter together for some time, and then the old man sighs and shakes his head with dismay.

'Go on,' insists Mulenga, and thrusts a bowl into his hands.

He scuttles sideways towards the children, his eyes down, prayers fluttering from his lips. His hand is trembling as he puts the bowl down near them. They eat a little, Luse spoon-feeding her frightened brother.

Soon they are told to clamber back into the Land Rover. No sacks this time. They squeeze themselves in amongst the jerry cans and tarpaulin. All three adults, praying again, squash into the front cab, and soon the engine has spluttered back to life and they are jolting along the track again.

With immense relief Luse slowly stretches and feels around for a clean bit of sacking in the gloomy canvas back. As they drive, bumping and creaking into the bush, she wipes Joshua's face and hands and rubs his bruised limbs and then does the same for herself. The jolting makes resting impossible so they cling together and wait for the end of the road.

12.

It is dark when the Land Rover finally grinds to a stop. Luse has no idea how long they have been rolling and weaving through the bush, but has noted the sun fading through the dusty plastic window, and guesses it is after sundown. She and Joshua wait, not speaking, just listening, as the three adults clamber down noisily from the front, stretching, spitting and talking in loud whispers.

'Hodi?' Mulenga is calling to someone.

'Ah mulibwanji, madam,' comes the deepest, booming voice Luse has ever heard, and an enormous shadow can be seen through the canvas sides of the filthy Land Rover.

Where are we? wonders Luse, gripping Joshua's hand hard and trying to peer through the murk.

Outside, the church folk are exchanging formalities with the giant. They talk about the journey, the road being bad.

'Maybe the rain will come early this year. The mud will make the return journey terrible...'

'Yah,' the giant agrees. There is a pause. What are they waiting for? She can hear the giant moving around the vehicle. He seems to be tapping the wheels.

'Ach, these tsetse flies,' whines the old man, slapping at his shirt.

'Chabwino,' the giant speaks again, his voice so low and deep that the Land Rover vibrates. 'You will need to sign the book while I call the Dome. Where are the goods?'

Frank says, 'We have the supplies ordered, but also we have secured two... err...' he seems at a loss.

'Two dangerous children.' Mulenga is clear. 'The Priestess sent them. They are expected.'

'Expected, are they?' The giant sounds faintly amused. 'Well then I will ensure they are collected too.'

There is the sound of an engine and the Land Rover is lit up by the headlights of an oncoming vehicle. Young strong voices shout greetings and instructions and several people approach the back of the car. Luse pushes herself backwards, grabbing for Joshua, but there is nowhere to hide. The canvas back is unhooked and the velcro peeled back to allow several slashes of torchlight in. Luse raises a hand to her eyes.

'Heh! What a stink!' The voice is a man's. It has the slight squeak of youth and the figure behind the torch is tall and skinny. He points the torch directly at Luse and waggles the light. 'Right. You and the boy. Out!'

When she doesn't move, he clucks his tongue but lowers the torch slightly. 'Look, come on out. You have arrived. There is nowhere to go but forward.'

Luse knows he is right. 'Hold on tight to me,' she whispers to Joshua, and they climb slowly over the jerry cans and the rolls of tarpaulin until they are within reach of the grasping hands of the tall man. He doesn't drag them exactly, but he isn't gentle either, and Luse and Joshua land heavily in the road.

Now Luse can see that they are at a checkpoint. There is a large guardhouse on the right of a heavy-duty barricade made of red-and-white-striped poles swathed in razor wire. The Land Rover is parked facing the guardhouse. A green jeep sits on a pristine tarmac lane, engine idling on the other side of the barricade. A twelve-foot-high wire fence fans out into the darkness on either side.

All this Luse takes in as she finds her balance on aching legs. Her face throbs, her nose is still clogged with blood and dust and she wants to lie down and sleep for a year, but Joshua is clinging to her and the electricity of anger is still flowing under her skin.

The skinny young man is hopping from one foot to the other. Luse sees his face in the security light's glare – small close-set eyes in a round face with a protruding jaw of buck teeth. Next to him stand two women, one hard faced with terrible acne scars, the other just hard faced. They move fast, helping the security guards unload the diesel from the back of the Land Rover.

The young people are all dressed in identical Chinese-style suits with short sleeves and buttons up to the neck. In the odd light Luse can't tell the colour. They each carry long canes as if to herd sheep or cows.

'Tiyende!' says the buck-toothed man impatiently. 'They are waiting for us.' He is speaking imperiously to everyone, but it is Luse he pushes roughly in the back. She staggers forward towards the barrier, Joshua dragging behind her. The security men at the gates don't bother to even look at them. Their guns are lowered; they stand relaxed as if battered, stinking children are delivered on a nightly basis.

As Luse and Joshua come level with the guardhouse, Frank, Mulenga and the old man come out. Frank has the paperwork in his hand. They look relieved – that is until they see the children, and then something almost like guilt passes over their faces. Almost. Luse looks around to see if there is anyone who looks kind, anyone who can help them. She points at Frank but doesn't know what to say. But it seems the pointing is enough. He actually whimpers, and, covering his head, runs for the Land Rover. Under other circumstances it would almost be comical, but Luse can only watch open-mouthed.

'Resist the devil and he will flee from you!' shrieks Fat Mulenga as she waddles after her husband, the old man close on her heels. Luse sees the young people are watching her too, twitching their sticks as if she might attack. She shakes her head in disbelief.

These people are frightened of you... Oh Ba'Neene, she thinks. *I can't do this.*

The young people begin to move forward, towards Luse and Joshua, menacingly raising their canes, but then an enormous shadow separates itself from the doorway of the guardhouse. It is Luse's giant – a soldier in full battle dress, so tall and broad that he blots out the night sky. He takes one long leisurely step forward and covers five feet of ground. Craning her neck, Luse peers up at his face, but it is shadowed by his peaked hat.

'Ahh, Bwana Kalulu,' he addresses himself to the tall boy, his voice so deep that it seems to come from the bottom of a well.

The young man scowls, trying not to cower too obviously. 'I asked you not to call me that rabbit name,' he says, sullen, rubbing at the bit of growth that constitutes his moustache.

'Seems we are getting children instead of scratch cards with our fuel these days, Kalulu?' The giant indicates Luse and Joshua. 'At this time of night they must be important.'

The soldier makes a noise that Luse thinks might be a tut of distaste as he hands the young man the signing-in board. A trickle of curiosity breaks through Luse's exhaustion. She peers harder into the shadow under the soldier's hat, moistens her cracked lips.

'Excuse me, sir,' she croaks. Pauses. Tries again. 'Excuse me, sir. May I ask where we are?'

'Be quiet!' hisses the young man, and his cane swishes near her legs, but the giant soldier is still and Luse feels his gaze wash over her and Joshua. Then he does something unexpected. He kneels down on one knee and gently removes his cap.

'Ulibwanji mfana,' he says. 'My name is Samuel Yomba. This place is called The Blood of Christ Street Child Rehabilitation Centre. It is a brand new educational establishment. A very special school.'

Samuel's face is wide and round, his cheeks like pillows, his nose as large as an upturned canoe. His hugeness is mesmerising and Luse and Joshua just stare and stare.

'They really put you through it, didn't they?' he growls and pulls a white handkerchief as large as a tablecloth from his jacket, reaching over to wipe some of the caked blood from around Luse's nose and mouth.

Neither Luse nor Joshua is frightened, but the young man steps back defensively. 'You don't understand, Samuel.' His voice is high. 'These children are dangerous...'

'Dangerous? Don't be ridiculous,' Samuel booms and he smiles at the children, his huge grin so magnificent that they can't help but beam back at him. 'They are just children.'

'Yes but...'

'Shut it, Kalulu. Go and get them cleaned up and give them something to eat. They look famished.'

Samuel gives his handkerchief to Luse and then stands up slowly, reclaiming the sky, and jerks the board from the young man's hands.

'They are children,' he repeats. 'They are our future.'

He replaces his hat and his moon face disappears into shadow. In one step he is over by the barrier, hauling it up with a single huge hand.

The young man hesitates. 'My name is Phillemon, *not* Kalulu,' he hisses at the children. 'Just ignore this...' Lost for words he indicates with his twitching cane and the others fall into line beside him, forcing the children forward towards the jeep.

'Now then, Bwana Kalulu,' booms the voice from over their heads. 'You be nice to these kids or I will know about it.'

'Yes-yes, Samuel.' The young man glowers and his fellows snicker. He pushes Luse into the jeep.

'I mean it, Rabbit-face...'

The young man ducks his head, ashamed and furious, but lowers his stick.

Luse is squeezed into the jeep with Joshua on her lap and the two grim-faced women on either side. The security lights are dazzling and as they pull out and drive away from the barrier, Luse can see that they are following the line of the twelve-foot-high fence with even more spotlights glaring down on them. Joshua seems to have shrunk into her. She can feel his bones through his skin, the bones of his bottom dig into her thighs. Luse tightens her arms around him and squeezes but he doesn't respond. When she glances down at his face, she sees his long lashes fluttering against his cheek. In spite of all the noise and the fear, it seems he has fallen asleep.

On either side of the road they are passing half-finished buildings; low single storeys with small windows and wooden doors. Ahead is a large square of dry lawn, the size of half a football field, with a flag pole but no flag. They drive around the lawn and alongside a larger building, two storeys high, much grander with large windows. The windows are glassless, but each one is covered with ugly thick black burglar bars.

Across, on the other side of the lawn, are more low buildings and a large concrete area with long wooden tables and benches. Luse has yet to see a light in a building or any sign of human habitation. The jeep carries on, its engine making a terrible din in the eerie quiet, the noise echoing from the buildings around the lawn. They round the corner and once again pause for an armed checkpoint. The guards just grunt at Kalulu and the barrier swings up. They are heading through a cultivated field now, towards another cluster of lights. Through the dust Luse can make out an extraordinary-looking building, again surrounded by piercing security lights and overseen by two armed guards on raised platforms. As the jeep passes beneath, one of the guards idly points his AK at them, mocks a shooting. Yawns.

The building ahead is one enormous dome and looks to Luse like a battered tortoise shell covered in spider webs of wires. There are no windows at all, but thousands of wires sprout from ragged holes and race up the sides to the roof where a very tall spike pokes up into the black night sky. Next to the spike is a massive satellite dish, bigger than any Luse has seen before. The whole building looks as if it might collapse at any moment.

There are several big cars parked outside, but the jeep doesn't stop and heads directly for a curved wall which slides open, allowing them to drive all the way inside. Inside it is very bright. Lights ping and hum. Luse, exhausted and confused, thinks for a moment that they have driven into daylight. *Did I fall asleep?* she wonders. *Have we been driving all night?*

She glares around, feeling Joshua rousing. They have parked in a big garage. The walls and floor are painted white and the light bounces around and around, dazzling Luse and hurting her already sore head. The air smells of antiseptic and something flowery... Luse can't place it.

'Right,' says Kalulu. 'Out. You are to be processed.'

Luse does not like the sound of this. She clambers out of the jeep but doesn't walk forward, standing instead with her arm protectively around Joshua. They are parked next to other green jeeps and the two hard-faced women have leapt out and are stretching and yawning as if their work is done. One begins offloading the fuel.

'Who have we here?'

Luse looks around and sees several people walking across the garage forecourt towards the jeep; two nurses led by a long-haired oriental man with a large puffy red mark on his face under his right eye. Walking next to him is an elderly Zambian woman in a grey trouser suit that matches her grey hair. The floor is so shiny, and Luse so tired, that they look a little as if they are walking in the air.

'Bwana Doctor, Madam Phiri,' Kalulu bows, not just with his head but with his whole body. 'These are the two orphan children from Siavonga, the ones sent by Madam Priestess.'

Luse is struck by the sudden deference and respect from Kalulu. The two mean-looking women also dip and fawn, grinning and actually blushing. Luse turns to face the elderly woman – Mrs Phiri – and is struck by her elegance, her glowing skin and beautiful eyes. She is almost like... Luse searches her vocabulary but the only word that comes to her is *angel*. Yes... Mrs Phiri is like an angel. Mrs Phiri is love and Luse loves Mrs Phiri.

Joshua pulls at Luse's hand, a violent tug, and Luse is abruptly woken from her hypnotic reverie.

'Luse, I want to go home. Tell them to take us home,' Joshua is asking her urgently, and there is something else now in Luse's head. She can hear a faint twittering and a fluttering of wings. As the Zambian woman and the doctor come closer, the noise of wings increases until for a moment it is all Luse can hear. She can see the Chinese man's mouth opening and closing but all she hears is flapping wings and the thrumming of feathers.

No one else seems to notice except Joshua, who shakes his head and scratches his ear, and Luse raises her arms to ward off what sounds like an almighty flock of quelea about to land... but then the sound is gone completely and there is just the Chinese man completing his sentence.

'... it won't take very long and then you can have a nice long sleep.'

Luse and Joshua just stare at him open-mouthed.

'I don't think they heard you, Dr Lin,' says Mrs Phiri. 'Perhaps they are too tired to take it all in.'

Her voice is low and rich and Kalulu and the women look as if they want to drop to their knees in adoration, but Luse is no longer captivated. It is as if the bird noise has cleared her head, brushing away all the confusion and now Mrs Phiri looks just like an everyday person. Just an old woman with a thin wrinkly mouth and a big nose. Nothing special.

Luse gets a waft of that rotten flowery scent again. It is coming from the woman but it isn't perfume as such. It is more layered, like the smell of the bush itself, night flowers and hyena piss. *More piss than anything else actually*, thinks Luse, wrinkling her nose.

'You smell funny,' Joshua announces to the lady in grey before Luse can stop him.

There is a shocked silence and Kalulu steps forward, raising his stick with an expression of fury flushing over his face, but the woman holds up a hand.

'Ahh chabwino, chabwino... these little ones, eh?' But her eyes dart to Luse and back to Joshua. She is unnerved. 'Chabwino,' she says again.

'Very well. The children have been through a very hard time in their lives. I am sure they will feel greatly revived after processing.'

Processing? That word again. Before Luse or Joshua can say another word the two nurses move forward and take them each by the arm.

'Food first! Plenty of water please, Sister Luo,' says the doctor with a jolly smile and a wink at Luse, and the nurses begin to lead her and Joshua away down the gleaming corridor. Luse's instinct is to fight, to pull away and run – but where would they run to? And Luse can see that Joshua is exhausted and frightened too. She will achieve nothing by causing more trouble and maybe the doctor is actually telling the truth and there is food and water coming. Sister Luo looks kind enough and the hand on Luse's arm is warm and gentle.

'Tiyende. Umvela?' asks Sister Luo and Luse nods.

'Yes, I am coming. I understand.'

She allows herself to be led from the large garage through the double doors and into a long white-tiled corridor with doors at intervals on either side. The corridors look similar – slightly yellowing walls, grey rubber floor tiles and dangerous-looking wires poking through the walls like creepers. The whole place looks cobbled together in a terrible hurry. Some of the wall partitions are unpainted and others a different colour altogether, there are holes in the floor and several dripping pipes.

Eventually they go through a door and into a large white room which not only looks clean and ordered, but also has a table in the centre with a large jug of water and several plastic cups. Just looking at the jug makes Luse rush for the table, grabbing at the jug with two shaking hands. She pours water sloppily into two cups. Joshua is already pressed against her side and his hands are reaching for the cup before she has finished pouring. They drink and the water is so delicious and so refreshing that tears run from their eyes and down their cheeks without them knowing.

'Pang'ono, pang'ono, slowly, slowly,' says Sister Luo, gently prising the cups from the gulping children. 'If you drink too fast you will vomit it all back up again.'

Luse knows the nurse is right but it is hard to stop. Her whole body is shaking now and her stomach whines, causing Joshua to grin. Sister Luo gets them to sit on the wooden chairs and the other nurse brings over a covered basket and takes out a couple of silver foil packets and several large white rolls. Cutting the packets at the corners she squeezes the contents into the middle of the rolls and hands one each to Joshua and Luse. The stuff inside the rolls tastes like peanut butter but even sweeter and very smooth, melting away with the bread in the mouth. Luse looks at the foil packets and reads 'Fatten-Up Nuts Therapeutic Foods' written over a picture of a peanut in a safari hat. She has seen the packets before, at the clinic where her mother worked in Siavonga, piled up in boxes marked 'Emergency Aid: Food Relief'.

Thinking of her mother makes her pause, hand hovering near her mouth. What happened to her mother? Suddenly Luse is no longer able to eat, her throat tight with tears. The two nurses have moved across to a white cubical at the back of the large room and Luse can hear the sound of taps being turned on and water being run into a bath. Now she notices that there is a line of empty beds in the room against a far wall, and an odd-looking stretcher on wheels with some kind of contraption at either end. *Are we in a hospital?* She is woozy and can't concentrate, even more so after eating the food. In fact the room seems to glisten and swirl around her and she really wants to lie down.

'Luse,' yawns Joshua widely. 'Luse, I want to go to bed now.'

She doesn't reply, seems unable even to control her own arms or her mouth, which is stuck open, still full of food.

'Time to get washed children.'

The nurses appear, swooping down in their white uniforms and plucking up Luse and Joshua, carrying them over to the cubical where a long wide bath is full of steaming hot water. Luse can only watch, raising her arms passively, as the nurses gently remove their filthy clothes and help them into the enormous bath, each nurse taking care to keep them propped up and their heads clear of the water. Joshua's eyes are half closed and Luse hears him begin to snore lightly as Sister Luo lathers a large cloth and soaps him down. The water around him becomes instantly grey with dust and dirt. The bath is big and Luse, being washed at the other end of the tub, doesn't even touch Joshua. She is so filthy that the nurse tuts and clucks and rinses her twice over. There is blood in the water and Luse feels her head stinging.

'Dear Lord Jesus,' she hears the one nurse say, her voice seeming to drift to Luse's ears as if from a great distance. 'Why do they always have to beat them up before they bring them in? Shame, shame.'

Then she is out of the bath and being wrapped in a soft white towel and there is another voice now, another person nearby, moving around in the bright fuzzy room. A man, the Chinese Doctor man with the red cheek. Luse yawns and yawns and her eyelids are like heavy curtains as the nurse helps her up onto what feels like a bed, and there is the doctor talking and her towel is gone and she is cold. She blinks but cannot clear the blurring from her vision.

'Female: approximate age eleven. Pre-pubescent...' the doctor's voice drones and the nurse says, 'Yes, Doctor'. Luse hears a pencil scratch on paper. Then there is a hand on her ankle and her legs are pulled apart gently.

The doctor's voice comes now from over there, between her legs. She feels breath on her inner thigh. Then something touches her most private part – a swift prodding finger – and she struggles, desperate to wake up, but her body remains unresponsive. Almost immediately the finger is gone and a hand pats her knee as the doctor's voice moves from between her legs to above her head.

'She is intact. Healthy. Mark her down for Hut Two. The boy too. The heavy bruising around her jawline will clear in a few days but she may require paracetemol for the discomfort.'

Luse tries to moan, to call out for Joshua, and feels a hand stroke her face, soothing her. Sister Luo leans down to Luse's ear. 'Sleep child. You will feel much better in the morning. Your brother is right next to you, umvela?'

The nurse's hand is gentle and warm and Luse is comforted. She feels a heavy blanket being laid over her naked body and she turns on her side and sleeps.

13.

Luse jolts awake, heart pounding. For a few terrible seconds she can remember nothing and has no idea where she is. She smells antiseptic, feels the warm roughness of a woollen blanket, but in the darkness is not sure which way she is facing. She waits for her panic to subside and the memories to rush back. *I am in a bed. In the tortoise hospital building. I am naked. The doctor touched me. He touched my doyo.* Gingerly she puts a hand down under the blanket and feels her vagina but there is nothing odd or different. She sits up slowly, still dizzy from the drugged food and there is light coming from under the door, enough to illuminate the bed next to her. It's empty.

'Joshua?' she whispers into the darkness. There is no reply and the darkness seems to thicken and move in the corners of the room. Luse swings her legs out from under the blanket, aware of how chilly the room has become. She pulls the blanket back around her body as she slides off the high bed to the floor, having to pause again to let the wooziness clear.

'Joshua?' she hisses louder but there is still no response. Somewhere a clock ticks. Behind her, Luse can make out a dim light coming from a window in the top of the door. She carefully walks towards it, one arm waving in front of her to protect herself from bashing into anything, and fumbles for a light switch. There! Low down on the inside wall. She clicks it on and the room floods with bright white light and the long fluorescent tubes buzz noisily. There is the table, clear now, the bed she has just vacated and the empty one alongside it. There is no one else in the room. She tries the door and it clicks open, but sticking her head out into the dim corridor reveals nothing. There is no one around, not even a nurse. The empty corridor stretches away to darkness but Luse has no choice.

She dumps the blanket and pulls the sheet from the bed, wrapping it around herself tightly so that her arms are free and her legs uncluttered in case she has to run. Her shoes, like Joshua's flip-flops, were left back in the bedroom when they were kidnapped so she will have to remain barefoot.

Out in the corridor she keeps close to the wall and edges along, her bare feet soundless. As she passes each door she carefully tries the handles but they are all locked, lights out, and there is no sign of Joshua. Up ahead are double doors and light floods from between them. There is more noise too; Luse can hear muffled women's voices and the sound of movement. A telephone rings and is answered. A louder buzzing voice sounds like it is coming from a PA system. There are windows at the top of the doors and Luse is just tall enough to sneak a quick peek and see what looks like a hospital reception area with a long curved desk, manned by two receptionists with bulky headphones and ear pieces attached to computers. The desk is littered with different coloured telephones and box files. Behind the desk more corridors and doors go off in every direction.

There is a clock above the reception desk. In fact, there are three, all with different times on them. The clock that says 'Local Time' on a small sign reads 02:42 but the women on reception don't look as if it is the middle of the night; they look like they have just walked in from a nightclub – thickly made up, with shiny jackets, lashes and fingernails. The nearest one glances around and Luse ducks out of sight, heart pounding.

She looks down the dim corridor she has just come from and counts the doors back to her room... seven. Right! Pushing against the double doors until they swing open with a tiny squeak, she creeps up to the back of the reception desk, keeping as low as she can. Her aim is to get to the far side where another set of double doors leads off. There is more light and noise coming from there, and although Luse isn't sure how she will keep out of sight, she feels strongly that that is where Joshua has been taken. Just as she is about to dash forward through them, they open from the opposite direction and Luse is nearly hit in the head by a large trolley covered in a green cloth, tinkling with glasses, jugs of water, orange juice and various bottles of beer on the top tier.

'Ladies, ladies,' says the man pushing the trolley. He is short and wiry and his eyes are firmly fixed on the receptionists. Without thinking it through, Luse lifts the green cloth and squeezes herself onto the bottom empty tier of the trolley. The glasses knock together but the man is fully focused on the women and is now leaning over the desk leering at them.

'Jackson, you're late. There have been two requests already for refreshments.'

Luse can hear irritation in the woman's voice. She is crammed in on the metal trolley bent in half, toes pushing against the cold frame. She sees a piece of her white sheet hanging over the edge, grabs for it in terror, and the glasses above her head tinkle again.

'What is going on in the kitchen?' Luse hears the younger receptionist ask.

'One of the cooks was caught stealing from the meat freezer. The Madam went penga.' He pauses, and Luse hears the woman speak into her phone.

'Yeo-bo-sae-yo.'

Another pause. A click.

'Pyongyang, line twelve,' she says curtly to someone else on another phone.

'... yeah man... penga, like a fly in a long drop!' continues Jackson. 'That muntu was lucky he didn't end up in the meat freezer himself!'

The receptionist giggles. Then her laugh cuts off as she takes another call.

'Dobry den. Yes, sir. Passing you through now, sir.' Click. 'Private bidder, line thirteen...'

'Jackson, you better get the drinks up then. I take it the food trolley is following?' The other receptionist sounds even more irritated. Luse curls up tighter.

'Hey, my dear, you need to loosen up... I should take you out one night. You and little sister here, eh? A bit of rumba at Omega Bar?'

The one receptionist giggles again, but the other hisses something Luse doesn't hear and the next moment she is jerked forward as Jackson, sucking his teeth, roughly pushes the trolley to the wall. There is a ping and a shushing noise and Luse realises that they are going up in a tiny shaking lift. She grips onto the bottom of the trolley, amazed that Jackson doesn't seem to notice the new weight. In the lift he croons to himself and farts horribly. Luse tries to cover her nose and mouth with her hand. She nearly falls off the trolley as the door pings open and Jackson pushes it back out of the lift.

Luse can see carpet now under the wheels, red carpet. The trolley stops and Luse expects Jackson to lift the green cloth and find her, and then she will be killed and Joshua will be left here and... She braces herself, bare feet ready to kick out, but nothing happens.

'Ah, at last,' comes a whispered woman's voice and above Luse's head someone takes a glass from the top of the trolley. Luse hears water pour from a jug.

'The food?'

'On its way, Madam Angela. Minor problem in the kitchen.'

'See that it gets here before the end of the bidding. And don't forget the cigarettes this time. And remember Jackson, I am not a goddamn idiot. I can count.'

The carpet absorbs all the other sounds around the trolley and Luse has to listen hard to keep her guard. Jackson's feet pad away and the lift door opens again. The woman takes more water and then picks up the whole tray from the top and moves away. Ever so slowly Luse pulls apart the green cloth and peers out. At first she thinks she is in a small cinema. The lights are low and there are several rows of fixed seats facing a screen... no... a window, which takes up the whole of the far wall. Each of the fixed seats has wide armrests and inset into the armrests are small red telephones. There are four rows of seats and those at the back are mostly empty, but the first two rows are full of people. Although Luse can only make out the backs of their heads, she can smell an unsubtle blend of perfumes and aftershaves. Every now and then someone picks up a red phone or their cell phone and speaks into it quickly. Luse pulls her sheet tighter around her body, wondering what is happening.

The woman who has taken the tray is walking along the rows of seats with the water. She has her back to Luse who has rolled quietly from the trolley and half stands up, keeping her back to the wall, aware that Jackson might reappear at any moment.

It is not a cinema but a viewing platform, slung together with old cinema seats nailed onto planks and patched with cloth where the stuffing is coming out. All the seats face the massive glass window. Luse edges closer to the seats to try and see what it is that everyone is watching. Standing on her tiptoes she narrows her eyes, looking down into a brightly lit white room bustling with figures in green, surrounding a table... a metal table bearing a doll-like form. They are watching an operation!

In the middle of the room a doctor and several nurses, dressed in caps and gowns with masks over their faces, are operating on a child. The child is wearing a white cap, and has a white tube sticking out of its mouth. All around the operating table are machines beeping and clicking and there is blood, bright red blood, everywhere. The doctor is covered in it and blood drips onto the white floor. Luse hears the familiar warning, fluttering wings, and immediately drops to her knees and rolls as far under the seat in front of her as she can, just as the door behind her opens and Jackson returns with the food trolley. The woman with the water is already moving towards him. She is tall and miserable looking with heavy-rimmed glasses on a long face. Her lips are the colour of cold sausage and her mouth is too big for her face. Luse hears the woman tell Jackson to open some Mosi bottles.

'Go and tell reception to count down. They are nearly at the heart,' she tells him quietly and Luse presumes she is talking about the operation going on below.

People are beginning to move jerkily in their seats and a man raises his voice, almost shouting to someone on his mobile in a language Luse can't understand. A massive black woman with long dreadlocks and a river of gold chains rises from her front row seat and moves forward, placing her hands against the grubby glass window. She looks down at the child on the operating table as if she is starving and the tip of a pink tongue comes out of her mouth and rolls around her lips.

'Je vous remercie de votre attention, Madame Bettina.' The woman with the glasses steps over, a tray of drinks still balanced on her arm, but doesn't touch the woman. 'S'il vous plaît pas de la fenêtre!'

The huge lady lets out a long hissing breath but the woman with glasses stands her ground. After a moment Madame Bettina takes a step away from the window, but without taking her eyes from the scene below. All around in the darkened viewing platform Luse can hear men and women speaking. She recognises French, German and American accents but there are other languages too. They all seem to be talking on their red phones. Luse hears the word 'dollar' a lot as she peers down into the white room again. The surgeon, although capped and masked, has long black hair tied back and a mark on his face under his right eye. Dr Lin. He leans in over the child, cutting away at the open chest, while white bones and bright red muscle stick up from between his fingers. There is a pause while he makes a small jerking motion and then he holds up the bundle of bloody red meat and brandishes it at the viewing gallery. There is an eruption, cheering and feet stamping and once more the garbled voices down the phone lines.

Luse is horribly upset, her teeth chatter and she hugs herself. Before she ducks down again she sees the nurse gently pull the tube from the child's throat. Now she can clearly hear the fluttering of wings again and knows she must leave. Without the tubing and mask on the face, the child looks horribly fragile and lifeless.

The sound of wings is getting louder and with it now comes a waft of sweet flowers and hyena piss. The lift pings and without even pausing to think, Luse crouches low and runs past it, sprinting as fast as she can through the door at the side and she is out, into the gloomy corridor, bare feet slapping against the uneven linoleum.

Another door and a short set of dark grubby stairs leads her gasping and sweating with fear back to the ground floor. At the bottom of the stairs she stops, leaning against the wall, trying not to think about the tearing jerking motion the doctor made before holding up the bright red thing. All she can think about now is Joshua, but where could he have gone?

Using a corner of the sheet, she wipes her face and hands and then slowly peers around the side of the stairwell to find she is nearly back at the reception area. There is only one woman, the younger one, on the desk now, standing with her back to Luse and talking into her headpiece.

'... the bidding is over now, sir. The next auction will be in seventy-two hours.'

She stops to jot something on a piece of paper and Luse dashes across the front of the desk and, squeezing her eyes shut, rolls back through the double doors she originally came through. Again she stops, heart smashing, hand over her mouth in an effort to silence her heaving breath, but once again she has managed to pass unnoticed. She slips down the dark corridor, passing the doors until she sees door seven with the lights still on. Her intention is to rifle through the drawers and cupboards and find some kind of clue as to where she is... maybe a weapon if she can... but as she enters she remembers with an almost physical spasm of relief that when she woke up the light in the cubicle was on and she hadn't checked it. She runs past the empty beds and smashes open the cubicle door and there, in the bath, is Joshua fast asleep.

Luse's legs go from under her and she sits heavily on the cold floor. She drags herself to the bath and leans over, shaking Joshua's naked shoulder. His skin is cool and dry but there is a sharp smell of ammonia.

Drowsily he half opens an eye. 'I did a pee-pee in the bed.'

'That's okay, Joshua. Come and sleep in my bed tonight. We can sort it out in the morning.'

Together they half-stagger, half-crawl back to Luse's bed and she drags the heavy grey blanket over them both. Joshua is chilled from lying in the bath, but Luse is warm from her dash down the corridor and soon they are both curled around each other fast asleep, the lights still on and the air conditioner droning in the background.

The Termite Tree

1.

'In the morning we were fed the peanut stuff again and given uniforms. Brown and green with The Blood of Christ logo on the pocket. We were also given new shoes, lace ups. It felt weird to have shoes on again. Joshua said his legs were heavy.'

Georgia hasn't been able to speak since Luse described the child on the operating table. She doesn't believe Luse's story, refuses to. She is trying not to look upset and sceptical, understanding that Luse, suffering from post-traumatic shock and grief, will inevitably make up these kinds of things. Now the story has become fantastical, she almost feels relief that she can distance herself from it all. She glances across at Bernard surreptitiously but the old priest is bent forward, totally focused on Luse. His hands are shaking and he drops his pen, bending over jerkily to pick it up.

'You said the doctor was called Dr Lin?'

Luse nods. Bernard wets dry lips, glances over at Gus. 'You said he had a funny mark on his face?'

Georgia feels herself going cold all over. Bernard knows something. Bernard is buying this ridiculous story. If Bernard believes...?

'Yes,' says Luse nodding excitedly. She puts a hand to her cheek. 'He had a red blotch on his cheek, a big red puffy blotch.'

'Please carry on, Luse,' he says. 'If you don't mind.'

'They let us sleep... I don't know how long. We were given more of that peanut stuff with bread and a bitter lemon juice that was disgusting but the nurse said would make us feel better.'

2.

The uniforms are a perfect fit. Joshua is in brown shorts and Luse in a brown skirt. Both have bottle green aertex shirts with a black Blood of Christ cross on the pocket and brown cardigans all scratchy and brand new. Joshua seems a little dazed but alright. The deep sleep has done them both good.

Not long after they have finished their breakfast there is a sharp rap on the door. It's the lanky young man from the jeep, Phillomen, otherwise known as Kalulu Rabbit Face. He sticks his head around the door and glares at them.

'Iwe! You two.' Luse realises he doesn't know their names. 'Line up and be counted.'

Line up? There were just the two of them. Even Sister Luo rolls her eyes.

'Quick quick. Times is ticking.'

'We are ready, Mr Kalulu,' Luse says sweetly. It's risky to taunt him, but the nurses are still in the room and Luse feels brave. Phillomen twitches his pimply nose.

'I will tell you only the once. Do not call me that.' He scowls but can do nothing. 'Come on then.'

They follow Phillomen's lanky frame down the corridor and all the way back to the carport and out of the front of the strange domed building. The sunlight, though blinding, feels lovely on Luse's skin, warming and massaging her aching limbs after the chill of the air-conditioned rooms. Phillomen barks instructions at them as they walk along a pristine, tarred track that runs from the Dome through a small wooded area alongside a field of what looks like cabbages and paprika. Luse is only half listening to Phillomen, revelling in the warmth, the smell of wood smoke from the nearby kitchen and the sound of birds and crickets. She hardly notices the high fence circling the field and the guards on their turrets as they pass beneath.

'You will at all times obey the Seniors,' Phillomen is saying. 'You will not mix with children outside of your allocated hut and classroom unless given permission to do so at mealtimes. You will take care of your own uniform and will be inspected at rolecall every morning. You will not take the Lord's name in vain – in fact any bad language will be punished. Any attempt to disobey will be punished. If you do not keep up with your lessons or refuse to participate you will be punished...'

Luse squeezes Joshua's hand as they walk, clumping along in their heavy new shoes, watching the little puffs of dry dust beneath their feet. Luse feels oddly calm considering all that has happened over the last week. She knows that her grandmother's spirit is close, watching over them. The fluttering bird noise that she has been hearing are warnings from Ba'Neene, she is sure of it. But, for now, all she can hear is the grass and insect sound of the bush around them, an engine noise from nearby and the chuk chuk chuk of the massive sprinklers in the fields.

They pass through another guarded gate and find themselves emerging through the back of the covered dining area. There are noises and wonderful smells coming from the doors that must lead off to the kitchen, but Phillomen pushes them on past and out towards the large central square surrounded by the imposing but half-finished buildings. They walk onto the green square, coming alongside an ugly, unfinished chapel that looks as if it has been thrown together with breeze blocks and mud. Part of the roof is missing and the steeple ends abruptly half way up. Several large crows have already begun to use it as a perch.

Luse and Joshua see at last that they are not the only children. Ahead, the path is crowded with others chattering and yawning as they congregate on the central green. Luse and Joshua are lined up next to thirty or so others, all in the same brown and green uniforms. They are pushed, shoved, encouraged and bawled at by several of Phillomen's fellow Seniors in the severe black Chinese-style suits. Only the Seniors seem to have any idea as to what is going on. Many of the other children, like Luse and Joshua, appear fragile, dazed, knocking into each other, shading their eyes from the sun, turning the wrong way around. Joshua isn't the youngest. A tall boy holds the hand of a toddler, a little girl. Another, even younger, is balanced on a Senior's hip. In the line forming behind Luse, there is a lone child who looks to be about three. He sucks his thumb, tears streaming down his face and, after turning in a confused circle calling for his mother, begins to wander away from the group. A young woman Senior runs after him, hauling him back roughly. The boy begins to howl and the woman pauses and then stoops down and gives the little boy a hug, pulling out a handkerchief from her pocket and wiping his face quickly. Then she pushes him gently back into line, but not before Phillomen has come storming over.

'No contact! No contact, you stupid girl!' he screams into the young woman's face, waving his stick. Spittle lands on her cheeks and the woman flinches and ducks away.

Luse looks around, but apart from the Seniors, can see only one older adult. The woman, tall and gaunt with heavy black-rimmed spectacles, that Luse saw in the viewing gallery, peers at the melee from the side-lines. She holds a clipboard and seems to be checking the numbers. Her face is manly and glum, the corners of her mouth point down almost to her hairy chin.

Luse, not sure who to ask, turns to a skinny girl in tight pigtails standing next to her. 'I'm Luse. This is Joshua. Who are you?'

'No talking in line!' shouts Phillomen. The girl, who opened her mouth to respond, shuts it again.

'Kalulu Rabbit says no talking!' announces Joshua just loudly enough to be heard by the children around him. There is a brief gasp of giggles from the children and Phillomen scowls at them, twitching his nose furiously, unaware of the affect this has on the children, but then the tall miserable woman takes a whistle hanging around her neck and blows it. Immediately there is silence and the two rows of children straighten up. The woman whistles again and the children all turn left. Luse and Joshua hesitate.

'Breakfast!' hisses the girl in pigtails and Luse turns Joshua to face the same way.

The Seniors lead the children across the central square, along the front of the ugly chapel and back to the large concrete and thatch dining area. As they round the corner, the smell of boiling porridge and baking bread hits the children in the face and several of them stagger. Many of the children seem as hungry as Luse and Joshua were when they arrived. There are a large number of tables lined with wooden benches, many more than the present contingent of children needs. They sit at the two large central tables and the miserable tall lady plonks herself into a solitary seat at the table on the left. Luse looks eagerly around for the source of the delicious smells but nothing appears. Instead the dour woman whistles for silence again and bending her head, begins to say a grace. The grace seems interminable and more than a little strange. There is the usual thanks to Jesus and God and all the heavenly things, but there comes some endless dirge about protecting all from the black witchery of the demon kings of the seventh domain of heaven.

The glum woman's glasses steam up as she recites, 'May we placate them with food and drink and divert them with prayer and with blood offerings...'

'Blood offerings?' A couple of the other children glance up at this point and the boy sitting across from Luse catches her eye, making a wordless universal expression of *What the hell?* He looks exhausted and thin, cheekbones jutting from beneath ringed eyes. He also has a fresh set of stitches holding together a wound that runs from the top of his head along the side of his face and down to his ear.

From under her lashes Luse sneaks glances at the other children. The girl with the pigtails has obviously done all this before. She has her head bowed and stares at the table mesmerised by a knot in the wood. Other children sit slumped and bored rather than anxious or starving. Luse works out that besides her and Joshua there are about sixteen other very new kids all looking famished and exhausted. A pale-skinned girl at the other table has a swollen eye and still has dried blood in her ear.

At last grace is over and several fat ladies appear, carrying trays of steaming food from two side doors that obviously lead out to the kitchens. Porridge, milk, sugar, tea, fresh bread and even jam are piled onto the tables along with bowls of water for hand washing and fresh water for drinking. The children eat.

Finally they are allowed to talk, although the Seniors seem to be listening to everything that is being said.

'I'm Eli,' says the boy with the head full of stitches when he finally comes out from the bottom of his breakfast dish. Luse introduces herself and Joshua.

'How did you get here?' she asks.

Eli grimaces. 'I don't really know why I am here... can't remember it all.' He puts a hand to his scarred head. 'It had something to do with me being told I was a witch, I think.'

'A witch?'

'Yeah... my mother died and my father accused me... well, not him exactly but his church did anyway. They said I killed her. That I was a witch. I was sent here to be cleansed of my sins. '

'Are you a witch?' asks Joshua, mouth wide and still full of bread and jam.

'I am in grade 10,' Eli replies calmly. 'I am an excellent student.' He looks at Joshua. 'But it's not a school for witches and wizards as far as I know. It's not a Harry Potter school. I think they only have those in England.'

'They have schools for witches in England?' Joshua is thrilled and Eli smiles but Luse is furious.

'Why would they say such a thing? They said the same to me and to Joshua. It was just a way to get us here.'

'That church group. Church of the Bloody something or other,' says Eli. 'They run this place.'

'That's enough talking,' a Senior cuts in, banging her palm on the table. It is the young woman who hugged the boy. She looks nervous. 'We don't need to discuss that kind of thing at breakfast.'

There is silence for a moment. Eli and Joshua return to eating.

'What's your name?' Luse asked the Senior. 'I only know Kalulu.'

This makes the young woman smile. Suddenly the strain on her face lifts and Luse sees she is not much older than the rest of the children. She has a sweet smile, a front tooth missing, a dimple.

'You mustn't call him that,' she whispers. 'He hates it.' She glances around and, seeing all the other Seniors have their attention elsewhere, ducks her head towards Luse. 'My name is Miss Chewe. But you can call me Rosie.'

'Madam Chewe,' Eli wipes his mouth on his sleeve. 'What is this place?'

Rosie glances around again obviously unsure what the rules are on releasing information. 'This is a school... a school for special children, orphans and vulnerable children who have been rescued by The Blood of Christ Church.' There is pride in her voice. 'We are saving the children of Zambia.'

'I wasn't rescued,' begins Luse, spitting jam onto the table in her outrage, but Eli gestures to her, one hand flat. Calm down.

'Are you a teacher, Madam Rosie?'

'I am going to be teacher some day.' Rosie dimples at the thought. 'Presently I am a trainee teacher. All of us are training, some for the police, some for the army, some for teaching...' She lowers her voice again, 'Even Kalulu – he is training too!' She titters.

Not the sharpest knife in the drawer, thinks Luse in her father's voice. It was his expression. He would constantly try and improve on it to make her laugh. Sharpest knife in the drawer. Brightest candle on the cake. Freshest fish in the fridge. Luse looks at her plate, the red jam congealing on her porridge. She isn't hungry anymore.

'The food is amazing,' Eli says through a mouthful of fruit juice and porridge. 'Where does it come from?'

'Trucks come from Monze. Everything is bought in South Africa.' Rosie is relaxing into the chatter.

Monze? Eli and Luse exchange glances. That gives them a location at least.

'Are we near Monze?'

'Sister Chewe!' A deep guttural voice comes from over their heads. The tall miserable woman with the heavy glasses is standing over them. Her eyes are small and close behind the thick glass, her eyebrows heavy as caterpillars and that sausage-coloured mouth looks raw and flaky. The accent is the same as the Priestess; a kind of French-American.

'Sister Chewe you are here to oversee this table, not prattle away like an idiot child. Pull yourself together or I will see to it that you are severely punished.'

Sunlight on the glasses flares briefly as she turns on her heel and stomps away leaving Rosie huddled and shivering with anxiety.

'Who was...?'

'Shut up! Shut up! You will get me in trouble you nasty little chilombo.'

Rosie stands, her lips trembling. 'Finish your food and clear your plates to the kitchen.'

She doesn't make eye contact with them again and eventually they lose her in the confusion of clearing up.

Luse tries to stick close to Eli. There is more they need to discuss but there is no privacy. After collecting plates, they are instructed to take them through to the back of the kitchens where several of the fat ladies stand at the water pipes and wash up. The ladies speak a Zambian dialect Luse hasn't heard before. They seem easy with each other and relaxed, rolling their eyes at the ever-present Seniors and laughing behind their hands at the tall lady. However they are careful not to speak to the children and when they make eye contact it is brief and cold.

Food after the trauma they have recently endured results in several of the new children feeling sick and tired. Luse is pleased to find that Joshua does not seem to have tummy ache at all. But neither has he asked a single question about Mum or Daddy or where they are now. He just seems to be taking it all in his short stride, watching, then absorbing and accepting the new situation.

She finds herself following Joshua and the others in line back towards the centre lawn without even considering making a break for freedom. Then ahead of her someone falls over. It's the pale girl with the swollen eye. The line disintegrates, some children running towards and some away from the small prone body. Luse stands still, watching as Kalulu brandishes his stick, clearing a path to the girl. He kneels down to shake her. She doesn't respond, just sags in his arms, a trail of white vomit running down her chin.

'Not another one,' snarls the tall woman striding up to Kalulu's shoulder, pushing him aside and kneeling over the girl. 'Brother Phillomen, tell Vincent to bring the stretcher and you and Brother Jonas round up this ungodly rabble and get them into the class. This gets more ridiculous with every new intake.'

'Yes, Madam Angela.'

The Seniors are directing the children into various buildings that line the square. These are temporary classrooms and Luse is told that the classes are segregated. For the first time she has to endure the pain of having Joshua pulled away from her side and taken out of her sight. This makes her feel panicky and breathless and she cannot get the image of the child on the operating table out of her mind. But Joshua says he is alright and allows Miss Chewe to take him over to join the small boys' line filtering into the end classroom, a white porta-cabin on blocks with Chinese writing down the side. Luse watches Joshua carefully as he disappears inside but he is not tearful or frightened. She too has joined a line – this one for girls over ten years old. Her classroom is on the other side of the green in one of the half-finished bungalow blocks. The girls sit on the floor facing the back wall where a teacher and a Senior write on a free-standing blackboard. The back wall has glass doors that have been partially bricked up. Every window has heavy burglar bars on it and the room is hot and smells of concrete.

The class is incredibly dull, as are almost all the classes Luse takes that day, and the next and the next. Each is based around a chapter of the Bible, but taught with indifference and some ignorance. The children are not given pens or paper, just expected to learn by rote and recite from memory. During the third class, as Luse sits fidgeting and bored watching chalk dust spiral in the sunlight, there is a loud knock at the door and Madam Angela's voice bellows from outside, 'Welcome your guests!'

Immediately all the girls in the class leap to their feet and the teacher, a short woman with an enormous bottom, runs to the door clapping her hands and curtseying. Luse hears the flapping and fluttering of wings and tenses as an elderly couple steps into the classroom. Luse recognises Mrs Phiri and smells the sickly tang of flowers and piss. She quickly steps backwards, behind the group of girls which has crowded forward in excitement. In spite of the stench, which only Luse seems to find unpleasant, there is no doubt that Mrs Phiri and her husband make a remarkably striking couple, both with shining skin, and halos of soft grey hair.

'Ulibwaji, wafana,' says the man with a regal raised palm. He is dressed in a grey silk suit, his wife in a gorgeous blue and purple flowered chitenje with matching headscarf. The teacher and Senior look as if they are about to weep with joy at the Phiri's visit. Luse looks at them all warily, remembering the effect Mrs Phiri had on her at first. Something tells her not to act differently to the others. She drops her eyes to the floor, curtseys.

'For you new girls, this is Mr and Mrs Phiri who are our hugely generous and loving hosts, praise Jesus,' says Madam Angela, looking even more sour and ugly by comparison. 'This is their home and their farm, and without them we would not have this wonderful school.'

The elegant old couple are light on their feet, laughing and joking with the teacher, who is so excited that spit glistens in the air around her mouth as she talks.

'Mushi mushi. All is very well in this classroom, Bwana Phiri.'

The couple move forward amongst the girls. They come closer to Luse, fixing her with bright, dark eyes and she gets an odd sensation of being pulled forward slightly, but then there is a quick fluttering of wings and she blinks, eyes filling with water as if scratched by a feather. When she has wiped them, the Phiris have politely moved on.

They are only in the classroom a few minutes, but when they go it is as if the very sunlight has dimmed and the class gets down to their lessons again, dulled and full of longing for things they do not understand. All except Luse who sits quietly thinking that nothing is right here. Nothing at all.

3.

The days have an easy routine. At lunch times they usually troop back to the dining area to join all the other children for bread and tea, and then in the afternoons they are given overalls and sent to work in the paprika or cabbage fields. Luse likes this best, being outside and able to keep an eye on Joshua. The Seniors, sweltering under the afternoon sun in their black Chinese suits, hang around like lost bank clerks in the shade of the trees lining the fields, happy to leave the childcare to siblings or other children.

From their first afternoon, Luse begins plotting escape. She needs to get back to the lake house to look for Mum. She scans the surrounding fields every chance she gets, but can always see the far-off glint of razor wire and often the cloud of dust as the Seniors in their jeeps patrol the perimeter.

She needs to find out how close they are to a main road. They could hitch a lift from it back to the nearest town and then home to... *to where*, she wonders, a grey bleakness washing over her as she realises there is no home. But she rallies. *There is Rachel in Lusaka and once at Rachel's we can find Mum and get Miriam to come and fetch us all.*

In the second week she finds herself walking to the fields at the front of the line with Kalulu. He is rapping to himself softly.

'Yo yo and I say
It's to Jesus we pray
Our Lord is the rock
From the base to the... top.'
He pauses, thinking about his rhyme.

'That's pretty good,' says Luse.

'Oh yeah, how would you know?'

'My dad used to manage a band in Lusaka. He was... kind of well known there.' Luse knows she is a terrible liar so she keeps her voice as flat as possible, doesn't look up.

Kalulu's little eyes widen. 'Really?' He is impressed.

'Oh yes,' Luse relaxes a little into the story. 'But that was before he got too busy with church business of course.'

'Oh... well, of course.' They walk along in silence for a while.

'So, you rap a lot? Like that?' Luse asks innocently.

'Yeah. I am creating lyrics all the time. Only it's not acceptable here, while I am at work. They don't understand that my music is for the Lord even if it is in the form of rap.'

'Well, perhaps they will realise when you become famous.'

'Yeah... you think? Does your dad know anyone who... oh sorry,' Kalulu, realising his mistake, has the grace to smack himself on the forehead and blush.

'It's okay. Obviously he is dead now but I might remember a few names...'

'Really?'

'Someone in this area perhaps? Close enough for you to take a demo to?'

'Yah! There is no one around here, not for a hundred kilometres! Apart from a few Chinese farmers and the old mine. No, it would have to be Lusaka.'

Luse is disappointed. She tries again.

'There was a guy Dad mixed records with. He came from Monze. That's near here, right?'

But Kalalu isn't listening. They have come alongside the tortoise-shaped hospital and he is glaring at it.

'What is that place?' asks Luse, feeling cold, remembering the child on the operating table. 'Is it just a hospital?'

Kalulu is uneasy, flicking the grass with the tip of his stick. A rainbow locust flies up from in front of him, bright green with the burst of red, purple and orange under its wings.

'That building they call the Dome. After you have been processed you can only go back there if you need serious medical treatment or, if you are really lucky, you are selected for relocation. Even us Seniors are forbidden to go past reception without additional training.'

'But it's a hospital, right? And what do they mean by "relocation"?'

Kalulu scratches his head and then says, 'I think... I have heard... the rich people go there to watch...'

'To watch what?' Luse wants to ask, but Kalulu is stomping off.

'Come on, come on. Time is short!' he calls over his shoulder.

4.

In the evenings Luse and Joshua go back to Hut Two after supper. They are with a dozen or so other girls and the youngest children and toddlers in a long unpainted room. It is pretty basic, rows of mattresses on the floor, a long-drop instead of a loo, a sink-and-hose cubicle at the far end and a table with two chairs in front of the door. Two other doors have been bricked up and the only windows at the front of the room have black burglar bars on them and mosquito mesh with no glass. There are three light-bulbs hanging from the ceiling and one wall crawls with wires that lead up to a CCTV camera above the door with its blinking red light permanently on.

'It's for your security,' a Senior told Luse when she asked why they had a security camera *inside* the room.

Hut Two is the smallest dormitory. There are several others and Eli says his room has over a hundred mattresses in it and there is a whole other block next door that is still empty. Every day more children are arriving. At breakfast Miss Chewe tells Luse and Eli that the school has only been open for two months and they are the second intake. She says they expect thousands.

'The Blood of Christ Church is going to heal the children of Zambia. Praise the Priestess! In Jesus' name.'

Then come the street kids. The first group of twenty boys and girls is driven over to the green on the back of a police lorry. Luse learns from Miss Chewe that these ones were arrested on the streets of Lusaka. They were held for several days in cells before being bought here for 'their rehabilitation into society'.

'Madam Priestess has rescued them. She has brought them to Christ,' says Rosie, clutching her hands to her chest with happiness.

Luse cannot help staring at the children as they drive towards the Dome for processing. They are filthy, skin and clothes crusted with dirt. Their hair is lumpy, short and dusty. They must be exhausted and certainly have been crammed into the back of the truck for hours, but they still yell defiantly from behind the wooden bars enclosing them.

'Hey, Baboon Face!' yells a boy in Bemba at Madam Angela. 'Show us your arse!' and the other children start howling with laughter and making monkey noises. Luse is impressed, fascinated. Mostly she is hopeful. These street kids come from Lusaka. They must know how to get back there.

The street kids are accompanied by a new recruitment of Seniors. These ones are older and even the tough-looking women wear military T-shirts and combat pants with boots. They carry batons not sticks. The batons are powerful and the new Seniors are terrifying to all but the street kids who seem to endure the blows with weary stoicism.

Even after being processed the street kids look famished and battered and they stick together in a group, refusing to mix with the other children. They are sharper, less trusting, dangerous. They hoard food and have to be searched after meals. Often their language is foul, full of sexual bravado, confrontational. Fights break out continuously and then the new Seniors wade in grinning, batons at the ready.

At the same time as the new intake arrives, Luse begins to notice that several children are disappearing from Hut Two and being replaced by new faces. She has made a tentative friendship with a girl called Lottie who goes missing the very day the truck of street kids arrive. No one knows where she has gone. Luse asks, but Rosie looks blank and Kalulu tells Luse to stop whining about it.

'She has probably been relocated. Good for her. You should be happy,' he says.

Far away, over the horizon, thunder begins to rumble as the rains edge closer. The children pause when they hear it, each raising their heads to sniff for rain, but the air remains like an open oven. It is still so dry and hot that every blade of grass disappears and field work is too harsh for the little ones who get dehydrated.

We must go, we must get out, thinks Luse each night. Still, she can't come up with a plan. Homesickness and anxiety about Baama give her constant tummy ache but they are all getting stronger now with the plentiful food and field work. Luse is more confident that they would survive an escape attempt. Eli, when they can speak at mealtimes, brings her more information. They seem to have more freedom in the other dormitories, although they still have a Senior on duty every night and are locked in.

'Apparently the razor wire goes all the way around the plot and is four feet deep so we can't dig under. We'd be spotted by the guards anyway... they patrol all night.' But Eli's heart isn't in the scheming, Luse can tell.

'It's just that it's okay here, Luse,' he tells her. 'There's so much good food and you know... there isn't anything to worry about. Our dormitory Senior told us that there is money coming for televisions and even DVD players for each room. And he said those kids who disappear are being *adopted...*'

'Adopted? He told you that? And anyway we haven't even got beds yet,' hisses Luse. 'I am sure that's just a lie.'

But Eli continues, 'They are clearing a football pitch on the other side of the cabbage field and he said there was even a rumour of a swimming pool.'

Luse sucks her teeth, but she can see why he is reluctant. There is something so soothing about the repetition of the days. The work isn't hard, although the hours are long, and there is always food and water.

They are overheard. A tall strong girl from the street kid group leans over and pinches Luse's cheek roughly.

'You just cannot appreciate,' she says. 'I am telling you, this is like being in heaven compared to the last shit hole we were sent to. Ndikumbukila... it was just a garage. Some stupid wazungus gave their ndalama, dollars, to this guy who just shoved us in an old car park and gave us pap with no relish. Sure! You remember, Lazurus?'

A tiny, bald boy turns to them. He could be any age between eight and eighty years old. His eyes are huge and liquid but his mouth is full of black broken teeth.

'Yeah, Regina. That guy was a serious kawalala bandit. Eh hee hee hee.' His laugh is high-pitched and catching. Luse and Eli laugh. Lazurus grins and bares his monstrous teeth. Luse's grin flickers.

'What happened to your teeth?' comes Joshua's voice. For a second Lazurus' face darkens and his huge eyes fix on Joshua who steps back behind Luse.

'I'm sorry,' begins Luse. 'He is only little... he didn't mean...'

But Lazurus's face clears as quickly as a wink and he laughs his squeaky laugh again. 'When I was your age, little brother, my teeth were broken. I used to belong to an Arab man who bought me from my father. He took these teeth from me. Made it better for him. You know...'

Luse doesn't know, but Lazurus mimes remarkably well and Luse makes an educated guess. She feels sick. When he was Joshua's age?

'Yes, that Arab. I'm going to find him again.' Lazurus sighs. 'I am going to tie him up with wet rope and then take his teeth out one at a time and then his fingernails and then – only then – am I going to give him his last ever...' Here he mimes again. 'And then I will cut it off with a knife and throw it to the dogs. Eh hee hee!' He laughs uproariously again and the big girl, Regina, joins in, slapping him on the back.

'Do your dance, do your dance!' she says and several other children from the group join in, banging on their table for a drumbeat.

'Lazurus! Do your dance!'

Luse, Joshua and Eli watch mesmerised as Lazurus begins to do the most remarkable dance, twisting his little hips and making his entire body vibrate. It is expertly done and so shamefully explicit that the first

Seniors who run over to break up the crowd stand, eyes wide, mouths hanging open.

The incident lasts barely a couple of minutes but resonates in Luse's mind all night. If she and Joshua ever get out of the school will they end up on the streets? Will she be able to protect Joshua from Arab men? To protect herself? Perhaps they should just stay put after all. If Joshua got hurt because of her she would never be able to live with herself.

'I don't know why you talk to those street kids,' says Rosie tetchily a couple of days later. Rosie is no longer quite so dewy-eyed about 'saving Zambia's children' since she had her skirt pulled up by a couple of the boys during morning parade. 'They are a bunch of ruffians.'

Ruffians isn't quite the word for them, thinks Luse. They are survivors, have faced more real monsters then any character in any book. Luse tries to sit closer to Regina, Lazurus and some of the other street kids at meal times.

'No goody-goody can last longer than a day or so. But you can always pretend to be a goody-goody for extra money,' Regina says. They are discussing sex again. They always talk about it. It was their only consistent commodity on the street, the only thing they ever really had to barter. Some of them boast about it, some of them cry about it, but they all resorted to it at one time or another.

Just by sitting among the group at mealtimes, Luse learns other survival skills the children use apart from sex; scams for hitting supermarkets and market stalls, where to go through the rubbish, how to find drugs, how to avoid the police and where to 'park cars' and beg safely. Most of them talk about drugs a lot. A petrol-soaked sleeve can be sniffed through the day to stop hunger. For that reason ganja has to be avoided unless there is food nearby. Booze is best and chikasu – moonshine – is easy to find in the compounds, but it can make your stomach bleed.

'Worth it though,' says a tiny wraith of a girl called Brenda whose hands never stop trembling. 'Makes you more relaxed if you have to go with a big man, you know, or more than just one.'

Again Luse doesn't know, but she can hazard a guess. She tries not to look as horrified as she feels.

A week after the street kid group arrives, Hut Two is segregated during meal times. Luse suspects Rosie has told someone about her getting friendly with the street kids and is furious but helpless. Now she has to sit at a table with the girls and little boys from her dormitory and hardly gets to speak to anyone else, not even Eli. More children are arriving and with them more Seniors. It becomes harder and harder for any of the children to have any privacy or space to play or chat. Now, even in the evenings, the night duty Senior refuses to let the children talk after lights out. Luse is forced to lie awake watching the blinking red light of the camera for hours, her mind racing around and around the school, trying to find a hole in the razor wire, a map, a plan.

Joshua is uneasy too. His mattress is next to Luse and often she wakes hearing him whimpering in his sleep, but in the morning he doesn't want to tell her about his dreams.

5.

In the third week of Luse's stay, Mr and Mrs Phiri start to attend the morning parades, walking up and down the lines, smiling and chatting with the children. Usually they are accompanied by one of the Seniors with a video camera and will stop beside a particular child, almost always one of the girls or the youngsters from Hut Two, and film the child singing a song or reciting a line or two from the Bible. 'We want to show the world,' says the lovely Madam Phiri, 'how beautiful the children of Zambia are.'

Within a week most of the children that the Phiris film go missing from Hut Two.

Luse tries to tell Eli in the paprika fields. 'Jojo and Beatrice have gone this time,' she tells him. 'Last night there were two new girls in their beds. It's really weird.'

'I don't know,' Eli says, not raising his head. He has become quieter over the last few weeks, his eyes never seem to focus on anything and he complains about headaches all the time even though his stitches are out and his scar is healing.

'Eli, I'm serious! Kids disappear and I'm sure it has something to do with the Dome. Remember the kid I told you about ...'

'You said you could have dreamt it.'

'No! I am sure I didn't now. Listen, those girls who went from my room, they were filmed by the Phiris just that morning. Maybe there is a connection.'

'Look,' Eli straightens at last. Despite the fact that he has put on weight he still looks somehow defeated. He rarely smiles that beaming smile of his now. Dark bruises are smudged under his eyes. 'The Seniors told us about that place. It's where you go if you have been selected to go to live with a family abroad! It's a good thing! You go and then you are interviewed and given new clothes and money and stuff and then you are taken to the airport and flown off to be with your new family.'

Luse is stunned. 'But I *have* a family. I don't want to go abroad with strangers!'

'You *had* a family,' Eli says, then pauses when he sees her face. 'Okay, I am sorry Luse. But you know maybe this is a good place to be. Maybe we are the lucky ones.'

But Luse won't be reassured. The next morning on parade she watches the Phiris as they walk regally down the lines of children. Mrs Phiri is wearing a damask shawl over a grey trouser suit. Her husband is in a simple dark blue Mao suit, like the Seniors' black ones, only his is silk.

Little Rosie Chewe is darting around them with the camera held up to her eye. The Phiris pause next to a gawky long-legged girl called Hannah, who blushes fiercely at something Mr Phiri says. Then she smiles and it lights up her long face. With an odd snapping gesture Mrs Phiri indicates to Rosie to move up with the camcorder. It is nearly breakfast and Madam Angela blows her whistle. The lines straighten and begin to move left. Luse has every intention of following them, but then from the corner of her eye she sees the Phiris approaching her. She notices that Madam Phiri hangs back behind her husband to shake the large basket she always seems to carry. From it the reek of flowers and piss wafts on the slight wind across the lawn.

Mr Phiri bends down towards Luse. 'Good morning, Luse. I believe you are one of the Priestess's personal finds? How wonderful to see you here looking so well. We were worried about you and your brother when you arrived.'

Mr Phiri's gentle dark eyes are thoughtful and Luse can hear no feathers fluttering. Not one. All she wants is Mr Phiri to speak to her, to love her, to be proud of her. His eyes seem almost completely black now and Luse cannot look away.

'What can you do, child?' he asks softly. 'For your fans out there? Can you sing for us?'

Luse nods, desperate to please him. 'I can sing, I can sing,' she whispers although there is no song in her head.

Mr Phiri lifts a manicured hand and gestures towards Rosie who comes forward, camera whirring. At that very moment there is a piercing cry from high above in the bright clear sky where a fish eagle wheels alone on the updraught. Immediately Luse blinks, remembering Gran, the cave. For a moment she doesn't know where she is, then she shivers and shakes her head.

'Oh sorry, Mr Phiri. I can't sing today... sore throat.'

Mr Phiri's pupils narrow. He turns away abruptly, too abruptly, and crashes into poor Rosie. She falls, grabbing hold of Mr Phiri, and pulls him down onto his knees. He falls clumsily and all around him the children laugh spontaneously and even Rosie, blushing and embarrassed, begins to giggle.

But Luse, looking down at Mr Phiri's face, sees him change horribly. She sees he is not handsome at all. His face is twisted with rage and wrinkles tear through his forehead as he shrieks at Rosie and his wife. Something has fallen from inside his sleeve and lies on the ground next to Luse's foot – a blackened thick, short tube stuffed with what looks like stained cloth. It seems to writhe.

Mr Phiri is feeling around in the grass, making an unpleasant mewling sound. Luse sees with horror that his eyes have gone completely white.

'... waaangaaa...' He is trying to say something.

Madam Phiri comes rushing forward and hastily kicks the bulging thing of cloth towards his groping hands. He has it and immediately is perfectly calm and still, sitting on his knees on the grass, holding the thing up tight to his cheek, eyes closed. His wife crouches next to him whispering in his ear and the smell of piss and flowers becomes overpowering.

'Let's go,' Luse says to Joshua. Just as they are turning away to catch up with the other children, Luse sees the bulging writhing cloth-tube wriggle back up into Mr Phiri's sleeve. She does not wait for him to lift his head. She knows that his eyes will be normal again, his skin smooth and soft and he will be searching for her.

6.

'Wanga,' says Father Bernard

'I beg your pardon?'

'Wanga. It could be what that foul old man dropped. His "wanga". It's the special medicine that witches carry with them... a kind of tool kit. If they become separated from it they can be exposed.'

'I knew it, I knew,' says Luse, clapping her hands together, her face fierce. 'I just *knew* that man and his wife were bad people.'

'Now just stop it.' Georgia is appalled. 'Come on. We all know that witches do not exist. It's just a cowardly way of accusing people of crimes they haven't committed... of scaring people.' She stands up, distressed and angry.

'It isn't as simple as that,' says Gus, a little surprised at her vehemence.

'No, it isn't,' says Bernard, looking sternly at Georgia over his spectacles. 'You are taking a most narrow-minded view of the world, Georgia, and I am surprised by your attitude. Ritual and superstition have been part of every cohesive society since man first settled. Your own British parliament is rife with it.'

Luse excuses herself and heads to the bathroom. Georgia sits back down.

'Oh, come on. Ritual and superstition is mostly innocuous these days. We are talking *witches* here. Should we be encouraging her?'

'Try not to get fixated by the word. It is more the idea, Georgia. As a doctor you must surely have come across all kinds of things that can't be explained.' Bernard is settling into his lecturer stance, hands folded behind his back.

Georgia shifts uncomfortably in her seat. 'Yes well... but I believe that is just because we haven't got the diagnostic tools yet.'

'And neither can anyone map a brain,' interjects Gus. He is enjoying this.

Bernard sits smugly and crosses his legs. 'Imagine this, Georgia. I tell you I am a witch. You say you don't believe me, but I say I don't care that you *don't* believe me and I am cursing you anyway. The rational part of your brain may dismiss the curse, but deep in a part of your mind, as yet unexplored, I tell you, there will come a little paranoid twitch. That twitch is just enough to cause stress. That stress gives you a rash, spots, hiccups. Maybe distracts you enough that you walk into a door and hit your head. Some here call that Chiposo. Now... is that witchcraft?'

'Very good,' chuckles Gus. 'Self-fulfilling witchcraft for the lazy sorcerer.'

'You are talking placebo effect.'

'And more. Here our brains are wired differently. More can occur than is in your known universe.'

'You are paraphrasing Shakespeare. Badly, I might add.'

Gus breaks in again, 'I always thought it was childish but it does lead to some fantastic stories; masabe dancers eating goats alive when possessed, if you tread on poisoned ground you may die, out of control lombas wreaking havoc.'

'Lombas?'

'It's a snake-like object that can be animated by the owner, doesn't even have to be a witch. It is used to steal money mostly or crops, but it can get nasty. Sometimes they get out of control, grow enormous.'

Georgia looks from the priest to the soldier. 'You are taking the piss?'

'Actually,' says Gus, almost apologetically, 'there was one in Mutendere only a couple of months ago. It was in all the newspapers. Killed a policeman.'

Georgia is silent for a moment. Then she remembers her question. 'What about that Doctor? Dr Lin wasn't it? You knew something, Bernard?'

Again the old man glances over at Gus. In that furtive look Georgia sees that they both know more than she does.

' "Cannibal witches and wicked Chinese"?' she quotes Gus, her throat tight, voice strained with anger. 'You knew that monster was out there?'

Bernard stands, tries to placate Georgia, but Gus nods. He looks at Georgia and she sees herself reflected in his eyes; his gaze is open, his pain clear to see.

'I told you the young man with the cold box full of body parts had described an oriental man? Well, they called him the Red Chinaman because of a large strawberry birthmark on his face. We looked for him. We all looked for him.' Gus puts a hand on Bernard's arm. 'No one more then Father Bernard. But the case...'

'Yes, I remember,' Georgia speaks bitterly. 'It was closed.'

'Are you alright?' Luse comes over to Georgia.

'Yes, Luse. All good.' She breathes out slowly, feels the two men relax a little too.

Georgia is tired. She feels a headache starting to tweak her neck and temple and she sighs, 'But this hysterical belief in witchcraft... you don't think it just makes Zambians sound so primitive?'

Gus gasps with mock outrage. Bernard tuts and pushes his glasses up his nose.

'If you mean does it connect us to our pre-literate ancestors... then yes. But we are clearly *not* uncivilised. We just accept limbo, the in-between, we embrace it. Perhaps this makes us more in tune with reality... Think of quantum physics.'

Gus coughs. 'May we discuss this later? I would really like to hear the rest of Luse's story before supper.'

Luse nods, stretches, then sits forward and continues.

7.

That night Luse lies awake. Cold sweat on her forehead, under her arms, trying to think of a way to escape. They are counted out and counted back in again so trying to hide out until darkness is not possible. She sighs and stretches. In the gloom she can just make out the woman Senior slumped in the hard-backed chair reading her Bible. Luse turns and reaches over to the next mattress to put an arm around her brother who is sleeping sideways, blanket thrown over to one side.

She dreams the fish eagle has landed in a tall flat-topped acacia tree. The magnificent bird blinks at her with its golden eyes and then throws back its head and makes its whistling keening cry and the tree rocks beneath it almost as if it is dancing. The eagle spreads its wings and begins to take off; the wings beat and the air fills with dust and... inswa! Inswa – flying ants – rising up all around like smoke. *Wooosh, woosh* beat the mighty wings of the eagle and up it rises, gripping the entire tree in its talons. With a creaking cracking noise the tree parts from the earth and rises up under the bird.

Luse wakes with a start and lies quiet and still, the plan already forming in her head. As everyone begins to stir she leans across and whispers into Joshua's ear and he looks surprised then excited and nods. Surreptitiously, he pulls his arm out from the covers and sucks at the inside of his forearm, hard, until a large raised mark appears. Luse grins.

'Keep sucking but don't let anyone see you,' she whispers and raises her eyebrows. 'And that includes the camera!'

As the rest of the children stagger to the bathroom to wash and change, the night duty Senior stretches and yawns, exposing pink gums and glistening white teeth.

Luse continues to fret about the finer details of her plan. Most importantly Joshua must not go on parade. Neither she nor he would get away this time. They would be selected and taken to the Dome and disappear like the others.

The children, still clumsy with sleep, with Joshua squeezed between them, line up at the door and wait while the Senior goes to wee and wash her own face in the bathroom, taking her time with the ageless pleasure of the prison guard. At last she pats her hair, flexing her arm muscles in the dirty mirror, and ambles over, flicking through the keys on her large keyring until she finds the one marked with a blue splodge of paint. She opens the door and the children drag the fresh air and early morning sunlight deep into their lungs. The smell of hot bread and maize porridge wafts over on the breeze. Joshua looks across at Luse with something like annoyance. He is going to have to miss breakfast today.

As they troop down the steps and join the other children marching onto the parade ground, Luse pokes Joshua in the back and he begins to cry, loudly. He holds his reddened arm up by the elbow.

'Madam Senior!' calls Luse.

The Senior turns around and glares. Her eyes are puffed up with exhaustion but they still glitter.

'Madam, my brother has been stung by a wasp.'

'So what. He'll survive.'

'No miss, he is allergic. He could die!'

On cue Joshua falls dramatically to his knees, groaning. The Senior's little eyes widen.

'I must rush him to the clinic. They have medicine there – especially for him.' Luse is taking a big risk here but it turns out she has judged the woman's disinterest perfectly.

'Yes – you take him then. I will let them know on the parade count.'

Next to the open dining area is a shipping container that is now being used as a little first aid hut for the minor injuries, allergies and stomach bugs that the children present with. Luse has not been inside before and, unsure of protocol, pushes through the heavy metal door which is standing ajar.

It is early morning and already hot and stuffy inside the container. The sharp smell of antiseptic is almost eye watering. A nurse in a too-tight blue uniform sits slumped at a little desk with a metal fan whizzing in her ear. She has her head propped on her hand and her eyes shut but even so, Luse recognises her from the Dome.

'Hodi?' Luse knocks on the door to rouse her.

'Eh? What, what?' the nurse splutters and knocks the book she has been reading to the floor, a thin book entitled *All For Love*. It has a picture of a very muscular white man holding a slender woman with long black hair tight to his chest. The noise of the falling book brings another nurse into the room, older and with a kind face. Luse recognises Sister Luo.

'Hello dear,' she says. 'You have bought your brother? We haven't seen you in here before have we?'

'My brother has been stung by a wasp, madam.' Luse pushes Joshua towards them. He has remembered to bite his inner arm hard again before they entered and the red mark is puffy and looks sore.

'He is allergic,' she says and on cue Joshua begins to make disgusting choking noises. They are a little over the top and Luse winces.

'Dear, dear! This looks bad, poor little thing!'

The other nurse steps over with a tube of hydrocortisone and slathers Joshua with it and then checks his heart with a pink stethoscope. She nods at the Sister.

Sister Luo brushes Joshua's forehead and pats one of the beds. 'Well, all seems alright. Sister Chilufia and I will keep him in here this morning however.'

Luse kisses an anxious Joshua goodbye and runs out of the clinic, but instead of turning back to the parade ground, she slips around the back of the container and darts over to the trunk of the towering acacia, diving between its roots, out of sight. Noting the crunch of the red termite-chewed soil beneath her feet, she puts out her hands and rests them on the tree trunk. It is smooth and cool. She remembers her dream, the termites and the tree pulled away from the earth by the eagle. She looks up at the towering branches. It seems impossible that this massive acacia would even sway in a storm. She quickly scans the ground around the bottom of the trunk and sees where the thick roots are pushing through the soil and the red termite tracks run. At the crook of a root, a few inches from the trunk, the termite debris is darker, older. She takes off her shoe and pushes with the heel into the crumbling earth and it immediately falls away to reveal a large hole about two feet deep. Now she feels the tree vibrate ever so slightly and more earth shifts around the base of the trunk. There is a slight creak and the earth suddenly gives way and the ground engulfs Luse's bare foot. She shrieks and falls back onto her bottom, pulling her foot that is now streaming with white-bodied ants from the hole. Gently, trying not to yelp again, she shakes the ants off and pushes herself away from the tree. Her dream was true. All around her she can hear loose earth falling away beneath the tree. She must be sitting on a very thin shell of earth indeed.

Time passes slowly, the heat builds and the far thunder creeps closer. Luse is just about to doze off when she hears a faint ringing from the container. A few minutes later the door opens wide and Sister Chilufia and Sister Luo appear with a trolley stacked with boxes of cotton wool and hypodermics. Luo stands in the doorway and calls back to Joshua inside; something about not being more than half an hour and then the two nurses head towards the Dome.

Luse waits patiently until she can no longer hear the jingle of the trolley and then approaches the container. 'Joshua, it's me open up!' she hisses.

There is the sound of bare feet smacking along the floor, the door opens and Joshua's round face peers up at her with relief. 'Luse! You went for a long time. What did you do? You are all dusty!'

'Shhh, Joshie! You did good, now back up on the bed. We haven't got much time!'

Luse looks around and frantically begins pulling out drawers and rummaging through already open boxes of pills. *Which ones, which ones?* she thinks. She has no idea what most of the tablets are for and time is ticking away.

'There are more in the cool cupboard, Luse,' Joshua says, pointing at the corner where a large fridge stands humming quietly and then gets back on the bed as Luse races over and pulls at the fridge door. Layers of pills and bottles are inside. Luse grabs a few and reads the boxes. Some of them have instructions and warnings and quickly she finds a set of little white boxes with 'WARNING: causes drowsiness. Do not operate machinery' in bold on the back. Luse grabs three boxes from the back and slams the fridge shut tucking the boxes into her knickers. From high above the roof of the clinic, way up in the blue sky, comes the melancholy whistling cry of the fish eagle.

She kisses Joshua and slips back out of the container across the strip of grassless earth and hurls herself once again into the protection of the tree just as Sister Chilufia and Sister Luo emerge through the kitchen looking hot and irritated.

'I need a cup of tea, praise Jesus,' says Sister Luo pushing open the door, not noticing that it is already ajar.

As soon as the nurses are inside, Luse dashes away to join the other children as they line up for class. No one bats an eye at her late arrival. The weather is changing. The rains are coming.

8.

That evening the sound and smell of rain approaching causes great excitement. Everyone is talking about it, watching from the dining hall as the sun goes down; flaming red and orange, fading to grey and smoky black. The bush sounds change too. The wind blows from the south, bringing across the dining area the smells of cooking fires from far off villages, the sweet smell of the irrigated fields and clammy taste of dust. For the hundredth time Luse lets her hand brush along the top of her skirt where she has tucked the pills.

'Hands under the table,' Luse says and slips a box of the pills into Eli's palm during the grace.

'Crush them into the night Senior's tea flask tonight. I don't know how many. Lots probably.'

'I can't, I can't.' Eli looks terrified and Luse feels truly sorry for him but she knows they have no choice.

'That tree!' Luse points at the acacia. In the darkness it fans out fifty feet above the ground.

'Yeah? Nice tree. What about it?'

Luse leans closer and whispers directly into his ear, making him flinch from her tickling breath. 'Its roots are entirely eaten away by white ants. We could easily push it over.'

'I still don't...' Eli's eyes slowly widen with dawning awareness. If they push the tree and it really is weak enough to topple, it will fall over the razor wire and provide a bridge to climb over.

Pills and an acacia tree... It isn't much of a plan, Luse thinks.

Now, as she lines up with the other children to go into Hut Two, Luse sweats, fretting about how it is all going to work. It is the night of the mean and lean Senior Bwalya, again.

'Madam, I have a message for you,' says Luse.

'What did you say?'

'I have a message. From that ka-tall one, that teacher with the hole here.' Luse gestures to her chin, and places a finger where the man's dimple is. 'Siza.'

Bwalya's face has changed. Her cheeks quiver. 'Yes. Yes... what?'

'He said to come out before lights out. He will try and meet you. If he can't make it he will try again later.'

'Why does he want to meet?'

Luse feigns boredom, yawns widely. 'Madam Senior that is all he said. I am tired now. May I go?'

She stomps over to the bathroom, rubbing her face and using the gesture to glance at the camera up at the ceiling. There is nothing to be done. The red light silently blinks on, off, on, off.

Bwalya sits perfectly still for a minute. She is also looking up at the camera. She hesitates for a moment then she stands and takes her chair in one hand, casually pulling it across the room until it is directly under the camera.

'All of you in your beds! NOW!'

The girls rush to their beds and lie down just in time for her to turn off the lights. In the darkness Luse can only see her as a dark silhouette as she climbs up onto the chair and gently knocks the lens of the camera a little to the left, pointing it away from her desk and the entrance of the dormitory. It is now only filming the far end of the dormitory and the last set of mattresses.

'All of you keep quiet and stay in your beds,' she hisses and is out of the dormitory in two long-limbed strides. The key clicks as she locks the door behind her.

Luse jumps up and runs to the desk, unscrewing the top of the regulation thermos of tea and pulling the foil sachet from her knickers. She careful empties the crushed contents into the tea and wipes around the rim, quickly replacing the stopper and the cap and giving the thermos a small shake. Now the other children are getting up from their beds, unsure of what is going on, curious and anxious.

'What are you doing?' whispers the newest one. 'You will get us all in trouble.'

'You mustn't tell her,' begs Luse. 'They are going to hurt my brother.'

Then the key turns in the door and the children scatter, each one to a mattress. Luse hits hers only just in time, but Bwalya is distracted and sits back at her desk, not still this time, but twitching. One long muscular leg bouncing nervously under the desk.

'Iwe...'

Luse jumps. The woman has crouched down by her head. 'When he said "later" what time did he mean?'

'I don't know, madam. Just that he really wanted to meet up.'

Bwalya growls and then goes back to the desk again and sits biting her nails. Luse can feel that all the other children are lying awake, watching in the darkness and when Bwalya lights a candle, several curious eyes glitter in the flickering light. Bwalya sighs loudly and pours herself a cup of tea.

They wait. Minutes tick by and eventually the generator kicks off and silence settles over the school and Bwalya topples forward onto the desk in a puddle of cold tea, snoring.

Joshua gets up first. Luse is so shocked that the drugs have worked that she can't move.

'Did you kill her?'

Luse gets up and steadies herself then comes over and prods the woman with a finger. Nothing happens.

'Nope. She is breathing still. Get your clothes!'

As Joshua grabs his uniform, Luse tentatively rifles through Bwalya's pockets and slides out the keys. The other children begin to get up.

'Don't get up unless you are coming with us!' Luse hisses loudly. 'The camera will see you moving and you may be punished later.'

'It is more dangerous to leave. How will you get out? How will you survive in the bush?' asks the new girl and turns over on her side as if she is angry but Luse can hear her weeping.

'Come on, come on.' Luse fumbles with the keys and then the door is open and the wide blue-black night lies ahead. She pushes Joshua out ahead of her, feeling the cool night air on her face and breathing in the smell of the coming rain. Wind knocks her off balance and dry leaves skitter and whirl. She locks the door behind her and throws the keys to one side, creeping low along the building line until they find their way around the edge of the parade ground. It is eerily empty and the green grass looks black in the flood lights. The wind is strong, rushing around the buildings and far off there is a crash of something breaking. They don't hesitate and soon are at the closed shipping container.

The huge acacia stands looking as solid as rock, but Luse knows better. 'Put your hand on it gently,' she says to Joshua as she pulls her uniform on over her nightdress.

'It's shivering!' Joshua is surprised. 'Poor tree. Is it scared?'

'No Josh. It's excited to help us escape.'

At that moment there is a scuffling sound and before either of the children can duck down into the tree roots, Eli appears with his eyes glittering, a huge grin on his face.

'I did it!' he whispers delightedly. 'It was too easy! The Senior always goes for a cigarette break before lock down and I stuck the pills in his tea. He passed out in minutes! I told the others to come but no one...'

Eli trails off, looking upwards into the thorny branches of the huge acacia.

Luse is beginning to get a little frantic. The dangerous part is only just beginning. The wind is tearing through the top of the tree and thunder booms around them. There is no rain, just the wild wonderful smell and the sound of the branches thrashing above them.

'Be careful where you put your feet,' says Luse. 'Joshua, you just hold tightly to me okay? Come on, Eli!'

The children place their palms flat on the trunk of the huge acacia, feeling the shivering increase to a steady vibration.

'One, two, three!' yells Luse, her voice whisked away in the wind, and they push.

The earth beneath the huge tree caves in entirely, almost voluptuously, with a mighty whumph and the children leap back as the ground falls away at their feet. Unable to see clearly now through the dust, Luse can only grip Joshua's hand tight, her free arm held over her face, as the noise builds. There is a terrible creaking, cracking sound and then a slow-building whine, a splitting shriek and then finally the air is blasted across their faces as the tree topples over onto its side. The ground vibrates and dust billows up higher and higher, thick and choking.

The noise must have alerted the whole school, thinks Luse, desperately peering through the dust to try and see if the tree has landed as they had predicted, bridging the razor wire fence.

'I can't see anything!' she shouts at Eli.

His voice comes from above her. 'It's not that difficult to climb up! Put your hands out and feel for the trunk. It seems solid and there are plenty of footholds. I am near the branches already and it's almost level.' His voice comes again, muffled and unclear. 'Be careful of the thorns. Hurry!'

From far off, Luse hears someone yelling, then a crack of a gunshot. But it isn't coming from the direction of the dormitories. It sounds like it is coming from the Dome.

Pushing Joshua ahead of her, Luse clambers up the trunk, the bark feeling cool and smooth between her legs. The tree has come to rest at a forty-five-degree angle, and they quickly find that they are entangled in the thorny branches. Hundreds of disturbed insects flutter and fizz around their faces as they inch forward still blinded by dust and darkness. From over by the Dome, Luse hears another snap of a gun. An alarm shrieks on and off, on and off.

'Keep on going, Joshie,' she whispers, trying to untangle a thin whippy branch from her hair. The branches become more slender and begin to sag beneath their weight and Josh cries out as he slips forward.

'It's alright, Joshua. You are over the other side. Let yourself slide,' comes Eli's voice.

'I'm down!' shouts Joshua and from his voice Luse can tell he is grinning wildly. 'That was fun, Eli!'

In a few seconds she has followed, dropping through the last thorny branches to land on the hard ground, covered from head to foot in red dust.

'Run!' she says, but thorns still grip her clothes, her hair and scratch at her face as she drags herself forward.

'If we run they will track us no problem. I say we use our heads,' says Eli.

'Oh...' Luse calms a little watching him. This is a different Eli from the boy in the school, defeated and broken. This boy is stronger, more courageous even than she is.

'We stick by the fence. Track back along it until we are as close to the front gates as possible. They will never expect that. We wait until mid-morning when all the fuss has died down and then we head off into the bush to look for the main road to Monze and Lusaka.'

Luse kneels down in front of Joshua and dusts him off as much as she can. She wipes his face feeling the fearful drag of responsibility on her heart.

'I'm okay, Luse,' Joshua says impatiently, catching Eli's excitement. 'I am okay!'

'Right! Let's do it,' says Luse.

It takes them at least two hours to crawl around the perimeter towards the main entry gates. Every few minutes they hear shouting, the sound of pounding footsteps and flatten themselves into the dirt of the shallow ditch, holding their breath and crossing their fingers. Each time they are lucky.

With the first orange tendrils of dawn blossoming in the blue-black sky, they can make out the main entrance gate floodlit from every side. Breaking away from the fence, they dash across the tarred track and clamber into the nearby bushes. They crouch down behind a termite mound and peer from between the thorn branches as the agitated guards march up and down the tarred road to the school, talking loudly to each other on their radios.

'Look, look!' Joshua points. 'It's Samuel!'

Luse follows his finger and sees the massive man striding from the school down to the gate. He looks furious. The ground-shaking rumble of his voice carries to them on the blustery wind and Luse thinks she hears '... breach in outer perimeter. They all climbed over...' Then he stands still and his voice is quite clear even from a distance.

'I cannot condone using excessive force on children. No Madam, I will not listen. There will be no "shoot to kill" on my watch.'

There is a pause, radio static, a shrill distorted voice. Samuel interrupts, 'I am very angry too, Madam, but even the most tenacious chief of security cannot control termites. I suggest you let me get on with clearing up the mess you made at the Dome. Give me those details again... the spy a Zambian Rastafarian, long dreadlocks, a beard, slim build. Anything else? And you are sure he and the three runaways are together?'

He strides off again, heading towards the main guard house, disappears briefly and emerges with three other men carrying torches and AKs. A jeep rumbles up, slowing just enough for them to jump on and they all drive off, passing the children and covering them once more with clouds of dust.

'What did he mean by "spy"?' asks Eli. 'There is no spy with us.'

'Don't know...' Luse says.

They dig themselves a little deeper into the ditch behind the termite mound and wait.

'I'm thirsty,' whispers Joshua, putting a hand to his dust-clogged throat. He sticks his tongue out. It is covered in red dirt and Luse too feels the horrible ache beginning in her mouth. It hasn't rained and they need water. How could she have been so stupid not to have prepared anything? The dawn light is getting stronger and the wind has dropped away completely, the thunder just a memory. Luse peers at the bushes around her and gives a shiver of relief.

'Dig here,' she hisses at the boys and they join her in scrabbling at the hard ground. Just beneath the surface is a thick root like a cable running under the gritty sand. Luse drags at it and it finally comes away from the ground. She holds it up to the light, looking at the surface of the root carefully, then breaks it into several pieces.

'Peel back the dark skin and chew the white inside,' she orders and shows them. 'Be careful though. If you get the dark bits in your mouth it will make you feel sick.'

They chew cautiously at first and then with pleasure. The succulent root releases a thin sugary water that immediately slakes their thirst.

'Don't swallow the stuff. Spit it out!'

Eli spits a white wodge of chewed up plant onto the ground. 'How did you know about that?'

Luse grins. 'Ba'Neene.'

9.

The sun clambers higher into the dry October sky, dragging all the dawn dew with it. The cool shadows disintegrate and soon all three children are exposed to the full sun and are panting in the heat. It is time to move on. Eli is confident and insists that they keep moving, trying not to leave footprints by keeping on the bare rocky outcrops alongside the sandy bush track. This is hard work as they have to sprint diagonally from one outcrop to the next, keeping a constant eye and ear out for movement or voices. Sweat beads Luse's face and her uniform is soaked through by the time they come over a ridge. Looking down into the long shallow valley, they see a wide tar road glistening in the boiling sun.

Luse is about to step off towards the road when Eli grabs her arm and pulls her back.

'Heh? You crazy? You can't go straight. We need cover from the road.' He points, 'Over there! A drainage ditch. Come on.'

Luse plucks a thorn from her hair and follows, creeping along to the large concrete drainage ditch that cuts through the field all the way to the road. They scramble down the sides into the cool half-shade at the muddy bottom.

They are very thirsty, but the water with the green froth looks poisonous. Instead Luse breaks apart some more of the cable-like root and hands it around. The water at the bottom of the ditch is shallow and sluggish and full of frogs and bugs. Mosquitoes and gnats cloud the air around their faces, mud squelches between their toes, but they feel safer, less exposed in the ditch. On Eli's signal they begin to move down towards the culvert that runs under the road, Luse holding her skirt and shoes up with one hand and keeping a grip of Joshua with the other. Slipping and sloshing, and occasionally pausing to let some small creature slide away through the brown water, they make slow but steady progress.

Then Eli stops and the tension in his back causes Luse to clap a hand to her mouth to stop from crying out. Ahead, slumped in the bottom of the ditch, just in the shadow of the concrete culvert, is a man. With his long dreadlocks hanging down over his face and skinny legs stuck out straight in front of him, he looks like a ghastly man-sized rag doll.

Joshua edges around them both and sloshes up to the crumpled figure sitting waist deep in filthy water. He bends down and carefully pushes a couple of dreads away from the man's face. 'Mulibwanji? Hodi?' he says, as if knocking at a door.

The man lifts his head.

Joshua jumps back and Luse and Eli jump forward, but the man only opens enormous red-rimmed eyes and stares at them, snot and blood dripping from the tip of his nose. His face is bruised and swollen and he has a shallow but jagged cut on his temple. The man moans and shakes his head as if dizzy but seems unable to speak.

'What's wrong with him?' asks Eli who has found a large stick and is holding it in one hand like a bat.

'I don't know.' Luse watches horrified as the man rolls his eyes, feebly raising a hand to his mouth and moans again, lips still clamped together. 'I don't think he can open his mouth.'

She hears fluttering wings and, as she moves in front of Joshua to look, feels a sudden cold sharp snap in the centre of her body. Old bones wrap themselves around her young ones and her grandmother steps into her body and clicks herself on like a key in a car's engine. It is the strangest sensation. Luse feels absolutely safe and unafraid but it is as if she is crouching in her own head, a passenger looking out through the window of a car. She senses Ba'Neene, smells her wood-smoke and dry grass scent, feels her bones in her own and she relaxes, letting her grandmother rush all through her. Ba'Neene's eyes peer through hers, searching the bushes at the side of the culvert, seeing every plant and insect in great detail. Her hands are compelled to reach out to a purple fleshy plant and crush it between her palms, releasing a sharp sour smell. Through her mouth her grandmother begins to chant under her breath.

'Luse?' The two boys are watching her, mouths hanging open.

'What's happening to her?' Eli backs away.

'It's okay, Eli. She is doing like Ba'Neene used to,' says Joshua and grandmother leans down and kisses him on both cheeks. Luse can feel Ba'Neene's love for Joshua like fire in her stomach.

Then she is turning to the bloody man with her handfuls of pulped flower. She pushes his head back and forces apart his jaws, pushing in the pulp, then squeezes his mouth shut again. Whispering into his ear, she stands up and punches him hard twice, right in the centre of his chest.

The man contorts, his eyes roll back into his head and froth appears at his nostrils as Luse steps sideways and feels her grandmother disengage and disappear as quickly as she came.

'Ahhhh!' The man opens his mouth wide, leans forward and vomits bloody purple liquid into the middle of the ditch.

He retches and retches and, as the children watch, a small black lump flies out from his throat and lands a few feet away in the water. As if released from a stranglehold, the man gasps and shudders all over, his eyes closing in the sensuous pleasure of breath, tears of relief trickling into his beard.

His hands come up to his face, he rubs his eyes, wipes his mouth and spits. 'Thank you,' he says. 'I was about to die...'

For a few minutes he sits and just breathes deeply in and out. Then the Rasta turns his huge sad eyes to Luse and asks, 'Who are you and how did you do that?'

Luse shrugs. 'My grandmother... is... was a healer...' her voice peters out, but the man nods, accepting it.

'Well I am grateful. To you both. That is some gift, little sister.'

'Luse,' she says. 'And this is my brother Joshua and our friend Eli.'

The Rasta grunts, wipes his hand on his very stained and bloody shirt and extends it to shake, clasping their hands firmly.

'I see you are from the school. Your uniforms...'

'It's a bad place,' says Joshua. 'We are running away.'

'It is indeed a bad place,' the man says, his eyes briefly widen with some terrible memory. 'I am running away too. I was trying to find out how the Priestess got her money. And I did.'

He is silent, then he shakes his mane of dreadlocks. 'We must get to Lusaka.'

He recovers quickly, but when he moves it is still with great pain and it takes all three children to help him to his feet and manoeuvre his long lanky frame out of the ditch, across the road and over to a large elephant-grey baobab tree.

Exhausted, dripping with stinking dirty water and sweat, all three children sit with the Rasta, backs against the spongy bark of the baobab and rest. Luse passes around more chunks of the fibrous root and the Rasta reaches deep into his shirt pocket and pulls out a roll of boiled cola sweets which they suck, watching the bright blue sky thicken with the pink and orange dust of afternoon.

On the other side of the massive baobab the tar road is still releasing heat in waves. There is not a car to be heard or seen. Luse gets up and moves away from the rest of the group to pee and when she gets back from the small bush, the Rasta and Eli are discussing how to hitch to Lusaka.

'We'll have to flag someone down,' Eli is saying, but the Rasta, holding his ribs, shakes his still gory dreads.

'There are four of us and we look exactly as if we are on the run. Look at my suit!'

The Rasta's suit was once a smart one. Now he is jacketless, tieless and his once-white shirt is brown with blood and torn in places. The trousers have no knees and are encrusted with green mud.

'Well, how then?' Eli asks sulkily.

'I know,' Luse says. 'I know how we can get a lift to Lusaka...'

It takes nearly two hours, but they are now all squeezed into the front of a small pick-up truck, its back laden with cabbages, driving away from an irate Chinese farmer. The farmer came to a screeching stop when he thought he had hit a child. He hadn't of course. They heard him coming from miles away, the tarmac started thrumming and they crouched at the verge and waited. Then, when the Rasta signalled 'yes', he and Eli threw a large lump of soil at the front of the pick-up and when the famer screeched over to the hard shoulder to see what he had hit, Luse leapt out wailing with Joshua in her arms. The Chinese man, possibly Mr Li of the 'Li's Fine Vegetables' logo painted in blue along the side of the pick-up, came towards them, waving his hands in front of him, horrified, shouting, 'No no! You no be hurt! I help you!'

Feeling very ashamed of themselves, Eli and the Rasta clambered into the front of the truck and pulled away, driving jerkily around the baffled farmer, pausing to sweep up Luse and Joshua before hurtling away into the early evening.

The Rasta is driving whilst holding his smashed ribs and Eli is employed in gear changes. He has had a go in a car before, he says, and his focus is intense and cheerful. Luse rummages around in the front looking for any food that isn't raw cabbage. She produces some strange dried fishy strips from a plastic bag in the glove compartment. She also finds a small battered hand gun, which she immediately stuffs back inside, feeling blood rush from her face. *Imagine if Farmer Li had been carrying it when he got out of the car?*

The journey to Lusaka takes them along the flats of Mazabuku and by evening into the bustling din of Kafue town with its roadside abattoirs and bright market stalls and pool halls.

They drive silently at first, with only the Rasta giving occasional instructions to Eli between his small groans of pain, but after a while as the night thickens around them and the hot sweet air blows cooler through the broken back window, they begin to talk. The Rasta has a gentle, easy way of including them all in the conversation and the children relax, letting the past few days disappear into the backs of their minds. Luse is impressed to find out that Eli was top of his class in school last year; won a prize of a set of encyclopaedias. She already knows that Joshua hates eggs and loves, almost more than life, condensed milk, but she is reassured to hear his light voice chirping away so happily next to her.

Luse, for her part, says she really believes it was their dead grandmother that had shown her the right plant to help the Rasta.

It turns out that the Rasta managed to escape from the Dome after being caught trying to film inside – he doesn't say what he was filming, just shudders. He says he was captured and that black thing was forced into his mouth. But he managed to break free, crawled from a window and ran blindly until he came across the fallen tree. Like the children, he had used it to breach the razor wire, kept running for a short while, but then he had begun to gag and his throat had closed up and if it hadn't been for them finding him...

The night is clear, no sign of rain tonight, stars glitter and the moon is full. Luse empties herself into the night, wishing for her grandmother to return, to come back inside her. She doesn't want to be alone and she wonders if the Rasta will make it all alright. There is fresh blood glistening in his hair. She turns her face to the broken window.

Joshua is sleeping when they top the ridge and see the bright lights of South End Lusaka ahead of them. The Rasta has become quieter and keeps checking in the rear-view mirror. He is finding controlling the wheel a little harder too and must be in considerable pain although he says nothing about it. Luse is still watching him out of the corner of her eye when they turn into the South End roundabout beneath the bulky shape of Findeco house. Suddenly, with no warning, he swings the wheel and swerves wildly across two lanes of traffic, narrowly missing an outraged wheelbarrow boy and a minibus and sending dislodged cabbages bouncing into the headlights of oncoming vehicles. The children shriek, clutching at the seats to steady themselves, and the pick-up teeters, nearly rocking over onto two wheels, but then it slams back onto the road and skids to a stop.

Dust billows around them along with the stench of petrol and hot rubber as the engine dies. The Rasta is gasping, holding his side, and Luse takes a moment to realise he is laughing.

'Sorry about that. We were being followed,' he says at last between chortles. 'They have been on our tail since Kafue. That black Mercedes... I would know it anywhere. Well they damn well got a pile of cabbages through the windscreen!'

Luse and Eli immediately stick their heads out of the windows straining to catch a glimpse of the cabbage-mashed car, but it is gone.

Joshua blearily opens his eyes. 'Are we there yet?' he says and then looks crossly at Luse and Eli as they burst into laughter.

When everyone calms down, the Rasta and Eli put the ragged truck in gear and move off around the corner of Cha Cha Cha Road. They are driving on petrol fumes now and the inner left wheel hub has been dented, the tyre blown. With Eli's help, the Rasta parks the pick-up behind an empty market stall made of sacking and tin. It is dark in this part of town, very few street lights and almost no people, most of the buildings are shuttered and dark, businesses shut until morning. A few charcoal braziers burn on corners where security guards keep watch on the shop fronts, but behind the stall they are out of sight of everyone.

The Rasta turns on the little cab light over the rear-view mirror and, while the children check themselves for further cuts or bruises, he rifles in the glove compartment again. Before Luse can say anything, he pulls out the hand gun and checks it for ammunition, then reaching further in he finds a used padded brown envelope. This he empties and, with an odd look at Luse, an almost apologetic shrug, he digs into his shirt pocket and pulls out the disgusting small black thing that had been wedged in his throat, choking him. *He must have grabbed it from the water in the ditch,* thinks Luse. Just looking at it makes her feel queasy. There are two other objects that he also drops into the envelope; a square bit of plastic with a photo on it and finally a heavy black cross on a chain.

'That's the Priestess's cross!' says Luse, involuntarily shrinking back.

The Rasta nods with disgust, sealing the envelope with obvious relief. He wipes his hands on his shirt, as if the objects are sticky with something unpleasant, then turns his large sad eyes to the children. In the low light Luse sees grey in his dreadlocks. He clears his sore throat for an announcement, 'Look you guys, I have to go and get help and I don't think it is going to be safe for you to come with me. You need to stay here with the truck and I will come back as soon as I can, okay?'

'No! Not okay!' Eli is horrified. 'You can't leave us here.'

'I have to, don't you see? You will be safer here until I get back. I need to move quickly, to find people who can help us, who will even believe us. I can't do it with three children in tow right now. It's just too dangerous.'

Luse watches as Eli's face pales, becomes stone. Her heart aches seeing the light seep away from him again.

'We understand,' she whispers, putting a hand on Eli's shoulder. He shrugs it off and turns away.

The Rasta delves again into the inside of his shirt and pulls out a small silver box. He wipes it clean of most of the blood and hands it to Luse. 'Look – to prove I will be back I am going to leave this with you. This is the most precious thing I own and it could potentially save all our lives. I have to come back to it and I will come back to you. Keep it safe, Luse. Promise.'

Luse nods solemnly and lets Joshua lean over and look at the silver and red box.

'What is it?' he asks, but the Rasta has already cracked open the car door, letting in the smell of charcoal fire smoke and hot concrete. Several mosquitoes attracted by the car light wail as they drift in. Clutching his side, the Rasta drags his legs out one at a time and then balances warily, holding onto the hood of the truck before shutting the door on the children. Then he remembers something, 'Luse!'

Luse sticks her head out of the window. She can already see fresh blood glistening as it seeps through the fingers laced around his ribs.

'Luse,' the Rasta gasps in pain. 'If anything happens... if I don't make it back in the next few hours, take the box to Doctor Geo... sh....'

Luse can't hear him properly. She tries to climb further out of the car window.

'What did you say? Who?'

The Rasta is already moving off. 'The muzungu. Doctor George Shapi...' he calls over his shoulder. 'But don't worry. I'll be right back.'

He wasn't.

10.

They wait all night in the cab, driven to distraction by the mosquitoes and the humidity. At some point it rains, cooling the air, and they sleep a little.

Screetch screetch! Luse wakes with a start, clonking her head on the steering wheel. Joshua is snoring, stretched out on the passenger seat next to her. Eli is not in the cab.

The scratching sound comes again and Luse can make out fingers pressed against the window above her. Out in the darkness she thinks she can see a face peering in but she doesn't call out. The glass window mists with the stranger's breath and Luse squeezes her eyes shut, arm tight over Joshua, until she hears whoever it is shuffling away. Silence descends once more but Luse can't relax. Where has Eli gone? Eventually, stiff and sore, scratching a dozen new insect bites, she sits up and watches the blackness around the car lessen, become diluted with pink and orange. Birds sing as the dawn light gains strength and after an hour or so the noise of traffic becomes louder as people begin to make their way to work.

'Joshua! Joshie wake up!' Luse shakes him gently by the shoulder, as always amazed by her little brother's ability to sleep anywhere.

Groggy and grumpy, he pushes himself up into a sitting position and glares at her. 'I have to weewee,' he says.

'We have to look for Eli. He went off last night.'

'Yes, I know. He said his head hurt and he was going to look for something to eat.'

'In the middle of the night?'

'I don't know. You were asleep. We were hungry. Are you angry?' His cheeks shiver with the beginning of a sob.

'Okay, okay,' Luse soothes him. 'I'm not angry, Joshua. I just wish you would have let me know.'

She pushes at the stiff car doors and helps Joshua out onto the sparse grass on the side of the road. Without looking around to see who is watching, Joshua pulls down his shorts and begins to pee.

Luse scouts around. No one has yet come to open the stall which is painted bright red and advertises a local soft drink and condoms. The ground around is bare and it doesn't look as if anyone is interested in coming over to check on the abandoned pick-up. The pavement is becoming crowded with pedestrians and other stall owners, and the cacophony from the nearby market is getting louder. The road is becoming crammed with cars, bicycles, women in chitenjes and men in suits trying to avoid the large holes in the pavement. The city is roaring into life.

I wonder what day it is? thinks Luse. They kept no diaries at the school but they had just celebrated All Souls Day in class, so she guesses it is the first week in November.

In the truck she finds a cloth that isn't too dirty and, spitting on it, she wipes their faces clean.

'Joshua, we can't stay here. We will have to go and find Eli.'

'What about the Rasta Man?'

'I don't know...'

Luse looks around again for inspiration.

'We need to fill the water bottles at least,' she says, pointing to the crowded pavement adjacent to the market where a line of people is patiently waiting to collect water from a single standpipe.

'You stay with the truck and I'll be right back.'

'You better come back quick,' grumbles Joshua. 'Everyone is just running off.'

Luse grabs an empty bottle from the back seat and dashes across the busy street, narrowly missing a minibus. She is back at the truck less than ten minutes later.

'We need money for the water. They won't even let us have a dribble for drinking. How can we get money? What are we going to do?' She is terribly upset and cannot hide it even from Joshua. Hot tears rise up behind her eyes.

Joshua holds out a fist full of sweaty 1000 kwacha notes.

'Joshua! How did you get that?' Luse is staggered.

Joshua gestures to the back of the pick-up, 'It was stuck between the seats.' At Luse's huge smile he relaxes, proud of his find. 'Are we rich now?' he asks. 'Can we take this to Baama?'

Hours pass with still no sign of either Eli or the Rasta. Luse knows she will have to think about what to do next, for Joshua's sake as well as her own.

They leave the truck and head into the market, locating lunch by the glorious smells emanating from 'Auntie V's Wonderful Café', and order from the sweet-faced woman behind the pots. Every mouthful brings a groan of pleasure from their greasy lips and they eat, staring vacantly at each other. Sighing, heavy with food, they head back to the truck with the intention of having an afternoon nap, but it is gone.

They both stand baffled by the empty space behind the still-empty stall. Tyre marks on the grass and one rotting cabbage are the only signs that anything has been parked there at all.

'It's not your fault,' Joshua whispers to Luse as she stamps her feet in frustration, but she knows that with the truck gone neither Eli nor the Rasta will be able to find them. They can't stay on the grass behind the stall for the rest of the day. They need shade and safety. For the moment she has no idea what to do. They sit down on the grass, snoozing on and off and digesting their lunch.

'Ahhh excuse me? You two children...'

Luse turns around to see a very pretty woman in a baggy brown uniform peering at them over the side of the stall.

'Mulibwanji madam.' Luse isn't sure if she has ever seen a woman security guard before, certainly not one who could have been modelling in a magazine.

'I am looking for Luse and Joshua.' She smiles and her perfect nose wrinkles prettily like something from a Disney film. *Bambi!* thinks, Luse ignoring the rustling, feathery sound in her ears.

'That's us.'

'Eli sent me,' says the woman. 'My name is Tina. I work as a security guard in town during the day and help a local street kid centre with their evening street safety programme. Last night the police picked up Eli who claims to have been kidnapped by a church of all things!' She laughs at the very idea. Her laugh is melodic, light and sweet.

'Anyway, the police thought he might be a bit... you know?' Here she makes the time-old gesture of whirling fingers at the temple. 'They brought him over to the street kid centre for some food and he told me about you guys and where the truck was parked.' She looks around at the empty space.

'The pick-up... someone took it.' Luse is about to explain, but Tina shrugs.

'Come on,' she says. Hand in hand, Luse and Joshua follow her, walking through the outdoor market and plunging into the cool dark of the covered concrete halls with the stink of fishmongers and the din of several hundred radios, CDs and cassettes all being played at different volumes by different marketers. Each stall is separated by an aluminium partition and the entire space is crammed from ceiling to floor with new and second-hand clothes, shoes piled high, cobblers, radio repair shops, tailors, vegetable stalls, bakers and take-away cafés.

The market is badly lit inside and the dirty floors have drains running through them which Luse and Joshua have to jump over, but near the far end sunlight seeps in from a large hole in the roof. Now Luse can see a small black and white sign over one of the partitioned stalls – South End Food Relief Centre. There are a couple of logos underneath that she remembers from the AIDS Day banners she had helped paint, a blue globe and a red cross and sickle.

Tina leads them under the reed matting hanging over the entrance. Thick soupy smells come from several large bubbling saucepans on a set of braziers at the back of the unit. Luse, already full from lunch, finds the combination of heat and meaty smell overpowering and she keeps hearing that annoying feathery sound. A cold sweat trickles down her neck.

The unit has a sole cook, a scrawny white woman with blonde hair braided so tightly that the pink scalp between the rows looks tender and raw. She glances over her shoulder and scowls when she sees Tina. The wrinkles that go with it are deep set and permanent. Tina, all delicate grace and doe-eyed sweetness, acts as if this woman has joyfully extended both arms in welcome.

'Hey there, my sister Ingrid. Eli was telling the truth all along! I found them all safe and well.'

The white woman grunts and turns back to the pot. A drop of sweat falls from her nose into the thick broth. Luse feels nausea climbing up her knees.

'Is Eli here?' she turns to Tina to distract herself.

Tina's smile wobbles just a fraction. 'He'll be along later. I sent him to play with some other children. To have some fun, you know.'

Luse doesn't know. 'Didn't he even leave a message?' she asks.

Tina clucks without irritation. 'He'll be back for the early evening meal. Now I've got to get across town to work but I will see you again this evening. This nice muzungu will look after you till then. Food, somewhere to sleep and everything.'

'Tina,' blurts Luse, 'we have a friend. A man... who said he would come and find us by the truck. But now...'

Luse isn't sure how to ask about the Rasta but Tina surprises her.

'Ah yes, Eli told us about him as well. I have sent messages with several of the other security guards and I am sure when he comes back they will let him know exactly where you are.'

Luse and Joshua are so cheered by this that they leap over and hug her, breathing in her scent of vaseline and rose water. Tina is heavenly.

On the other hand, the white woman just ignores the two children. When Luse asks if there is anything she can do to help, Ingrid doesn't turn to look at her for several uncomfortable minutes. Eventually, she gestures over her shoulder at them, 'What's with the school uniforms? They were talking about them last night with your friend.'

When Luse says nothing, Ingrid puts down the large metal spoon she is stirring with and comes closer. Her eyes are watery blue, red-rimmed from the smoke. She looks exhausted.

'I asked you a question,' she says, irritated, but Luse isn't afraid. She and Joshua have money. They don't need to stay here and Luse has already decided it is time to try and contact Auntie Miriam.

'Come on, Joshua,' she says, grabbing his hand.

'Oh no you bloody don't!' Ingrid sounds panicky. She lunges for Joshua's other hand.

'Ow! You're hurting me!' he cries.

'Ingrid, what are you doing?' a man's voice comes from behind them. Ingrid looks up and her sour face goes red and blotchy with embarrassment.

A white man is ducking in under the matting. He looks strong and is very tanned, with dark brown eyes and yellow blonde hair. Around his neck is a leather thong and a silver cross and he has several friendship bracelets and copper bangles on his wrists.

Ingrid releases Joshua, throwing up her hands. 'I'm doing my best. Some of these kids though... Kawalalas and troublemakers, Duncan,' she mutters but Luse can tell she is ashamed.

'Really? You don't look like trouble, little man,' Duncan smiles and extends his hand to Joshua who grins bashfully. Duncan's dark eyes look down into Luse's and he winks at her. 'Ingrid is quite new here. I am sure she didn't mean any harm.'

He reaches up overhead and pulls at the matting which slithers to the floor, opening up the kitchen to the next-door partition where there are more pots on the go and buckets full of clean plastic bowls. A large door opens out onto the back of the market and Duncan, with Luse's help, puts up an awning that extends from the back door into the late afternoon sunshine. It is coming up to four now and cooling off a little. The endless traffic of wheelbarrow men has slowed and most of the market is shutting down for the evening with only a couple of rickety bars and improvised cafés still blasting music.

Other volunteers, all colours of white, beige and black, begin to arrive and there is much high-fiving and hugging. The volunteers, all American Peace Corps and British VSOs are ebullient and excited and none of them particularly clean. Luse doesn't mind though. They are, Ingrid aside, warm and charming, hugging and cooing over Joshua like he is a puppy and shaking her hand with earnest interest. How does she come to be on the street? What is the uniform she is wearing? Is she hungry? So many questions, but never enough of a pause for Luse to respond. She tries to ask about Eli but no one knows where he has gone.

At about 6pm half of them don orange tabards and organise into groups.

'We are taking half the food to the street,' says Duncan. 'The guys in orange tabards are counsellors who walk the city at night searching for children and young people who are new to the street and need help. We tell them about the different centres in town where they can find shelter and food. It's incredible, man, I mean how any kid can survive alone out there. Blows me away. Hey... it's Tina! Come on guys, let the lady through!'

The crowds of volunteers and children part slightly and Luse is delighted to see Tina has returned.

'Hey Duncan,' she says and pecks him on the cheek. Duncan glows golden pink and wraps an arm around her delicate shoulder. Together they make the most beautiful couple that Luse has ever seen, except Tina pulls away, ducks under Duncan's arm and Luse sees her grin is a little fixed, almost irritated.

'Hey Luse! Good that you are still here.' She bends down to Luse's eye level. 'You were okay with Ingrid then?'

It's not really a question that Luse wants to answer as Ingrid is staring at them both with a furious sulky expression, arms crossed against her skinny chest.

Tina shows Luse a hand-drawn map of the city and the routes each small group usually takes at night.

'Isn't it dangerous?' asks Luse. It is obvious that the wazungu must stick out like sore thumbs in the night. Not just their colour but their appearance in general.

Tina smiles and raises a delicate eyebrow, reading her mind. 'We have a couple of policemen with us when the wazungu are on roster. Otherwise they can get too... err... emoshono. Mostly they mean well. They just don't understand the Zambian way sometimes.' She glances over at Duncan and again Luse notices that odd twist of the lip.

The teams with the tabards head off and street children begin to arrive at the back door. A few at first; little groups of ragged wary creatures with half-closed suspicious eyes and dirt around their mouths. The volunteers, led by Duncan, take a few details and help Ingrid to fill plastic plates with steaming mounds of food and the kids squat down and eat. Only when they are finished do the volunteers approach to ask more questions.

'What's your name? How did you get here? Have you any family? Friends?

Gradually the food is exhausted and the children begin to head off again into the mosquito-filled night.

Looking around at the emptying room, Luse thinks this might be a good time to ask Duncan about phoning Auntie Miriam in Canada. Then she and Joshua will slip away and get a taxi to Rachel's house... She will remember the place when they get close. She still has a little money in her pocket. She is about to tug on Duncan's arm when the sound of beating wings in her head intensifies. All light from the doorway is blotted out as two very fat men squeeze through into the room, bringing with them the smell of stale alcohol and old fishy sweat. They are identical – flattened noses and wide high cheekbones with small long-lashed eyes – apart from a large puckered scar that crawls across one of the men's faces from scalp to lip. They are wearing the same thing too, green tracksuits and gold chains, huge colourful trainers with the laces hanging loose. Behind them comes another man, taller, and although dressed well in a blue shirt and chinos, he is hardly able to stand straight, he is so drunk. From behind him a pack of rough red-eyed teenage boys erupts into the room, laughing and there, in their midst, is Eli. Eli isn't laughing. Eli looks strange, his body is twisted when he walks like he is in pain and even from a distance Luse can see that his eyes are red like he has been crying. He is trying to creep away from the big boys along the back wall.

Luse wants to run over to him but the atmosphere has changed completely. An ominous cool settles over the room in spite of the men's noisy entrance. They take up all the air, hugging the volunteers too hard and shaking hands too vigorously. One of the muzungu women cries out in pain as a fat twin pinches her breast roughly before slapping her bottom. Luse notices several street kids flattening themselves against the walls like Eli, sinking low, trying to remain unseen as they creep towards the door. More than a few dash away silently into the darkness.

'Duncan, my brother,' says one of the fat twins, the one with the puckered scar across his face. He whacks Duncan on the back so hard that Duncan lurches forward and the golden god of the Peace Corps brigade seems to diminish, his light doused like water thrown over a candle.

'Hey Spider. Howzit?' Duncan is tense and uncomfortable. 'Umm look guys... I thought we agreed you wouldn't be coming here anymore.'

'Oh yah yah,' says Spider. 'We agreed, sure, but that was last week. Today is another day and we are running short of supplies. You know what I mean.' He makes a thrusting movement with his pelvis and the pack of teenage boys howls and whoops. 'We have lost another couple of workers and our business could be damaged if we don't replace them and pay their funeral costs soon. Plus...' he raises his bulbous toad-like head and peers around at the children, 'we have heard that you are harbouring fugitives. Bwana Duncan. It is our duty, my friend, to collect them. I believe they are...?'

He stands on his toes and makes a play of looking around, twisting and turning, his grotesque belly sliding out over his trousers. Then covering his eyes, he sticks out his arm and spins around until he staggers to a stop, his finger pointing.

Too late Luse realises Spider is pointing directly at her. She feels a sharp push from behind and, unable to stop herself, steps forward. Shocked, she looks to see who has pushed her and there is Tina, lovely silky-skinned Tina, smiling peacefully, blowing the fat man a kiss.

'Thank you, my baby,' says Spider, returning the gesture. He steps over to Luse and gestures dramatically, his hand sweeping over her clothes.

'This uniform bro... this is not the uniform of a street kid. No. This is the uniform that says "Property of Madam Priestess". This one and...' he looks around, twisting his thick neck so that the fat splurges over his collar, 'yes, and this one.'

Spider reaches out an arm and plucks up something, holding it aloft in the air. Spider is holding Joshua by one leg. He hangs upside down, his mouth open in a howl of fear.

Luse screams whilst the rest of the drunken men and boys laugh, slapping their legs and braying.

Duncan pushes forward through the other volunteers. 'Look they are just kids, Spider. I am sure they ran away because they wanted to be back with their friends on the street again. It's no crime.'

'Ah, but you are wrong Duncan, mwana. It is exactly that. A crime. You see if someone feeds you, clothes you and keeps you, then you should be grateful always. Honour thy father and mother, right bro? Well the Priestess became their mother and her heart has been broken by their ingratitude. They stole from her, they spied on her... they are traitors to Zambia.'

'We didn't!' shouts Luse, furious and very frightened.

'Traitors?' Duncan is pale. 'Come on, Spider, I mean, for crying out loud man, he's just a kid.'

Spider swings Joshua in the air, almost to the wall, and Luse claps her hands over her mouth, agonised. Joshua is choking in fear, his eyes wide, tears flying through the air.

'These kids helped a spy. That makes them what, Bwana Duncan? That makes them traitors. A spy, a bad, bad man who was threatening all Madam Priestess has been trying to do for these ungrateful cockroaches.' He holds Joshua up higher, staring into the child's face. 'I should tear you apart. It would be easy to take your leg... like a chicken drumstick.'

Luse is faint with fear, but just as she is about to move, she feels two heavy arms closing around her shoulders. The tall drunk man has crept up behind her, giggling. He is breathing in her ear and the stench of beer and worse is coming off him in waves.

'I will punish this one too, right Spider, my brother? It's my turn. You had the other...' He stops to belch loudly and Luse kicks out, pushing the man's sticky, grasping hands away as they reach for her skirt. In his drunkenness he slips sideways, dragging Luse to her knees.

'Ha! This is a fiery one!' he titters and the big boys yell encouragement and clap. Luse is vaguely aware of Duncan and some of the volunteers shouting too, but in anger. From the corner of her eye she sees Ingrid step forward as if to help, but then, shuddering, stepping back, turning her face away.

'Stop it!' A young Chinese volunteer, pale and outraged, comes forward to stand next to Duncan. 'We are going to call the police! Right, Duncan?'

But at this Duncan lowers his head and again the fat twins chuckle. Spider's brother thrusts out his chest and waves a finger in the boy's face. 'You can call the police. Sure, sure. Ask to speak to the Deputy Chief Inspector at Central. He is my brother. The first born.'

'Or,' says Spider, 'you could call immediately for... now what is your rank again, buti?'

The drunk man, who has pushed aside Luse's flailing hands and grabbed her collar, looks up blearily.

'Detective Inspec...' he burps again loudly and the young men howl with mirth again. 'Detective Inspector,' he says. He twists Luse's collar and she chokes. Tears of fear and rage flood her eyes as he pushes her forward onto the filthy floor. She tries to claw at him but he puts a knee on her back, twisting her arm roughly behind her. Her shoulder explodes with pain and his weight is overpowering. She just manages to raise her head and sees Duncan talking again, pleading, and now several of the other volunteers, upset and frightened, are closing around him but Luse can't hear what is being said. The man's weight is crushing her. Black waves are rising up under her eyelids and she feels as if she is floating away, watching the drunk man pushing up her skirt, exposing her buttocks, scrabbling at her pants. She hears her heartbeat and the sound of beating wings getting louder and louder. The sound seems to be rushing up from deep under the concrete and the earth beneath her body, rushing towards her, huge and furious and...

11.

Screaming. Terrified screaming. It's not coming from her though. No...
Luse is standing up in the middle of the room and the screaming is coming
from all around her. There is smoke too and the snapping cackling fizz of
fire. She tries to move but can't and looks down to find Joshua hugging her
tightly, howling into her breastbone.

'Luseeeee!'

Confused, she pats at his head. She isn't sure where she is but she feels
odd, tingling all over. She feels pretty good in fact.

'Joshua? Hey Joshua... what's wrong? What's going on?'

'Luseee! Stop it!'

'Stop what, Joshua? Hey, hey...?' She reaches down, pulls his arms away
from her sides, and looks at his face. His eyes are tightly shut, snot bubbling
from his nostrils.

'Joshua?' She has to raise her voice above the noise. 'What's going on?
What's all the shouting?'

Out of the corner of her eye she sees a tongue of flame reach out and
lick a pile of bamboo matting. There is a cracking, splintering sound and
the matting seems to explode into flame.

Luse is calm, so calm. She pulls Joshua around so that her back is facing
the flames and gently pushes him forward into the clogging black smoke.
Her body feels cool in spite of the roaring fire behind her; not a drop of
sweat trickles down into her eyes. She knows that the back door is open and
now can feel the suck of air. There are still screams coming from behind
her and she turns and yells, 'Follow my voice! The back door is here and
it's open! Follow my voice! Tiyende! Tiyende!'

Within seconds panicking bodies are flying past her, coughing and
sobbing for breath.

'This way!' she yells again, still terribly calm. Then, with Joshua wrapped
around her, she walks steadily out and into the crowd of shouting red-eyed
people gathering in a frantic mob outside. She sees Duncan, very pale and
wide-eyed, counting heads, shouting names as volunteers and children
mill around him.

A hand on her shoulder. It's Eli, his eyes huge, reflecting the flames
coming from behind them. Next to him is another boy, possibly the ugliest
person Luse has ever seen.

'Luse, is it you now?' Eli whispers as if he doesn't want the other boy to hear.

'What are you talking about?' Luse is baffled. 'Of course it's me...' She is becoming irritated by Joshua who refuses to slacken his grip.

'Come on now, Joshua. Stop it... you are fine now.'

'We have to get out of here,' hisses the ugly boy and points to where a gang of people is organising a line of buckets from the standpipe. Several policemen have also arrived on the scene and one of them is shouting orders.

'Shouldn't we help?' asks Luse.

'Help? There are *police* there. Police, Luse!' Eli looks flummoxed. 'Don't you remember?'

Luse can remember, if she wants to, but she doesn't. She is still feeling too good, too powerful.

'Really... there might still be people inside.'

'Luse! Stop messing around!' Eli prods her and pain shoots through her shoulder.

No. I will not remember, she insists sulkily to herself. *Not yet.*

'Okay then. Where shall we go?'

'You need new clothes,' says Eli's ugly friend. 'There is no way I am going to hang with you in those uniforms. We'll get picked up in no time.'

Luse looks down at her scuffed and filthy skirt. She can't think of anything she would like to get rid of more. 'Yes,' she says eagerly.

'Look, over there.' Ugly Boy gestures to the left of the crowd. One of the marketers running from the fire has abandoned their salula bundle. 'We need to drag it to somewhere where we can get the clothes out.'

Luse and Eli nod and, peeling a still distraught Joshua from around Luse's waist, they scuttle sideways to the bundle and haul it away from the crowd and the fire, behind a nearby wall.

'No dresses,' says Luse. 'I am going to have to be a boy from now on, okay?'

Ugly Boy grins and slaps her on the back. 'Good, you are thinking of survival. Like a ninja!'

'Come on then!' she orders, throwing clothes to each side. Joshua has steadied himself and now comes over to help.

'Take these!' Luse thrusts T-shirts at him. 'Quick, put on as many as you can. One over the other!'

Joshua manages to put on five and a huge grin breaks through the snotty, tear stains on his face. The noise beyond the wall is increasing and there is the sound of a fire engine. Arms laden with stolen clothes, Luse, Joshua and Eli follow the ugly boy further into the maze of the partially empty market, keeping out of sight of the people who rush past in the direction of the fire.

'Who's that guy?' whispers Luse to Eli as they jog along the outer wall. She gestures at Ugly Boy.

'His name's Bligh. He is cool. He knows loads of stuff.'

'Is he... is he ill?' Luse isn't sure how to ask about Bligh's bulging eyes and stick-thin limbs.

'I don't think so. I think he's just like that.'

Luse is losing that wonderful tingling feeling of strength and energy. Her shoulder feels bruised and her throat is becoming increasingly hoarse. She is gradually becoming aware of other scratches and bruises on her legs, the backs of her hands, her chest. And like that she remembers the drunken policeman in the market, choking her, kneeling on her. His hand pulling at her pants... She stops, bends over and vomits. Joshua runs over but she holds a hand up, warding him off.

'It's alright,' she gasps. 'I am alright.' The others wait, Bligh's eyes roaming around, Eli's ashamed, looking at his feet. At last she straightens out and now all the sweetness has fled from her body.

'Did I kill him?' she asks Eli directly.

'I don't know,' he mutters, not looking up. 'He was going to... well he was trying to... and then you just stood up from underneath him and kind of pushed him, but really hard. He fell into the cooking mbaula and went on fire.'

Luse stares at him.

'Yes,' whispers Eli. 'I think you killed him.'

'I hope so.' Bligh astonishes them. 'I hope that fucker burnt long and slow. I wish I had been the one to kill him! There will be hundreds of kids thanking you all over Lusaka, I am telling you.'

'And the others? Those...?'

Bligh laughs but without humour. 'The Twins can't die as far as I am aware. Once someone tried to blow up Spider in his car. He didn't even stay one night at the hospital. Come on. We need to get moving.' He jogs off ahead down the dark alley. 'Keep close!' he calls and Luse, aching and shaking now, is the one who is pulled forward by Joshua.

Bligh guides them artfully out into Kabwata township but he won't let them rest, except for a few minutes behind a garage to change their clothes.

'You are lucky,' says Bligh when she comes out. 'You all still have your school shoes.' He sticks one of his feet up in the air. His soles are grey, cracking and leathery and he has scar tissue on the end of lumpy misshapen toes, no nails. Joshua makes a face.

'You need to know that until your feet have hardened, they are your weakest point,' Bligh says proudly. 'A cut gets infected easily.' He peers at

Luse, head on one side as she comes over. 'Yah, good. You make a good boy. You look tough enough,' he adds, winking one red-rimmed eye at her.

Eli is holding his head, still walking as if in pain, but when Luse tries to ask him about it he spits on the ground and tells her, without making eye contact, to just shut up.

'I'm hungry,' says Joshua for the tenth time. He is also tired and has a bad cough from the smoke in the market. Luse can tell that what he really needs is a long good rest.

'Where are we going, Bligh?' she calls over to the two boys who are staking out a long empty piece of land to see if it is safe to cross.

'Shhh,' he says. 'You really never can tell who is about in the dark.' He sidles back to her side. 'We have to get beyond the Twins' boundary. There is not one person we can trust otherwise, no other kids, security, bus drivers... no one.'

'The Twins' boundary?'

'Yeah, they control everything south of Church Road. And several blocks along Great East too... but we should be safe once we hit Northmead.'

'How far?'

'We are going to have to head through to neutral zones. George and Chaisa compound.'

Luse's stomach turns over. The Flight Deck Bar is in George compound. Her dad's old place! Maybe she can find Daddy's old friend, Masuouo? But even as she thinks this she dismisses it. She has seen enough men like Masouso in the last few months. Without her father's protection she knows that he will not be her friend. *How changed I am*, she thinks. *Am I a bad person now?*

12.

The first few days on the street are a blur for Luse. She is constantly terrified and hungry and they never seemed to find anywhere to sleep for more than an hour or two before Bligh is shaking them to move on. 'Trust no one' is Bligh's guidance at all times, in all situations. He doesn't have to remind Luse that she murdered a policeman, a cop. She might be arrested and beaten to death before they can even get to a trial.

In the second week Luse knows she is going to have to sharpen up. There have been rumours circulating among the street kids that the Twins have offered a reward for Luse and Joshua. She has noticed that Bligh has started looking at them differently, as if assessing how much they are worth. She knows they are holding him back, that he is considering dumping them. Kindness is not a useful commodity on the street. It can't be sold or bartered. There is safety in numbers to be sure. More kids together mean more eyes to keep watch, more hands to rifle through rubbish, more muscle to fight off stray dogs, rats and the older boys and men who find raping children faster and more satisfying than trying to date adults. But Bligh is used to working alone and now, with three new kids, he is having trouble finding enough begging time. Sooner or later he will hand them over or they will find him gone.

Luse and Joshua are camped under a stairwell in a half-demolished block of flats. They are trying to sleep on piled up rubbish and the flies and mosquitoes, even at his time of night, are dreadful. The stink they hardly notice anymore. Bligh and Eli have gone to beg outside the Omega Bar, a popular night spot near the Lebanese supermarket, but Joshua has had a bad bout of diarrhoea and Luse can't leave him. It is hardly surprising. The rain has failed to make a proper appearance and the heat means everything rots so quickly that any scraps they find in the trash are already putrefying. All of them, except Bligh, have been sick and for the first time Luse has to deal with the fact that being homeless means there is no way of finding adequate and private places to be sick in or to clean up afterwards. They shit balanced precariously over open sewers, sometimes, if the cramps are bad, just in the nearby bushes. Sickness leaves them weak and dizzy and vulnerable to attack from other kids or adults. Luse's bundle of spare clothes from the market has been stolen and Joshua no longer has any shoes, which means she has to lug him around on her hip when she feels strong enough.

God, how Luse hates never being clean. On the occasions when they find a working tap unattended, Bligh stands guard while Luse washes Joshua all over and then rinses and rings our their quickly greying clothes. Eli has less interest in washing and, more worryingly, almost no interest in food. He has pain when he goes to the toilet and sometimes screams out but refuses to let Luse help him. His head has become worse too and he moans constantly, even in his sleep. When he is awake he scratches around his scar until it bleeds and Luse has noticed that his eye bulges slightly on that side.

He doesn't want to talk and he doesn't want to help beg. All Eli wants is drugs. 'Nifuna nifuna nifuna' – I want I want I want – he whines pitifully, badgering Bligh until Bligh drags him off to score some grass or get a hit of glue from a supplier at a nearby garage – a petrol-soaked patch on his sleeve that he can sniff and suck on for a few hours.

When drugged, Eli can sleep and Luse and Bligh find it easier to talk and try and make plans to find their next mouthful of food. As soon as Eli wakes it starts all over again. 'Nifuna bostick, nifuna chaamba,' on and on. *He is more of a baby than Joshua*, Luse thinks. She is beginning to hate him.

Now sitting in the virtual toilet of the stairwell, flies clogging the corners of Joshua's mouth, Luse realises that they are going to die here if she can't pull herself together. Now, more than ever before, she feels the weight of Joshua, the responsibility of having another life to drag around, to care for and to love. For a fleeting second she considers leaving him in the rubbish and just running away, she could just keep going until...

'Luse?' Joshua's voice is croaky. He doesn't sound six years old. He sounds old like Ba'Neene. Luse sighs and tries to stop crying, puts her hand out and takes his little one, squeezes it hard.

And there it is. All this time she has been staring out at the vacant lot in front of the flats. It is covered in rubbish, plastic bottles, bits of cardboard and plastic bags flapping about in the dust. But there, right there, is a scrubby thorny plant with little yellow-tipped leaves and small pale flowers clustered at the ends of the branches. Luse slaps her forehead.

Nakasanza. Gran's favourite cure-all. She has seen it growing before but in woodland where it was lusher and taller. She didn't recognise it here, hidden among the rubbish and dust.

By the time Eli and Bligh come back from the club, Luse has a fire and, boiling up a little of their precious water, has made a paste of the leaves and roots of the plant. Joshua has already had several doses and is feeling much better, sitting up with Luse, prodding at the fire with a long piece of wire. Eli barely notices anyone, just staggers past into the foul-smelling stairwell and goes to sleep. Bligh, however, comes over and sniffs at the goo, looking askance at Joshua.

'You can make medicine... mankwala?'

'Yes,' says Luse. 'But I need a proper metal pot to cook with. This piece of tin I was using cracks too easily.'

'What is it for?'

'I can make stuff from that plant for stomachs,' Luse says pointing. 'And I can make stuff from the one over there for cuts and bruising. I think I can anyway.' She pauses, not looking up, then casually adds, 'We could sell it.'

'What about food?'

Luse moves aside to show Bligh a small pile of hard fruit. 'I found a musikil tree! This fruit needs peeling and cooking for a really long time. Then you have to mash it all up and dry it and then you cook it all over again. It is a lot of work but it makes a kind of porridge.'

'Is it good to eat?'

'No, it's gross.' Luse pulls a face. 'But my Gran told me it makes you strong in times of drought. When I am stronger I can find more fruit. Better. And maybe plants for relish.'

'Cool,' Bligh nods. 'Okay. I am going to sleep now and then I am going to steal you a pot.'

13.

From that day, Luse becomes an adept scavenger. Her eyes constantly seek out every shrub, bush and tree for potential foods or medicines. Bligh is fascinated and watches her closely. After a few weeks he is almost as well versed in the local fruit trees and roots as she is.

They still have the problem of protein and protection. Eventually Luse feels that she has to consider a strategy for stealing from some of the bigger supermarkets. She can't beg like Bligh and she won't let him use Joshua, but he is the only one sourcing the money for Eli's drugs and their occasional buns and sausages. She agrees with Bligh that they must join forces with some of the other ragged groups of children who, like them, drift around the outskirts of the city.

'I can't be found out. I can't be a girl.' Luse is nervous, but Bligh reassures her.

'You are probably going to have to have at least one fight then, just to prove yourself. When it happens you must attack first and keep on attacking until the other one is down. You hesitate and it won't go well.'

And he is right. Her first fight is quick and pretty painless. It happens one night when the first heavy rains come and their current ditch floods. They are forced to shelter in a culvert with several other young children led by a brutal-looking boy called Franklin. He says they can't come in, stands in the way with his hands on his hips, and without even having to think about it, Luse jumps on him, shouting as loud as she can, knocks him to the ground and punches him in the mouth. He surrenders immediately and later she gives him a bit of salve for his split lip and they make grudging friends.

But Eli, trailing along behind Luse and Bligh, is no longer able to hold down Luse's medicine. He is all stick bones and huge swollen head, his eyes constantly drug red.

'We have to get him to a doctor,' says Luse. She is thinking about the Rasta and the doctor George Shapi. Maybe they should try and find him? They still have the silver box. Bligh and Eli wanted to sell it for drugs but Luse refused, hiding it from them, tying it into Joshua's clothes.

'The only doctors who will see street children are on the Twins' side of town,' Bligh says. 'One in Kabwata and two on Cairo Road. And even then they will not give us free medicine.'

At this Luse feels her stomach turn over. They can't go back there. Not ever. She stops thinking about it and instead tries to block out Eli's constant moaning. He sleeps most of the day now. When awake he can only manage a tiny bit of food and then cries for a toke or a sniff of something to take away his pain.

The Rushing World

1.

Luse stops speaking. She holds her hands up, shaking her head, still seeing Eli lying on the sodden newspaper on the cold concrete. Georgia gently takes her flailing hands and rubs them. 'It's alright, Luse. It's alright.'

Luse looks up at her, Georgia's eyes are so clear. *How can I explain how it is out there?* thinks Luse. The fan clunks overhead and the fridge chatters and quiets.

'Eli didn't wake up one day and... we had to leave him and... I didn't get him to a doctor in time.'

'Luse,' Georgia says. 'It sounds to me like he had a subdural haemorrhage. That he had bleeding in his skull. There was nothing you could do. There was probably nothing anyone could have done.'

Luse looks down, pulls her hands away. She knows Georgia is being kind, but the words do not ease the thick greasy knot of guilt in her stomach.

'Luse,' Gus takes her gently by the shoulders and gives her a tiny shake, 'you are one amazing little girl! I have met plenty of armed soldiers with less chutzpah, less resourcefulness and courage.'

'I agree.' Bernard smiles solemnly and clasps Luse's hand. She doesn't even notice. She is seeing Eli, alone, lying on the newspaper as if he is asleep... except his chest is still and there are already flies inside his mouth and eyelids.

They work out the rest together as Luse has been unable to keep a clear track of time during her months on the street.

'By my reckoning, I put you and Joshua on the streets from the first week in November. That's over four months, Luse.'

There are still so many questions but there seems to be an understanding between the adults that Luse has spoken enough for the moment.

'We need her Aunt Miriam's married name,' Gus says. 'After all this time I bet she is frantic.'

'I will ask her,' says Georgia, watching as Luse heads to the fridge to help herself to a Mazoe orange juice. 'You know, I see those kids at the clinic once a week and I have never, even once, considered the idea of not having access to clean water. As a doctor too. It is pretty disgraceful. And *no*, Gus, do not even think of wheeling out the do-gooder muzungu bullshit.'

Gus grins, exposing rather sharp white canines, 'I wouldn't dream of it.'

Georgia refuses to smile back, turns to the priest, 'Bernard, who deals with all this? With these street children?'

'There are several government initiatives, UNICEF, Red Cross... several small voluntary organisations. It all rather crept up on us. Previously we always had the extended family. Suddenly aunts and uncles were dying as quickly as everyone else. There is such stigma around HIV and AIDS that the orphans of people who have died tend to be scapegoated. Sometimes these children are demonised, treated like dogs, abandoned.'

'Oh for God's sake.'

'I don't think God has much to do with it,' sighs Gus.

'Try telling that to the Priestess,' snaps Father Bernard.

2.

The next morning Georgia is in a flap. She hasn't slept well; her brain is clogged with Luse's story, with the weight of her responsibility to the children, with thoughts of Gus. All night this has kept her fretting, tossing and turning. Now, trying to put on mascara, her hand slips and she smudges black goo across her nose.

'Shit,' she says, not for the first time this morning. She is already running late for work. Nearly 7am and she is going to hit rush hour.

'Shit,' she says again.

Georgia quickly checks on the children, who are still mounds under the bed sheets. Gus is on his way to pick up Luse. He has promised to be her bodyguard while she buys some clothes for herself and Joshua. For Luse's safety he is not taking her to the markets but to the main mall at Manda Hill.

'You awake, honey? Gus will be arriving at about nine, okay?'

There is a muffled 'Okay' from Luse and Georgia tiptoes out and flies down the stairs, braiding her hair and scanning the floor for her shoes. She gives Yvonne a look that says 'Don't ask' and thanks her for getting in so early again.

'Sure, sure, Georgia,' says Yvonne, bustling into the kitchen and coming out waving a banana. 'They are good children.' She sticks the banana into the pocket of Georgia's white medical coat and points to the teapot on the table. Georgia shakes her head.

'I'll get coffee at the clinic, thanks.'

Marta and Joshua are already at the dining room table, drinking milky tea and eating sugar-encrusted cereal that Georgia doesn't remember buying. Joshua smiles at her, milk running down his chin. She kisses the tops of their heads before grabbing her car keys. She hesitates, looking back at Joshua. He is tipping his tea carefully into Marta's cereal bowl.

'Go on,' Yvonne calls from the kitchen. 'They will be just fine.'

Georgia's morning is packed and she doesn't get a chance to call home until just gone 11am. There is no answer. *Odd*, she thinks, twirling the phone cord absently and looking out the window. There, washing Georgia's car, is the pretty woman security guard. It is with a cold twisting in her gut that Georgia remembers it is the very same woman who was selling talk-time to the fat twins two days previously. Twins... one with a puckered scar. My God! The Twins? And that must be Tina, the woman Luse described, the one who lured the children to the volunteer centre. Tina must have been spying on the clinic... on her! Without thinking, Georgia bangs hard on the glass and the woman raises her head and stares. She is very beautiful but her expression is like a dog bite. Georgia steps back from the window, shocked by the hatred in the woman's eyes.

'Get away from my car!' she shouts and bangs again on the window. Tina shrugs, raises her hands and drops the hose, backing away slowly, then she whips around and runs out of sight. Georgia fumbles for her mobile, calls the house again. Nothing. This time it doesn't even ring and Georgia knows that something is very, very wrong. Shaking, she calls Gus. He answers immediately.

'Augustine.'

'Gus! It's me. They are here!'

'Who? Calm down, Georgia. I will just get some space.' There is a lot of background noise, syrupy shop muzak and the ping of tills.

'Tina, that security guard Luse told us about. She's been working here all along. I saw her with the Twins just a couple of days ago. I think... I don't know... they're after the children... Is Luse safe?'

There is a pause. She hears Gus shift the phone to his other ear. 'Hang on, Georgia.'

She hears him call Luse. Hears a faint response.

'We are fine. But now I want you to stay where you are, keep in full sight of people, your staff and the nurses. Just wait and we'll come.'

'No! I can't stay here! Yvonne isn't answering the phone!'

He gives a muffled curse. 'Okay, I am closer than you! I am going to go there right away and I will call you from the house. Stay put! Do you hear me?'

But Georgia has grabbed her medical bag and is already half way out of the room. For a moment she thinks about telling one of the nurses to call the police, but what would be the point when they still don't know how many of the Lusaka cops are involved with Blood of Christ and the Twins.

She sticks her head around the door of her colleague, Doctor Chisanga. 'Could you cover for me, Leon?' she asks. 'I've got a home emergency. Only Mrs Bannerjee and her husband to see.'

Leon groans, 'Mrs Bannerjee. She of the terminally fallen arches? Alright, but you owe me!'

Outside, Georgia looks around for Tina but she is nowhere in sight and the main gate has swung wide open. Telling herself she is overreacting, that she is overtired, head full of scary stories, Georgia clambers into her car and reverses out of the tight parking space and turns right into Cairo Road. She takes the North End roundabout too fast, overtakes a spluttering Datsun on the inside and speeds into Great East.

Stop panicking you bloody idiot, she thinks, but her foot stays heavy on the accelerator and she tips the car into fifth gear. The dual carriageway is busy and she is forced to weave through traffic. She feels a slight lurch on her right side and hears a dull thumping sound, but then the road ahead is clear and she puts her foot down again. Only the road isn't clear. There is a funnel of what looks like smoke ahead, dense black smoke or thick dust spiralling upwards like a mini tornado. She is wondering about whether she should drive through it when she realises it is birds. Thousands, maybe millions, of tiny birds in the strangest formation she has ever seen, twisting around and around each other and upwards. Amazed, she brakes, slows right down until she is almost at a stop, with the traffic forming a hooting queue behind her. Suddenly the car lurches violently to the right and with horror she sees in her rear-view mirror that her back wheel is rolling away down the road.

Had she been going any faster, she would have veered into the oncoming traffic, possibly flipped over. As it is, at the speed she has reduced to for the birds, the heavy four-by-four fishtails wildly, metal screaming against the tarmac, but she is able to keep control, hauling at the steering wheel with her entire weight, taking her foot off the brake and sliding across the slow lane into a deep ditch at the side of the road.

She turns off the engine and sits in shock, hanging slightly forward in her safety belt, breathing in the thick cloying smell of burning rubber and feeling her heart trying to break through her ribs.

'Shit,' she whispers.

Already a crowd is gathering. A man taps at the window. 'Madam, are you hurt?'

She shakes her head.

'She is fine,' the man informs the other people gathering around the car. The small crowd cheers and faces beam at Georgia through the windscreen. She braces herself against the back of her seat and unclips the safety belt, before gingerly opening the door. The kind young man helps her out.

'You better shut and lock your car, madam,' he advises, glancing around at the little mass of people. 'The police will be here soon and will help organise a tow.'

'Did you see them? Did you see the birds?'

The man widens his eyes. 'Birds, madam?'

Georgia looks at the road and sees nothing but the stream of traffic. The air above the road is clear.

'Did you bang your head?' the man is asking kindly. 'Do you want to sit down?'

'No... no. I am fine... Thanks. I must have imagined it.'

A couple of dusty street kids have skipped through the traffic to collect her tyre and one has even found her hubcap and a couple of wheel nuts. They present them to her solemnly, helping to throw them into the boot.

'Evidence,' says the young man.

'Evidence?' asks Georgia trying to be surreptitious about handing the street kids their finders' fees.

'Your tyre. How can such a one fall off? It has six nuts. It is not a common accident.'

Georgia has a headache and her mouth is terribly dry. She reaches back into the car for her water bottle and medical bag. The young man looks as if he is about to move off.

'Please, you have been so helpful,' she says. 'Would you be able to wait with my car for the police? I have a sick child at home.' She hates to lie but she doesn't know what else to do. 'I will leave you my purse and my address and phone number and if you could just hand it to them? I will be right back.'

The young man cocks his head. He has a dreamy, thoughtful face and a wide philosopher's brow. 'There is no need to leave the purse. But may I take your number? Payment will be a drink?'

In spite of all that has just happened, Georgia cannot help smiling. Slightly abashed, she takes back her purse and nods. The rest of the crowd is dispersing and she quickly jots down her name and number on a page of prescription pad, tears it off and hands it over. Meanwhile the kind young man has flagged a taxi down. She thanks him, shakes his hand.

'I will call you!' he shouts as she drives away. 'Jabulani Kongwa is my name!'

The taxi is very old and battered and has no front seat, in fact there is a small hole right through the car and consequently the exhaust fumes funnel up into the back. By the time they reach Georgia's house her headache is monstrous and she is nauseated and trembling.

'Hey Mummee!' The driver has been talking to her the entire journey but she has barely been able to respond. 'We are arrived.'

Throwing kwacha notes at him, Georgia staggers out of the car and hammers on the main gate. But it is already opening and Gus is there and behind him Eddie is looking anxious alongside another man that Georgia doesn't recognise.

'Georgia? Where is your car?' She sees Gus's eyes widen as he takes in her dishevelled state. 'What hap...?'

She can only hold out her hand and shake her head. He understands. *Don't worry about me*, she is saying.

'Have you got your medical bag?' he asks.

This she can cope with.

'Yes,' she says, immediately calming, stepping into her doctor's role like pulling on rubber gloves. 'Take me through.'

The house is a wreck, but Georgia has eyes only for the two bodies on the kitchen floor.

'I will need you to help me, Gus,' she says kneeling next to Yvonne. Her assessment is quick, thorough.

'Yvonne, can you hear me?'

Yvonne groans loudly, 'Marta? Is my little one alright?'

Georgia looks up and is relieved when Gus nods. 'She's absolutely fine. She hid outside in the garden. Didn't see a thing.'

'I tried to stop them...'

'Shh now. Yvonne, you have a broken arm and some cuts and bruises that I can see. Is there anywhere else that is causing you pain?'

The other person down is Wilson, the complex's gardener. He has a nasty-looking head wound and there is a lot of blood, but it is relatively shallow and Georgia finds that he is otherwise unhurt. She has given Gus the numbers for the clinic emergency ambulance and, as she finishes dressing Wilson's head wound, she hears its peeping horn at the gate.

'Gus! Where is...?' But then she sees Luse, sitting on the sofa in the living room. Eddie is next to her, with a wide-eyed Marta on his lap. Luse is silent, staring at her feet. Georgia is about to run forward when Gus takes her arm.

'Georgia. You must know that Joshua was taken. Luse and I got here too late.'

'Oh no.' Georgia feels emptied out. 'By who?'

'We don't know yet, but we can guess. Yvonne said the men were dressed as police but there was a woman who didn't get out of the car. It was a black Mercedes.'

Georgia takes it in and feels the weight of it around her neck. 'Okay... how is she?'

'Not good. She blames herself for leaving him here.'

Brushing hair from her face, Georgia picks up her medical bag and heads over to the girl. Eddie stands, gives her a small sad smile, hefts Marta on his hip and moves discreetly away to the side of the room where the paramedics are helping Yvonne and Wilson prepare to travel.

'Luse? Are you alright?'

Luse nods. Her face is stone, her eyes are dry and clear.

'You must *not* blame yourself for this. Do you hear me? Not even Wilson and Yvonne could stop those men. If you had been here you might have been killed.'

'No. I would have killed them.' Luse's voice is small and harsh like ash in the wind. 'If they hurt Joshua I will kill them.'

Georgia takes Luse's pulse. The child's hand is cold and lies unresponsive in hers. 'I am going to give you something that is going to make you feel calm and drowsy. I think you are in shock and I don't want you to get sick. We are going to need your help to catch these people and I will need you to be full force. Alright?'

Luse doesn't move a muscle.

'Luse?'

A small tip of the head.

She gives Luse half a sedative and a glass of water and watches her swallow. 'Good girl. Now I want you to curl up on the sofa and wait for me. I am going to change and then go to the clinic to make sure Yvonne and Wilson are alright. Then you, me, Eddie and Gus are going to go and find Joshua, okay?'

At this Luse finally looks into Georgia's eyes. 'Yes,' she says quietly. Then she curls up on the sofa, eyes shut. 'He is not dead,' she says without opening her eyes. 'I can feel him in my tummy.'

Georgia nods. 'Good. I don't think they will hurt him.'

Not yet, she is thinking and knows Luse is doing the same.

3.

Gus is standing at the kitchen table with Eddie and the other man, a short wiry Zambian with a gleaming bald head. They have pulled a lamp onto the table and it is illuminating a dozen open maps. Georgia should go over and join them, but she aches terribly, only now aware of how bruised she must have been when the car veered off the road into the ditch. She is also spattered with Wilson's blood. She wearily makes her way up the stairs to her bedroom and sits heavily on the bed. She is still wearing her white doctor's coat, but as she tries to shrug it off she gets stuck. Her entire shoulder is frozen, bruised and swollen from the seat belt. Now she is trapped half in and half out of the jacket, hands behind her back, stuck in the sleeves. Tears of frustration and pain pop hot from her eyes.

'Hodi?' Gus sticks his head around the door. 'You decent?' he begins then catches sight of her and his face is such a picture that she can't help but grin through her tears.

'I'm okay Gus, just a little bruised. Could you help me with this jacket?'

He comes into the room, bringing a slight scent of sandalwood and sweat with him. 'We just had a call,' he says, very gently releasing her arms from the coat. 'A man called Jabulani? Says the police are going to impound your car and that they are threatening to arrest you for leaving the scene of an accident.' He looks at her carefully. 'The accident sounded pretty bad.'

She winces and tells him about the wheel coming off.

His face tightens with anger. 'On Great East? Georgia, you could have been killed!'

'I know... I was so lucky... something slowed me down...' She doesn't want to tell him about the birds. She isn't sure he will believe her. Without asking, he has begun to help her peel off her vest top, once white and now caked with gore. He is very gentle, rolling it up over her back and shoulder. Shyly she thanks him, holding her arm up over her bra.

'That's some bruise,' he says and heads into her en suite bathroom to start the shower. 'I'm going to send one of my guys to negotiate with the traffic cops and get your car back,' he says over the sound of gushing water. 'We are going to need it. Right now I am not sure if you and Luse should stay here or not.'

Georgia looks at herself in her dressing table mirror. A thick red and already purpling stripe runs across her body. There is a small cut on her belly where the buckle of her seat belt cut in. She shivers. It was a close call.

Gus comes over and carefully helps her over to the shower.

'Err... Gus... I can take it from here,' she says and he smiles. His eyes are amber.

'Sure? I am extremely good with a sponge.'

Georgia laughs and it hurts. 'Augustus! Be very careful or I will tell you exactly what to do with that sponge!'

'Okay, okay. I'm leaving. I've got my eyes shut,' he adds, closing them before she can say anything and makes a great show of feeling his way back to the door of the room. 'However, with my eyes shut I am afraid my imagination is on overtime.'

'Get out you...!' says Georgia who has gone a little pink, attempting to throw a towel at him with her good arm. She hears him wolf whistle from outside her door.

'You should see what I'm seeing!' he hollers as he heads down the stairs.

4.

Luse is drifting around the room, unfettered by her body which lies curled in on itself like a cat on the couch. She is cool, floating, singing to herself as she flits up, down and around and all the time she can feel the other heartbeat, Joshua's heartbeat, a fast frightened pitter-patter like water dripping on stones right alongside her own steady pulse.

She concentrates on her brother's blood beat, willing to find a way to reassure him, to tell him that they are connected, that she will find him. The thought of the men hauling her terrified brother from the room makes Luse fly higher and faster. She is pinned against the ceiling like a moth. She breathes out, concentrates on Joshua's pitter-patter heartbeat. Frees herself.

She flits around the head of the bald man who stands next to Gus, poring over the maps at the table. He has a small razor nick on his thick neck and smells of coal tar soap.

'So, if we go with Luse's description of the place, we know the school is on an abandoned Chinese site.' The bald man points to the map, 'There are six abandoned building projects in that area. Three road building settlement sites, one farm and a hotel and conference centre. The Chinese Embassy is sourcing the information as quickly as possible.'

Another smell, apples and coconut, and Georgia, long hair still damp and loose around her shoulders, comes down the stairs holding herself stiffly straight, her arm in an improvised sling. Luse notices how Gus turns to her, sees his eyes lighten. He holds out a hand to her as she comes off the bottom step, bringing her within the arc of his body as if they are dancers.

'I have to go to see Yvonne and Wilson at the clinic. Can someone drive me?' she asks, sounding to Luse as if she is speaking from a long way away.

'Sure. The Commander will take you.' Gus introduces the bald man to Georgia, 'This is Commander Peter Mhone. He is our Army Liaison and will be coordinating the special task force on this. He and I have seen a good deal of action together in the past. I trust him with my life.'

The bald man smiles and his long, narrow eyes wrinkle. 'I would be happy to run you in, Doctor. I need to speak with the two casualties if they are strong enough.'

'Has anyone contacted Yvonnes's husband?' Georgia is looking for her handbag, which Luse can see has fallen behind the sofa. 'He has a taxi that he runs out of the airport.'

'Yes, he is already on his way. Father Bernard will be here to help in about an hour. We'll need to pull together everything we have on Selena Clark and The Blood of Christ Church.'

'Good, thank you. I'll try and be back by then.'

Luse, from high above, sees them all look over at her body as she lies on the couch. She sees Gus take Georgia's good hand, squeeze it. 'I'm not leaving her, I promise.'

Georgia leans into him momentarily, then nods at the Commander and they are gone. Gus turns back to the map and the laptop and Luse carries on whirling slowly around the ceiling with the spider webs. He is tapping his nose with a pencil stub. The stub has a silver ring at the bottom that holds the eraser. Luse is entranced by the light glinting off the silver. It reminds her of something.

Silver. She feels a faint weight. Drops down closer to her body.

A silver something... a silver.

She has it. The silver and red box that the Rasta gave her in the car the night they arrived in Lusaka. The night of the fire. The night she killed a man. What had the Rasta said? Something about it being important. 'It could save our lives' he had said.

And like that she is back inside her body, awake, wide awake.

She sits up with a gasp and Gus turns to her from where he is standing at the table.

They have to wait for Georgia to return with the key to her office drawer. Gus could break in, but he thinks there has already been enough vandalism. The fake policemen already ransacked everything, taking Georgia's laptop, but by having overturned the desk, they missed the small locked drawer underneath.

'What's going on?" asks Georgia as she, Bernard and the Commander come through the door to be met by Luse jumping from foot to foot, with Gus obviously equally excited behind her.

'Why did the Rasta give me that silver box?' Luse asks Georgia now.

Of bloody course, thinks Georgia. The silver cigarette box. It isn't even really silver, only nickel-plated and the inscription is sweet but not the most precious thing Harry had owned. Why had he told Luse that it held all the answers? Georgia dashes upstairs as quickly as her bruised body will allow and unlocks the little drawer, plucking out the box.

'Gus!' she calls from the top of the steps and drops it down into his now gloved hands. Once more they all gather around the table as Gus lays down plastic and white paper and opens the box. It is stuffed not with cigarette papers and tobacco, but with something small wrapped tight in a torn dirty piece of bubble wrap and then tighter still with sellotape. Gus uses a scalpel to slice the plastic and then he rolls out...

'It's a memory card,' says Gus.

'What's that?' whispers Luse.

'That is the card that fits into a camcorder,' says Georgia.

'The documentary? Do you think...' Bernard can hardly speak and they all fall silent as Gus pulls his laptop over and checks the connections.

'This one here, I think....' he says and inserts the card. The computer hums energetically and they all lean in, eyes wide.

5.

There are sixteen files on the memory card but only four that can be opened. The first starts in darkness.

A voice: '... on here, Emil, and then hopefully we will pick up no matter how far away you go.'

A second voice, obviously Emil, responds: 'Is it recording now, Jens... Jens... the lens cap? How much do you cost an hour, you fucker?'

Jens: 'For helvede! Sorry.'

There is a crunching noise as the cap is unclipped and a whine as the camera adjusts automatically. Now they can see a long beautiful stretch of pristine lawn, with little white gravel paths leading down to a kidney-shaped turquoise swimming pool.

Jens: 'Okay, Emil. We have picture and sound.'

Emil: 'Right, let's test these mothers! Hey, Rasta Man, can you speak normally and keep walking?'

As they watch the screen, they see a tall man with dreadlocks step in front of the lens. He has his back to the camera but Georgia puts a hand to her mouth. It is Harry. She feels Gus tense beside her and she reaches out for his hand, feels his fingers and squeezes. On screen, Harry walks down the grassy slope towards the pool. He is singing 'The Hills are Alive with the Sound of Music' and the camera fizzes.

Jens: 'Quieter, you crazy Zambian! Too loud and you mess with the pick-up mike!'

Harry blows a loud raspberry and there is laughter.

Emil: 'Just talk!'

Harry: 'Well hello there, ladies. I wonder if I could present to you the two gentlemen of Copenhagen and their talking bear...'

Emil: 'Hey, how far is that? The sound is still crystal.'

Jens: 'Sure is. Tell him to walk to the far end.'

Emil: 'Keep walking, brother! In fact, try going into the pool house.'

Harry begins impersonating a wildlife presenter.

Harry: 'Here, in the wilderness of the Danish Ambassador's garden, we search in vain for the cold beer once promised by foreigners to the local men of this country...'

Jens: 'Okay, very funny... So these radio mikes rock. I reckon we could get clear sound through concrete. Okay, let's get a cold one...'

The second file is an interview. At first Georgia thinks the camera is broken, but it becomes apparent that it has been placed deliberately low. Bodies move past the lens in different directions. There is the sound of cutlery and a hum of conversation and what looks like a tablecloth hanging down over a corner of the lens. Two voices cut clearly through the hubbub – a woman and one of the Danes.

Woman: 'You know that we are only protecting our children by refusing the filming. It would not be in their interests. Many of them have gone through severe trauma in their lives. The last thing we want is to have them exposed to further…'

Emil: 'Madam Clark… or should we call you Madam Priestess now? We understand that of course.'

Now the white cloth is stealthily pulled up, allowing the camera to focus on a small square table in the midst of a busy restaurant. The sharp-boned face of the Priestess is visible, sitting diagonally across from Harry and Emil. She looks relaxed, sipping a Coke with her legs neatly crossed. Emil is hunched forward, a pen poking through his fingers, sweat rings under his arms.

Emil: 'However we are not just interested in the children. We have, as you know, been interested in documenting your new role in this church and your life since leaving Evil Eye Productions. You have acquired a great deal of land and property over the last year.'

Priestess: 'All generous gifts and legacies from our church members. All legal. I believe you already have the names of our lawyers.'

She waves to someone passing, a languid gesture, but the camera picks up her foot tapping pell-mell under the table.

Emil: 'Yes, but we are especially interested in how it is that you seem to have secured so many of the contracts for child-based projects in Lusaka, especially with your previous history. You yourself were rescued off the street we understand, back in Nigeria in the early 70s?'

He bends to consult his notes and does not see the Priestess's face contort. Her foot stops tapping.

Priestess: 'How did you…? No. No, you are mistaken… Slanderous!'

She looks panicked and Harry holds up a soothing hand.

Harry: 'It was just something we heard, Madam. There are rumours of children being taken from the streets, supposedly taken off into the bush to a boarding school?'

The Priestess, regaining her composure, patting her lips with a napkin, replies, 'It is a rehabilitation centre. The first of many I hope and yes, it exists and we are very proud of it, but we insist on it being kept out of the view of any press. In fact its location is restricted to our staff and drivers. The children must be protected.'

Emil: 'The children... I see. Well then may I ask how the families of the children can find it to visit? Who ensures the health of the children? The teaching standards?'

Priestess, laughing: 'I don't know what you are implying! Our children are all abandoned by their families or orphaned. It is rare for them to have any family but us. If they do, of course we insist the family comes to visit. As to standards, we are regulated by several international bodies. Just speak to my secretary Mr Thomas and he will get you copies of our certification. I am afraid that is all I can do for you. Now, if you will excuse me?'

The Priestess gathers up her phone and her handbag, but Emil carries on talking.

Emil: 'We have followed you and your church for some time now, Madam, and we are aware that, although now banned in Nigeria, you still insist your church members watch the video *Witch Children*. Wasn't that very film, one in which you were a producer, implicated in the torture and murder of a great many children?'

A man appears in a suit, standing behind Emil but his head is out of shot. 'That's enough now,' says his disembodied voice.

A hand is on Emil's shoulder, preventing him from standing as the Priestess, visibly upset, gets up. She walks out of shot but a second later she is back. Her face is twisted in maniacal fury and her eyes are black pinpoints. She slams her fists on the table, knocking over the glass. Other diners turn to stare.

Priestess: 'Who are you? Who are you? A milk-fat muzungu and a half-caste Rasta who will never see Babylon? How dare you continue to persecute me? Have I not already suffered? I do the Lord's work! I have been chosen as his handmaiden! I am a good woman!'

The camera whines, focuses in on her face. She looks absolutely demented. She has gripped Emil's arm and he is trying to pull away in pain, her red-tipped fingers look like talons on his white shirt.

Priestess: 'I HAVE BEEN CHOSEN BY GOD!' Spit lands on Emil's face. 'You are nothing more than rats in the sewer to me...'

Someone comes up behind her, there is movement, a murmuring and the Priestess calms, standing over the table panting. Her face is still congested with hate.

Harry: 'All we ask is the location of your school. An interview with your teachers. A few interviews with the children you purport to protect...'

The Priestess jerks around and walks away. Harry and Emil sit there for a moment, mouths open, Emil rubbing his arm.

Emil stands and looks over in the direction of the camera.

Emil: 'Did you get that? Skøre kælling.'

The camera is pulled upward from beneath the table, the focus blurring.

Jens: 'I got it... and yeah, Emil, I agree. Crazy bitch!'

The third clip is shot from the back of a moving car. They can see the back of Harry and Emil's heads. Harry is driving. A hand turns the viewfinder and Jens' smiling face appears, his blonde goatee bobbing. He is filming himself. *He looks so young*, thinks Georgia.

Jens: 'Well it appears the crazy lady has relented and we have won ourselves an interview at The Blood of Christ Rehabilitation Centre. We are en route to join up with a convoy of food trucks which we have been told will lead us to the secret location.'

Emil's voice comes from the front seat and Jens turns the camera on him. His blue eyes are wide in his chubby face.

Emil: 'I'm still not comfortable about this. I mean, don't you think it is all too sudden? I didn't get a chance to call to let anyone know where we are heading. What happens if...?'

Jens: 'Call yourself a journalist? Come *on*, Emil. We might have an Emmy-winner here. Thanks to Harry we now know that the police are being paid to coordinate sweeps of the city to collect children for this place... I mean, that's creepy.'

Harry: 'Yeah, but not unusual.'

Jens: 'Well, then why all the secrecy? What about those rumours of children being adopted?'

Emil: 'Trafficked more like...'

Jens: 'Well exactly.'

Emil: 'Yah, I know, but we should have told someone we were heading out of Lusaka. They think Harry is on a flight to Johannesburg and you and I are on a safari. What if...?'

Jens: 'What if? Emil, man, you gotta relax. There are three of us. My father is a diplomat. Nothing is going to happen to us. But we are going to uncover a huge story, I know it. Come on!'

Emil sighs and Jens flips the camera around.

Jens: 'And look...'

He is filming the rolling wooded hills of the escarpment.

Jens: 'It's going to be a beautiful ride.'

The last clip they watch is the most upsetting. The camera whines and blackness becomes a silhouetted scene of thick bushes and dust.

'Look! That's the place... the Dome!' whispers Luse, hugging herself tightly. Now in the frame they can see the strange tortoise-shaped building through the trees.

Georgia leans in to Luse, 'You don't have to watch this. I will tell you...'

'No,' Luse shakes her head, keeps staring at the screen. 'I am fine.'

They hear a voice coming from behind the camera.

Emil: 'Jens? Are you in? Are you alright?'

Harry's voice is a hoarse whisper: 'We have to go in, Emil. He's been quiet too long. Something's wrong.'

The view of the bushes shakes and tips to film the ground.

Emil: 'I'm *not* going in there. They have armed guards for God's sake. Guys with guns everywhere.'

Harry: 'Calm down, Emil. We can't just leave him. I'll go.'

The camera moves again, rises and now they see Emil looking very frightened with dirt streaked across his cheek. *Harry must have the camera*, thinks Georgia, willing him with all her heart to just put it down and run away, knowing he doesn't.

Emil: 'Please be careful, Harry. We need to get this stuff back to Lusaka.'

The camera moves and they are dashing forward. At a small service door there is a pause. The camera shows a broken lock and the door is slightly ajar.

Harry: 'Hang on, Jens. We are coming through...'

They are inside. The camera picks out the grey walls of a badly-lit corridor.

Emil: 'Jens! Where are you?'

Emil: 'Jens?!'

There is a terrible scream from along the corridor. The camera drops and is picked up again.

Emil: 'Fuck! Run!'

There is yelling, several voices, but everything is blurry and confused.

'What's happening brother?' whispers Gus at the monitor and Georgia's heart lurches, knock-knocking in her chest.

Harry: 'Jens!'

The camera focuses on a reception desk. The receptionists look shocked as the men rush past. Then there is brighter light and the picture steadies, a whine as the camera adjusts and Harry gasps.

Harry: 'Oh dear God.'

Harry is slowly turning the camera, filming everything. They are in the operating room and Dr Lin is standing with his nurses over the prone body of a child. The Priestess is there too, hand raised in salutation, as if they are expected. Next to her is Jens, slumped across the shoulders of an elderly man. Jen's face is horribly puffed up and his eyes are bulging.

Dr Lin smiles at Harry, almost bashfully as the camera scans up, whines, adjusts and picks out several shadowy faces staring down from the large window overhead. There is an almighty CRACK of a gunshot and Harry shouts, his voice hoarse, 'Run, Emil!'

The camera smashes to the floor and the picture goes blank.

6.

They are on the road at dawn. Gus and the Commander are ahead with a small convoy of soldiers. Father Bernard has the loan of the Bishop's ancient land cruiser. Georgia is driving with Bernard and Luse in the back.

The previous night Gus took Georgia to one side.

'Look, you need to stay here with Luse...' he began but Georgia turned on him, eyes blazing.

'Don't you dare, Gus. Don't you bloody dare! I agree it is dangerous but Joshua was under my care. I am a trained medic. I need to be with you!'

She saw his distress, but there was a growing tightness in her body after watching the film clips, a rigid anger that made her distrust even Gus's touch.

She has been unable to get Harry's quiet gasp of horror out of her head, keeps seeing his broken body in the morgue, his poor face all bloody, and she can't help wondering over and over what happened between his leaving the children in the car and his death. She knows Gus is not to blame, but she twisted away from him anyway, feeling ugly, petulant. 'We are all coming with you and that's final.'

Now Georgia can feel every jolt in the road through her shoulder, but it is looking at Luse that causes her more pain. She has tried to tell her that they still don't know for sure that they will find Joshua at the school. He could have been taken anywhere, but Luse is adamant that Joshua is in the Dome. She sits stiffly next to Bernard, staring ahead, hardly blinking.

Georgia hasn't slept and, as the heavy cruiser rumbles down the road, a slight numbness comes over her. She drives almost on autopilot, while rifling through her memory for the correct treatment of gun shots, stab wounds and – remembering the blackened finger – poisoning.

After two hours of fast and silent driving, Luse feels Joshua's pitter-pattering heartbeat become stronger. She puts a hand on Georgia's arm. 'We are right. He is this way. I can feel him better.'

Up ahead, the convoy has pulled over to the side of the road and the men are standing around the bonnet of the leading car looking at the satellite photographs they have pulled up on the laptop.

The Commander speaks over Gus's bent head as Georgia and Bernard approach. 'We believe that the school is on the site of what was originally a Chinese work settlement for the Monze road project. The funds were pulled two years ago and the settlement has been deserted ever since.'

Luse isn't paying much attention to the adults. She drops out of the car, needing to run around, to jump up and down on the spot, anything to stop the fearful jittery feeling. That is when she sees a beautiful fish eagle drop from the sky and land on the top branch of a thorn tree nearby. It turns its snow white head and looks right at Luse with one golden eye and blinks. It seems to be waiting.

Luse turns and calls out, 'We have to follow the eagle. This is the way.' She is pointing across the mottled shrub away from the turnoff to Monze. She runs into the bush. Georgia lunges for her but misses and falls over onto her sore shoulder, crying out.

'Shit!' Gus runs after Luse. Meanwhile the Commander sweeps up the maps and shouts to the other men, 'Form up! We have our co-ordinates.'

'What? Wait!' cries Georgia. 'Luse said it was in the other direction.'

The Commander shakes his head, 'I'm sorry Doctor but Luse is a child and has already been through a hell of a time. I wouldn't trust one of my own people to know what direction was up after experiencing what she has been through. The facts are that the school is on an area previously utilised by the Chinese. Their Security Service has identified it. We know the place.'

Georgia knows that he is being rational but still she wavers. She turns to Bernard who stands looking upwards at the eagle in the tree, 'I trust her, Father.'

'And I do too.' Bernard looks fierce. 'Commander Mhone, with respect sir, we are not dealing with the usual sensible clear-cut world anymore. Luse's grandmother was a –'

'I don't want to hear it, Father. I am sorry. I am not going to jeopardise Joshua by driving blind into the bush in the wrong direction. Now please, move out of my way and let me go and find these children.'

Bernard steps back and the Commander begins to make his way to the convoy.

Gus is heading back towards them, holding a struggling, crying Luse tightly in his arms. Georgia and Bernard run over. Sweat is dripping from Gus's face and Luse is in danger of sliding from his arms. He looks extremely confused.

'She tried to bite me!' he says. He puts her down and immediately she tries to run back the way they have come. Gus just manages to catch her wrist. He drags her back to the group.

The Commander strides over and stands in front of Gus, gesturing at the convoy. 'Gus, we must hurry.'

Gus looks sheepish. 'I don't know why, but I am going to trust the kid on this one, Peter,' he says quietly. 'It's a gut feeling.'

'Your call, Gus. Keep in radio contact at all times, please.'

They watch as he sprints back to the convoy. Engines are grinding and sunlight glints off metal as the cars turn back onto the road and head south.

Luse is pulling on Gus's arm, 'Hurry up. Hurry!'

'Luse you have to calm down. Do you hear me?' Gus holds Luse's face in his hands. 'We have to be careful and that means not rushing. More haste, less speed. Do you understand?'

Luse nods, biting her lip and twisting her feet in the sand. She doesn't care about careful. She only cares about getting to Joshua as soon as she possibly can.

Bernard stands back, scratching his head while Gus, Luse and Georgia clamber back into the Bishop's land cruiser. 'Kufwafwa ni kafwafwa, praise Jesus,' he mutters under his breath, looking uneasily up at the still circling eagle.

The Bishop's land cruiser is very old, but it rolls and bounces over the tussocks and bushes with little problem. Soon the windscreen is encrusted with dust and Gus has to drive with his head out of the window. Some of the bush is so thick, Georgia and Father Bernard must get out and walk in front to search for clearer pathways while the eagle keeps just ahead, swooping down to land in nearby trees, watching them with its golden eyes, occasionally tipping its head back into its whistling sobbing call. It takes a slow hot hour before Luse sees the eagle perch on something that doesn't quite belong in the surrounding bush. She points.

'When is a tree not a tree?' asks Gus.

'When it's a phone mast,' replies Georgia smiling wearily, thinking, *Shit, we have bloody found it.* She has been hoping that following the eagle would take them on a wild goose chase, leaving the Commander to face the danger of the school. 'Well, your goose is cooked, Georgie,' she imagines Harry saying to her with wicked delight at his own wit.

Just beyond the mast they get stuck in the thick black clay. Luse is twitching with nervous energy. The bush has changed since she last scrambled through it. Back then it was the end of the dry season and everything was hard browns and thorny scrub, easy to see through. Now, at the end of the rains, the bush is lush and green, softer and muddier underfoot and impossibly thick. She knows they are close though and puts a hand over the little pattering heartbeat next to her own. *We are coming, Joshua!*

She takes her feet out of her sandals and steps into a small brown puddle while Gus and Georgia try to work out where to put the dry branches to manoeuvre the land cruiser out of the slick black soil. The water is warm, but the mud beneath is deliciously cool, and her toes sink in deep, mud squelching between them. She sees something.

'Father Bernard! Come here and look,' she calls. Bernard walks over, carting a dead branch. 'Over here!' Luse says again. She is crouching over a thick mass of green and purple. She pulls at the stems and holds out a small purple posy. 'This is the flower I told you about. The one my grandmother used on me and I used on Bwana Harry.'

Bernard takes the flowers. 'Thank you, Luse,' he says and sniffs. He doesn't recognise the flower and collects a posy to identify later.

'You have to crush them together and squeeze the juice,' says Luse.

Behind them sounds a whine from the engine and then a shout of triumph as Georgia calls out that the cruiser is free. They are off again.

When they get a few feet from the first mast, they pause while Gus radios the Commander with their estimated location, telling him about the masts. Georgia and Bernard confer on the far side of the cruiser.

'How do we do this?'

'If we are right and we are close to the school then we have to wait for the Commander to get here.'

'We can't wait.' Luse has come around and is standing, hands on her hips glaring. 'They are going to chop him up. Tonight.'

The child-like phrase silences both adults. Georgia swallows.

In a few minutes the bush breaks apart abruptly to reveal several long fields of maize. Between them and the field is a twelve-foot-high fence topped with a tiara of razor wire. They have found it.

'Ya vah. They aren't kidding around are they?' says Gus as they turn left and follow the fence, the land cruiser rolling and pitching over the rough ground.

Then Luse grabs him by the shoulder. 'Stop, stop! Pull over into the bush, someone's coming.'

Gus rams the land cruiser hard into the thick thorny shrub on the right and jumps out, pulling branches down over the car as camouflage. They can hear the whine of a small engine coming along the track behind them.

'Get behind the cruiser,' orders Gus and grabs his gun.

It's a small green jeep, like the ones Luse described. There is only one man in it but he takes up the whole of the front of the vehicle, which lists a little to his side, tyres bulging beneath his weight.

'Samuel!' Luse shouts. The jeep lurches to a stop. She pulls away from a horrified Georgia and runs towards him, waving her arms.

Georgia plunges out of the bush after her and Bernard stands helpless as Gus follows, his gun aimed at the huge man who is clambering slowly from the jeep ahead.

Samuel stands now, a towering goliath. His eyes take in all four people running towards him, including Gus and the gun. He slowly raises his arms, enormous palms facing out.

'Am I under arrest, little sister?' he asks Luse gently as she gets close.

'Samuel, Samuel! Give me back my brother! Give him back!' Luse runs right to his feet and punches him in the stomach.

'Luse! Don't ...' Georgia is circling the huge man, trying to gauge the reach of his arms. 'Please don't hurt her. She is very upset.'

Samuel gives Georgia a tight small smile. 'I don't hurt children, madam. But I would suggest that your friend there lowers his weapon before someone gets hurt.'

There is something about his voice. Georgia looks back at Gus, imploring, and he slowly lowers his gun but doesn't take his finger from the trigger.

'Now,' Samuel's voice is like a low booming drum roll. 'Little Luse, tell me what you think I have done.'

It takes only a few minutes for Samuel to understand that Joshua has been kidnapped again and they suspect he is being held at the school.

'I can feel him, Samuel sir,' says Luse, 'Here.' And she puts a hand over her heart. 'He is frightened but he is alive and he is here... I know it. In the Dome.'

Bernard pushes past Gus, eyes glittering behind his glasses. 'Did you see anyone bringing Joshua, or any children, in last night?'

'There was only one vehicle in last night, Father,' Samuel is thinking it through. 'The Priestess and her Mercedes. I don't search that car.'

'Could it have been...?'

'Enough, Father, with respect.' He tries to soften his voice but he is obviously angry. 'This is a school for orphaned children and street kids. It is a good place. Why would you accuse the Priestess of such things? What would she gain by stealing a young boy?'

'Joshua is special... or at least I think the Priestess thinks he is special.' Luse turns to Georgia and Bernard. 'Please, you have to help me explain...'

'Bwana Samuel. There are some very suspicious and unpleasant things going on under your jurisdiction.' Bernard is rolling up his sleeves. He looks as if he is about to start a fight. 'I tell you here and now Samuel, on my faith, that these people you are protecting are using children, worse, killing children and selling off their body parts. We have proof!'

At the word 'proof' the giant blinks at Father Bernard and then freezes, his eyes flicking back and forth.

He is putting it all together, thinks Georgia, watching him swiftly scanning through his memories. *He knows something is wrong here.*

'I almost never go into the Dome,' Samuel says at last. 'They told me it was the medical centre and I hate hospitals. I was not happy that they had separate security at that place but I did not question.'

'Samuel, the night Luse, Joshua and Eli escaped,' says Georgia, 'there was another man you were looking for, right?'

'Ach, that night. There was some poor white boy who got shot...'

'Poor Emil,' moans Georgia.

'... and the man who did it escaped from Mr Phiri's custody. He found the fallen tree and jumped the fence like these little ones. I was told he was a spy but it seemed strange to me. I met the man when he arrived. A good, funny Rasta man. We shared a joke at the gate. Why would he suddenly shoot his colleague?'

'Harry...' Gus's voice cracks and he looks away.

Samuel peers at Gus's face keenly then blows through his nose in sorrow. 'Ah, I see now. There is a brother here. Sorry, sorry.' He is silent a moment. 'Did he not make it back to Lusaka?'

'Samuel, Harry was my friend and Gus's brother,' Georgia says, trying not to cry. 'He was beaten and murdered not long after helping the children get to Lusaka.'

Samuel's face drops, he slumps. It is like watching a landslide down a mountain. 'I have known in my heart that it was wrong to keep quiet about that night. But I was under orders. I presumed that the Church would take responsibility for the mess. Now you tell me there is worse... much worse going on here? I can't believe...'

Samuel lets one enormous hand come to rest on Luse's head. 'Have I been protecting the wrong people?'

'We are going to need your help, Bwana Samuel.' Bernard steps closer. Next to the soldier he looks the size of a child. 'We need to get into the Dome to find the boy.'

Samuel nods then shakes himself. Taking a breath he seems to swell up again, his head hits the sky. 'I am going in for my shift. You all better come with me. You,' he gestures at Gus, 'you better hide your gun.'

'Is it safe?' Georgia asks Gus and Bernard as they head towards the jeep. Luse has gone ahead with Samuel, jumping from one foot to the other with tension and urging them all to be faster. 'Surely we should wait for the Commander?'

On the pretext of shutting up the cruiser, Gus has already radioed in and told the Commander that they have found the school. The response was distorted and hard to hear but Gus is sure the Commander has told them to stay with the vehicle. They are at least two hours away.

Bernard looks up at the sky. The eagle is nowhere in sight now but the sky is turning pink as dusk approaches. In an hour it will be dark. 'I don't know what to suggest, Georgia. If we wait we could be too late.'

'With Samuel's help,' Gus says, 'I think we might be able to get in and out without causing too much of a stir. We just need to find Joshua. The rest we can leave to Commander Mhone and the boys. There is certainly no way we will be able to convince Luse to stay behind.'

Samuel is already helping Luse up into the jeep. 'Come on,' he calls. 'We will need to get supplies from the guard house. There isn't a moon tonight. We are going to need torches.'

'I can't leave Luse.' Georgia hefts her medical bag over her good shoulder and heads to the jeep, her heart fluttering in her throat.

'And I can't leave Georgia,' she hears Gus mutter to himself and in seconds they are all in the jeep and moving off.

Before they round the corner to the main gate, Samuel gets Luse to crouch down and covers her with a tarpaulin.

'The rest of you follow my lead and stay quiet. My men will think you are just the usual foreigners coming through. We get a lot of funders and VIPs coming each week. In fact a helicopter dropped off a small group less than an hour ago.' He glances over at the four of them as he changes gear, his mighty hand engulfing the whole gear stick. 'Try and look like you are wealthy,' he says, shaking his massive head. 'And Father... your collar? Best removed I think, for the moment.'

7.

At the gate Samuel signs them in as guests. The three guards on duty seem completely uninterested. Only one asks, 'But what happened to their car?'

'They took a bad route through the bush. Tore off their exhaust pipe. Luckily I was passing by or they would have had to call the Priestess directly.'

The soldier nods, stifles a yawn. 'Will you be back for the briefing?'

'Not tonight. But I will expect a full report on my desk by twenty hundred hours.'

The security guard sighs, 'Yes sah!'

Once they clear the gate, Samuel allows Luse out from under the hot tarpaulin. The fresh air revives her, but driving back through the school grounds is difficult. She feels unreal, ghostly, as if all the school is a movie set and she is just the audience. Things have changed a great deal, it seems. There are more lights on in more of the half-finished buildings and several of them have scaffolding up on the outside and new building material piled up at the walls. The central green has another flag pole and a banner fluttering overhead that reads 'The Children of The Blood of Christ Rehabilitation Centre Welcome You!'

'That's Hut Two!' she says to Gus, pointing at the building opposite the square. It still has the heavy burglar bars across the windows but now, painted white, they seem almost cheerful.

'Do you think Joshua is in there?' Gus asks, shading his eyes, but Luse shakes her head with solemnity.

'He's in the Dome,' she says. 'For sure.'

Wonderful smells from the kitchen are flooding out into the evening air and Luse reckons that most of the children will be coming in from the fields now, washing up in readiness for supper. She has a sudden pang of longing for that early evening of weary, contented expectation. Got through another day and food coming. For a mere second she wonders if she shouldn't have just stayed put. Maybe she would have been alright. She is surprised by the emotion and feels suddenly tired and numb. *No, we would already be dead,* she admonishes herself. *Come on, Joshua needs you.*

They drive past the kitchens and are on the track to the Dome, passing several of the children as they walk in from the fields. Luse doesn't recognise any of them but they all look up, cheerful and strong, waving at the jeep. The sun is setting the world on fire.

They drive under the guard towers and into the Dome through the carport. Georgia notices with curiosity that several old lorries are parked outside. They look half loaded. She is just about to ask Samuel about this when her eyes adjust to the gloom of the bunker and she becomes aware of two people standing in the slipway ahead of them. She hears Luse give a small gulping scream and Gus shouts, 'No!' Then there is a terrible crack and Samuel rocks back in his seat, knocking into Father Bernard. Samuel's huge hands come flapping off the steering wheel, the jeep jumps, the engine stalls and cuts out.

As the gunshot echoes around the concrete walls and Samuel slumps forward over the bonnet, Georgia folds herself in half and somersaults under the seat she is sitting on. Next to her Bernard, rubbing his head and readjusting his glasses, sees what is being pointed at him and raises his hands in the air. Now Georgia can hear Luse's sobbing and Gus trying to comfort her and then another voice.

'Shit man! You shot the Captain! Totally shot him Siza!'

'He was resisting arrest, okay. Now shut up!' There is a pause. Booted feet clumping. 'You in the jeep. Step down slowly, slowly. No sudden moves, right.'

The voices are those of young men, a little tremulous, as if the speakers are frightened... or excited. For a second Georgia sees Bernard's legs begin to twist as he turns to her and she grabs his trouser cuff and pulls hard twice. How does she think she will get away with this? God, she doesn't know, but Bernard seems to understand. He doesn't bend down but stands and steps over her medical bag, leaving it close to the seat. The jeep shifts as he and the others clamber down, leaving her behind.

'We were told there were five,' Siza is suspicious.

'Can't you count?' Gus's voice is flat. He sounds cool, unruffled. There is a tense pause.

'Hey Siza,' says the other young man. 'Maybe they thought the big bwana was two people? He is surely the son of an elephant.'

Siza makes a snorting noise that could be a laugh.

'You have shot one of the Big Five, mwana!' brays his friend. 'Ha... next a lion!'

'Ya... that's a good one,' Siza begins, but then his friend spots Gus's belt.

'Hey, he's armed!'

'Okay, keep calm. If he moves I'll shoot him and the old guy. You, buti, take his gun and let's get going! We need to tell the others we have them!' The triumph in the man's young voice is obvious and Georgia shudders.

And then that is all. Blood pounding in her ears means Georgia doesn't even hear their footsteps as the two young men herd Luse, Gus and Bernard away from the jeep. She doesn't know how long to wait, grinds her teeth in terror and desperately tries to control her shaking. *Hang on until you are quite sure...* but she can't. The claustrophobia and not knowing is too much and, gasping like a fish, she pushes herself back out from under the seat.

She and Samuel are alone in the large concrete carport. Behind the jeep the Dome door is still half open and Georgia sees soft pink evening sky, smells maize porridge cooking. She could run away from all this but she doesn't. Instead she tugs out her medical bag and clambers over to the front seat.

'Bwana Samuel,' she whispers, steeling herself.

Samuel has been shot high in the chest and blood is oozing out between every button of his jacket. It is a terrible mess but he is still alive. In his current position, however, Georgia knows he will go into shock and bleed out. Her inner doctor assesses the damage and rifles through her mind for correct procedure whilst she frantically tries hauling him off the steering wheel. After a couple of attempts she sits back, breathing hard. He is too heavy and she is scared of complicating the injury. *Oh my god. What next?* She is holding down the panic, scanning the space, the car for inspiration, anything. Then, an idea! 'If Mohammad won't come to the mountain...' she says under her breath as she jumps over the side of the jeep.

She has seen that the handbrake is off. By racing around to Samuel's side and opening his door, she can push the jeep forward a little. Inch by inch, with sweat stinging as it drips down her face, she shunts the jeep out from the doorway and into a shadowy corner away from the other parked vehicles. With brute strength she grabs Samuel's arm and yanks him once, twice until his own body weight spills him out of the jeep and onto the white-washed floor.

'Sorry, sorry big guy,' Georgia whispers, trying to ensure his head doesn't hit the ground too hard. He gives a soft 'ummmm' but doesn't open his eyes.

'Shhh,' Georgia hisses. 'Don't speak. Samuel, you have a serious gunshot wound. I need to dress it and it is going to be very painful, but I need you to keep as still as possible.' She isn't sure if he has heard her but she is whispering in part to herself, to calm herself down. *They will be back to get the body any minute,* part of her mind screams. *Run away, run away!*

Thanking all deities for her medical kit, she does everything she can, controlling the blood flow, improvising a plastic vent over the wound and hanging the drip bag up on the jeep's wing mirror. She has treated gun shots only twice before and both times she had a full surgery and a team of nurses behind her, but there is no time to second-guess herself. She works fast and her hands do not shake. Samuel is more conscious now as she grabs a tarpaulin from the jeep and begins to cover him. He tries to say something. Georgia leans over him as she tucks her cardigan under his head.

'I'm... sor...'

'It's alright, Samuel. You couldn't have known they were listening in on the radio.' She takes his plate-sized palm in her two hands and squeezes. 'Samuel – this is going to be very hard for you. You need to try and keep awake and quiet. I am going to go after the others but I will come back for you soon, okay.'

It's a lie. She isn't sure what will happen but she wills it to be true. Samuel manages a faint squeeze in return. He seems to be pulling her hand down, gesturing to his leg. Is he hurt there? Georgia feels carefully down from his knee and finds a small revolver strapped to his ankle.

I'm going to shoot myself in the arse, she thinks hopelessly.

'Okay then. I am going to hide you in the tarpaulin, which should also keep you warm. The jeep is blocking you from view of the rest of the car park in case anyone comes through.'

It's all she can do.

From far off there comes the sound of angry shouting and running feet. *You could still get away,* screams her mind as Georgia, with wooden feet and trembling lips, collects her bag of tricks and, giving Samuel's hand one last squeeze, turns towards the noise of the struggle.

8.

Luse is so frightened that she cannot think straight. If she didn't have Gus on one side and Bernard on the other, she wouldn't be able to move forward at all. Her legs would freeze and her brain would freeze and they would just shoot her too. *Must find Joshua, must get Joshua,* she thinks, keeping the words buzzing under her tongue, trying not to gag at the memory of the gunshot and Samuel's chest opening and his life whooping out of him.

Joshie, Joshie, Joshie... In the gloom of the corridor, and with the constant noise of fluttering feathers in her head, she nearly trips over a large piece of rubber flooring that has come unstuck and curled over. Gus's hand, warm and strong on her shoulder, steadies her and he keeps it there even though Siza tells him to stick his hands up in the air. Luse thinks Gus isn't scared of Siza and this gives her comfort.

Bernard whispers to her that Samuel will be fine, but his voice is trembling and Luse knows he is scared too. Having Samuel with them was like having their own army. Now the only strong person is Gus and he can't fight Siza without a gun.

There is another hole in the floor. As they step over it, the stench of sewage from a cracked pipe wafts up making them all gag and blink.

'This building is falling to pieces,' hisses Bernard to Gus over Luse's head.

'Quiet,' shouts Siza and then flinches as his own voice ricochets around the empty corridor.

Now Luse hears noise ahead. Through the next doors she sees the reception desk. People are running about looking frantically busy, carrying boxes and waving clipboards. They ignore Siza and his prisoners, dodging around them to carry on packing.

'Fifty minutes!' shouts someone and one of the box carriers groans, 'Impossible! We can't pack it all in under an hour!'

'Have you got the camera down from Hut Two?' shouts another voice.

Siza pushes them on through the milling people. 'Pah, this is your fault,' he snarls from behind Gus, gun still cocked. 'We have to pack up, clear out before the army gets here. Why couldn't you have just stayed lost, you stupid kid?'

Luse sees a flash of white from the eyes of one of the receptionists as they go past. The woman points at her and turns to her colleague as they pass, her mouth making a round shape: 'Witch.'

In seconds they are through yet more doors and enter a large bright space with cracked white tiles and three long strip lights hanging from the ceiling. The fluorescent lights are crackling, encrusted with excited moths, flying ants and rose-beetles.

Above Luse's head a platform juts precariously out over the room, casting a shadow. The platform bounces and squeaks as people move around on it, unsettling dust and rubble which trickles down from the wooden struts. The platform's fourth wall is a large scratched window and Luse feels her stomach tighten. She knows exactly where they are. This is the operating theatre where she saw the child being cut open. She grabs Bernard's hand and he squeezes hers back, hard.

'I know,' he sighs. 'You have been here before.'

Luse looks around the room for any sign of Joshua. It is as if she has stepped into a nightmare. There is an operating table surrounded by machines. On it, unconscious and half covered in a green cloth, is her brother.

The scream doesn't come. It lodges like a fishbone in her throat, choking her, preventing her from leaping forward. She can't get air, she can't get breath. She scrabbles at her neck, eyes bulging as the tall, sharp outline of the Priestess detaches itself from a group over by the far wall.

Father Bernard, ignoring the Priestess coming towards them, kneels in front of Luse, clutching her heaving shoulders. She manages to make out his words: 'I've got you, Luse. You are panicking. Breathe out first. Out. Trust me.'

After a terrible second Luse manages to exhale and then inhale; breath rushes back into her lungs, hot as steam.

Gus rubs her back. 'Okay, you are okay. We are going to get through this together,' he says quietly.

'Joshua,' Luse's voice is hoarse, just a whisper. Tears drip down her nose and her chest aches. Mr Phiri is there too, hovering like one of the moths up above. He is wearing delicate blue-grey and next to him the Priestess smiles down at Luse. She is in her purple regalia and clutching her large black Bible.

'Well done Brother Siza and welcome all!' Mr Phiri is greeting them as if they have arrived at a lunch party. 'We were waiting for you!' He pauses, sniffs the air like a wary animal. 'But where is the big man?'

'He was resisting arrest, sir. I had no choice,' Siza mutters.

Bernard bristles with fury. 'Rubbish! This boy shot the man in cold blood. He is a liar as well as a coward.'

'Ah, Father Bernard. It's very good to meet you. Without you I fear our rehabilitation centre might not have been possible. We are very grateful.'

Bernard turns pale and he drops his head.

The Priestess moves in on Gus. 'Who are you?' she asks, but then her face freezes. 'Wait – no need to speak. You have the same eyes. You must be a relative of that Rasta spy? A brother perhaps?'

Gus, hand warm on Luse's shoulder, speaks quietly but his voice is clear, 'I am here to tell you that your filthy business has been discovered. The army will be here in minutes. You will all be placed under arrest.'

'Not minutes. We also have radios here, Brother Spy,' says Mr Phiri. 'We still have plenty of time.'

'And our own security force,' adds the Priestess. 'The Lord's work will continue.'

Bernard, in spite of Gus trying to stop him, steps forward, letting go of Luse's hand. 'Please, I implore you. Just let us take the children and be on our way.'

Mr Phiri claps his hands in good-natured delight. 'That is good. Indeed you can have all the children you want, you can take them all. We only need this one and the boy.'

His hand reaches out for Luse's wrist.

'No. I don't think so,' Gus's voice is still very calm. He pulls Luse close and stands with her pressed tight into his side and she turns and buries her head into his shirt, smelling soap powder and sweat.

Mr Phiri withdraws his hand and cocks his head, assessing Gus. 'The decision has already been made I am afraid. He...' Mr Phiri gestures up at the viewing platform, 'he picked her and the boy out himself. He has come a very long way and is especially excited now that it is apparent how powerful a witch she truly is.'

'I am not a witch,' croaks Luse, keeping her face buried in Gus's side.

'Hey!'

Luse's head jerks up at the strange voice.

A white man is standing in the middle of the room. He is very pale and fat with itchy-looking red spots on his cheeks and bags under his eyes, sweat dribbling off him in torrents. He is wearing a T-shirt emblazoned with a skull in a motorbike helmet and he carries a large black camcorder on his shoulder. His accent is American, his baseball cap on backwards, greasy hair tied back in a thin ponytail. He moves gum to one side of his mouth to yell out, 'Who the hell are these guys?'

'Nothing to worry about, sir,' Mr Phiri soothes without taking his eyes from Gus. 'They have delivered the witch girl for the exorcism.'

'Oh right. Cool. Well come on then. We gotta hustle. This goddamn country!' He slaps his neck. 'I better not get malaria or some fucked up shitty disease...' He puts a hand up to his ear, grimacing and scratching as he looks up to the viewing platform. 'Say again...?' There is a pause and a tinny sound from his headphones. 'Okay, okay already. I'll tell 'em.'

He turns back to Mr Phiri, 'Oh and the boss says keep the new guys out of shot. He just wants the kids.'

'I don't know who you are,' Gus speaks over Mr Phiri's head to the white man, his voice still low and controlled. 'I do know that these people murder children and you really do not want to be involved with them. I warn you and your boss that the Zambian army are on their way. You would do well to leave immediately.'

'Oh ho. Wow dude, seriously chill out. I am just the camera guy, okay? We will be outta here quicker if you just shut the hell up. C'mon, Phiri man. What's with this guy?' He cracks gum, mouth open in a pout.

'Take no notice, sir. We will deal with this.' Now Mr Phiri waves at his wife where she has been waiting with Dr Lin. She swings an old canvas-seated wheelchair around and begins pushing it forward with one hand. In the other she is holding a large plastic bottle of clear liquid. She waves it at her husband. 'I am coming dear, chabwino, chabwino. Brothers,' she crooks her finger at Siza and his friend, 'I am going to need your help.'

Siza raises his gun and Luse feels Gus's body tighten. The feathery noise is so loud now that she can hardly hear her own self moaning, 'Noooo.'

Bernard turns to the Priestess. His voice is crackling with fear but he stands straight in front of her, 'Madam, what is going on? You can see this is all a mistake. This child is not possessed... She is terrified and rightly so. Let us just take her and her brother home and...'

Even in the midst of her terror, Luse thinks the Priestess looks different. She is sharper all over, all elbows and angles and her bat clothes hang as if they are too big. Luse remembers Daddy standing in the doorway of the lake house with his clothes all baggy and him getting so skinny underneath them. Peeking at her from within Gus's strong arms, she sees that the woman's eyes are sunken, her high cheeks hollow as if all the cheek padding has been chewed away. *Maybe she is ill*, thinks Luse. *Maybe she will die too.*

'You understand, Father,' she is saying. 'As a man of God you understand that the devil can hide deep inside a human body. Every right and true Christian knows that evil can possess even children. I am *never* wrong because I am directed by God himself in this matter. I am given signs, I am sent messages and now I have proof. Your witch is proof. She conspires with termites, directs the wind to knock down solid trees, sets men on fire and now corrupts your mind with what you think is love. The child is evil through and through. My exorcism didn't work before but I will succeed this time.'

Siza prods Gus in the back with his gun. 'Put the girl in the wheelchair.'

Gus stands straighter, turns around and just stares at the young man until Siza drops his gaze. The gun, however, remains pointed at Gus's belly.

Desperately Bernard tries again. 'Okay then, I am a Jesuit Priest and I too believe that there are demons, there is possession. Leave her in my care and I will exorcise her myself.'

'No! Her parents were in my care and I failed them. It is my duty. The Lord has spoken to me. I alone am strong enough. I alone will triumph and I will be healed, praise Jesus!'

'Healed?' Bernard's voice sharpens. 'How will her exorcism heal you? I don't understand. Are you sick? Your hatred of children is certainly...'

'Hate children?' the Priestess interrupts. 'I love them. Is it not obvious how much I love them? We have nearly three hundred children here now. Where would they be if not here? On the street, infected with disease, starving, in pain. Here they are cared for, given an education, love. And yes, the miracle which provides this sustenance to all these children is other children. One little life for every twenty. One who would die in pain and fear alone anyway.'

'You are lost and confused. You mutilate and torture for a business. For money, Selena Clark. That is *not* the work of God. Listen to me, you need to think who it is that is actually possessed by evil. This innocent child or you, you and your band of torturers and child killers?'

The Priestess seems momentarily confused. She has stopped waving her Bible and stands looking lost as if she has forgotten her script.

The Priestess sees Mrs Phiri. 'Did I say "healed"?' she asks in a little, child-like voice.

'Yes, dear,' Mrs Phiri's eyes slide to her husband and then back to the Priestess. 'Remember now. The witch's blood is very powerful. You will feel so much stronger. You will be able to start afresh in a new place with a new school.'

'This is wickedness, Selena!' Father Bernard's voice is rising. 'You must stop before someone is hurt.'

But it is too late. The Priestess is shaken from her reverie and kisses her Bible, holds it aloft. 'This demon child killed her father, attacked her mother. Remember Exodus, Father. Exodus 21:15: "Anyone who attacks his father or his mother must be put to death".'

'C'mon guys!' the fat white man shouts. 'Dr Lin is ready to rock.'

'Sorry gentlemen. Time has run out,' Mr Phiri steps back graciously to allow his wife to approach. In her hand is the large plastic bottle that might have once had cola in it. Now she swirls something milky and gaseous.

'Try not to breathe it in,' Bernard shouts. 'Luse get behind us.'

'She is not to be given the muti. Not the witch,' the Priestess shouts. 'Drug her and you drug the demon.'

Mrs Phiri, smiling, takes the lid off the bottle.

9.

Georgia only realises she is still covered in Samuel's blood when she puts her palms on the double doors and leaves a perfect handprint. For a strange moment she admires it and the crazy nightmare that she is in recedes into the lines on her bloody palm. She recognises that she is slipping into shock, her brain is skipping beats.

Come on. Buck up, she admonishes herself and, wiping her gory hands on her filthy trousers, pushes through the double doors. Spinning to her left, she dashes down another long curved corridor, feeling in her gut that she needs to get more central, that Luse and Joshua will be in the middle of the Dome. But every door she sees is locked or the rooms beyond are dark and empty.

Then, turning the corner, she sees movement and light. Feet slapping along the floor and a shout, 'Hey mwana! It's about to start! We should be clear in twenty minutes!' Instinctively she turns out of sight into another doorway and sees a set of grubby stairs. She pulls the gun from her waistband, feeling both terrified and ridiculous. She has no idea if there is a safety catch on the thing.

'For fuck's sake,' she hisses to herself, realising that she is holding it up to her face to check. She points the barrel in the right direction and, taking a big breath and hitching the medical bag up on her shoulder, takes the stairs two at a time.

10.

Mrs Phiri moves very quickly for an old woman. One moment Luse thinks she is in front of them and the next the old lady has dodged right behind Gus and reached over his shoulder to squeeze the bottle of smoky stuff into his face before he can block it with his hands. Gus gags, his eyes roll back and he drops to the floor like a bag of wet cement without another word, leaving Luse standing there shrieking in fright. She reaches for Father Bernard but Siza and his friend have already grabbed the old man, trapping his arms. He tries to twist away, but they grip his chin and force his face into the path of the vapour. Eventually he has no choice but to take a breath and down he goes too, leaving Luse standing alone, desperately looking for somewhere to run as Mrs Phiri pushes the wheelchair closer.

Can't he see what is happening? thinks Luse desperately, trying to signal to the fat white man, but he is indifferent to her shrieks. She can see his fat bottom squeezing over his waistband as he hunches over, filming Dr Lin and the nurses at the operating table.

'Help me!' she screams at his back but all he does is turn, without even lowering the camera, and yell at the Priestess, 'Get those drugged guys out of shot and shut that damn kid up. I'm getting feedback!'

Luse stops screaming. She realises, perhaps for the first time, that she really is going to be killed. The noise of beating wings drowns out the creak of the wheelchair, the fat man's directions, and for a moment she closes her eyes, deaf to everything else. *Why, Ba'Neene? Why do they want to do this? They are bloody bastards, bloody shit-eating, cock-sucking bastards.* Street words begin to come into her mouth, hot and filthy words, angry words and her fists clench and her stomach muscles tighten as fear and rage collide, growing until they can no longer fit in her body. She opens her eyes and sees a hand reaching for her.

'Get away from me!' she hisses and kicks out at Mrs Phiri, her tennis shoe making good solid contact with the woman's knee.

'Aieee!' screams Mrs Phiri, half letting go of Luse's arm, and Luse wrenches herself free, launches herself forward, and rams the Priestess right in the guts. Luse can feel soft stomach and then hard rib bone against her forehead as she slams into the woman and she shrieks right into the Priestess's belly, 'Get away from us!'

She is caught up in the flapping purple robes as they tumble down together, but she carries on kicking and punching with all the techniques she has learned in four months on the street. 'Leave us alone!' she screams and screams until her voice is hoarse.

It's over in a matter of seconds. Hands she barely feels roughly drag her away from the Priestess and force her backwards into the wheelchair where she sits, still shrieking and snarling with rage, her knuckles bloody, skin between her teeth.

'Jesus!' She finally has the fat man's attention. He has come running over to film it all, talking on his headphones. 'They weren't kidding about this freakin' kid, boss! Shit. She is like some kind of cage fighter.'

Dr Lin moves quickly to the Priestess and kneels to help her up, pausing in shock at the damage. He glances up at Luse with his mouth open. Luse spits at him and strains against her captors. The Priestess's face is a mess. Her nose is bleeding and one eye is swollen shut, scratch marks run down her face and she is terribly winded and having great trouble getting to her feet. Eventually, leaning heavily on the doctor, she stands, gulping air, her hair a tangled mess and her robe torn completely from one arm. Luse wishes she could hit her again, harder, so she will never get up again.

'Sheesh! Enough already,' the fat cameraman is no longer enjoying the spectacle. 'We are overrunning. Looking at your Priest lady, I think we'll have to make do without the exorcism, Doctor. Just get cutting.'

A very subdued Mr Phiri and his limping wife are at Dr Lin's side. 'We will look after Madam Priestess and get her out to the vehicle. You carry on.'

Luse is tied to the wheelchair with gaffer tape. The tape is tight in places, especially over her mouth, but Siza's fingers pulled away from her skin as if it burnt him and in his hurry to get away from her he hasn't taped all the way around the legs of the wheelchair. Already she can feel pieces of tape coming loose, but she still can't break free.

Now, as the fury subsides and she is left with just the deafening, endless fluttering wings and her own short panting breaths, she begins to cry. She has nothing left in her at all. She can't kick herself free of the tape, she can't call out, and Dr Lin is standing over Joshua wiping her brother's little chest with antiseptic. On her right, Father Bernard is moving feebly, but Gus remains slumped on the floor. She turns back to her brother but her eyes are so full of tears everything is just slices of light. She blinks and in the blinking she feels as if her lashes are feathers brushing her cheek. All over her body she can feel tickling prickles as though tiny feathers are pushing through her skin. Up overhead the lights flicker near the ceiling and a pattering sound, like heavy rain on the roof, builds louder and louder. Luse knows it is a river of birds pouring down from the night sky, a hurricane of dark-winged birds that will thunder down and flood the entire room. *Ba'Neene!* thinks Luse and closes her eyes.

11.

She is flying in the night, her body so light and delicate, her feathers warm and firm. The cool night air tickles her, a warm eddy lifts her, and below she sees the bush, the three melele trees and the cave. She sees everything in extraordinary detail, the veins on the leaves, the spider webs at the entrance. The darkness parts for her as she swoops hooohoo-ing softly into the mouth of the cave, threading her way between blind ghosts and blind bats. She emerges into the cavern of Ba'Neene's shrine.

In the musty grass-scented darkness she senses thousands of birds roosting, their small breasts rising and falling in sleep. Starlight comes through the open roof and makes the waterfall sparkle, each water droplet a gemstone.

Luse is herself now, barefoot, a piece of gaffer tape still sticking to her leg. She plucks it off, stretches, wondering if she is dead. This would be a peaceful, if lonely, heaven. *I must have done it. I must have killed everyone.* She thinks of Joshua but can feel nothing, no pitter-pattering heartbeat next to her own.

I am evil. Like they said. She watches a firefly dart-pulse-dart over the dark water of the pool where the fish sleep too. The firefly joins another and another and soon there is a cloud of tiny pulsing lights hanging in the air in front of her. Behind the cloud she can make out a shape, as if through a veil.

'Ba'Neene, am I dead?'

'No, Luse. You are there, in that terrible place still.' The fireflies are a face glowing in the air.

'Are Joshua and Georgia... are they okay?'

'Now. For now.'

Luse breathes out a long hissing breath of relief. She walks to the stone basin by the edge of the pool and splashes her face, washes her feet. The water is bitingly cold and when she drinks it she can feel it going all the way inside her, into her bloodstream, her muscles. It feels wonderful. The cloud of pulsing lights has grown. She turns to it.

'How can I be there and here at the same time?'

'Here? This place is inside you, Luse. There is no "there" and there is no "here". It is all the same.'

Luse bites her lip, not sure if she understands.

'Can I stay here? I mean, wherever I am in now, just to rest?' *I will curl up on the grass*, she thinks *and just sleep and sleep.* The pulsing lights swarm closer, around her.

'It is your choice. But Joshua needs you. Others need you too.'

'I can't help anyone, Ba'Neene.'

'Why do you say that?'

'I killed a man. A whole man,' Luse begins to cry. Her tears are cold like the water from the pool. 'And then I left Eli to die.'

'Luse, little one, you are very strong. When that man hurt you you pushed him very hard with your body and also with your mind... but *you* did not kill him. For you it was instinct to protect Joshua and to push him away. For him it was a choice. His choice was to be there. His choice was to attack you. The consequence of his choices was that he fell into fire. As for Eli, he was already very sick. Not even I could have helped him. Not even Doctor Georgia.'

Luse is silent for a while. Her tears are cooling her hot face. 'So I am not... a witch?'

The fireflies part and converge again and the waterfall makes a tinkling, laughing sound.

'A witch... ach. For shame!'

'But...'

'Luse, do you know what makes you and me special?'

'No, Ba'Neene.'

'Nothing,' says Ba'Neene. 'Absolutely nothing. You and I are no different to any other person born. Nyika yonse ila balika kwiinda muli ndiwe mbubona mbuli mbwibalika kwinda muli bonse bantu lyonse. The whole world is rushing through you just as it does through all people all the time. It rushes backwards as well as forwards, connecting you to all your ancestors and all your children and grandchildren at the same time. The thing is that you choose to listen. Most people choose to pretend they cannot feel or hear it.'

'Wow,' says Luse.

'Yes. Some people are more aware of this than others. Like you, they are open. But for most people it is too difficult to carry on with their day to day lives knowing that they are part of something so enormous. They teach their children not to listen to that rushing world, to their ancestors, their "kusonda", their intuition. They want to feel separate from the air and the earth around them. But you and I and those ancient ones who still love us, we can hear the world rushing through and we can sometimes feel it too. Then it is ours to use as we will for that moment.'

The fireflies again become person-shaped and the shape dances a little in the air making Luse smile. She is thinking.

'Ba'Neene? Does that mean you are not really dead?'

'When there is drought and a river dries, the water doesn't become nothing. It becomes fragments, tiny particles, it becomes air and rises or dust and sinks into the soil. Eventually it becomes rain again, a river again and the cycle continues. Mubili wangu ulifwide pele nda swaangana anyika ibalika. My body is dead but I have joined the rushing world.'

'There isn't death?'

'Death is change, a dispersing and reordering. You remember me and I am here. Our ancestors can only protect those that remember.'

Luse wrinkles her nose. 'So... I am not full of evil even if I feel like it sometimes? I am not a witch?'

Again the waterfall tinkles and the fireflies bombard her head.

'In a way there are no witches. There are just people who can hear the rushing, like you, but who make choices based on power, greed and fear.'

Sitting on the bank, Luse plucks at the soft grass. The fireflies caress her cheek and for a while Luse sings to them. A song about fish eagles and acacia trees, good spirits and termites. After a long time she has no more of the song in her. She sits quietly.

'Come and sweep the shrine when the time comes. Sweep and clean for us, for the ancestral spirits.'

Luse nods. She is so happy here in the cavern, but she can feel her brother's pitter-patter heartbeat again and now her skin is beginning to prickle with feathers.

'I have to go now, Ba'Neene.'

'Yes my dearest. For now.'

Luse stretches and her arms swing wide and she flies.

12.

The door sticks so Georgia, gun in one hand and medical bag over her sore shoulder, bashes it with her hip and is off balance when it jerks open. She staggers, can't stop her momentum on the sloping floor, and falls forward onto her hands and knees, ending up with her nose pressed up against a large glass window. The platform bounces beneath her from the impact of her tumble and she feels old red carpet under her hands, and breathes in a far off reek of popcorn. *Luse's viewing platform!* Lifting her eyes she looks down into the operating theatre below and gets a snapshot of utter hell. Bernard and Gus are on the ground. Luse is tied to a chair and the Chinese doctor is standing over a patient with his scalpel shining, a patient that looks like a small boy. She smashes her hand against the glass. 'Stop!' she shouts.

'What the hell! Who the fuck are you?' An angry nasal whine comes from behind her and Georgia glances over her shoulder to see three enormous black-suited men leap to their feet from their padded seats, causing the whole platform to sway. They look incongruous, out of place, as if they are nightclub security who have turned up at the wrong venue. Squeezed between them is a short and very skinny person in black drainpipe jeans and a white frilly shirt. Georgia notes the pancake white skin, thinning black hair and blood red lips. One eye is blue, the other completely black and when it opens its mouth, its teeth glisten, specialist orthodontic metal, canines filed to points.

Georgia feels as if her brain is bending the wrong way, that perhaps this is all some terrible joke. She knows exactly who the little prick with the metal teeth is but she has no time to process what or why he would be here. She focuses her mind on what is going on below. *I'm coming*, she thinks, and rolling onto her belly she aims Samuel's gun at the plastic window.

'Gun! Gun!' shouts one of the hulking men.

The huge window bulges and cracks squeak away in all directions from the bullet hole until the pressure is too great and the glass explodes outward in a thousand shards. The platform lurches down to the left, nails tearing away from the wall struts and the entire structure plummets to the ground in a thundering whooooosh, sending recycled cinema seats, pieces of plank, concrete, red telephones and people flying. Georgia is catapulted through the air and lands heavily on her back amidst falling rubble, all breath knocked out of her. One of the huge bodyguards lies next to her, face down, a bloody sliver of glass window sticking up between his shoulder blades.

Georgia's head swims as she battles for air and she thinks she sees birds, millions of tiny birds flying in torrents around the room. Almost in slow motion she sees holes appear in the concrete at her feet and hears the splat-splat-splat of bullets hitting the ground around her. Someone is shooting from the gaping hole of the platform but she can't get her legs to move. People are screaming in pain and anger and sparks fly from the strip lights now hanging down like loose teeth. She can smell burning wire and feathers. Is she hurt? She isn't sure and for a moment she has no breath in her to try and stand. She manages to raise her head and sees Luse standing, free from her binding, head thrown back and arms outstretched. Her eyes are shut, her expression peaceful, relaxed.

A scream comes from behind her and the Priestess steps right over Georgia's body.

'No! I will not let you win! I cast thee out! I cast thee out!' The Priestess is wading towards Luse through the clouds of feathers, smashing at the birds with her Bible. Something long and sharp glints in her free hand and her face is contorted with her ecstatic howling. 'I cast thee out!'

'Luse!' screams Georgia, finally finding breath. 'Run!'

But Luse is calm, unflinching, her eyes still shut. The Priestess stumbles, looking confused as the birds whirl faster and Georgia can hardly make out what happens next through the rush of dusky wings. The Priestess stops, shaking her head as if she has something in her ear. She belches and a feather flies from her lips. Bulges appear in her throat, her eyes widen, whites glistening, and she opens her mouth wide but instead of words out come more feathers. She retches and spits as feathers spill soggily from her mouth, her cheeks puffed full, little downy feathers squeezing from her nostrils. She raises the knife, still trying to lunge for Luse, when all at once her skull cracks open and birds fly out in a torrent from the top of her head.

Oh for fuck's sake, thinks Georgia. *I must have concussion!* She watches with horrid fascination as the Priestess, still clutching her Bible, falls to her knees and then keels over, landing in a pool of blood and feathers at Luse's feet.

The noise abates and Georgia can see that there are fewer birds pounding the air. They have begun to fly upwards through the hole in the roof, back into the night sky, dissolving into the darkness. The sound of people shrieking and yelling has moved from the operating room into other parts of the Dome. From further out comes the whack-a-whack roaring of helicopter blades gearing up, trucks roaring away and sporadic gunshots.

Luse opens her eyes and Georgia sees her become aware of the room, of the destruction all around, of her.

'Georgia?' she shouts, startled.

'I'm alright. I'm just a little...' but Luse has already turned, darting to the operating table without seeming to notice the still twitching Priestess.

'Hey, you are squashing me,' comes Joshua's groggy voice as Luse leaps up on the table and wraps her arms around him.

'Let me help!' Bernard appears, limping through the debris. His glasses are cracked and he is covered in concrete dust, but he is unhurt. Georgia feels a little of the tightness in her chest dissipate at his familiar owl-like blink.

He helps Georgia to her feet and together they turn to the children.

'Little brother, how are you?' asks Bernard, as Georgia quickly checks them both for injuries.

'I'm tired, Father,' Joshua holds out his arms sleepily and Bernard picks him up, hugs him tight.

Georgia, checking Luse for any cuts, pauses, feeling like she might faint. She looks around her, at the bodies and the blood. 'I need my medical bag.'

Gus is limping towards her, blinking. A block of cement from the roof has fallen on his foot but he is ignoring the fact that he is leaving a trail of bloody footprints. He has found his gun and has been hobbling around checking for survivors.

'Gus! Your foot!'

'I'm okay.' He winces and holds it up. 'Just leaking a lot. We have a few casualties though. Mrs Phiri is under the platform, I am afraid. And Siza, well you saw. He shot the Priestess. I think it was a mistake.' Gus gestures with his gun to where Siza is kneeling among the blood and concrete next to his friend who stares lifelessly up at the cracked roof.

'Siza *shot* her?' Georgia looks around. There are no birds. Not a single feather. 'You shot her?' she says again, disbelieving.

Siza nods, 'Yebo! Right in the head. I was aiming at the kid though, so it was a mistake, okay! Eish... I never saw that before. In the head, man... Hey, can you help my friend?'

'Your bag is here,' says Bernard, sliding it over to her and Georgia's hands stop shaking as she assesses the damage. *I am trained for this,* she thinks. *I am in charge of this moment.* Her heartbeat slows, the terror subsiding.

'It's too late for your friend, Siza. I am sorry.' She turns to Gus and Bernard. 'I need to see the other casualties and Samuel is going to need airlifting.' She looks over at Gus who nods.

'I'm on it. There must be a radio somewhere. Siza, you better come with me. We need to get hold of the Commander and an army helicopter.'

More shots come from outside and they all flinch.

'What about the other children? Are they safe?' asks Bernard, still clutching Joshua tight.

'We locked everyone in the rooms,' says Siza, sullen and ashamed. 'They should be alright if they stay lying down.'

Georgia kneels beside a nurse with what could be a fractured femur. She signals to Bernard but the old man is shaking with exhaustion. No good.

'Luse, I need your help.'

Luse's eyes are clear. 'Yes, Georgia,' she whispers.

'I need you to come here and apply pressure. Can you do that?'

Luse looks down at the nurse, recognises Nurse Chilufia, spattered with blood, eyes half shut, groaning. Remembers Harry in the ditch.

'Okay, lean in hard as I pull away. One, two, three!'

When Gus returns he tells them the Commander's team has broken through the perimeter and Samuel will be airlifted as soon as possible.

'I'll need to prep him!' Georgia jumps up and instantly feels nauseous from the pain in her back and shoulder. Gus puts an arm around her until she steadies. He reaches a hand up to her cheek and she holds it there tightly.

Epilogue

1.

Georgia and Father Bernard are sitting beside Samuel's hospital bed. It's after lunch and Samuel is awake and propped up on several pillows, his feet sticking out over the end of the bed. Father Bernard is showing them a posy of tiny purple flowers he has wrapped in his handkerchief.

'These are what woke me from that awful drug. Luse's flowers! In that half-concious state I reached into my pocket for my handkerchief. I was very confused, wanted to clean my glasses, not realising they had fallen off, which was why I couldn't see. Anyway, a few of these flowers were crushed inside the hanky and when I brought it up to my face it was like eating a teaspoon of mustard! Brought me to my senses quicker than smelling salts. I reached over and stuffed them up poor Gus's nose too and luckily they had the same effect. It meant we were able to crawl out of the way when the platform collapsed!'

'Amazing,' says Georgia, rolling the tiny flowers in her palm. 'They look so innocuous.'

'Not sure what they are yet,' Bernard chews his lip. 'Probably best not to ingest them.'

'Hey there,' says Gus, appearing around the ward door. He limps in, right foot in a cast to his knee. Pulling a squeaky chair over, he squeezes in next to Georgia.

'You haven't been driving with that?' Georgia narrows her eyes at him and he grins.

'I would never go against my doctor's orders! No, Eddie's in the car. But I wanted to speak to you all. There is news at last. They arrested Danny's bartender, Watson.'

'Watson?' Georgia is shocked.

'Apparently he is a member of The Blood of Christ Church. Has been for over a year. The Commander thinks he was the one who saw Harry at Danny's bar and told the Twins. He might even have been the one who...' Gus pauses and sighs '... who took him.'

Georgia remembers Watson's face when he saw her with the envelope. 'Was Danny involved?'

'We don't know. He is corrupt as hell, we know that, but I don't think he is a murderer.'

'A trafficker?' Samuel rumbles from the bed.

'Possibly. We are running his books now, interviewing his staff. Might take a while.'

'What about that revolting little pop star, the one Georgia saw on the platform?' asks Bernard.

'Don't you get the paper at the seminary, Father?' says Gus, not unkindly, and lays a copy of *The Postal Times* on the bed.

Georgia thought she might have imagined the pop star Jackie Ripper up there in the viewing platform but his arrest back in New York has been the headline of every newspaper in the world. On the front page, surrounded by airport security, a skinny white man in sunglasses holds two fingers up to the camera.

'Charming,' says Bernard, clearing his throat with distaste

'From B-list celebrity to the most famous man on earth in a week. That's quite a stunt.' Georgia sounds calm but she is so angry she can barely sit still.

'You're sure it was this ka-little one?' Samuel puts his finger on the photo, looking flummoxed.

'He was definitely in Zambia. We have his passport and ticket details. He took the flight out from Lusaka that same night. Turns out the FBI had him under investigation. He is known to be part of a group that drinks human blood regularly and are rumoured to try cannibalism on occasion.'

'Ya!' Samuel sinks back into his pillows and the bed creaks horribly. 'A witch from the USA! Eish!'

'But he's a fraud!' Georgia is irate. 'His vampire image is just a PR stunt. I mean, this is a man who dates supermodels and fakes eating live snakes on stage.'

'His publicist claims he was on safari...' Gus is saying.

'A goth on safari!' Georgia laughs mirthlessly, waving her hands in the air.

'What's a goth?' Samuel is asking Bernard.

'It's insane. These people.' Bernard is cleaning his glasses, eyes red and watery. 'Either they buy our children or they eat them.'

'Bernard has a point,' says Georgia, remembering the camera in Hut Two. 'There were other buyers, weren't there? Other people watching the children?'

'Oh yes. The Dome was rigged for live internet feed,' Gus nods. 'They destroyed much of the computer hardware but not all. They weren't just selling human parts either. It seems the monsters had a trade in virgins.'

Bernard sighs heavily. 'Virgins are very valuable. The ignorant believe that sleeping with them cures many illnesses, including HIV/AIDS.'

'You know,' says Gus. 'I am beginning to think the Priestess wasn't in charge of it at all. The Phiris and Dr Lin have been working together for years on the black market. We found a man who had been a mule for them in Mufilira back in the 90s and Dr Lin was known as the Red Chinaman in several parts of the Niger Delta. He was initially on the wanted list for trafficking rhino horn.'

'You think they forced Selena?' Bernard puts his glasses back on.

'No, not forced exactly. She was ill, perhaps she was vulnerable, but she also bought into the idea entirely. They might have engineered some of her hallucinations, her visions of God, but she was the one who brought them the children.'

'And what of the children?' Samuel asks, his face slack and grey.

'Many have gone missing,' Gus says, understanding that Samuel must feel responsible. 'But Luse says she saw a couple of kids she recognised back here on the street yesterday, so we know that at least some of the runaways have made it back to Lusaka. Altogether we counted 375 children, all uninjured. The US is putting a multi-sector aid package together – possibly in an effort to play down Jackie Ripper's involvement.'

'And Blood of Christ?' asks Georgia, pinching the skin between her eyes to try and reduce the tension of a mounting headache.

'You can leave that to me. We have a meeting with the Council of Churches tomorrow,' Father Bernard says, standing up. 'I believe lawyers will be present.' He pauses, clearing his throat. 'I hope you don't mind but there is a passage in Romans which I have always treasured and I would like to share it with you. I think it might be helpful right now. Now let me get it right.'

He begins and as he speaks he looks at each of them, Georgia, Gus and Samuel, 'Never pay back evil with evil, but bear in mind the ideals that all regard with respect. As much as possible, and to the utmost of your ability, be at peace with everyone. Never try to get revenge: leave that, my dear friends, to the Retribution. As scripture says: Vengeance is mine – I will pay them back, the Lord promises. And more: If your enemy is hungry, give him something to eat; if thirsty, something to drink. By this, you will be heaping red-hot coals on his head. Do not be mastered by evil, but master evil with good.'

Samuel and Gus clap hands, grinning, but Georgia wrinkles her nose. 'Ever thought of Buddhism, Father?' she asks and smiles.

<h1>2.</h1>

They are watching *Mary Poppins* again. It is the second time today but Joshua insists. He has been trying to learn the words to 'Supercalafragalistic' and is crouching close to the television screen trying to catch the mess of words as they fly out of the actors' mouths. Luse is lying behind him on the prickly brown sofa. They have drawn the curtains of the living room to stop sunlight shining on the TV but behind them the glass doors to the garden are open. Soft, warm air makes the white curtains billow. Luse watches them move, remembering the way the purple robes flapped on the Priestess's dead body.

More than ten days have passed since they got back to Lusaka. For the first few nights Luse and Joshua stayed at the Jesuit compound with Father Bernard. They slept, mostly, on camp beds in Father Bernard's study, listening to people quietly coming and going from the library. Luse refused to let Joshua out of her sight but no one disturbed them or tried to ask difficult questions.

Then Georgia came to pick them up. She was pale and smelled of hospitals. She took them to visit Samuel in the clinic.

'Hello little brother, little sister,' he growled. 'Any more adventures to tell me today?'

Luse felt greatly relieved to see him alive and so well, but she couldn't speak to him for long. Being in the hospital made her think about Joshua on the operating table. The smell of antiseptic made her nauseous, but she smiled, or tried to. Samuel wasn't fooled.

'You know, little sister, that when you ring a bell the sound goes on for a long time after?' Luse nodded looking down at her hand engulfed in his. 'Well a night like that night is the same. It will be ringing in your ears for a while, but it will go, I promise.'

Now they are back at Georgia's and Joshua has rewound the song again, his brow furrowed with concentration.

'Hodi? Hello?' A voice from the doorway makes them both jump.

It's Georgia but what is she doing calling to come into her own house? Luse sits up and looks over the back of the sofa. The sun is shining in the kitchen door so she can only make out silhouettes, Georgia and... there is a woman next to her and the light streams through her hair, bright as a bush fire.

'Luse? Joshua?' calls Georgia again and there is something in her voice.

Joshua is standing up, moving around the sofa to see who has come in and Luse hears a scream and a thud and the red-haired woman has fallen to her knees.

'Joshua!' she is screaming. 'Thank God! Thank God!' Auntie Miriam is on the floor, her arms open wide, tears running down her face.

'Joshua... Luse...' she sobs again but more quietly now and Luse can see she is trying to control herself so as not to scare them. Luse takes Joshua's hand and pulls him gently forward. She can see Joshua trying to process it all, his eyes widening. Then he realises and he remembers and he looks up at Luse.

'It's Auntie Miriam,' he says slowly and carefully, tasting the words. As what that really means begins to filter into his head, he twitches, jumps with excitement, runs in a circle. 'It's Auntie Miriam!' he shouts and abruptly he bursts into huge racking sobs and collapses, head on his arms on the floor in front of her.

Ever so gently Miriam crawls to him, pulling him into her arms and cuddling him tight, rocking on the floor while Luse and Georgia stand, watching. Miriam's eyes are tight shut, tears glittering and slipping down her cheeks and she is saying softly, 'Oh I have you darling, we have you back little ones.'

'Luse,' says Georgia quietly and takes her hand. 'Come outside.'

In the hot morning sun, a tall white man with a black beard is standing by Georgia's car. In his arms he is holding a very pretty little girl with hazelnut skin, long tumbling curly hair and Miriam's eyes. And someone else. On the far side of the car, the passenger side, someone else is slowly climbing out of the car. Georgia is talking, saying words like 'hospice' and 'missing records', but Luse hears nothing.

Baama.

Her mother looks different, so thin and she is leaning on a stick. As she moves around the car, the light reflects off the bonnet and blinds her and she puts a hand up to shade her eyes. Luse has moved too without knowing and now she is standing in front of her mother and still they say nothing and still they gaze at each other. And then slowly and with difficulty, as if she is an old woman, Esther kneels down in front of her daughter and opens her arms.

Acknowledgements

Thank you to my sister, Rachma, for being my ally and defender and an excellent critical reader and commentator.

To my MA fellows at Bath Spa University circa 2009–10 and for the great support and guidance of my supervisor Richard Kerridge and my other tutors, Tessa Hadley and Mimi Thebo.

To Will Francis for crucial and timely feedback.

To Simone Chalkley for the first MA manuscript proof-reading and to Shreeta Shah for her clever guidance, passionate feedback and volunteering to do the final manuscript copy editing.

To Ruth Hartley for her wonderful resources, stories and knowledge on all things 'plant-wise'.

To Polly Loxton and Megan Biesele for reading with pleasure, hooting with joy and kicking me forward. That goes too for the inspirational Suzanna Coleman, who didn't just read and hoot but slammed my manuscript into the hands of every contact she had.

To Colleen Higgs from Modjaji for saying 'Yes, we can!' and to Karen Jennings for doing much needed surgery. A wonderful edit!

To all the children and adults who took part in the research, development and production of *Choka - Get Lost!*, for showing me another side of Lusaka and of life.

To all at the Mother of Mercy Hospice in Chilanga for sharing your incredible spirit of hope through these terrible years of HIV/AIDS.

To Catherine Nyirenda for planting the seed.

To Beene Banji Hang'omba for giving me so many tales, inspiring Luse, and translating the Tonga. I will never forget what happens to Tonga women who whistle!

To Miranda Rashid and Tamara Guhrs for cheering me on whilst gently correcting all my terrible Chinyanja spellings!

To Bente, Charlotte, Martin and Ilan, for their love, encouragement and those Danish Christmas Eves.

To Connie Rawlinson for her stalwart wisdom and continuous support and Cath, Daisy and all the Cambridge folk who were there when things got tough.

To my aunt Jackie for the long and much needed walks.

To Paul and Sandra Ray for the advice you gave and the lifeline you threw.

To Colin and Jenny Carlin for helping me to acclimatise to Bath.

To Jane Amanda for giving me a roof.

To Wendy and John 'Sarge' Cooper who brought Grace and me together and in doing so changed my life.

And to Grace, who is absolutely full of the stuff.

For more about Modjaji Books and any of our titles go to
www.modjajibooks.co.za